(818) 461-3 Beachwood

818/814 8000 ext 104

213) 465 1427

465 05 71

PINBALL

464 4869

Grace St = 465 6523

653 0410

670 8283

TUESDAY

Bourgeois Pig 465 5066
area

461 4944

1845 Gramercy 465 7998
pL

1848 Gramercy 463 3537
pL

1848

1740 Gramercy 466 3585
(Devonshire)

1803 Wilton (200) 661 9155

Beachwood 851 1224   466 450

818 209   (812) 284 5305   46 -206

5648   -   446 9056

PINBALL

Beachwood 462 2 500

Jerzy Kosinski

This edition, first published in 1983 by Arcade Publishing, Inc., New York,
incorporates minor textual changes and revisions.
First Grove Press paperback edition published in October 1996

Published simultaneously in Canada
Printed in the United States of America

Library of Congress Cataloging-in-Publication Data

Kosinski, Jerzy N., 1933–
Pinball / Jerzy Kosinski. – 1st Grove Press pbk. ed.
p.   cm
ISBN 0-8021-3482-3
1. Missing person   n.   2. Musicians—Fiction.   I. Title.
                    P5   1996
                          96-24958

ACKNOWLEDGMENTS

Grateful acknowledgment is made to the publishers named below for permission to reprint the following material:

Excerpt from "Under Which Lyre" from W. H. Auden: Collected Poems *by W. H. Auden: copyright © 1946 by W. H. Auden. Courtesy of Random House.*

Excerpt from Ulysses *by James Joyce, copyright © 1914, 1918 by Margaret Caroline Anderson, and renewed 1942, 1944 by Nora Joseph Joyce. Reprinted by permission of Random House, The Bodley Head, and the Society of Authors, literary representative of the Estate of James Joyce.*

Excerpt from "Hypocrite Auteur" from New and Collected Poems 1917–1982 *by Archibald MacLeish. Copyright © 1985 by The Estate of Archibald MacLeish. Reprinted by permission of Houghton Mifflin Company.*

Excerpts from The Book of Rock Quotes *by Jonathan Green used by permission of the Publishers, Omnibus Press, UK/Music Sales Corporation, USA/Angus & Robertson, Australia.*

Excerpt from "His Confidence" from Collected Poems of W. B. Yeats. *Reprinted with permission of Macmillan Publishing Co., Inc., M. B. Yeats, Anne Yeats, Macmillan London Limited, and A. P. Watt Ltd. Copyright 1933 by Macmillan Publishing Co., Inc., renewed © 1961 by Bertha Georgie Yeats.*

Excerpts from The Legacy of the Blues *by Samuel Charters, copyright © 1977 by Samuel Charters. Published by Marion Boyars, Ltd., London, and Da Capo Press, Inc. All rights reserved.*

The excerpts and translations from "Chopin: The Man" by Arthur Hedley, "Studies, Preludes and Impromptus" by Robert Collet, and "The Songs" by Bernard Jacobson, which are included in Frédéric Chopin: Profiles of the Man and the Musician, *edited by Alan Walker (Taplinger Publishing Co., Inc., 1967; © 1966 by Barrie & Rockliff), are reprinted by kind permission.*

The man that hath no music in himself
Nor is not moved with concord of sweet sounds,
Is fit for treasons, stratagems, and spoils;
The motions of his spirit are dull as night,
And his affections dark as Erebus;
Let no such man be trusted. Mark the music.

SHAKESPEARE
Merchant of Venice

For he who has once had to listen
will listen always, whether he knows
he will never hear anything again,
or whether he does not . . . Silence
once broken will never again be whole.

BECKETT
The Unnamable

I

∧∧∧∧∧∧∧∧∧∧

1

∧∧∧∧∧∧∧∧∧

When Patrick Domostroy turned the ignition key of his car, no sound came from the engine and no lights showed on the dashboard. He tried again and again, and still nothing happened: the battery was dead.

Knowing that in his neighborhood it would take at least an hour to get a mechanic to show up and not wanting to lose the time, he unbolted the battery from its brackets and put it in an old canvas bag he kept in the trunk of the car. Then he carefully lugged the bag the full length of the parking lot, and when he reached the street, he hailed a taxi.

In a few minutes he was at the National KnowHow, the largest automobile service station in the South Bronx. A big sign reading "Wouldn't You Rather KnowHow?" loomed above the main entrance.

Canvas bag in hand, Domostroy went to the manager, a big-bellied guy in a blue work shirt, with JIM stitched on his white coveralls.

"Will you charge a battery for me?" asked Domostroy.

"Sure," said Jim. "Just bring her in."

"Here," Domostroy said, setting down the bag on the floor.

Jim looked at the bag, then at Domostroy over his glasses. "The car," he said, pronouncing each word deliberately; "bring the car in."

"I can't," said Domostroy. "It wouldn't go with a dead battery."

"Couldn't you jump-start it?" Jim asked.

"A jump-start is not enough: It needs a full charge. I just took the battery out, grabbed a taxi and here it is!" He prodded the bag open with the tip of his shoe.

Jim lifted his eyes wearily and asked, "Where is the car?"

"In the Old Glory's parking lot," Domostroy replied.

"You brought this"—Jim pointed at the battery—"in a cab?"

"Sure. It was too heavy to carry all the way here on foot," said Domostroy.

Jim's expression changed. Taking his glasses off, he kicked the bag shut. He called to another mechanic. "Pete, will you come here for a minute!"

Pete, a slim young man, looked up, saw Jim and Domostroy, and put down his wrench. "Coming," he said.

Turning to Pete, Jim pointed at the canvas bag. "Guess what's in that?" he said brightly, with the air of a host on a TV game show.

Pete's eyes circled from the bag to the visitor, back to the bag, then back to Jim. "I don't know," he said with a shrug.

"Just guess," said Jim, clapping him on the back.

Pete's eyes measured Domostroy, then the bag. "Dirty laundry," he said.

"Wrong," Jim answered triumphantly.

"A bowling ball?"

"Wrong again! Try once more," Jim prodded.

Pete took his time. "A dead dog," he ventured.

"Dead—right! Dog—wrong," Jim announced, kicking the bag open. "It's a dead battery! And this guy," he said, pointing at Domostroy, "brought it here." After pausing for effect, he added, "In a cab!"

"But where's his car?" asked Pete.

"Couldn't come with its battery dead," Domostroy broke in, "so the battery had to come without it."

"In a cab?" asked Pete.

"In a cab. To save time."

Shaking his head, Pete wandered away.

Jim started to write out a work order. "I've been twenty years at National KnowHow," he said, bending over the form. "Plenty of people tow in cars with dead batteries. But you're the first to haul in a dead battery without a car." He paused. "What kind of work do you do?"

"I'm a musician," said Domostroy.

"You have an accent," said Jim. "Where are you from?"

"South Bronx," said Domostroy.

"I mean—before that. Where does that accent come from?"

"The New Atlantis," said Domostroy. "But accents don't show up in music."

Jim laughed. "What kind of music?"

"Serious," said Domostroy. "Dead serious."

"If it's as dead as this battery," said Jim, "you should have brought your music here to charge it too." He kept on laughing as he glanced at the work order. "You know, I don't think I've ever heard of New Atlantis," he said. "Where is it?"

"The Land of Sounds," said Domostroy. "Francis Bacon wrote a book about it."

While the battery was being charged, Domostroy opened his mail, which he had thrown into the bag with the battery. He pocketed the bills and the usual credit-card statements; then he glanced through the junk mail. A letter from the National Vasectomy Club asked in large print, "Had a Vasectomy?" and then suggested, "Now Encourage Others! If you're one of the thousands of men who have had a vasectomy, join the National Vasectomy Club and inspire others to follow your lead in bringing population growth under control." For only a few dollars, the club offered to send him a sterling silver lapel pin or tie tack, a membership card, and a bumper sticker.

Domostroy stopped to think. If he should ever undergo a vasectomy—although he could imagine nothing less likely—what right would he have to proselytize? Furthermore, if in search of external identity—again, a concept quite foreign to him—he should decide to define

himself as an American Vasectomite, where would he feel
confident wearing the National Vasectomy Club lapel pin
or the tie tack? To cocktails? To dinner with a date? To
church? And what about the membership card? Why and
where would he need it? To whom could he show it? He
imagined being stopped by the highway patrol for speed-
ing and saw himself producing, in addition to his driver's
license, his National Vasectomy card: "It's like this, Offi-
cer: I've got to get to all those guys who aren't keeping
population growth down, and there's not much time left!"

In another letter, an illustrated flier advertised
Candypants—the hundred-percent edible underwear.
"Comes in butterscotch, cherry, banana, orange and lime
flavors. One size fits all." Domostroy tried to imagine
eating such panties off Andrea. Why, he asked himself, if
he were aroused by her, would he want to waste his time
eating her panties? Wasn't eating underwear in itself time-
consuming? And what would Andrea be doing while he
filled up on her banana, cherry, or butterscotch panties?
Watching him chew? Asking him how they tasted? For a
moment he imagined a court case involving poisoning by
Candypants, and their manufacturer, faced with a wide
range of questions: Were edible panties more life-threat-
ening than, say, candy? Did they improve family rela-
tions? Speed up courting? Did they increase or diminish a
healthy sexual appetite? Should students engaging in
campus panty raids be prohibited from ripping off more
panties than they could chew? And finally, what was the responsibility of the manufacturer as tastemaker in such a
business?

When the battery was ready, he hailed a taxi for the
trip back to the Old Glory, once the South Bronx's largest
ballroom and banquet center. It was empty now. The rise
in crime and gang warfare in the neighborhood had driven
out most of the Old Glory's mostly Jewish clientele—who
once flocked to it for their wedding parties and bar mitz-

vahs. Its owner, an aging slumlord, had finally closed the place, put it on the market, and retired to Florida.

A decade ago, when Domostroy was at the height of his success, he had given several benefit concerts at the Old Glory to aid the displaced children of the South Bronx, and for the last two years the slumlord, remembering those benefits, had allowed him to live in the dressing room off the ballroom.

Hoping that any potential buyer would want to reopen the Old Glory just as it had been in its golden days, the slumlord had left in it all the original furniture and fixtures. The vast kitchen stood ready to feed twelve hundred diners, and on a low stage next to the dance floor loomed an ancient grand piano backed by an impressive array of other musical instruments, all badly used and in need of repair, ranging from a harp and a cello to electric guitars, accordions, and— a mark of modern technology—an electronic music console that could simulate the sound of several instruments.

There was still no buyer in sight. Until one came along, Domostroy had taken it upon himself, in return for the owner's beneficence, to be guard and custodian of the Old Glory and everything the great shell contained.

Now he asked the driver to stop the taxi next to his car, which stood alone in the vast space of the parking lot, and as he got out of the cab in the twilight, he saw the ballroom as if it were a huge starship that was grounded on a temporary landing pad. He had had similar feelings before. His room was the ship's command post, and when inside he was the ship's sole passenger, about to start on his latest voyage of discovery. At night, the sounds of a faraway street-gang gun battle or the howling siren of a police car or an ambulance or a fire engine were like signs of life calling out to him, and as he listened, he felt that he existed alongside that life as well as within it.

Domostroy installed the battery and started the engine. He enjoyed the car's quiet motor, the bulky leather seats, the power and speed that resulted from the slightest pressure on the gas pedal. He had always liked to drive, and of all the cars he had ever owned, he felt the greatest fondness for this one. It was an old and venerable vehicle, the largest convertible Detroit had produced at the peak of showing-off its industrial power. When Domostroy had bought the car in a showroom some fifteen years earlier, he recognized in it a symbol of his own mobility and affluence. In his concert performing days he often had the car shipped to him wherever he was—California, the Caribbean, even Switzerland—as if it were a small package, but now the convertible was the only remaining object from his opulent past—and one of his last links to it. But wherever he worked he took his car—his sole impressive possession. Patrick Domostroy's old sedan was to him what a private customized superjet—a space-age flying saloon—was to a rock star.

His musical talent was the other link. No longer composing, with no income to speak of from the sales of his past records, Domostroy had been making his living for the last decade by hiring himself out to play any of a number of instruments—piano, accordion, harpsichord, even the electronic synthesizer so popular with the rock and pop musicians half his age—in small out-of-the way nightclubs. He worked either as a combo stringer or as an accompanist for other performers—singers, dancers, jugglers, or magicians. If he was pressed for cash, he even did stints at private parties, dances, and bingo parlors.

For the last year, he'd been working at Kreutzer's. The crowd there never varied much. There were couples in their late fifties, locals mostly, but some came from as far away as Queens, Brooklyn, even New Jersey, lured by the newspaper ads listing free parking, live music, two drinks for the price of one, a salad bar, and as much homemade garlic bread as you could eat, all included in the price of the dinner. There were also middle-aged out-of-town salesmen, on the prowl, alone or with flashily dressed pickups from the nearby singles bar; young neigh-

borhood couples who came mainly for the dancing; a birthday or anniversary party of eight, twelve, or sixteen people—
usually families; and at the bar, several solitary men of
various ages, watching the TV set, listening to the jukebox, playing an occasional pinball machine or electronic
game, and casting furtive glances at the three or four
ladies of the night who, in exchange for extending their
favors to the manager and sharing part of their income
with the bouncer, were allowed to sit at the bar and
solicit, as long as they looked good and didn't get out of
line.

Before this crowd gathered each night, Domostroy
ate his dinner at one of the corner tables, usually alone,
sometimes with one of the headwaiters or the manager;
then he went into the men's room and changed into his
tux, always checking himself carefully in the mirror. He
was glad the job called for him to accompany singers and
other musicians, never to play alone, because it made the
break with his past—as a solo performer—clean and complete, and thus his own tradition was not abused.

Since he no longer composed, he could devote his life
to his own existence rather than the existence of his music.
And because he could predict with relative ease what his
life would be like in periods ahead—something he could
not do with his music—his life had become fairly simple
and devoid of anguish. He maintained it in somewhat the
way he maintained his car—a minor repair here, a little
polish there—and he was pleased when it rolled along
smoothly.

Had he lived among the Victorians or during Prohibi-
tion, or had he remained in totalitarian Eastern Europe
where he spent his youth, he would undoubtedly have
found the imposition of moral rules of any kind to be
arbitrary and overly restrictive. And he was sure that the
world of tomorrow, full of computerized technology and
standardized behavior, depleted of natural and human
resources, would neither challenge nor interest him in the
least.

Freed as he was from the deceptive security of accu-
mulated wealth and the chimera of success—his freedom a

useful by-product of his composer's block—he rejoiced at being able to live his life as he pleased, at the time and in the place he was living it, and at being able to follow his own ethical code of moral responsibility, competing against nobody, harming no one, not even himself—a code in which free choice was always the indisputable axiom.

But he was lonely. He had no friends. Most of the people who had been his friends when he was on top assumed that success and failure ran parallel and were therefore not supposed to cross paths, and because he had once felt the same way himself, he could hardly burden them now with an explanation of his failure, making them feel guilty of their own success or uncertain of their own talents and place in society. In their eyes, he knew full well, his current way of life—particularly his way of making a living—represented not just failure, but failure with something of the contemptible, ridiculous and grotesque about it. He could never persuade them of the truth: that even though, by chance, he had reached the bottom, he was, by choice, comfortable sitting on it.

Often, long after everyone at Kreutzer's had gone home, he would get into his car and drive over the Third Avenue bridge to Manhattan. At dawn, the long avenues opened before him like lines of music stripped of notes. He would park in a deserted street where no sound broke the silence and sit and imagine that one day the well of his music, now as empty and soundless as the avenues of the huge city, would fill up again. Until then, he knew that he had to live each moment, making sure that the significance of it did not escape him.

Thus, owing not only to the circumstances of his career but to choice as well, Domostroy had come to fashion his life as if he had always lived it only in the present. He chose for companions people who, because of their age or upbringing or taste, neither recognized his name nor cared that he had once done things to make it famous. Their judgment of him, like his of them, depended only on how he presented himself in any number of chance meetings, never on knowledge of his past. He avoided the company of those who were informed about

his composing career and who might seek to convince him
that his past accomplishments far outweighed his diminished popularity, his recent musical sterility, his failure to
achieve lasting financial success, and his present obscurity.

He had gradually succeeded in turning his private
universe into a well-guarded fortress, and up to now he
had kept out anyone who might disturb the peace he
found there.

On the way to see Andrea, Domostroy played his
favorite tape on the car's stereo. His mood was often
determined by music, as if the waves of compression and
dilation in the air around him influenced the pitch of his
emotions. He perceived himself in terms of how he felt,
not just in terms of who he was. In this age of video he
often felt that he was an anachronism, trained to respond
with his cochlea, not his retina; a creature of sound, not of
sight. He speculated that, as mankind's insecurity about
its overcrowded physical world increased, so did its dependence on concrete space that could be seen and measured, and hence on visual art that portrayed it, from
television to photography.

But Domostroy was guided by the auditory, and his
art was music, which enlarged his spiritual world by de-
molishing boundaries of time and space and by replacing
the myriad separate encounters and collisions of men and
objects with a mystical fusion of sound, place, and distance, of mood and emotion. His spiritual ancestors included poets, writers, and musicians, especially those who,
like Shakespeare's pair of lovers, could "hear with their
eyes."

The two-hour tape he was now listening to contained
about a dozen musical pieces, or fragments of pieces,
some of them only a few minutes long. These pieces,
selected over the years, were ones he trusted to ease him
into a desired emotional state.

By learning to give himself up to the proper music,
he had become expert in the process of self-induced re-

flex. He could trigger in himself a variety of mental states: anticipation, tranquility, enthusiasm, sexual hunger, and in his composing days even the need to compose music. In "Life's Scores," his last published interview, he had said: "Composing is the essence of my life. Whatever else I do provokes in me a single question: Can I—would I—should I—use it in my next score? Whenever I hear my music played, I feel as though my whole life were at stake and that a single wrong note could mess it all up. I have no children, no family, no relatives, no business or estate to speak of; my music is my sole accomplishment, my only spiritual cast of mind."

Only once in a while, recalling his creative past, did Domostroy wonder what had happened to the essence of his life. Had the music critic of the influential *Musical Commentary* who had once accused him of composing himself into "radical isolation" been right? Was his music really so bleak and naked that it would one day tempt its creator, as another critic had once suggested, to cut his own throat?

Domostroy remembered when, also some ten years earlier, he had appeared on *Tuning to Time*, a TV talk show. The other guest on the show was a foreign military leader who was living in exile in Florida. Although until his exile the leader had been backed by the United States in a war that had lasted for years, his country—and his cause—had eventually been defeated. "We still have a minute, gentlemen," said the TV host cheerfully at the end of the program, and he turned to the military leader. "Tell us, General, after such a brilliant career—what went wrong?" Had the question been addressed to him, Domostroy would have panicked and not known how to answer. The military leader, betraying no emotion, casually glanced at his diamond-studded watch, then at the smiling host, then at the appreciative audience. "What went wrong?" he asked. "First, I was betrayed by my allies. Then I lost the war. That's what went wrong." To a military man, a lost war was the sufficient, obvious explanation for his life's failure. But what wrong note was sufficient to mess up the life of a composer and make him lose, in the prime of his life, the will to compose?

Domostroy parked the car in front of a renovated brownstone. Once inside, he ran upstairs and was out of breath by the time he reached the apartment on the fifth floor. He waited a minute for his heart and lungs to calm down, then he knocked. Andrea opened the door and let him in. She hung his jacket in a closet that was full of her dresses and coats and asked him to sit down on the low, oversized bed-couch, made up with a multicolored spread and flanked on one side by a table with a radio on it and on the other by a TV set. The room was comfortable, although sparsely furnished, and the few pieces were, he knew, fine antiques, complemented by several excellent copies of Pre-Raphaelite paintings, and, on a separate table, a large collection of antique perfume bottles.

The kitchen and the bathroom were both at one end of the room, seeming to steal space from each other, and he watched as Andrea moved about the tidily arranged apartment to fix him a drink. She was dressed simply but expensively in a silk blouse and a voluminous skirt of fine wool.

The day before, when he had seen her for the first time at Kreutzer's, he had managed to take in her youth, her formidable presence—expressive eyes, wide mouth, soft wavy hair, shapely rib cage, long legs. He had been aware instantly that she awakened in him a need, not for her exactly—not yet anyway—but perhaps for someone who looked like her. Perhaps, like a chord sounded from his past, she had simply awakened a longing for the feeling of wanting a woman.

"I didn't believe you would actually show up," she said, giving him his drink and perching on the table next to the couch. "Last night at Kreutzer's, handing you that note, I felt like a Band-Aid."

"A Band-Aid?" he asked, uncertain.

"An aid to the music band, a groupie!" she said and laughed.

She slid lightly onto the couch, her drink in hand, and leaned back against the table, facing him, her legs stretched in front of her so that her shoes were only inches away from his thigh. "At Juilliard, where I study drama and music, lots of students are into your stuff. They say you're a pro."

"A pro, with no new record in years, and all his old ones in the Memory Lane department."

"Not all!" she said. "Last month Etude Classics presented the Juilliard library with a gift of all its finest recordings, including every single one of yours."

"It's good of Etude to keep my masterpieces in print— and to get rid of them as gifts."

Andrea got up and went over to some shelves filled with books and records on one side of the room. Slowly, one at a time, she pulled out all eight of Domostroy's records and stacked them on the record player. Then she started the machine, announcing in a confidential disc jockey drawl, "Tonight's program, ladies and gentlemen, will be devoted to the complete works of Patrick Domostroy, the distinguished American composer, the National Music Award winner." As she sat down on the couch again, she brushed against him, and he caught the scent of her hair.

The music came to them from two large speakers placed on wall brackets at opposite ends of the room. As always, when he listened to his records, he was surprised by his own music, by the sounds he had once been able to hear only with his inward ear. Once again he was uncertain of his reaction; he could never decide whether he liked his music or not. Rather, he identified with it, knew each note, each phrase; he recalled how long—and where— he had worked on it. He even remembered his reactions to each piece when he first heard it in a concert hall, then on the radio, then occasionally on TV; and he remembered as well the anguish of waiting for each record to come out, the not-to-be-uttered expectation of success, and then the further anguish of waiting for the reviews.

"Don't you feel good about being a composer?" she asked, looking at him intently.

"I don't compose anymore," he answered.

"Are you ever going to give another big concert?"

"No more big concerts," he said firmly.

"Why not?"

"I lost my following," he said.

"But—why? They used to love you."

"They—the critics, the audience—changed, and I didn't. Or maybe it was the other way around."

"You're still a recording star," she said. "Your records touch more people than any concert would."

He felt her eyes on him, pleading, as soft and inviting as if she were a child, and he was tempted to kiss her.

"If my records touch you—can I?"

"Do you want to?" said Andrea, and she leaned back on her elbow and faced him. As she did so, her breast brushed against his hand.

"Only if you want me to."

"What makes you think I don't?" she asked, inching closer, her lips parting.

As he faced Andrea, he pondered what to do. He recalled a time in Oslo, during one of his European concert tours, when a young woman reporter interviewed him over dinner and then came back with him to his hotel. She asked him if she could spend the rest of the night in his room rather than drive all the way home, and although he found her tempting, he was perplexed, for during the whole evening she had not been the least bit flirtatious. He announced in the most straightforward way that his room contained only one bed, and she said that sharing it with him wouldn't bother her one bit, for as a girl she had often shared beds with her friends. Given that gratuitous admission and the Scandinavian reputation for sexual openness, Domostroy felt confident enough to tell the young woman that all through dinner he had imagined the two of them making love in a variety of ways and that he was therefore pleased and anxious to share his bed with her, as well as everything he had fantasized.

The woman became indignant. "I think you have this all wrong," she said. "All I asked was to share a bed with you, not you with the bed. For me," she said, "sharing your bed would be like going swimming with you. When swimming, you don't talk about it; you don't ask each other whether you like to swim or whether you prefer swimming on your back or stomach. You just swim. Making love is the same way. Why don't you try thinking about things that way!"

Angry, she left. As for her lesson, it was lost on Domostroy, who as a boy had almost drowned and ever since had been afraid of water.

"What makes you think I don't want you to touch me?" Andrea repeated. "After all, I came to hear you at Kreutzer's and slipped you that note about how much I liked you, didn't I?" She shifted again, and now her breath was on his neck, her breast against his chest.

In an instant he could cover her with his body, but he did not move. "Have you been with other musicians?" he asked.

She looked at him quizzically. "Been with?"

"I mean—"

"You mean slept with. Sure. I'm a music student, remember? What about you? Don't you fuck the girls who hang around Kreutzer's?"

He sat up and moved away from her. "You weren't just hanging around. You came with a purpose."

"I did," she agreed. "To know you."

"But—you already knew my music; wasn't that enough? Music doesn't make demands. Composers do."

"I don't mind your demands."

"You don't know me!"

"I know myself."

"Would you come to see me if instead of what I am, I were, say, a piano tuner?"

"Piano tuners don't interest me. Patrick Domostroy does."

She moved closer. Her hand rested on his thigh, and pulling him to her, she gently kissed his earlobe.

When he didn't respond, she pressed her breasts against him, then kissed him on his neck. He shivered lightly and reached for her, an excitement surging through him, propelling him toward her. Suddenly she stopped and pulled away, and his yearning subsided.

"I won't pretend that sex with you is all that excites me," she said, her eyes searching his. "There's one thing you—and only you—can do for me."

A slight discord was growing between them. "What is it?" he asked, fearful that she might ask him for money.

"I want you to introduce me to Goddard!"

"To Goddard? Which Goddard?"

"*The* Goddard. The one and only."

"Goddard the rock star?" he asked, feeling lost. He could see no connection between himself and the world of headlines, success, money, and popular music that Goddard's name evoked.

"That's right," said Andrea. "I want to meet Goddard. In person. That's all I ask."

Domostroy had to smile. Was she joking? Behind her slick facade, the girl was peculiar. "Is that all?" he asked sarcastically.

"Yes," she said, "that's all. Find out who he is. Better yet: find him. I want to meet him."

For a moment he felt disillusioned. Her girlish confidence annoyed him. So that's what she needed him for. An older man helping a young woman to fulfill her adolescent fantasy.

"What on earth makes you think I can find Goddard?" he snapped.

"Why can't you?" she asked, looking at him. "Aren't you a name too?"

He became impatient with her. "Look, for five—or is it six?—years," he said, "Goddard has been the biggest recording star in the country. Yet he's still nothing but a voice and a name—a complete mystery. Nobody has ever seen him or managed to find out the least bit of information about him. Nobody! And since the day his first big record was played on the air, every magazine, newspaper, TV and radio station, every professional, and every dilettante in the celebrity business has tried. But nobody knows any more about Goddard today than they did when he started. And you want me to find out who he is?" He laughed. "Are you sure you know who I am?"

"Of course, I do!" she said, also annoyed. "And also that you could find him. You could—but only if you wanted to badly enough. If you felt it was worth it to you, you could track Goddard down," she said emphatically. "All you have to do is want to find him. I've researched you," she said, "and I found out a great deal about you. I know you won the National Music Award for *Octaves*, and that both the Music Writers Guild of America and the British Academy of Film and Television Arts voted your music for *Chance*, the best film score of the year."

"What else?" asked Domostroy, a part of him pleased by her childlike belief in his power.

"Also, that for some twenty years or so, you were known all over the world and that in those days, you knew every big shot in the music field and the arts. I saw photographs of you with pop singers, business types, movie stars, TV anchormen, dress designers. I read the resolution the composers, lyricists, and performers of MUSE International drew up to honor you when you finished your second term as president of that association. They said you had shown an imaginative and protective sense of responsibility toward musicians all over the world; and that the fruits of what you had achieved would extend far into the future. Well, if you did all that for them then, don't you think they would do you a favor now? All you'd have to do would be to call, ask a few questions, and follow a few clues, to Goddard. Don't you see?"

He was impressed by her breezy rundown of his past success and her thoughtful disregard of his stalled career.

"It's not so easy to call people I used to know years ago and say I'd like to use them!" he said softly, trying not to discourage her. "Don't you think that all the reporters, disc jockeys, columnists, commentators, and musicians in the country would give just as much as you would to find out who Goddard is? What makes you think that all I have to do is phone a few old acquaintances and say, 'This is Patrick Domostroy. Tell me, who is Goddard?' "

"I'm not that naive," she said, ready to appease him, "but surely, somewhere out there are people who really do know who Goddard is, and where he is and what he looks like—and what he eats and whom he fucks and what he takes or smokes or shoots to get high. There must be a fair number of them—his family, relatives, friends, lovers, record company bigwigs, tax accountants, IRS agents, attorneys, clerks, secretaries, doctors, nurses, music technicians. No matter how great—or cunning or clever or rich—Goddard is, he could not have made it all alone! Look, every serious musician can tell that only one ear—yours!—wrote every one and all of your musical pieces! Yet, because, to guard the integrity of your work, you hand picked your own music-editors, that radical scandal sheet went after your entire reputation by alleging you didn't write your music alone! Can't you see there had to be people who helped Goddard? And who work with him now? All you have to do is find one of them. Just one!"

"Even if I could come across one of them, would anybody who has remained silent all this time break that silence—for me?" He shook his head.

She was adamant. "Find one before you say no! And persuade him—or her." She paused and waited for him to react, but when he did not, she continued. "If you say you'll try to find him, I'll do anything I can to help you. Anything, Patrick. I'll pay you in cash now what you make in six months at Kreutzer's. And I have enough money for us both to live on. It all comes from my family."

The prospect of living with her and of ready cash—his car needed repairs—was overpoweringly tempting.

He got up and walked around the room. "How long have you thought about all this?" he asked.

"About meeting you?"

"No. About finding Goddard."

"For a year or so."

"Have you talked to anyone else about it?"

"No."

"Why not?"

"I didn't have the right connections. Until recently, I was afraid to approach you because I didn't think I had anything to offer that would interest you." She paused, and a sly smile spread across her lips. "I read just about all the crap written about you since you first played in public long before I was born. Then, just as I was about to give up my research on you, I came across a most revealing article. It was written years ago—but it spoke of your true inclinations, and it gave me hope that you might not be indifferent to me after all."

"Was it my cover profile in *The New York Times* magazine?" he asked.

"It wasn't." She laughed mischievously. "It was in *Hetero*, 'the magazine of the morally liberated'—though not exactly a moral majority publication. Have you read it?"

"I might have at the time," he said. "There was so much nonsense published—"

"The article was written by one Ms. Ample Bodice," she interrupted, "a one-armed porno star who moonlights as a reporter of the sex scene. In it, Ms. Bodice described a weekend at the Sorcerer's Apprentice, a private club in the Catskills for 'sexual seekers,' where she ran into Patrick Domostroy. She said you were there with a sinuous young thing who behaved like a sex slave. Throughout the weekend and the various 'sexually imaginative' activities that supposedly filled it, your little leather-and-lace girl kept changing from one costume into another—sometimes looking pubescent, sometimes whorish, sometimes like a coed—each costume perfect, down to the smallest detail of dress and makeup. And not once did she repeat herself." Andrea stopped and waited for him to react. She moved and sat directly across from him, her calves crossed, her thighs spread wide, her flesh on display. She watched him calmly, as if he too were on display, with nothing hidden from her scrutiny.

"You've come a long way—from composing great mu-

sic and giving sold-out concerts at Carnegie Hall to living
at the Old Glory and working as a stringer at Kreutzer's, a
pinball joint that tries to pass for a nightclub! A long way!
Wouldn't you like to change all that?"

"That 'long way' happens to be my life, and I don't
complain about it," he said, wishing he could deflect her
argument. "And don't be so quick to knock pinball joints!"
He assumed a lighter tone. "After all, Earle Henry, the
man who invented the pinball machine, also invented the
jukebox. And where would your precious Goddard be
without jukeboxes?"

Andrea disregarded him. "All I'm saying, Domostroy,
is this: become as inventive in life as you once were in
music—and, apparently, in sex—by working for me. Help
me find Goddard. You won't regret it: I too can play sex
slave and wear kinky costumes, you know."

"I'm sure you can—but I'm wrong for the role of the
master," said Domostroy, standing up abruptly to get his
jacket and leave.

She walked over to him and put one hand on his
shoulder; with the other, she unbuttoned his shirt and
slipped it off his shoulders so that it fell to the floor. Then
she stretched to her full height and stared at him, forcing
him to look her in the eye. She knew she had won him
over.

"Money will be only half of your payment," she said.
"And this"—she nudged him with her thighs and glanced
at the bed—"will be the other half. At least you won't be
wasting your time playing pinball joints anymore."

"But wasting it, instead, on Goddard!" he said.

"You won't be wasting it!" She laughed and kicked off
her shoes. Her hands slid down to her waist, and she
slipped off her skirt and pantyhose and unbuttoned her
blouse, letting it fall from her. As she lay down naked on
the bed, another of Domostroy's records dropped onto the
turntable.

While she waited for him to speak or react, her
fingertips began to brush and circle her breasts, then
move slowly to her belly and below, to stroke and rub her
thighs. Standing there under her gaze, he felt clumsy and

ill at ease: here he was, trying to save his dignity while
trading his middle-aged wisdom and experience for sexual
favors from a young woman. He would have preferred to
undress her. Now, instead, it was she who was watching
him, as if with a magnifying glass.

Before his last record ended, he switched to the
radio, already set on her favorite station.

The mechanics of undressing further distracted him,
and for a moment he sensed a loss of arousal. Afraid that
she would notice it, he pretended he had to sit down to
take off his pants, and he remained sitting, with his back
to her, while he removed the rest of his clothes. Then,
still hiding his now limp flesh, he crawled over to her and
began stroking her shoulders, kissing her neck, bringing
his body slowly over her belly while keeping one hand
between his thighs, lowering his head to her breasts,
kissing, licking, and rubbing her nipples with his lips and
tongue. He was aroused again.

When he felt her prompting and hurrying him, he
was tempted to restrain her. He always took the initiative,
and tended to establish dominance over any woman who
in the heat of lovemaking strained insistently to bring
about his orgasm, which she seemed to need as a proof
both of his arousal and of her control. To him, his own
climax brought a definite end to his excitement and
stemmed, temporarily at least, the flow of his passion.

Andrea reached over and turned off the light beside
the bed, and in the darkness, in the midst of the music
pounding from the speakers, Domostroy allowed himself
to become engrossed in the images of her he conjured up,
sensing her body with every part of his—until he was
jolted by what seemed like a man's whisper, uneven in its
tone, almost like a cough. He strained to hear the sound,
which seemed to come through a hole in the ceiling or
high up on the wall. Realizing that the noise had thrown
off his concentration, he made a strong, conscious effort to
regain it and gave himself entirely to the task of lovemaking.

Andrea began to play more forcibly with him, to
fondle, finger, stroke and caress his body, and he was
about to yield to her, to make her scream and toss and

fight as if he were splitting and tearing her, when the
sound came down to him again, no longer a whisper, but a
deep voice with a Latin accent.

"C'mon, José, what did you say, man? Say it again,
man . . ."

Then the voice was gone and the music returned.
Frightened, hot and wet, his heart pounding, Domostroy
pulled out of the girl. "Who was that?" he asked, grabbing
for the spread and covering them both with it.

"What? Oh, that!" She sprang out from under him
and turned on the light. He watched her smooth back her
hair and study his perplexed expression. "They," she said,
flavoring the word with mystery and laughing, "are probably taxi or truck drivers. Every once in a while, usually
in the middle of the night—by electronic miracle—my
tuner picks their voices up as they talk to each other
on their citizens' band radios."

The voices interrupted her again. Chattering, they
seemed to be talking for the sake of talking and of having
someone to listen to.

"Really, I'm telling you, man . . ."

"C'mon, José, you know what I mean . . ."

Soon the voices dissolved again in the music.

"You're shivering," she said. Then she laughed again.
"They frightened you, didn't they?"

"I guess they did. Weird. But it's also cold as hell in
here. Can I turn on the heat?"

"You can try, but the valve is stuck. The super has
never come to fix it."

He walked from the bed to the radiator casing under
the window. Consciously keeping his back to her, he
squatted down, opened the metal flap, and tried to turn
the valve. But it was stuck tight, and although he as-
saulted it several times, he couldn't get leverage. The
valve wouldn't budge. As he crouched on the cold floor
with the draft from the window blowing in on him, he
began to shiver and, feeling awkward and embarrassed, he
mustered all his strength and leaned with both hands on
the valve. He felt it give, and then he heard it snap off
under his weight. As he pitched forward, a jet of scalding

steam shot from the opening, barely missing his lower arm and thigh. In catapulting backward to get away from it, he fell over a chair and went sprawling under a table. Vaporizing steam began to fill the room, obscuring its contours. Near him he heard Andrea laugh, but he could only barely distinguish her nude form as she rose, ghostlike, in front of the brilliant haze of the lamp near the bed. Then, he could not see her at all. In the white steam he, too, stood up and groped his way toward the hissing valve and the window above it. He and Andrea kept calling to each other, then—soaking wet, covered with thin, warm rivulets of water—they collided, only to cling to each other. Finally, Domostroy found the window and opened it. A wave of cold air rushed in, sending them both back to bed, shivering and laughing as they huddled together under the blanket. Minutes later, when the built-up steam had run out of the radiator, the air cooled and the fog lifted. Like a garden after a rain, the ceiling of the room, the walls, and the furniture were all dripping water.

"Storm's over," said Andrea. "I'll put a towel over the leak." And without pausing, she asked, "Why do you think I went to bed with you? Because I'm in love with you, or because I want to use you?"

"I hoped it was because you needed me," said Domostroy.

"Really? You mean you don't mind being used?"

"I can handle it. Being used comes with a clear motivation."

"What about love?"

"Love does not. And it doesn't fit in with the trappings of my life."

Located in the South Bronx, a twenty-minute drive from Manhattan, in the old days Kreutzer's had attracted a fairly chic crowd who went there to hear some of the country's best saloon singers. Domostroy recalled a period some twenty years ago—it was about the time when he'd finished his studies and *The Bird of Quintain*, his first work, was being performed by major orchestras—when he used to take dates to Kreutzer's for an evening of great music, elegant dancing, and good Italian cuisine, served in the club's famous Borgia Room. Also during that time, Kreutzer's, like so many other clubs, used to discriminate against blacks. Unable legally to prevent black patrons from entering the premises, the manager would seat them at the least desirable tables, well back in the room, and then tell the waiters to ignore them until they either left of their own accord or provoked a disturbance by complaining too loudly, in which case the management would call the police—always friendly to the establishment—and have them thrown out.

One evening, dressed to the teeth in a silk-lined vicuna coat and tails and accompanied by a glamorously attired date, Domostroy arrived at Kreutzer's well before the scheduled time for the floor show. In a heavy East European accent, with urgency in his voice, he asked the captain to set up the two best tables in the house for a dozen of his distinguished United Nations friends, whom he had invited to dinner. Prompted by Domostroy's generous tips, the staff flew into action setting up the club's best silverware and linen with vases of fresh flowers on two center tables.

The room soon filled to capacity, and to the great delight of Kreutzer's management, a number of press photographers, alerted by Domostroy, arrived to take pictures of the international dignitaries.

Just as the show was about to begin, a commotion at the entrance proclaimed the arrival of Domostroy's guests. The captain and a fleet of waiters rushed to the door to greet them and lead them to their tables; the photographers in attendance set their cameras and flashes at the ready. As the new arrivals proceeded through the aisles of tables to take their places, the manager, captain, and waiters discovered to their horror that the distinguished guests they had been anticipating so eagerly were black and, judging by their dress and speech, were Americans— from Harlem. As the Negro men and women sat down and raised their glasses of champagne, the photographers snapped their photographs, and the following morning the picture of these blacks prominently seated in Kreutzer's appeared in most of the city's newspapers. The papers remarked, tongue in cheek, that, of all the big New York nightclubs, Kreutzer's still took the lead in attracting the smartest clientele in town. With that, Kreutzer's color barrier was broken, and the club was never the same again.

That was more than two decades ago. There was no one at Kreutzer's now who could remember—or would even care to remember—Domostroy's place in the club's history. Just as Domostroy's looks and fortune had changed since then, so had the looks and fortune of Kreutzer's. As the South Bronx deteriorated, fewer and fewer Manhattan patrons wanted to risk their safety traveling there, and without them the nightclub could not maintain its luxurious standards. Eventually the place changed hands and later on became a dive, with rows of pinball machines, a jukebox, and electronic video games filling what once had been the polished dance floor. To attract customers and make the food seem palatable, the Oboe d'Amore Room still offered nightly entertainment, but these days it consisted of a seedy opera singer, an occasional combo of local rock players, a female stripper who could no longer get decent bookings in Manhattan clubs, and—four days a week—Patrick Domostroy, accompanying or backing up these acts on a Barbarina organ, an electronic spinet with a panel of preset tone selectors to provide the sounds of most major instruments, including piano, accordion, saxophone, trombone, guitar, flute, and trumpet, as well as a rhythm section and a mixed chorus.

When Domostroy first saw Andrea Gwynplaine walk through Kreutzer's, he had felt a moment's anguish, aware of an impression she made on him, of his need to impress her. But he'd had no expectations, and when she came over to him, handed him a letter, and humbly asked him to read it, he was surprised to the point of disbelief to have her so suddenly reverse his whole frame of thought.

He looked up and saw Andrea staring at him. She edged closer, piled up the pillows and cushions in a heap, settled back, and ran her hand through his hair.

"None of the articles I read about you explained why you called your first work *The Bird of Quintain*," she said. "Why did you?"

Domostroy wasn't sure whether her interest was genuine and he hesitated before he answered her.

"In the Middle Ages," he said, "a quintain was a practice jousting post with a revolving crosspiece at the top. At one end of the crosspiece was a painted wooden bird and at the other a sandbag. A knight on horseback had to hit the painted bird with his lance and then spur his horse and duck under the crosspiece before the heavy sandbag could swing around and unseat him. I thought the bird of quintain was an apt metaphor for my work—and for my life as well."

"None of the articles I read mentioned a wife, children, or a family," she said.

"I have none," said Domostroy.

"Why not?"

"I lost my parents early in life. Then music took my time and energy. To compose music was, for me, to belong to everyone, to speak every language, to convey every emotion: As a composer, I was the freest of men. A family would have imposed on my freedom."

"And what about sports and hobbies?"

"Never had time for much."

"Except for sex, according to *Hetero*."

"Even sex only on occasion."

"Which occasions?"

"When I have a partner. I don't play solo."

"Who were your favorite partners?"

"Women friends—artists, musicians, writers."

"Who are your partners now?"

"A groupless groupie now and then. A jazzed-out jazz songstress, Those are the only women I share these days."

She eyed him sadly. "It looks as though these days love is all you compose. Don't you mind not sharing your life with a woman of your own?"

"I don't. After all—I'm being shared as well."

"Would you mind sharing me?" she asked, stroking his flesh.

"With whom?"

"With my lover. A rock star."

"He fills your need. You fill mine."

She laughed. "I was just joking. I don't have a lover but—aren't you in the least possessive?" she asked.

"I am—of new experience. Of time passing."

"Then pass it with me. Finding Goddard."

"Why do you want to find him so badly?"

"Obsession. I also badly want to own a Tudor mansion and to fill it with original Pre-Raphaelite paintings. But—long before that—I want to know Goddard."

"Of all people—why Goddard?"

"Why not Goddard? He's a public figure, and I'm his public. I have a legitimate right to know all there's to know about him."

"And he has a right to hide his name, his face, and his life."

"Not from me. I don't separate him from his music."

"But he obviously separates himself."

"Too bad for him," she said, and she leaned back, giving Domostroy another chance to marvel at the smoothness of her belly.

"Tell me, Patrick," she said later that week, "have you ever been completely free with a woman?" She was lying seductively on the bed near him. "I mean free to share with her all that's alive or perverse or just plain spontaneous in you? To lay her any time, any place, once or twice, many times—or not at all? To let your instinct guide you to discover all that you want to know about her and yourself, all that you want to touch and take and taste in her?"

"I'm free with you," he said.

"If you are, it's because you're not in love with me. Because you have nothing to lose by being yourself."

"Surely you don't want your kept man to fall in love with you," he said, laughing off her remark. " 'In love, money shared increases love; money given kills it,' says Stendhal, and he's right: Think how obstreperous I could become if I started to resent your obsession with Goddard!" said Domostroy.

He stopped speaking and began inching closer to her again, until he pressed tightly against her.

Andrea took her knowledge of sexual matters as seriously and studiously as she did her music and drama studies. She was concerned about the ill effect on women's health of the birth-control pill, as well as of the other available products—the IUD, the diaphragm, even spermicidal jelly—and was proud to advocate instead the cervical cap, which she would insert with great care, quite unashamedly, right in front of Domostroy.

She routinely bought a number of magazines and tabloids devoted to the fast-changing fads concerning sex and the mores of intimacy and regularly visited some of the more sophisticated shops dealing in sexual aids, costumes, and novelties. Her closet was a veritable pleasure chest of sexual and, as Domostroy noted with some wonder, bisexual hardware.

She was, he knew by now, an efficient lover, forever anticipating and coaxing and satisfying his needs, as if she had somehow been able to research not only his   sical career but his sexual appetites as well. She liked to bring him just short of the peak of his excitement and then separate herself from him—under the pretext of changing the tape in the stereo set or getting something to drink. She would often surprise him then by coming back to bed, not naked as she had left it, but in various costumes. Once she dressed up like a punk performer, all in black: steel-studded leather collar, tight red leather jacket and short leather skirt, elbow-length leather gloves, and red high-heeled knee boots that clung to her feet and calves. Another time she emerged from the bathroom heavily perfumed and looking like a stripper, with a platinum wig, dark eyeshadow, and thick red lipstick, wearing only a black lace brassiere, lace panties and garter belt, silk stockings, and stiletto-heeled shoes whose leather straps wrapped around her ankles. One night she disappeared in an instant and reemerged with no makeup on at all—with every inch, every pore, every orifice of her body fresh and clean, her hair silky soft, wearing the simplest cotton dress and sandals. With each change of dress and appearance, her manner changed as well. One minute she would be so aggressive as to suck the strength out of him; the next, totally submissive, letting him sap her energy and use her body in whatever way he wished. But no matter what she wore or how she looked, there was always an aura of sensuality about her, at once vulgar and delicate, demure and shameless, so real, so overwhelmingly manifest, that he felt subject to it as he might to a figure of authority or a contagious illness.

At first, given the lengths she went to to excite him, he suspected her of pretending, of acting parts, of creating a sexual masquerade in which he became both audience and participant while she remained merely an instrument of his amusement and pleasure. But later in their lovemaking, as he listened to her rapid breathing and watched her shapely breasts rise and fall in rhythm with the excitement building up in her, as he felt her heartbeat speed up and heard her lose her breath and cry out as she raced into orgasm, he realized that she liked sex just as much as he did and that all of her efforts to bring him to the peak gave her as much pleasure and excitement as they gave him.

"When I want to have a man, he could be the hunchback of Notre Dame," she said. "His looks, his age, his business just don't matter. Only his mind matters—and I don't care if it's crooked. I must get to him as he really is.

When I do—and no holds are barred in the process—I feel free, safe, abandoned to all that pleases him, to all that pleases me. It's natural with me, and to have it I've gone after every man I ever wanted. And I've always gotten him. Always." She rested her chin on his shoulder. "Except for one: Goddard. And getting him is only a matter of time now."

"I remember this guy," said Domostroy pensively, "who for years, every day, rain or shine, dressed in filthy rags, used to stand on the sidewalk in front of Carnegie Hall and sing well-known arias from operas. His voice wasn't bad, and God knows it was strong—it carried for a block—but when he sang, his face turned bright red from the strain, and he grimaced, showing toothless gums. People passing by were so put off by his appearance that they paid no attention to his voice; they thought he was insane. In all those years of singing opera, he only inspired discomfort, even fear. In a way, Goddard is the reverse of that man; we don't see him—we only hear his voice—and therefore we wish to know who he is."

"What if," said Andrea, "Goddard has rebelled so strongly against rock's dependence on visual hype, on the looks and gestures and personal lives of the big stars, that he's decided to literally remove himself from it? Suppose he thinks that by hiding his own face, he is saving the face of rock?"

"He must have a very strong reason for hiding," said Domostroy. "It has to be something much more than a mere publicity gimmick. And it costs him a lot of money, too!" He paused. "Some years ago, six million people sent for tickets to Bob Dylan's rock tour—and there were only six hundred and sixty thousand seats. Don't you know that if Goddard were to give one live concert tomorrow, say, in New York, or Los Angeles, or any big town, hundreds of thousands of his fans would storm to it, no matter what the ticket price? If he would come out of hiding, any TV network would give him millions for just a single performance, and any Hollywood film studio would triple the TV figure for the rights to his life story." He hesitated. "So why doesn't he? Maybe he's a cripple, so hideous, so unsightly that he has to stay out of sight?"

Andrea looked at him skeptically. "He's probably just allergic to people," she said. "Hideous or not," she added, "we still have to find him. I still want to know him."

She waited for Domostroy to respond again, to press her against him, and when he did not, she took his hand as if it were an object and pushed it inside herself, twisting it until his fingers were moist all over, then withdrawing it and slowly raising it to his mouth while the fingers of her other hand spread his lips apart. His tongue felt and tasted her moisture before it combined with his own.

Her voice floated dreamily. "One day, when I know who Goddard is, I'll show up in front of him and surprise him with the truth about himself!"

"What if he already knows the truth?" said Domostroy.

He had accepted her offer and taken her money, worth six months of drudgery at Kreutzer's, all paid in one lump, in cash, in bills so crisp he felt he was the first to use them.

But he didn't know where to begin to crack the nut she had tossed him. Even at the height of his popularity, when he had been composing and making records and performing regularly in public, Domostroy had been, after all, a creative artist and, as such, relatively detached. His connections in the music business had been limited mainly to the staff of his own publisher, Etude Classics. Since then public interest in classical records had diminished, and profits had fallen to the point where Etude could no longer maintain its own sales and distribution arms. For the last several years all Etude records had been distributed by Nokturn Records, a large Manhattan-based company devoted primarily to rock music. Because of this recent affiliation, Domostroy had met, on various occasions, a few executives and employees of Nokturn, but he had not come to know any of them well.

His other professional associations consisted mostly of

lawyers he had hired over the years to advise him about his contracts. He had never even had an agent, preferring to act on his own behalf, and he only consulted his lawyers from time to time, usually when, as it was often the case, he was derided and smeared by irresponsible, inaccurate and biased journalism, and they advised him to sue for libel the paper, magazine or publisher of a scandalous book about him and his work. As a firm believer in uncurbed freedom of the press and, for decades, an activist of the American Civil Liberties Union, he always refused to follow their prompting.

As for the rest of the music world, the composers, performers, impresarios, managers, and media executives, though he had known them all in his heyday—he had served two terms as president of the musicians' and performers' union, sat on the board of the New York Chamber Soloists, and been active in the National Academy of Recording Arts and Sciences, the Recording Industry Association of America, and the National Academy of Popular Music—he rarely communicated with any of those people now.

If he was to find Goddard through such regular channels, he would have to try to comprehend the music industry as a whole and then to decide which part of it, or which individuals in it, could help him in his search.

The irony was that if he were living in a totalitarian state—as he once did—dealing with a monopoly run by a single leader or party, he would only need to befriend or seduce someone in a position of privilege—or insinuate cleverly to others that he had done so—in order to gain access to any information he wanted. It would be far easier to find the button that would open all the doors in a closed, one-party, totalitarian regime than to find the one closed door—the one leading to Goddard—in an open, freely competitive American society.

Besides, just as he would not ever enter into a public dispute with his slanderers or ask the courts to intercede on his behalf when he was viciously libeled by the yellow press, as a free-wheeling self-employed artist, Domostroy had always mistrusted the federal and state government as well as large companies and conglomerates. They were so organized and bureaucratized that they allowed the individuals who made them up to display, as proof of their adherence, only those parts of their personality that coincided with their colleagues' personalities, never those that showed the individual in question to be truly an individual.

Thus, rather than look for assistance from within the music industry, Domostroy was inclined to seek help from someone who, like himself, acted as a free agent, whose access to the world of music was unhampered by corporate or collective considerations.

Sidney Nash was such a man. A freelance journalist, not yet thirty, he had for almost a decade been successfully covering the complex world of corporate musical America. His recent study on the intricacies of the music industry, *Music to Their Ear: The Record Business in America*, had won him a Pulitzer prize, and his major book, *Moonlight Sonata: Music, Self and Profit in American Society*, was already considered a minor classic and a model of journalistic inquiry and documentation. Owing to his meticulous research and his innumerable contacts, nothing in the modern music business was a secret to Nash.

During his late composing days, Domostroy had known Nash pretty well and had been an object of the young critic's admiration, but he hadn't seen Nash in several years. He knew, however, that Nash, typical New Yorker that he was, preoccupied largely with his interests of the moment, would still be willing to stop to take a call out of the past. Also, Nash would understand better than most people the reasons for his old friend's prolonged absence from the city's success-oriented social scene.

Nash told Domostroy to meet him that evening at the Fuzz Box, a popular showcase club in Greenwich Village where he had to catch a new punk group. When Domostroy arrived there, four kids with gaudily dyed hair were into their frenzied finale on the tiny stage. Nash, alone at a table, spotted him and waved. In spite of his big income and his growing popularity, Nash hadn't changed. He still looked like a dissipated graduate student, with his horn-rimmed glasses, baggy tweed suit, and polyester wash-and-wear shirt that made him sweat.

He stood up and greeted Domostroy affectionately, like a prize student seeing his favorite old professor after a number of years. Remembering that Domostroy liked to drink Cuba Libres, he ordered one and another beer for himself. He also rolled a joint, which he held under the table when he wasn't pulling on it.

After they had inquired about each other's health and well-being, Domostroy went straight to the point.

"I need a favor," he said. "I'm working on a project with someone in the record business, and she wants me to find out whatever I can about Goddard. The truth is, I haven't the slightest idea how to go about it." He sounded apologetic and embarrassed.

Nash gave him a forgiving smile. "What does she want to know?" he asked.

"Anything I can find out," Domostroy blurted out awkwardly. "As long as it's more than what's known generally."

"What's known generally," Nash said, spreading his arms, "is his music—and nothing else. Doesn't your friend know that when it comes to Goddard, more is less? Hasn't she heard that he's the man who isn't there?"

"Of course she has," said Domostroy. "She just thought that with my contacts . . . you know . . . people like you . . ." His voice trailed off.

"I see," said Nash. "Well, all I can give you are the facts," he added with a sigh. "As you must know, from the day WNEW first began to play him, Goddard has sold more records than any other pop star. In six years he has produced six LPs, each of which has stayed at the top of the charts for many months. Four of them became platinum, selling over a million albums each. In addition, he's probably had at least a dozen single hits, including six gold ones that grossed over a million dollars each." He sipped his beer. "What can I say? The guy wants to be a mystery."

"You've never met him?" Domostroy asked meekly.

"Not likely," Nash said with an amused smile. "He's a very well-guarded secret. The largest entertainment con-

glomerate in the country, American Music Limited, created Nokturn Records not only to manufacture and distribute
Goddard's records but expressly to guard his secret, to
protect his invisibility—not to mention the shareholders'
investment in him and his music." He paused. "Keep in
mind, we're not just talking cheap hype. We're talking big
money. Record sales in this country equal the combined
grosses from films, television, and all professional sports,
and Goddard is the biggest grosser in the business! Ever!
Now—did you know all that?"

"I did," said Domostroy. "I read it in your article in
the *Times*."

"Good for you. Then you also know that in rock,
nothing succeeds like excess. That's why as long as Goddard's records are selling that way, nobody is about
to crack through Nokturn's hype and invite Goddard to
dinner. That is," he corrected himself, "they can invite
him—by writing care of Nokturn Records—but I have
a hunch he won't show up!" He signaled the waitress
and ordered more beer and another Cuba Libre for
Domostroy.

"What do you think of his music?" Domostroy asked.

"It's good—maybe the best. Bigness has always eaten
up greatness—but not his. He just keeps getting better.
Granted, you can hear influences in his work, but he's
coherent, always plugged into the best. He knows what
he's after, and out of all the shreds and borrowing from
elemental Latin and domestic folklore he's come up with
the finest pop sound we've ever had. Don't tell me you
don't like him!"

"Not much," said Domostroy.

"Generation gap," Nash replied, teasing him. "Or
jealousy, perhaps? How many really coherent works of art
are there?"

"What about his lyrics?" Domostroy asked defensively.

Nash began to roll another joint. "As far as I'm concerned, his taste in lyrics equals his taste in music. Look
at a song like 'Out of Rock.' What other pop star would
sing words by William Butler Yeats?

Out of rock
Out of a desolate source
Love leaps upon its course.

Or how about 'A World Ends'? Imagine anybody else
setting a magnificent poem by Archibald MacLeish to
music!" With fervor he began to recite:

"A world ends when its metaphor has died.
An age becomes an age, all else beside,
When sensuous poets in their pride invent
Emblems for the soul's consent
That speak the meanings men will never know
But man-imagined images can show:
It perishes when those images, though seen,
No longer mean. . . .

And that's the single that sold millions! That's hard to
beat, don't you think?" Nash asked.

"Maybe so," said Domostroy, "but what about a song
like 'Acne Lady'? All the cute wordplay on pharmaceuti-
cals: Blondit, Nudit, Moisture Whip, Lush Lips. Or that
other one—'Pornutopia Is Utopia'—where he says, 'Pro-
creation is creation, contraception true deception, mastur-
bation—sex probation.' You don't think that's pretty silly?"

"If it is, so is the culture that daily promotes all that
stuff," said Nash. "Goddard is obviously making fun of it,
Domostroy! What's more, that's the stuff his young fans
understand. You may not like it, but that's probably because of your age. Keep it in mind—"

"I mind keeping it," said Domostroy. "Childish jin-
gles on TV and in all the jukeboxes don't make growing
old any easier for me."

"Be fair, Domostroy. Musically and in terms of lyrics,
Goddard is the culmination of all his rock 'n' roll predecessors—Elvis Presley, John Lennon, Bob Dylan, Elton
John, Bruce Springsteen—as well as of what's best in
funk, soul, reggae—and, of course, the influence of such
master saloon singers as Nat King Cole and Tony Bennett.
In Goddard's music you can hear the whole vocabulary of

Karlheinz Stockhausen and electronic gizmos—from the
Sound City Jo'anna and Pianomate through the Hammond,
the Moog, the Buchla, all the way to the ARP, the Putney,
the Synthi, and the Gershwin. You name it, he's played
it!"

Domostroy listened carefully. After a pause he said,
"I still can't believe that in this free-wheeling media-crazy
society, no one can find out the identity of our most
popular music star!"

"Everybody is free to try to find out," said Nash, "and
believe me, almost everybody has tried. Do you remember when all the fan magazines were offering rewards to
anyone who could name Goddard or produce a verifiable
photograph of him? When hundreds of guys came forward, each one claiming to be Goddard—and some even
singing like him? When, after the real Goddard failed to
show up to accept his first Grammy Award—the first of
three he's won so far—the news and wire services all
went after him. And so did every Dick Tracy, every disc
jockey, every sleuth and gumshoe of the Record Industry
Association of America, every frustrated music critic, song
writer and rumor-monger—and everybody else on Tin
Pan Alley—the central coterie of songwriters, music plug-
gers, and record companies! And what did they uncover?
Nothing, apart from all the usual red herring and guess-
work: that he stays out of sight because he's crippled; that
his face was destroyed in a car accident; that he has Saint
Vitus' dance; that he had a premonition early on that if he
ever came out of hiding he would get a bullet—instead of
flowers and kisses—from one of his fans or envious enemies.
Others, who claimed to have fucked him or supposedly
helped him to write his music or lyrics or both, say that
he's heavy into smack—a heroin addict who doesn't want
to be cured; or get this, that he's a wireheading freak, with
wire implants in his brain that give him hallucinogenic
jolts and let him and his wireheaded lovers trip for hours
on electrosex! Still others say that his invisibility is nothing
but clever record company hype—the best ever. It keeps
the public excited and it keeps the star safe from all the
crazies; because as long as nobody knows who Goddard is,

nobody can take a shot at him. A singer who loses his head over his public will be publicly beheaded. Remember John Lennon?"

Nash finished his beer and glanced at his watch. "I'd give up if I were you," he concluded. "Everyone else has. Goddard says it all when he sings those lines from Joyce's *Ulysses*:

> *I am the boy*
> *That can enjoy*
> *Invisibility.*

And why shouldn't he enjoy his invisibility? If anybody as good as he is wants to be a mystery, I say let him. And I wonder if anybody really gives a fuck, any longer."

"My partner does," said Domostroy. "What do I tell her?"

"Tell her to go after me instead. I've got a sound mind, the looks of a rock star, and what's more, I don't hide!"

In the New York Public Library, Domostroy pored over one article after another, and they all bore out what he already knew without offering any fresh clues. Each year Goddard's records continued to top the charts of best-sellers, and each week the sound of his music grew in popularity until it seemed to fill the airwaves, yet no one had managed to discover who he was. His mystery remained inviolate, in spite of elaborate efforts to crack it. One San Francisco textual music scholar claimed that Goddard was an ex-student of his at Berkeley who followed the Descartes credo "*Larvatus prodeo*—I walk about masked" and who had written essays that sounded a lot like the lyrics of Goddard's bestselling song "The Passion of the Soul." The scholar related how, when he tried to contact the student, the man had disappeared, and none of his friends would provide any reliable information about him. A Manhattan disc jockey announced with similar assurance that Goddard was a farmer with a wife and three children who lived on a remote farm in upper New York State. And a well-known English rock guitarist was convinced that he and Goddard used to hang out in a certain London jazz club before either of them had made it.

Each of a number of psychics hired by tabloid newspapers and fan magazines had come up with a different composite of the man. One saw Goddard as a pathologically shy small-town youth holed up in a private asylum where with the collaboration of his music editors he wrote and recorded his music; another clearly pictured him as a drug addict in an industrial city, requiring periodic hospitalization; a third said that before he turned invisible, Goddard was known to the world under another name as a second-rate country singer and that only by means of a CIA conspiracy, coupled with the help of hired professional music writers and of his influential big business friends and his mistress, who was a well-known Hollywood agent, Goddard had managed to go so long unmasked.

Reluctantly, Domostroy decided to take a look at the Goddard Beat, a popular West Side discotheque that was named after Goddard and featured his music. The Goddard Beat differed from most discos in that, instead of hiring disc jockeys to program records, it employed live performers, often the most inventive rock 'n' roll and pop groups available, to whom doing a gig at the Goddard Beat was tantamount to reaching Mecca.

Domostroy abhorred discos and had stayed away from them even when, at the time of his own popularity, he'd been invited to go to them with friends. His reason was simple: mixed by a computer, amplified by a robot, and danced to by human automatons, disco music was not art.

As Domostroy entered the Goddard Beat, members of one of the alternating bands of the evening were noisily removing electronic gear from the stage while another band's members were setting up theirs. Before Domostroy could push his way through the sweaty crowd to a place at the bar, the new band hit its first number, and all around him couples began to sway, tightly embraced.

When he finally reached the bar and ordered a Cuba Libre, the bartender, a Latin with a fierce mustache, glared at him and asked, "What was that?"

"Cuba Libre!" Domostroy repeated in a louder voice.

"Cuba what?" asked the man angrily.

"Cuba Libre," said Domostroy slowly, controlling himself. "You're a bartender, aren't you? That's rum with coke and a slice of lime!"

"I know what a Cuba Libre is. I'm Cuban!" snapped the bartender. "But *Libre* means 'free,'" he went on, "and I happen to know that Cuba is not free, Señor, so instead of calling your drink a Cuba Libre—which is a lie—I suggest, Señor, that you call it a Big Lie! Do you understand?"

"I understand," said Domostroy, deadpan. "Then give me a double Big Lie. With two slices of lime, please."

A girl sitting at the bar next to Domostroy started to laugh, and Domostroy turned defensively to face her. She was also Latin, with expressive brown eyes, jet-black hair, and teeth that seemed almost too white.

He felt out of place as she continued to stare at him and laugh, but he neither shifted his gaze nor neglected to take in her full, high breasts and compact figure.

"Don't be mad, Dad!" she said to him. "Next time, ask for a Tequila Sunrise."

"I'm not your dad," said Domostroy.

"You could be," she said, and she turned toward him on her bar stool, ready to start up a conversation.

"I could be a lot of things," he said, trying to figure out whether she was a lonely flirt, which he wouldn't have minded, or a professional hooker, whom he knew he couldn't afford.

"You could also have a better haircut," she said, studying him.

"Why?"

"It's cut too short," she said with conviction. "All wrong for your face."

"What should I do about it?" he asked with a grin.

"Let it grow for a month or two. Then have it cut right."

"By whom?"

She gave him a coquettish look. "By me, for instance."

"Why you?"

"I'm a beautician. Fully licensed to cut hair." She promptly reached into her shoulder bag, pulled out a business card, and handed it to him.

He read the card: "Angelina Jimenez, Beauty Expert. Formerly of Hotel Casa de Campo, La Romana, Dominican Republic." The address was in mid-Manhattan.

"Everybody calls me Angel," she said.

Domostroy introduced himself and apologized for not having a card to give her.

"I cut their hair," she said, pointing proudly at the band on the stage. "I cut most of the big New Wave musicians." She paused, as if expecting him to register surprise, and when he didn't, she said, "Any time you see a great haircut that stands out on a new punk, funk, rock, or pop album cover, you can be pretty sure it's mine. I make them all original—and I know them all personally!"

"I'm impressed," he said, sensing an opportunity. He moved his stool closer to her.

"Don't tell me you cut hair too," she said.

"No. I cut—used to cut—records."

"No kidding. What kind of records?"

"My own music," he said.

She gave him a long look. "Should I know you?" she asked then, a touch of awe in her voice. "I mean, would I know your stuff?"

"I doubt it. When I wrote it, you weren't born yet."

"You're not that old," she reassured him. Then she added, quite seriously, "I'll bet you still have most of your own teeth."

"Most," he told her. "Capped, some of them, but mine."

" 'Your teeth are clean, but your mind is capped,' " she recited. "That's from John Lennon. But what about your music?" she went on.

"It's nothing I could play here," he said with a vague gesture.

"Did you ever play at the hall?"

"The hall?"

"Carnegie Hall. A lot of the big pop stars play there."

"Yes, I've played a few times at Carnegie Hall," he said.

"And at the Garden?" she pursued.

"No. Not there. Madison Square Garden was too big for my music."

"Could I find your records in a store?" she asked.

"You might," he said. "By now, many of them are collectors' items."

He ordered another round of drinks.

"What are you doing now?" she asked.

He smiled. "Having a drink. Letting my hair grow."

"Not now! I mean—in life. You know."

"I'm between—" he halted "—records."

"Well, before you do the next record, promise you'll call me. I'll cut your hair and make you up for the album photo. Believe me, a good picture makes all the difference!"

"Tell me, Angel," he asked her as they sipped their drinks, "have you ever cut Goddard's hair?"

"I wish I had," she said, flashing her white teeth.

"Maybe you've cut his hair without knowing who he was."

"Maybe you're right. I wouldn't know, would I?" she reflected.

"He might even be one of those guys there," said Domostroy, pointing at the band.

"No way," she said. "All of these guys know every note of each other's voices from records. They could tell Goddard just like that!" She snapped her fingers.

"Are they curious about him?"

"Of course they are," she said. "They've been trying to figure him out for years now. They go on and on and on talking about his out-of-the-ballpark sticks and his two-beats and his barrelhouse, his singsongs and his trances and his harmolodics and his fizzles and fuzzboxes and his overdubbing—you name it—and they still can't figure it out."

"Figure what out?" he asked.

"Why he plays such a mean pinball—why you can never tell which way the guy's going in a song—like the ball in a pinball machine!"

"What's so different about him?"

"His licks, for one thing. The way he leans on some notes like nobody else around. Some punks swear that Goddard rehearses with an audience—did you know that? They swear that to come on so strong and so good he has to get kicks from real people."

"Do they think he has his own studio?"

"Oh, sure," she said. "Look, having your own recording studio is not a big gig these days! I cut a lot of people's hair in their own places. There's one punk rock guy who has a penthouse studio with all the sound-track equipment and electronic gear you could imagine—right on York Avenue, overlooking the river! And not one of that guy's funkadelics has ever even hit the top forty!"

"Who do they say the people are who work with Goddard?"

"Some guys think that with Nokturn behind him, he's got the best people in the business working with him. But I cut a lot of hair," she said with a wide smile, "and quite a few say Goddard might be doing a lot of stuff all by himself. If Stevie Wonder, who's blind, could play, record, and produce an album like *Music of My Mind* all alone in his own studio, which he bought with his own money, why couldn't a smart guy like Goddard do the same thing? Why couldn't he record on his own gear—you know, his own synthesizers and sidemen and bandboxes and ribbons and wheels, and whatever all the rest of that stuff's called—just like Stevie Wonder?"

"Do you know anyone who says he knows who Goddard is?" Domostroy tossed off.

"Oh, sure! Everybody I know says they have some idea," she said, shrugging, "but between you and me, they don't. All they know is that there's nobody like him."

"Where do they think he's from?" he asked. "Is he black or white?"

"Everybody keeps guessing," she said. "Most don't think he's black, but you really can't tell. I should be able to tell if he's Spanish-speaking, but I can't."

"What do you mean?" Domostroy asked.

"He put out some songs in Spanish. Didn't you know that?"

"I didn't," said Domostroy.

"Oh, sure. They're Mexican. 'Volver, Volver, Volver' and 'El Rey.' Old folk songs. Every Latin person knows them!"

"And how good is Goddard's Spanish?"

"Not bad, but he's got a funny accent. Some people think he's American-Mexican, but he also might be like me—an American from Santo Domingo!" she exclaimed with pride. "I once cut the hair of a guy who knew everybody at *Billboard*, *CashBox*, and *Variety*, and he said Goddard was—" she searched for the word "—a Jewish musical egghead."

"Meaning?" Domostroy asked.

"That he is smart!" She touched her head with a forefinger. "That if you listen to Goddard real close, you can tell he's gone to a good music school. Not at all like those guys!" she said, gesturing with her head at the band.

Two young men from the band came over to tell her they were about to leave, and Angel got up to go. As she thanked Domostroy for the drinks, she gave his face and hands a last hard look. "Your skin's getting a bit dry," she said. "You should use a moisturizer. Did you know that pure petroleum jelly is best?" She grinned. "For the hands, glycerin and oxide are also okay. Or, if you want to be fancy, buy yourself some preparations with stearic acid, propylene glycol, glycerol stearates, or purcellin oil." She obviously enjoyed showing off her professional knowledge. "Purcellin oil is really super. It comes from the glands of ducks and geese. It's the stuff that makes water roll off a duck's back!" With that, she left to join her departing friends.

*   *   *

By now, Domostroy was convinced that any attempt
to trace Goddard through music societies, business con-
cerns, or government channels would be useless. Even
with Andrea's help he had neither the means nor the
energy to undertake that sort of investigation; furthermore,
he had no reason to believe he would succeed where so
many others had failed.

There had to be some path that would lead to Goddard. But which one?

Domostroy began listening to Goddard's music, hour
after hour, with his eyes closed. The melodic shape was
always original: the tempos created an exciting pulse; the
singer's voice remained strong and vibrant, with good
diction and coloration; and the lyrics, now turbulent, now
tender, seldom robbed the music of its own drama.

After a while Domostroy began to suspect that Goddard cleverly mixed the sounds of live instruments with a
synthesizer, which, by electronically storing the sounds of
several instruments, allowed him, at a touch of the keyboard, to accompany himself with a number of instruments or even an entire band. He noticed that only once
had Goddard ever recorded music written by anyone else—
the two songs in Spanish that Angel had mentioned—and
even then he had tailored the songs radically to match the
famous Goddard sound. In the past, both of these selections had been performed time and time again by Latin
singers, so if Goddard had gone to the trouble of rearranging,
translating, and recording them, these simple, folk songs
must have been important to him. But nothing on his
other records indicated any Latin influence. Had he, perhaps, in his travels, heard the tunes in Mexican nightclubs
or at Latin music festivals and liked them enough to
commit his time, talent, and effort to popularizing them in
the States? Who could tell? There could have been a
dozen other reasons equally as plausible.

*   *   *

Some days after his meeting with Nash, Domostroy went to see Samuel Scales in the offices of Mahler, Strauss, Handel, and Penderecki, a large law firm representing many clients in the field of the arts, and principally musicians. A few years before, Scales had negotiated Domostroy's contract with Etude Classics, and at that time the two men had often seen each other socially. Scales's firm—until recently housed in an East Side brownstone—reflected perfectly the mushrooming of the entertainment industry in America, for it now occupied six floors of the Hammerklavier Building, one of the tallest futuristic additions to the Manhattan skyline.

Domostroy shared the waiting room with a still glamorous aging movie star and a couple of black rock musicians. As he followed the receptionist to Scales's office, he passed rows of desks and dozens of cubicles buzzing with the noise of electric typewriters, telexes, telephones, and photocopying machines. The sight of so many secretaries working with the newest electronic word processors surprised him, and he suddenly felt intimidated as well as embarrassed at the thought of why he was there.

Scales stood up behind his large rosewood desk, which was centered in front of a wall-sized window fifty floors above Madison Avenue. Deeply tanned, his silvery hair combed back, his forehead and cheeks smoothed out by plastic surgery, Scales looked like a middle-aged Beverly Hills playboy. He waved Domostroy in. "Well! I'm surprised to see you looking so fit," he joked, "after all the terrible things I've been hearing about you."

"What terrible things?" asked Domostroy, forcing a big smile.

"Gypsy living. Moonlighting in wild places. Mickey-Mousing." He laughed and motioned for them to sit down. "True or false?"

"True," said Domostroy, sitting. "They keep me fit."

Scales pushed some papers aside and leaned forward on the desk. "What can I do for you, Domo?" he asked. "Got a new masterpiece? Another *Octaves,* by any chance?"

"Not quite. I am working on something—with another person," said Domostroy, mustering courage.

"Be careful! I still recall those press hatchet jobs about your 'secret' collaborators and what their headlines did to your reputation. But this time is it really a musical collaboration?" Scales asked with interest.

"Only of sorts. And no more than were all those others. But this time I need advice. It won't take long at all," he said, recalling Scales's extravagantly high fees in bygone days.

"I'm all ears," said Scales.

"Well . . . my partner and I are wondering . . . what are the chances of our tracking down Goddard."

Scales raised his eyebrows. "Goddard? *The* Goddard?"

"Yes."

"What for?"

"For a good reason, believe me," said Domostroy.

"Like what? Murder? Can you prove Goddard killed someone?" asked Scales a bit impatiently.

"No, but—"

"Because if you can't, I'd advise you not to waste your time." He paused and reflected. "In fact, even if you could prove such a thing, finding him still wouldn't be easy. I once handled a rather famous case involving a prisoner at Leavenworth." He paused, then opened up to tell Domostroy yet another favorite story. "This man, starting when he was twelve, had spent some twenty-five years in the clink for various crimes, including killing a fellow prisoner and badly wounding another. While he was in prison, invisible to the world, he wrote country and western music and lyrics and he sent the stuff to some music luminaries on the outside. They were convinced that they'd discovered a genius, and they hired me to help them obtain the man's parole. So at the age of thirty-seven he arrived in Nashville and was welcomed by the country and western establishment as if he were a Johnny Cash clone.

"Even though his music—at best, mediocre—was gentle, his lyrics were not. They expressed contempt for the faceless masses whom he saw as ignorant, cynical and basically evil. The fellow believed that to be a man, you must, to save face, kill anyone who threatens you with force. But once his arrival turned into a rags-to-riches publicity event, everyone hoped that the man to whom violence was music would now be just a music man, a noble savage, a gentle prisoner of the keyboard, with a musical talent that would free his soul. Needless to say, as if on command, in spite of his hateful lyrics, his music received some of the most laudatory front-page reviews country and western had ever seen and—visible as hell— our genius was launched, like no other, into a musical career. However . . ." Scales slumped back in his chair.

"However," he went on, "barely two weeks later, he was in a coffee shop, where he asked to use the washroom. The counter man, a twenty-two-year-old musician—a recently married gentle fellow who worked there part-time— told him that the place didn't have a public toilet. Actually, it didn't, but our noble savage chose not to believe the guy, and—possibly to save face in front of two young women who were with him—he knifed the young man to death for lying to him. Then he vanished. He managed to stay clear of the police, write many more songs, and, possibly in collusion with some of his past sponsors, have them published under another name, and sung by some of our best country and western stars, before tipping off the newspapers to who he was. He's still writing, as far as I know, still at large and invisible again. Nobody has any idea what he looks like these days, whether he has killed anyone else, or who—if anyone—is helping him out. And that man is a publicized murderer! If he can hide and write his music in secret, think of what Goddard, with Nokturn Records behind him, could get away with!" Scales looked sadly up at Domostroy.

"Do you then think looking for Goddard would be a complete waste?" Domostroy asked.

"In my opinion, it would," Scales said. "At least it's been a complete waste for, I guess, quite a few thousand people so far."

"You mean I don't have the smallest chance of finding him?"

"That's exactly what I mean."

"What about Nokturn Records? Surely they deal with him, don't they? How? How does he get his music to them?"

"By mail probably. From their very first press conference on Goddard, Nokturn has stuck to the same story: they say that no one in the company has ever met Goddard in person and that no one there knows who or where he is. Therefore, Nokturn could not divulge his secret even if they wanted to."

"Do you believe them?" asked Domostroy.

"Do I have any proof that they are lying?"

"But what about the government?" Domostroy was insistent. "Someone in the government must know who Goddard is."

"C'mon, Domo," said Scales gruffly. "What does the government care? Goddard is a rock singer, not the head of a foreign state in disguise or a Soviet or CIA master spy on the loose!"

"But Goddard gets money from Nokturn, doesn't he? What about taxes? Doesn't the government go after his taxes? They certainly went after mine—checking my returns year after year—when I used to compose and record!" Domostroy was feeling more and more frustrated.

"I know they did," said Scales softly. "I represented you then." He straightened in his chair. "As I recall," he went on with exaggerated calm, "about a year after Goddard's first big album came out and the first big money started rolling in, a congressional inquiry prompted the IRS to do a scrupulous audit of all of Nokturn's dealings with Goddard. The IRS found nothing illegal in Nokturn's handling of their Goddard business. On the contrary, as Oscar Blaystone, Nokturn's president, revealed, the company paid all Goddard's royalties to a Swiss bank's numbered account, but only after all New York state and city taxes and all federal taxes had been withheld. That meant, as an agent of the IRS publicly pointed out, that by remaining incognito, Goddard was voluntarily waiving massive tax deductions he would be entitled to under U.S. tax law as a self-employed artist." He paused. "It also means that as long as his income is properly taxed to the fullest, Goddard is free of any hassles with revenue agents. And given the extraordinary secrecy the Swiss guarantee people with really big accounts—can you imagine how big Goddard's account must be!—he can move money from there with the greatest ease to accounts in his own name, or in the name of John Doe, anywhere in the world, without fear of discovery. What else do you want to know, Domo?" he asked, glancing at his desk calendar.

"Nothing. I guess you've said it all." Domostroy got up. "Do you have any advice for me?" he asked as Scales escorted him to the door.

"Write music and don't make new headlines. They don't do you any good," said Scales, shaking his hand. "I mean that. Besides, isn't Etude still your publisher?"

"Yes," said Domostroy. "They keep my records in print."

"Well, Etude records are distributed by Nokturn. So if you write some more music, you'll be in the same boat as Goddard! What better way to find him?"

"But how will I know the other guy in the boat is Goddard?" asked Domostroy.

"You won't. And that's the catch," said Scales, laughing as he closed the door.

Listening to Goddard's music and speculating about his own fate, Domostroy recalled his own better days, when he traveled to give a concert or plug his latest release on a publicity tour. All during the time when his records were selling and his music was at its peak of popularity, he often appeared on TV and radio talk shows and music programs across the country. His fan mail then was so voluminous that Etude would ship to him only the cream of the fan letters, for he could never have read them all. One of the secretaries at Etude Classics did the sorting out, sending him by express mail only letters from critics, serious listeners, and music students. The straight-into-the-wastebasket stuff, comprised largely of naive assurances of adoration, was answered by the secretary herself with the usual form letter.

Domostroy's thoughts wandered to a conversation he had once had with a handsome Hollywood star. The actor had said that most of the letters he received from his countless female fans—even when they contained photographs showing the writers as beautiful and voluptuous women—were so predictable and banal that he had never had any interest in meeting the women.

"A typical fan letter from a woman," he had said, "is all about how much she loves me, how much she wants to meet me, how much she would cherish a moment with me, how much she hopes I might go to bed with her! It's all about *her* and what *she* wants. But how about me? Am I here to fuck America's darlings just because I'm the star they want?

"If any one of these spoiled cunts ever for a moment thought about me," he had continued, "she would know that the way to meet me is not to offer to let me lay her—I can get laid by anyone I want—but to show that she understands me in some other way. Has she seen all my films, including the early ones, where I played bit parts? Has she read all that's been written about me? Has she figured out from my interviews why I've said what I've said—and whether I've told the truth? Why I like some of my films and hate others? Why I'm proud of some of my roles, but not of others? After she's done all that, let her convince me that she knows what I need and that she can deliver it better than any other woman I could pick up on my own. It would be fun to meet such a fan! But if there is one like that, she certainly hasn't written to me yet—and so I've yet to go on a date with her. How about you, Domostroy? Did you ever have a fan who understood you?"

"Maybe one," Domostroy had answered evasively, "and I didn't understand her."

*   *   *

"All the ways I've thought of up to now," said Domostroy to Andrea, "are wrong. They're wrong because they all go one way—from us to Goddard."

"Is there any other way?"

"Yes. From him to us. We have to make him come out of his hideaway and then unmask him, rather than the other way around."

"He probably doesn't have one hideaway," she said. "The whole world could be Goddard's hideaway."

"It probably is. So then, what we have to do is compose the right invitation from you to Goddard, send it to him, and hope it intrigues him so much that he shows up here to find you."

"And what would attract Goddard to me?"

"What you say in your letter. You have to trigger in him a longing for you. For your understanding of him. If you can succeed in doing that, he'll show up to claim you soon enough."

"My understanding of him?" she repeated. Then, folding her arms over her breasts, she exclaimed, "You're a composer, Patrick; you have more understanding of him than I'll ever have! In one of your old interviews you said that music was 'the only spiritual accomplishment of your life'! In another, you said, 'There is anguish that only composers recognize in each other.' Think of his music, Patrick! His music is his spiritual address. It might tell us who he is!" She halted—excited—then went on. "Why can't you figure out who influenced him as an artist. Was it a particular composer? A music teacher? Someone who determined his choice of instruments or his arrangements? A particular engineer or sound expert or one of those new electronic music wizards? Can't you find out who he is from his music?"

Her enthusiasm and her line of thought were contagious.

"I could try," said Domostroy. "Goddard's melodies and harmonies and rhythms and musical forms probably tell more about him than his handwriting or his astrological charts or the lines in his hand. So do his lyrics." He paused. "For instance, one of his songs is called 'Fugue.' Now, of course, in music, *fugue* signifies contrapuntal imitations, but in psychiatry it means a state of flight from reality. Such things may indeed tell us much more about Goddard than, say, we would be likely to deduce from his looks."

"What do you mean, from his looks?" She rose on the bed and hovered over him.

"I mean, he is not about to come to you as Goddard. He might be anybody."

"What if I have already met him?" she said. "What if that tall creep next door who always says hello to me is Goddard?"

"If he is, he certainly won't admit it—even to you. If he's remained in a state of fugue and secrecy all this time, you don't expect him to walk in, shake your hand, and introduce himself as Goddard, do you? And I'm sure his everyday voice sounds quite different than his recording one—as is the case with so many other pop singers. A lot of work has gone into Goddard's staying hidden, and a lot of money comes out of it. He, or the people behind him, are not about to give that up just because of a clever letter from an amorous fan. Even if he likes your letter and is tempted to meet you—in person—he or his associates will probably send someone to check you out, to make sure you're not trying to set a trap for him."

"Send whom, for instance?"

"Who knows? A man, a woman, even a couple. Anybody—a guy making a pass at you at a cocktail party, a door-to-door saleswoman, even the creep next door! We don't know who works for him! In fact, if Goddard does fall for you, I'm quite certain he would have to come to see you incognito, as an ordinary man, without ever admitting to the handicap of his success, wealth, and fame— or to any knowledge of your letter. You might make love

to Goddard, listen to his heart—or the story of his life—
and never know he's Goddard."

"You mean that after my magic letter is sent off, I
have to embrace every ordinary slob who makes a pass at
me because he might be Goddard?" said Andrea.

"You might have to, yes. And when you do, try to
figure out if he is the one who read your letter."

"But I don't want to share my body with any ordinary
slob."

"In that case, you might miss altogether the chance of
knowing Goddard. What if the sole reason for his invisibility and secrecy—and his success—is that he enjoys being
an ordinary slob?"

She considered the idea in silence. Then she said,
"Where do we send the letter?"

"Care of Nokturn Records," said Domostroy.

"Doesn't Nokturn get hundreds of letters to Goddard
every day?"

"They probably do. There's no other place to write
him. Nokturn even admits that his fan mail amounts to
about a thousand letters every week, and they have a
special staff to process it. Out of that mass I'm sure they
forward him only a small handful of mail."

"What would make them forward my letter?"

"I don't know yet. Something about it should make it
unusual—and convincing."

"Keep in mind, Patrick," said Andrea, "that the letter
might not even reach the invisible boy. What if he has better
things to do than read fan mail the week our letter arrives?
What if he's traveling? What if . . ." Her voice trailed off.

"What if he reads the letter and doesn't think much of
you?"

"That too," she said.

"Then we'll send several letters," said Domostroy.
"One after another."

*   *   *

Domostroy dreaded death—not illness or pain or the humiliation of disability associated with dying, but death itself: the sudden cessation of the self, the end of being, the final, arbitrary dissolution, as it were, of the entire concrete history of Patrick Domostroy.

The thought of it came to him often, both in the daytime—during a spell of joy or pleasure—and at night, when nightmares about dying would wake him up to conscious fear of it as he lay alone in the dark.

All men were subject to death at any time, and, he knew, for most men their past—their lived life—was the only reality death could not take from them. Still, whereas death could terminate the existence of Patrick Domostroy as a physical being, it could not terminate the existence of his music, which, being an abstract entity, would extend into the future. His music was a shadow cast before him, and as long as he was composing, Domostroy regarded himself as existing without a history, as creating the means to outlive himself.

In his composing days Domostroy thought of his music as a key that could open the door to the future. Since many of his admirers were young, they would outlive him and thus become his standard-bearers and messengers in the years ahead. When his music was widely known and he himself famous, he kept the lock and hinges of that door well oiled. He would answer piles of letters from young men and women enthusiastic in their praise of his talent—all of them sincere, a few actually perceptive. Occasionally, for the sake of vanity, but even more for the sake of securing his future, he even encouraged them and went so far as to make an appointment and talk to one or another of these eager fans.

He recalled one in particular, a college music student from somewhere in Michigan. She had written to say that his music meant so much to her that it would be the high point of her life if she could discuss it with him. She assured him that she would not be a nuisance and that the most she would ask of him would be to autograph her copies of his sheet music and albums. She would come to New York whenever it was convenient for him to see her, if only he would call her—collect—and say when. Enclosed with the imploring letter was a photograph of the girl looking slim and young and pretty. Domostroy telephoned her and named a weekend when he would be in New York. Sounding like an innocent, she thanked him profusely; she was not familiar with the city, she explained, and so they arranged to meet at her hotel.

He was seated at a table in the hotel bar when she arrived, and she recognized him immediately. Tall and graceful, with wide blue eyes and an oval face framed by auburn hair, she walked over to his table and introduced herself. She wore her simple clothes well—with a sort of stylish slouch—and yet she was obviously shy. She was so flustered when she went to shake his hand that she dropped the armful of scores and albums she was clutching. As she and Domostroy scrambled to retrieve them, their heads colliding under the table, she admitted that she had been terrified he would find her clumsy and dull; surely, now he must think the worst of her.

Domostroy tried to put her at ease. He ordered drinks for the two of them, and as she sipped hers, and blushed with shame, he playfully said that he was the one who should feel insecure, faced with someone as young and attractive as she was. Slowly then, she began to open up. She talked about herself and her studies, told Domostroy how a fellow student who was a fan of his had first recommended his music to her, and confessed that through his music she had discovered emotions in herself she had not been aware of before.

As the evening wore on, he tried to sort out his feelings about the young woman. Should he prolong their time together and eventually take her to bed, or should he leave her and join a group of his friends who were having a birthday party for a young, apparently very sexy French cellist they thought he would like. The party was being held at the Rainbow Room, a nightclub high atop the RCA Building.

Domostroy was prone to these moments of conflict over unimportant matters—where to dine, what to wear, whom to call for a date, how long to stay at a party. His

literary friends chose to read into his chronic indecision a
Jekyll-Hyde syndrome; his friends who believed in astrology saw him simply as a typical Gemini, forever torn
between pairs of conflicting impulses.

He could, of course, take his Michigan fan to the
Rainbow Room, introduce her to his friends, and then
take her back to her hotel; or he could go alone to the
Rainbow Room, meet the French cellist, make arrangements to take her out in a day or two, and then go back
and spend the night with his out-of-town visitor.

He tried to assess the situation in terms of responsibility. Was it fair for him to take her to bed, treat her as if
she were a thing, an image of youth and purity that he
could use to shore up his self-esteem?

On the other hand, he reasoned, she saw him as the
artist who personified maturity, creation and many lively
though now forgotten public controversies. And since she
had created her concept of him in order to satisfy herself,
she had made him a part of herself; but that image controlled her as the drug controlled the addict who sought it
out. Yet by seeking him out, wasn't she declaring herself
able to decide on her own that she wanted to keep him as
the source of her obsession—to become his lover and take
him to bed as if he were an object, a thing created purely
to satisfy her own needs?

The girl must have sensed his restiveness, he thought,
for she glanced at her watch and said she had taken up too
much of his time. She thanked him once again, then went
on to say that she had a confession to make: perhaps she
was wrong to tell him this, she said, but the reason she
had wanted this meeting so much was that she was suffering from acute myelomonoblastic leukemia, a degenera-
tive disease that attacks the bone marrow as well as the
liver, spleen, and lymph nodes, and according to her
doctors—and all the books she had read on the subject—
she would be dead within the year. Inasmuch as she was
sure to be confined to a hospital for the final stage of her
illness, she had decided to forgo her normal timidity and
do everything she could, while she was still able, to meet

Patrick Domostroy, the person who had most enriched her life.

He looked at her carefully. Nothing in her looks or manner indicated the ravages of disease; on the contrary, she seemed almost glowing with health. He told her that in this day and age she might very well be cured of her illness and live for many years, even outlive her family and friends. Or, her life might be stopped in its course not by leukemia but, say, by a car accident. Only chance stands up to the predictable in our lives, he said; chance, in the end, provides man's only excuse, and therefore his comfort in the face of the irrational.

He watched her as he spoke, noticing how soft and unblemished her skin was, how thick and shiny her hair. Her breathing seemed perfectly even, and when, under the pretext of picking a bit of lint off her collar, he touched her neck and cheek, her skin felt dry and cool.

He had the feeling that she was not ill at all; that she had invented her illness to justify her visit, as well as to make him feel sorry for her, thereby exciting his interest in her and inducing him to stay longer with her than he would with any other visitor who had nothing to offer him but youth, innocence, and naive admiration. And so he became determined not to play into her hands, but to extricate himself then and there. He called for the check and while waiting for it, quickly inscribed to her all the scores and albums she'd brought with her. Then he politely escorted her to the elevator, kissed her gently on the cheek, and said good night.

Minutes later, the high-speed elevator in the RCA Building flew him to the Rainbow Room, sixty-five floors above the lights of Manhattan.

During the months that followed, in the busy course of his life—writing music during the day, going out at night, traveling, performing, seeking out women with imagination and men with wisdom—he forgot all about his Michigan visitor. When one day a lawyer from an Ann

Arbor firm called him, mentioned her name, and suggested that Domostroy must have known the young lady very well, Domostroy became annoyed. He asked what could possibly have led the man to such a conclusion. After a short silence, the lawyer apologized for having been presumptuous and then went on to inform Domostroy that the young woman had just died—the victim of a fatal blood disease—and to the surprise of her family and friends she had bequeathed all she owned to Domostroy. Ironically and touchingly, all she owned of any value consisted of a collection of Domostroy's sheet music and record albums, which the composer had so cordially signed for her several months before when she visited him in New York. The lawyer told Domostroy that she referred to that visit in her last testament as the most moving experience of her short life. Did Domostroy know, the lawyer asked, that his fan had spent most of her meager savings on that trip?

"No performing artist who's any good can dispense with fans altogether," Domostroy said to Andrea. "Listening to Goddard's records, I have the distinct impression not only that he sometimes needs a real audience, but also—" he paused "—that he occasionally has one—in a live performance. That would rule him out as a psycho, a hermit, or an elephant man."

Andrea looked up in disbelief. "Did you say live performance?"

"Yes. A girl I talked to at the Goddard Beat suggested it, and I think she may be right. The way Goddard pronounces words and times certain phrases in his latest album—and the sheer energy of his performance—convinces me that he must have sung some of the songs in public prior to recording them."

"Would Goddard risk a live performance just to test his songs?"

"Not his songs. Himself." He leaned over her. "Like every popular singer, Goddard knows that singing in a recording studio is a bit like singing under a shower. Instead of hearing your own voice, you hear the resonance created by the shower stall. The same with saloon singers; they know that peiforming in a cramped nightclub is not like performing in Carnegie Hall, or the Kennedy Center, or Madison Square Garden. A large live audience forces the singer to sing at the highest pitch of his ability, to give a performance in which his energy has to top the collective energy of the audience. When he makes a studio recording, a good singer will attempt to imitate his own live performance, recapture the aliveness of it, and even use a tape recording of it as a cue."

"But where could Goddard give live performances without being recognized through his voice?"

"Any big town, actually," said Domostroy. "Half of today's young singers do everything they can to sound like Goddard—and many of them succeed. The last thing anyone in the world would expect would be to see Goddard performing in public. And besides, no one knows his real name or what he looks like."

"Where do you think he might have performed?"

"Perhaps a Mexican town—near the U.S. border," said Domostroy.

"Why there?" she asked, stunned.

"South of the border, Goddard would probably attract no more attention than any other young American with a guitar on his back. In any square or sidewalk cafe he could sing and play—and study his impact on a live audience—without much danger of revealing himself."

"Then why wouldn't he try Paris—or Amsterdam—where they all know and play American music too?" asked Andrea.

"For a good—personal—reason, I suspect. Of the seven songs in the newest album, two are adaptations or paraphrases of Mexican folk songs, 'Volver, Volver, Volver' and 'El Rey,' which Goddard sings in English except for a few Spanish lines. The other day I went to a Latin record store on Broadway and bought the Mexican originals, and when I compared them to Goddard's adaptations, I dis-

covered that some of the Spanish phrases Goddard sings
are not in the originals. Goddard wrote them—in Spanish!"

"I know those songs," said Andrea. "They seem more
sentimental than most of his stuff." She started to sing
"Volver, Volver, Volver":

> *"My love is restless*
> *to come back;*
> *I'm walking towards madness and*
> *while all is sadness*
> *I want to love*
> *and I'm dying to return."*

Then she asked, "What do the Spanish lines he wrote
say?"

"In 'El Rey,' they follow right after these original
lines:

> *With money, or without money*
> *I do what I want . . .*
> *And I keep on being a king,"*

he intoned. "In one he speaks of being lonely, 'like Del
Coronado'; haunted like 'the useless warships—on the
border—I cross to see her.' In the other song he talks
about 'hiding and singing—in El Rosarito—where she comes
back—and comes back—and comes back—each time—her
last time.' He also talks about being 'weary of peace and
quiet . . . the price of loving,' and he says that 'lovers
who part commit a crime of passion.' "

Andrea was getting excited. "Are there any more
clues?" she asked.

"I think there might be. On the last band of the
album, Goddard cleverly interlaces motifs from three Schubert pieces: 'The Town,' 'By the Sea,' and 'The Double.'
He repeats the somber chords of 'The Double' over and
over again, only to interrupt them by changing, in a final
series of chords, to a cleverly interwoven though intrinsi-
cally different harmony that is clearly Arabic in nature—as
if, after all his monotonous hiding, Goddard—'the double'

—had suddenly revealed himself—or his true feeling!"
Domostroy was silent and pensive for a moment.

"Arabic?" asked Andrea.

"Arabic," he answered. "As recognizable in music as
the arabesque is in filigree work or fancy embroidery."

"Well—go on!" said Andrea.

"There's a U.S. Navy shipyard just a few miles from
the famous old Hotel Del Coronado and the border between San Diego and Tijuana. Maybe Goddard was there
for some reason, and perhaps he was anxious to communi-
cate what he felt to someone—someone, I think, whom he
loved. Maybe he didn't have time to compose a piece that
would properly express his feelings and instead hastily
latched onto some popular Mexican songs, to which he
added an Arabic motif and new lyrics—his secret message."

"A message for a woman?"

"Why not? And if he sang for her in Spanish, she was
probably Mexican. He could have met her in the Hotel
Del Coronado. Many Mexicans visit it when they go to
San Diego, having passed those haunted ships at the border. Then, who knows? Maybe she was engaged, even
married." He paused. "If she was, the only way he could
see her without raising the suspicion of her family or the
other man in her life would be by performing in public
places—cafés or restaurants. In your letter," he said, pursuing his own suppositions, "we ought to ask him if it was
his Mexican love who attracted him to those Mexican
songs and inspired him to change their original lyrics. If
we're on the wrong track, and he invented all that Latin
stuff by simply attending El Festival Latino at the Village
Gate in New York, he'll dismiss the idea as your fantasy.
But if not, we may have hit the bull's-eye."

"Speaking of bulls," said Andrea, now in one of her
reflective moods, "did you know that a lot of Americans
from Southern California routinely go to see the corridas
in Tijuana?" Without waiting for him to reply, she continued, "I've seen bullfights in Spain, and you know, they
never struck me as a macho duel between a brave matador
and a ferocious bull. Somehow, I always saw the bull with
his huge dangling black cock as the essence of maleness,

and the matador as a female in courtship—a pirouetting, fancily attired maiden pretending she's hunting, but who is, in fact, eager to be caught, enticing and provoking the male, letting him brush against her seductively in each pass, her cape as red as if it were already soaked in the blood of her deflowering, of her goring, by the bull. And only when the bull is finally too tired, or too fed up with the pursuit, with his feet square on the ground and his head down low, only then does the matador, like a rejected woman out to punish her now spurned lover, raise his sword and plunge it down into the world's most vulnerable spot—the male heart."

Occasionally Andrea spoke about her family. She said that her grandmother, a stubborn old lady, had been so proud of her beautiful thick hair that for years she had refused to cut it. To the despair of the rest of the Gwynplaine family—who considered it unseemly for an old woman to wear her hair long—it eventually reached well below her waist. Then Andrea, still a very young girl, had decided to take it upon herself to teach her grandmother a lesson. Late at night she would sneak into her grandmother's room when the old lady was sound asleep and thin out her hair with scissors, leaving all the wispy cut-off hair scattered about on the pillows. Assuming that her hair was falling out because of its length and weight, Andrea's grandmother panicked, and in an effort to save what was left, promptly had it cut so short that it barely covered the back of her neck.

Andrea also told Domostroy about a trick she used to play on her dates when she was a high school senior. She would let a boy lure her into his room and start to fondle and kiss her passionately. Then, when he wasn't looking, she would nonchalantly bend down and remove from her bag a feminine hygiene tampon soaked in red wine and toss it high and hard enough in the air so that it hit the ceiling and remained attached to it. The boy would stare horrified at the oozing ball of cotton and the red droplets falling from it onto the floor—his face registering irrational male fear of handling anything soiled by menstrual blood—and he would apologize profusely and take her home untouched.

Listening to these and other, similar stories, Domostroy sometimes wondered if Andrea would ever play pranks on him; and although he frequently found himself struck by her insights, he was baffled by her as well.

Late one night he had to leave Andrea—already asleep—and drive to the historic Passion Play Church on Long Island to play for an early-morning requiem mass. But about ten minutes after leaving her apartment he realized, to his dismay, that he had forgotten his wallet. He went back and tiptoed his way through the apartment, careful not to disturb Andrea, only to find that the bed he had shared with her was empty—she was gone. He wondered where she would go—alone—in the small hours of the morning, and why she would lie to him, telling him to wake her up for breakfast when he came back.

At the church, the coffin stood at the head of the center aisle, and as he played, Domostroy couldn't help glancing at its black presence and thinking of the dead man inside, a reminder to the living that they were merely the next link in the chain of the dead. Instead of upsetting him, the thought cheered Domostroy. Confronted by death, he was happy to be around to accept life's other ultimatums.

When he got back to her apartment later that morning, he found Andrea asleep in bed, as if she had never left it at all. Hurt by her betrayal, he woke her up and asked her how her night had been. Stretching and yawning, reaching out to kiss him good morning, Andrea said that for once she had slept through the night really well. Enjoying the heat of her young, firm body, he let her hug and kiss him and, reluctant to confront her, said nothing about his surprise night visit.

At another time, she told him that she saw herself, spiritually, as half man, half woman. From time to time, she said, she liked to dress up as a man and make the rounds of Manhattan's lower West Side gay bars and dis-

cos in the company of some of her male friends, a group of
punk rock musicians.

She said that her fascination with male sexuality had
begun when, as a teenager, she fell in love with a boy who
was actively bisexual. She would accompany him on his
clandestine prowls in search of a male lover, at times even
offering herself as bait to lure sexual partners for him. In
return, her boyfriend would let her watch him make love
with a man. It had come as a revelation to her, she said,
that watching the two of them seemed to arouse not the
female in her, but the male. In such moments she always
wanted to make love to her boyfriend and to satisfy him as
another male would, a male he was in love with, and when
she made love to him, she fantasized about having a penis
of her own—a replica of his.

Andrea prided herself on being an accomplished sexual tease. Often, in the middle of the night, when she was
unable to sleep, she would select a man's name at random
from the telephone book, dial the number, and in a husky
voice introduce herself as Ludmila, or Vanessa or Karen,
saying that she had just woken up and that to put herself
back to sleep she needed "a sexy talk." If the man hung
up, she would dial another number and repeat her introduction. She would ask the unsuspecting man to introduce
himself to her, conning him into a long conversation—and
more than that. Watching Domostroy in bed next to her,
she would gauge by his reaction the impact of every word
she uttered.

"I want you to be free with me, baby," she would
whisper into the phone, "as I am now with you. I want
you to touch yourself where I touch myself. You want me
to start first? I will—because it excites me. I like your
voice—it makes me feel you so close. Let me guide your
hands—to where you want to go—yes, that's where I want
you to touch me. Now, touch yourself, and as you do,
think that your hands are mine, touch it again—and
again . . ."

Aroused by her voice and by the fantasy of her, her
telephone love partner would whisper to her words
Domostroy could not hear, and as she whispered and

moaned into the phone, her breath rasping and broken, she would sprawl over Domostroy, her breasts on his chest, her face next to his, the telephone receiver in her hand the only barrier between them.

She would continue her verbal charade, at the same time licking Domostroy's ears, kissing his lips, her free hand wedging between her flesh and his, raking and squeezing.

"Love me faster, lover, harder, deeper—faster now," she would breathe into the phone, and listening to the sounds from the receiver, she would pull away from Domostroy, leaving him in the midst of his own excitement, and replace the receiver. "Another bastard just came on me," she would exclaim in mock anger. "Imagine the nerve—on our first date!"

One morning, just as Domostroy was about to tell Andrea of his latest discovery, she startled him by anticipating him. "Goddard is like a writer who uses a pen name," she said, rolling over and looking at him. "Usually such a name has no relationship to the writer's real name, or to his life, because it is meant to be an artistic cover-up, a creative camouflage. But the other day you said you thought you know why Goddard picked that name for himself. Tell me what you think."

"I have a clue," said Domostroy. "As I was listening to his records, I picked out two musical themes, both of which I was sure belonged to other composers whose records I'd heard before. They were subtle paraphrases of music I thought I knew, and for days I listened to hundreds of records and tapes—old and new, American and foreign—but I couldn't track down the sources, mainly because both of these elusive themes evoked the music of a number of past and present composers. Finally, I traced one motif."

"To whom?"

"To—Lieberson, a man I used to know," he answered, "who died some years ago. Lieberson was president of Columbia Records Masterworks, and he was responsible for launching some of our finest contemporary composers, both classical and popular, as well as for bringing about the productions of *South Pacific*, *My Fair Lady*, and *West Side Story*. He won seven Grammy Awards, and at least as many Gold Record Awards, and he was one of the most erudite and admired men in the music industry."

"Wait a minute," she interrupted impatiently. "You're talking about a corporate executive. What's that got to do with the themes in Goddard's music?"

Bending down slowly and inhaling her tart odor, Domostroy brushed one cheek against her inner thigh, hard and cool, and pressed the other against her mound, shaved of its hair, its flesh rippled, steamy, and coiled. "Lieberson was also an inspired and accomplished composer," he said softly. "I've spent time listening to all of his work again, and he wrote a goodly amount: incidental music for *Alice in Wonderland*, a ballet, a suite for string orchestra, a symphony, settings for three Chinese poems for mixed voices, a suite for twenty instruments, a piece called 'Complaints of the Young,' another called 'Nine Melodies for Piano,' a quintet, and a number of songs to texts by Ezra Pound, James Joyce, and others. I even reread his novel, *Three for Bedroom C*. Gloria Swanson played in the film."

"Come to the point," she said as she moved back and trapped him between her calves, their roundness not marred by the slightest muscle bulge, their smoothness not disturbed by a single hair.

"The point is that Goddard paraphrased a whole section of one of Lieberson's works."

"Big deal," she interjected. "Everyone paraphrases. In my piano literature course I just learned that in the 'Fantaisie Impromptu,' Chopin, who so massively and unashamedly borrowed from Polish folk music, also paraphrased an impromptu by Moscheles that had been published by chance in a volume along with Chopin's Opus 15 nocturnes. Chopin was so ashamed to acknowledge his indebtedness to Moscheles, that for twenty years he refused to publish his masterpiece. "Like any other artist, the composer transforms the already existing forms,

motifs, techniques into a new musical entity," she lectured
him. All Goddard did was paraphrase one musical passage
from a piece he might have heard anywhere!" She was disappointed. "That's not enough to be a meaningful link."

"I agree, that's not enough," he said, kissing her, his
tongue tracing the folds and curls of her flesh, roughing it,
pressing and withdrawing.

His touch sent shivers through her, and her breathing
came in rasps; with her eyes closed, turning her head from
side to side, she twisted her body.

He stopped, then said softly, "There is another link.
Guess what Lieberson's first name was?"

"Why?" Pushing her hands against his shoulders, she
stopped twisting.

"Just guess," he said.

"Victor. No, wait: Hector."

"Wrong."

"What does Lieberson's first name have to do with
Goddard?"

"A lot," said Domostroy, "because Lieberson's first
name was Goddard."

Sweeping the hair off her face, she sat up.

"What?"

"Goddard Lieberson." He stared at her.

"That's unbelievable," she said. "Could it be a
coincidence?"

"Coincidence? First Lieberson's name, then his music!
That's a connection, not a coincidence." Domostroy paused.
"But what can the connection be? When Goddard Lieberson
was in his heyday, our Goddard was probably like you,
Andrea, a teenager in high school."

She sat and thought. "You said that Goddard had
paraphrased the themes of two composers. One is Lieberson. Have you traced the other one?"

"Not yet," said Domostroy.

*   *   *

A few days later, as if checking on his progress, Andrea said, "Did you find the other theme that you thought Goddard paraphrased?"

"For the life of me I couldn't place the composer or the piece," he said. "There was something bright and evanescent about it, a bit foreign and old-fashioned, in the vein of the late-nineteenth-century Russian Romantics—Borodin, Balakirev, Mussorgsky. Yet I had the strange feeling that I had heard the piece played by the composer himself at some time or other, which meant it had to be much more recent. Then it hit me. Goddard got that motif from Boris Pregel, another composer I knew—as I knew Lieberson."

"Boris Pregel? I don't think I've ever heard of him—or of anything by him."

"He was also somewhat before your time. Pregel was born in Russia, and starting at the age of six, he was trained by his mother, who was an excellent pianist and singer. He later studied music at the conservatory in Odessa, but then he switched to engineering and escaped to the West—to France. Then he came to the United States. Like Lieberson, Pregel became known, not for his music, but for other reasons—in his case, primarily as a great expert and inventor in the field of atomic energy. And he was an enormously successful entrepreneur, dealing in uranium and other radioactive materials. For his achievements and service to mankind, Pregel was made president of the New York Academy of Sciences, and he became one of the most decorated men in the world, right up there with De Gaulle, Eisenhower, and the Pope."

"What about his music?" Andrea asked.

"It was first-rate," said Domostroy. "In the Russian Romantic tradition. His 'Romantic Suite,' his Fantasy in D Major, and many of his other works were performed in America and in Europe, by the Rome and Milan symphony orchestras under D'Artega." He halted. "Strange how things come back," he said. "I'd forgotten that D'Artega, the conductor, also acted. He played Tchaikovsky in the film *Carnegie Hall*."

"You know all kinds of musical tidbits, don't you?" she said, impressed.

"Stick around, and so will you," said Domostroy. "For example, Boris Pregel's songs, like Lieberson's, were usually settings for works by well-known poets."

He stopped and reflected. "There's one tidbit that I would like to know: how did Goddard happen to pick up motifs from both Goddard Lieberson *and* Boris Pregel? I can't figure out the connection."

"Maybe he just liked their music," said Andrea.

"Still, what a coincidence! Even when Pregel and Lieberson were alive, their music was not widely known. Most people wouldn't be familiar with the work of either one, much less both. I wonder if our Goddard's family was somehow connected to them. Could Goddard possibly have known both Lieberson and Pregel?"

"Why not?" she cried, excited. "Goddard might be a young corporate executive, a sort of contemporary Lieberson or Pregel! Could that be the connection?"

"I doubt it. For one thing, Lieberson and Pregel were hardly typical executives. Both were creative artists and intellectuals, men with extensive education, exposure, worldliness."

"Do you think that in his way Goddard is up to their standards?"

"Definitely not. They were both talented and accomplished musicians. Despite what Nash and the other critics say, our Goddard has no real understanding of the piano; his music is elemental, flat, without depth; his treatment of rhythm, harmony and melody is a synthesized mishmash. In my opinion, he has also failed to develop as a singer: his voice remains as ordinary as his repertoire. He can't darken his vowels, and for volume he depends entirely on electronic amplification."

"At least he doesn't merely try to entertain," said Andrea. "Goddard writes to broaden his audience's musical experience. That's why they love him. That's why he's not just another rock star. He's an innovator, like Gershwin."

"The mass public is by nature indiscriminate and gullible," said Domostroy. "Easily influenced by mass media, it cannot distinguish between what's authentic and what's merely believable, between originality and sham novelty. At best, Goddard is a mildly gifted singer and a clever electronic-music improviser, that's all. Chopin once said that nothing is more odious than music without hidden meaning. But Goddard has no meaning to hide. Instead, he has cleverly hidden himself in his music! His invisibility is still his greatest asset." He looked at Andrea and saw that his words had annoyed her. "Innovator or not," he continued in a gentler voice, "his music alone will not tell us how he linked himself to both Lieberson and Pregel. But perhaps the files of Columbia Records—or the New York Academy of Sciences—will."

Andrea read the letter. "It's wonderful," she sighed, "and so moving. If I were Goddard, I would certainly want to know the woman who had written it." She read it again, slowly, her lips moving as she lingered over each word. Then she looked up. "Do my sexual feelings have to be spelled out in such detail?"

"What you say about sex in this letter has to work like the sustaining pedal on the piano. It has to keep you resonating in his fantasy."

"I wish I had written it," she murmured sweetly. "It's beautiful."

"It will come from you," said Domostroy.

"Yes, but the signature will be my only contribution."

"It won't be signed," said Domostroy. "And there won't be any return address on it."

"Why? If the letter is telling the truth—"

"Truth needs no signature," said Domostroy, taking the letter from her. "If he's convinced by what you say, not knowing who you are will intrigue him all the more. He'll count the days until you write again—and hope that the next time you write, you'll sign your name so that one day he'll be able to meet you."

"Can one letter do all that?" she wondered aloud.

"I doubt it. But several—let's say five—might," he

said. "Long ago, during my *Sturm und Drang* period," he continued, "when I had received enough fan letters to know how similar they all were, I received one unusual one. The writer, a woman, said she knew me only from my work and a few concert and television appearances, but her analysis of my music was so acute, as were her perceptions of my needs and longings—the undercurrents of my life, which I'd never talked about with anyone—that I was flat-out enthralled.

"If, without meeting me, she had detected so much of my innermost being, you can imagine how tempted I was to let her study me face to face, with no emotional or professional niceties to mask the encounter. But when I reached the end of the letter, I realized with dismay that she had not signed it, or rather, that she had signed it only with a musical phrase from Chopin. I assumed that she had simply forgotten to add her name, and I earnestly hoped that, in spite of not hearing from me, she would write again.

"A few weeks later a second letter arrived, and this time, with uncanny insight, she speculated as to what sort of musical composition I was working on—its length, its mood, my sources of inspiration for it—and everything she said was mystifyingly close to actual fact. Again the letter was signed only with a phrase of Chopin's—a different one—and now I knew this was by design, not oversight.

"Other letters followed—all signed with Chopin phrases—in which she continued to speak about my work, but also included more and more reflections about her own feelings and desires, and in time the letters became specific regarding her sexual thoughts and fantasies. She would describe in graphic detail scenes of the two of us in bed together, complete with dialogue—what I would say to her and how I would say it; what she would reply; and the exact positions of our bodies at every step along the way. With uncanny insight she would speculate with surprising accuracy about the entire range of my sexual desires—from those I would admit to freely to those I would never dream of confessing, much less pursuing.

"In most instances she was so close to the heart of the

truth about me that I began to believe she had extrasensory perception. Worse, I feared that my mystery correspondent might be someone I knew or a friend of someone I knew—a past mistress, a casual lover, an associate, or an acquaintance. And yet I was certain that I had never come across anyone so lucid—or so obsessive.

"For the successful pursuit of both my creative efforts and my sexual fantasies, I came to rely completely on her letters, as if she were the vital force in my life. For months, each time a letter arrived, I was convinced that she would reveal herself in it so that we could at last meet, so that I could tell her what she had come to mean to me. But she never did, and after about a year the letters stopped. I felt at first as if my brain's lifeline had been cut without warning. Then I started to comfort myself with various theories: that she was old and ill; that she had died; that even if she were alive, she must be—however brilliant—neurotic, unstable, probably schizophrenic. Finally I reduced her to banality—imagining her as physically plain, or ugly, maybe a bit repulsive—and in time, I shut out the memory of her altogether.

"Some years later I participated in the Musical Weeks festival at Crans-Montana, a Swiss resort favored by artists. The honorary guest at the festival was a woman pianist who was considered, in spite of being only in her twenties, one of the world's greatest piano players, and who, because of her unusually good looks, was a special favorite of the public and the media. I had heard and seen her play several times, and each time I had found myself positively distracted by her sensual appeal.

"On the last evening of Musical Weeks, I was seated—along with several other guests—at the head table with the pianist and her husband, a youthful businessman. During the meal I noticed that the pianist would glance at me furtively; at one point I even caught her staring. Intimidated by her beauty, as well as by the presence of her husband, I managed to exchange only a few remarks with her—on the subject of the artist's need for both seclusion and public exposure, which seemed obvious to the two of us, but appeared as a contradiction to some of the others at the table.

"At one point I left the table to go to the men's room downstairs, and on the darkened staircase I heard a woman behind me calling my name. It was the pianist. 'I want to apologize, Mr. Domostroy,' she said, 'for staring at you during dinner.'

" 'I was flattered,' I said. 'I have wanted to meet you for a long time.'

" 'You have already met me—even before tonight!' she said, moving closer until her face was under the light. Once again I felt the full force of her beauty.

" 'I've heard you play, but I don't think we've ever met,' I said.

" 'Not in person,' she said, and she put her hand on my shoulder. 'I've written to you, though,' she said, 'many times. I didn't sign my letters. I closed them instead with musical notes.'

"I felt my body jolt. My heart was racing. 'From "The Wish," a Chopin mazurka,' I said, and I started to recite the lyric to the musical phrases she had sent.

> *If I were the sun in the sky,*
> *I would not shine except for you;*
>
> *If I were a bird of this grove,*
> *I would not sing in any foreign land;*
>
> *Only for all time*
> *Under your window and for you alone.*

"Overpowered by the memory of her letters, and by the images they conjured now that she stood in front of me, I took her arms and drew her toward me, then locked my hands behind her back and put my face against hers. 'I loved your letters,' I said. 'They made me think about you constantly and wait for you more anxiously than I've ever waited for anyone. That was five years ago. Five years! Think what those years might have been had we met then.'

"She took my hands in hers. 'I looked at your hands at dinner,' she said, 'and thought of the time when I'd have given the whole world to feel them on my body. I had such a crush on you, on your music, on everything about you. I watched you on TV, read about you in the papers, went to every concert you gave. All I wanted was to have you fall in love with me.'

" 'If you had only introduced yourself, you would have succeeded,' I said. 'I was in love with the woman who wrote those letters. I dreamt continuously about her and about the life we could have together. I would have given up everything for a new life with her.' I drew her toward me, buried my face in her hair, pressed her body against mine. She swayed in my arms. 'I still would,' I said. 'I still love her. Tell me what you want me to do so that we can be together.'

"She hesitated, not looking at me, and reminded me that she was married.

" 'Do you love him?' I asked.

" 'Love? Perhaps not, but I care for him,' she said. 'And we have a child.'

" 'We could still be lovers,' I urged her.

"She turned her face away from mine. 'I wrote you once that I was in love with you. I still am,' she said, 'but if I had to hide my love, I would feel I was perverting it, turning what's natural into something shameful.'

" 'Then why hide it?' I asked, holding her tighter. 'I don't want to lose you again.'

"She freed herself from my embrace and said, 'My husband loves me. He has been very generous. Without his support I couldn't have become who I am. I can't leave him.'

"As she turned to go, I blurted, 'Please write to me again.' Then she was gone, and the next day she and her husband left Crans-Montana.

"I was left at first with the thrill of knowing that I had held in my arms the woman I loved, and only later did I become aware of my loss. As I waited for her to write, I fantasized about her more and more, always imagining her naked, making love to me in clandestine meetings—after her concerts, in big anonymous hotels on New York's West Side; in out-of-the-way hotels in Paris, Rome, or Vienna; in motels in Los Angeles; in private rooms of the secret sex palaces in Rio de Janeiro. But she didn't write, and I began to spend hours on end reading and rereading her old letters. During these periods I would despise myself—my music, my whole existence—because I'd failed to have her the only time I'd had the chance. The sight of a telephone filled me with pain, but I dared not call her. Like a desperate schoolboy in love with his music teacher, I made elaborate plans to follow her, to arrange things so that we would accidentally run into each other, but I always abandoned these adolescent designs out of embarrassment.

"A few months ago I learned that her husband had died in an automobile accident."

"Really?" Andrea asked, casually reaching for a hairbrush. "Then why don't you get in touch with her?"

"What for?"

"To be with her." She brushed her hair slowly, letting it fall on her shoulders and neck. "You're the best part of her past."

"But she isn't the best part of mine," said Domostroy in a voice deliberately calm. He got up and stretched. "Anyway, she wrote to me when I was a composer. All I compose now are letters—somebody else's." He chuckled, then reached for Andrea and laid her down on the bed. He covered her breasts with her hair and gently smoothed it out over her nipples.

"How soon after that meeting with the pianist did you stop composing?" Andrea asked the next day in an emotionless voice.

"A year or so," said Domostroy. With a smile he added, "You might say creation petered out as abandonment set in."

"Aren't you still in love with her?" Andrea asked.

"Not with her. Only with her letters," he said. "Which

reminds me, your first letter to Goddard went out last night. I mailed it in an official White House envelope, one of a few I've saved as souvenirs over the years. They're embossed inner envelopes, the kind you get wedding invitations in. They've never been postmarked or addressed."

"Where did you get them?" Andrea asked.

Domostroy looked at her before he answered. "Each time I performed in Washington, I got congratulatory notes enclosed in them from a fan of mine, who was then an adviser to the President. If any fan letter ever reaches Goddard, that one surely will."

"He'll probably think I work in the White House."

"Perhaps. Or that you're the wife or daughter of one of the country's big bosses—who, like Goddard, maintains invisibility. That will make him despair of your ever abandoning your own anonymity, but you can be sure it will also make him keep his eye peeled for the next White House envelope, and the one after that."

"What will be in those?"

"More of your perceptions about him, his music, his life—maybe some photographs of you to show how beautiful you are."

"Should we let him know what I look like so soon?" she said, and then she promptly answered her own question. "Maybe they could be shot from a distance or taken with my face turned away."

"That's a good idea," he said.

"If I'm not signing the letters, I shouldn't show my face either. Isn't the face the body's signature?"

He smiled. "Do you have lots of good pictures of yourself?" he asked her.

"Not many." She paused and added, "Hey, maybe we could take some! Sexy ones. I could even undress for him."

"Another good idea," he said, then added, "but I wonder if he'll resent your posing for another man."

"Of course he would," she declared, "so we won't let him know. Can't we arrange the shots so that he would think I used a self-timing camera?"

"I guess so. What purpose do you think the pictures should serve?" asked Domostroy.

"Purely to excite him. To make him aroused by the very sight of me."

"You think of everything, don't you?" he said, impressed.

"Someone has to," she said, "because, Patrick, if Goddard has kept his secret from the world all this time, he's got to be smart. That means we have to be smarter, right? I think we must also make sure that there are no fingerprints on my letters to him—or on the photographs. If he does become interested in me, I wouldn't put it past him to check for them, and we don't want him to check me out before I've checked him in, do we?" She rolled her eyes and burst out laughing.

"What's so funny?" Domostroy asked her.

"After all this," she said, "what if Goddard turns out to like men?"

"If he does," said Domostroy with a wide smile, "you two will have something in common right from the start."

They lay naked, sunning themselves on the roof of her brownstone. Stretched out next to him, her head propped up on a folded towel, Andrea was asleep. He watched a single drop of sweat gather on her neck, roll onto her breast, stop at the nipple, run sideways, and with not a single wrinkle to stop it, roll down the smooth, dry surface of her belly.

He then looked at himself. Streams of sweat poured out from small pools that had formed between the folds and wrinkles of his skin. Unable to stand the heat any longer, he put on his trunks and got up. The steaming streets of Manhattan stretched out below. A faint breeze brought the smell of tar, and on the Hudson a nuclear aircraft carrier, escorted by a flotilla of tugs and pleasure boats, was on its way toward Ambrose Light, the folded wings of the planes on its flight deck catching the sun like an open accordion.

"I don't believe you about the White House stationery." Andrea's voice caught him from behind.

"Why not?" he asked without looking around.

"All that mail-inside-mail stuff sounded fishy," she said calmly. "So I did some checking. They don't use double envelopes in such cases at the White House. You lied, Domostroy. Now, why?"

"I thought the envelopes might benefit our cause, not the truth about how I came upon them."

"Truth is not supposed to benefit," she said. "Truth just is."

"Then I have merely withheld it," he said, still watching the aircraft carrier.

As he said it, for a moment he wondered: had he also withheld his life's truth from himself? Would his life be better served if instead of enlisting in the service of the young woman behind him, he were an enlisted man, one of the crew of that aircraft carrier? To remain truthful to himself, shouldn't he be adaptable, as changing as was the life of music, where it made little difference that "The Star-Spangled Banner" was, right up until the War of 1812, "To Anacreon in Heav'n," a London supper-club drinking song? Or that Chopin's majestic Polonaise in A-flat Major had reached masses of listeners for the first time in A *Song to Remember*, a vapid movie about the composer's life, and also as "Cheek to Cheek," a swing version of its leading melody?

"So how about trying the truth, Patrick? How did you get those envelopes?" Andrea persisted.

"All right, I'll tell you," said Domostroy. "Over a decade ago, I taught musical syntax at the drama school of one of the Ivy League universities. Among my students was one whom I—quite frankly—liked a lot, and when she applied to become my assistant, I hired her on the spot."

"So much for impartial hiring practices in Academia," interjected Andrea. "I bet the same goes on at Juilliard."

"She lived on the ground floor of a large country house near the university." Domostroy went on. "The owner, who occupied its top floor, was a retired attorney, once a partner in a prominent Washington law firm and in his younger years one of the top White House counsels."

"And did he leave White House stationery lying around?" asked Andrea with a smirk.

"Even if he had, at that time I had better things to think of than filching fancy stationery for letters I might one day write—as a woman at that!—to a rock star with a disappearing act."

"Better things? Such as?" asked Andrea.

"Musical compositions. That was the year I wrote *The Baobab Concerto*."

Andrea smiled disparagingly. "Which, just a few years later, as I recall, you chose to rewrite because you said it wasn't good enough. Obviously you had other things on your mind the first time through. That young assistant, to begin with."

"Correct," said Domostroy. "Without her, my teaching would have been a drab routine.

"The old man, by the way, lived alone, and despite his advanced age, he insisted on preparing his own meals— thus saving the cost of a cook.

"One Saturday morning my assistant called me and asked if I could come over right away. She had a surprise for me, she said, which might just inspire a musical piece.

"When I got to the house, I found her in the garden wearing an almost transparent chiffon gown from an earlier era and a pair of old-fashioned high-heeled shoes, and as she walked toward me a breeze made the gown cling to her shapely body. Like the Lady of Shalott from the Waterhouse painting in the Tate Gallery, she took me by the hand and led me to the house, where she blindfolded me with a scarf and led me up a flight of stairs.

"We entered a room. From the smell of books and old leather, I guessed we were in the old man's study.

"The girl led me to a leather sofa and pushed me down onto it. Suddenly, as she placed a wet kiss on my lips, she pulled off the blindfold. I opened my eyes and saw him sitting at the desk not ten feet from us, his head resting on his hands as he stared at the two of us in blind fascination."

"Him?" asked Andrea.

"The old man, who else?" said Domostroy. "But he didn't move—he was dead."

"How long had he been dead?" asked Andrea matter-of-factly.

"Just a few hours. That morning the girl noticed that he hadn't come down to pick up his copy of the *New York Times*. When she went upstairs, she found him at his desk, already cold, and on an impulse she propped his head on his hands and telephoned me. She had a taste for the bizarre, you see."

"And silly me, I thought I could surprise you with my punk leather outfit!" Andrea moaned. "Tell me what happened next."

"Nothing much," he said. "We went through his things— drawers, files, letter cabinets. His presence definitely excited her—the idea of Death watching Life. She said that the two of us making love then and there would have made a perfect subject for Hieronymus Bosch or Dali."

"With the old man, I hope, just watching," interrupted Andrea. "Or was your assistant ready for a more bizarre experiment?"

The aircraft carrier was gone now, and all the small boats had scattered.

"And the stationery?" asked Andrea.

"I took a packet of White House stationery from his desk. As a souvenir," he said.

"A souvenir," murmured Andrea. "I wonder of what?"

At odd and unexpected times, Andrea liked to throw Domostroy off balance.

"When my grandfather retired," she once remarked to him, "he did not want to eat anymore, and when the doctors saved him from starving himself to death, tired of his useless life, like Hemingway, he blew his brains out with a shotgun. Why haven't you?"

"Because I'm still useful," said Domostroy. "To myself. To you. I'm happy to be alive."

"That's not being useful," she said, laughing at him. "That's having an ego!"

Occasionally Andrea would remind him that once she knew who Goddard was, Domostroy would have to go. She would say this perfectly calmly, as if to point out what was obvious: that finding Goddard was the only reason she and Domostroy were together. And she would sometimes say it right after their lovemaking, when she would let him excite her and then, switching roles, would tease and arouse him to cross all thresholds. When there was no more tension in him to release, after begging her to stop pushing him beyond his limits, he would fall asleep, exhausted by excitement, and wake up at her side satiated and serene. Then she would tell him.

Her words inevitably brought back the terror he had often felt before he met her—the terror of driving back each night—alone—from Kreutzer's to the Old Glory— the black hole of his shrinking universe.

Domostroy knew that if the letters from Andrea and the photographs intrigued Goddard sufficiently, the star would eventually track her down to claim her. The trick would be to make it impossible for Goddard to positively identify Andrea before she could identify him. For if he found out who she was, there would be no reason for him to reveal himself, and all their efforts to discover him would have been in vain. Even if Goddard found Andrea and became her lover, Domostroy reasoned, he must never—not even with her naked body stretched out next to his—be able to make a positive identification on the basis of her looks. Rather, in order to identify her as the White House woman, Goddard must be forced to talk to her at length in hope of making her betray herself by alluding to a thought, a phrase, or an association in one of her letters to him. Domostroy hoped that, during their long verbal exchange, Goddard would trip and reveal himself first, by involuntarily referring to something Andrea would recognize as having its origin in the letters.

To give Andrea the fullest advantages in the match, Domostroy decided to photograph her in an anonymous motel room rather than in her apartment, which Goddard would probably recognize instantly. He also decided to disguise her. By washing her hair with a color rinse and blowing it dry, he changed its shape and consistency. Then, using body makeup, he slightly altered the indentation of her navel, enlarged and darkened the aureoles of her breasts, and covered several conspicuous moles on her back and thigh. Because she regularly shaved off her pubic hair, he made her put on a pubic wig, a device popular with transvestites and hermaphrodites, which made her vagina look higher set, larger, and more elongated than it really was.

In the many photographs Domostroy took of Andrea, he himself had to be completely invisible. There must be nothing in the picture or in Andrea's expression or pose to indicate the presence of a man in the room. After preparing her for each pose, he would disengage himself from her, get up, and position the camera so that the photograph would show Andrea's body—but not her face—and the camera itself, solitary, reflected in a mirror.

As Andrea lay naked on the bed, with the pillows and sheets in disarray, Domostroy would pour oil on her shoulders, neck, breasts, belly, and thighs, and then on himself. Sitting next to her or straddling her, he would massage her with even strokes, starting with his palms at the top of her spine and descending along her back until his thumbs spread her buttocks. Turning her over on her back, he would guide his hands to the circles of her nipples, then press the tips of his thumbs on the nipples, stretching the coronas; he would slide his hands lower and with his thumbs trace oil on her loin, over the contours of her buttocks, on the lips of her vulva. He would pause to pour more oil on her and then, hard, rigid, tense, and oily, raising her up without warning, her calves slippery against his arms, his chest against the backs of her thighs, he would slide into her with all his force and weight and push in and out of her. Just as her breasts started to rise and fall and she began to twist and moan and scream and toss and strain under him, he would pull away, dash to the camera, and direct it at her as she lay contorted, midway in her need. Then, after the undeveloped picture rolled evenly out of the camera, he would study its emerging contours and colors, checking critically the sharpness of every detail of her body and flesh as they gained contrast and density second by second.

He would move the camera, massage her again, change her position—or the position of her hands on her breasts, her belly, or her mound—and take more pictures of her, glistening as if her body were bathed in sweat. Again he would return to her. Heaving, seeking his mouth, she would strain under him, shuddering, and her hands, slipping along his hips, would grab him and guide him into her flesh. He would thrust into her then, but only until she started to quiver and heave against him. Then he would pull out again and run to the camera.

He took one picture after another, leaving her unfulfilled, screaming, calling him cruel and heartless. When she grew frantic, he would go over to her and with one hand slap her face back and forth while with the other he roughed up her flesh, until she would whimper and let him force her own passive hand between her thighs into her groin. As he rushed back to the camera and moved it closer to photograph her breasts, her thighs, her flesh and her fingers on it, she would start to abuse him again, and he would go over to her. Shouting that it was her idea to excite Goddard by showing him how aroused she could get, he would hit her on her breasts and belly and hips, like a jealous husband in a fight over his wife's lover. Turning her face down, restraining her in a powerful grip, he would mount her from behind, then dive into her time after time, hurting her more with every thrust, while she thrashed under him, her face buried in the pillow, begging him to let her be.

He photographed her also when she was poised and
calm, standing or sitting in the bathtub or with a dryer in
her hand and her hair floating over her face to shield it
from the camera. Then, to assist his memory of her, he
photographed for his own possession each step of her
dressing: in panties, putting on stockings and shoes, with
her blouse open, with it buttoned up, stepping into her
skirt, buttoning it at the waist.

With the passage of time, Domostroy changed his
attitude toward Andrea's place in his life. He still needed
her, but he began to resent his need. Though he would
rush to be with her, anxious not to miss a single moment
of the lovemaking she dispensed so obligingly, as he got to
know her better he rebelled more and more against his
dependence. He feared that in his relationship with her
he had begun to resemble those sexual addicts for whom
he had always felt contempt, men and women who came
to rely so completely on the guaranteed fulfillment of their
own brand of sexual pleasure that they looked for it only in
the safety and predictability of private sex clubs such as
the Sorcerer's Apprentice.

There was another reason for Domostroy's rebellion.
In Andrea's incessant curiosity about Goddard the man, in
her never-ending speculation about his life, his money, his
lovers, and his travels, she consistently relegated the most
important thing about him—his music—to a position of
no great consequence, a view Domostroy found crude and
offensive.

"One day," said Domostroy, gathering Andrea into
his arms until their lips touched, then breathing his words
into her mouth, "one day you might be lying like this in
somebody else's arms—somebody who might be Goddard—
and he might ask you about something—an image, an
idea, an association—that he read in one of our letters—

and you'd better be ready for it!" He squeezed her by her shoulders until she twitched in pain. "To make it easier for him to trace you, I plan to refer to some of the subjects you're currently studying at Juilliard—Chopin's life and letters, for instance. But you'll always have to be on guard. Even in the heat of the sack, you'll have to remember exactly what it was that I wrote and be able to recognize his slightest nuances in trying to find out if it was you who wrote the letters."

She freed herself from his arms and said waspishly, "Don't be a fool, Patrick. When Goddard's in bed with me, he won't be—like you—cross-examining me. He'll have other things on his mind."

"Do you think Goddard will miss not seeing my face, or think I'm ugly or scarred?"

"Maybe, but by then he should be in love with the rest of you."

"He might already be in love with someone else."

"He might. But if she's his intimate friend and knows who he is, then he has no mystery for her, and she none for him. If she takes his greatness for granted, she leaves his vanity starved, whereas you in your letters fulfill it. Being his lover, she can at best only fuel his lust—but you can awaken his self-love, the drum major of love. With her, he feels understood. With you, he's wanted and admired. Imagine his temptation to be with you!"

"Imagine mine!"

"I do. I also know that once Goddard knows where to start looking for you, you and I will have to find new places to see each other. I wouldn't be safe here, or even at the Old Glory; he—or his spies—might be watching. And you wouldn't want to lose Goddard merely for the sake of keeping Patrick Domostroy, would you?"

"I certainly would not!" she replied. Then she said, "How will Goddard ever know who I am?"

"From clues I drop in the letters to him. I'll make him succeed in tracing you, don't worry."

"What if he fails?"

"I'll send more letters. With more clues."

She stretched and yawned. "I wonder what our mystery man is doing right now," she said.

"He might be wondering who you are!" said Domostroy.

II

James Osten stopped in front of a Fifth Avenue watch shop, studied the window display, and went inside, where he was promptly accosted by a young salesman.

"Good morning, sir," said the salesman in a heavy Italian accent, smiling at Osten with unconcealed admiration and swishing behind the counter like a ballet dancer. "Can I be of service to you?"

"Yes," said Osten, "indirectly." And pointing at a gold wristwatch in the window, he said, "I like that watch."

"My compliments on your taste," the salesman breathed, all smiles, as he removed the watch from the window. "This is the thinnest watch ever made. And," he added with a suggestive flash of his eye, "it's a unisex design."

As Osten examined the watch, he pictured it on Donna's dark wrist. "How much is it?" he asked.

Naming the price, the salesman forced a casual smile. "It is truly a timeless timepiece. Its value will never go down. Therefore, it's a very good hedge against inflation— even at the price of a Cadillac!"

"I don't plan to hedge inflation with it," said Osten. "It's a gift for a friend."

"Marvelous choice," purred the salesman. "You know, it's water-resistant."

"Good," said Osten. "My friend hates water."

The salesman pretended not to hear the quip. "Your friend is sure to find the black face very dramatic," he said.

"More than likely," said Osten. "My friend is black."

"He's sure to cherish such a gift," the salesman said primly.

"He ·is a woman," said Osten as he took a roll of bills from his pocket and counted out the exact amount in a neat stack on the counter.

"That's a lot of money to carry around like that!" remarked the salesman, impressed with the stack. "Aren't you afraid somebody might rip you off?"

"Not at all," said Osten. "I've learned how to make myself invisible!" He laughed, then added, "That reminds me: I want the face of the watch replaced by one without the watchmaker's name."

"No name?" The salesman was horrified. "But then it would be invisible—no one will know it's the world's most exclusive timepiece!"

"Exclusive or not, a timepiece merely pieces time, right? Only music lets you hear time passing. My girl friend is into music—not time."

Without a word, the salesman picked up the watch and carried it to the back of the shop. In a matter of minutes he returned. "Here it is, as you requested it," he said, handing the watch to Osten. "It's just lucky that to please your black friend you didn't also want the watch thickened," he murmured with a sneer, opening the shop's steel door for Osten. "That couldn't be done on the spot, you know!"

Without taking the slightest notice of him, Osten walked out.

He selected a small hotel buried between two burlesque theaters off Broadway. He woke up the porter, an elderly black man in a Mexican hat and mirrored glasses who was dozing next to the switchboard, and asked him for a room with a bath.

"For yourself? Or will there be two?" asked the porter sleepily, rubbing his eyes.

"I'm alone," said Osten.

"Sure, that's what they all say," said the porter with a sigh as he reached for a key. "How long you staying?"

"A day. But just in case I get hooked on somebody

from the shows next door, I'll pay for two." He handed the man some bills.

The man muttered, "No luggage?"

"It's all up here," said Osten, pointing at his head.

Osten stayed in his room only long enough to use the toilet. Then he went down the corridor to the public telephone. After carefully closing the folding door of the phone booth, he dialed Nokturn Records.

"Nokturn Records, the house of Goddard, good morning!" answered the operator, her voice almost a recording and as out of place as Nokturn's advertising pitch which, given Goddard's anonymity, had always struck Osten as patently ridiculous.

Before Osten spoke, he coughed. By slightly straining the muscles of his throat in this way, he was able to lower the pitch of his normal voice and make it sound raspy and guttural. The little trick, employed so often, had become habitual. Osten asked for Oscar Blaystone, the president of the company. When Blaystone's secretary answered, Osten asked to speak to him.

"May I say who's calling?" asked the secretary.

"Mr. River," said Osten. "Swanee River."

"Mr. Swanee River?" she repeated suspiciously.

"That's right."

"Mr. Blaystone can't be disturbed at the moment. He's in conference. I'm afraid you'll have to give me your number, and I'll—"

"Be brave," Osten interrupted. "Just tell him Swanee River is on the line. He's expecting my call. I'm his swan song, so to speak!" he chuckled.

Soon he heard Blaystone assuming a cordial b   ess-like voice on the other end. "Hello? Mr. River? Swanee River? Let me call you back on my private line. Where are you?"

"In a melting pot," he said.

"A melting pot?"

"Yeah. Manhattan in the summer," said Osten, and he read Blaystone the number on the phone.

A minute after he hung up, Blaystone called back. "I got your cable with the new code name two weeks ago," he said reproachfully. "I've been waiting for your call ever since."

"I've been busy," said Osten. "Anyway, we talked recently."

"Recently? That was six months ago!" said Blaystone. "You must keep in mind," he continued with exaggerated emphasis, "that I have no way—absolutely no way—of getting in touch with you when I need you. And I *do* need you. There are a lot of papers to be signed by Goddard— and soon. But all I get is your phone voice, these talks and your various code names, each one canceling out all the others. Do you know what I'm saying?"

"I do. You say it every time I call you. Anything else?" asked Osten.

"Yes! For starters, I need a new authorization from you for transfer of your foreign royalties from the last album. In less than a month that LP earned back your advance. In Great Britain, you have established an all-time record. Imagine—Great Britain alone! In Latin America, your Spanish-language songs sold over—"

"Use the same Swiss account, the same number, I gave you last time," Osten broke in.

"All right. But I need your Goddard signature on the new tax forms. And please don't change the shape of the G in your signature the way you did last time. We have no way to reach you to have it confirmed! It's the only ID you have, at least as far as we and the IRS are concerned. Then there's this matter of Etude Classics. I put through that renewed two-year agreement whereby you—Goddard— reimburse Nokturn—including agents' fees and all the rest—for distributing and promoting Etude Classics. The whole deal is absolutely secret—just like the one that's about to expire—and Etude has no way of knowing, or even suspecting, that you keep them in business."

"And it better stay that way," said Osten. "Etude isn't

the only company I keep in business. I keep Nokturn going too."

"Yes, of course," Blaystone agreed hastily, "but that's no secret." He paused. "You do realize, don't you, that without your subsidy, Etude Classics would have gone under years ago! And if you continue to support them at the present rate, so could you. Do you have any idea how much money it costs you to float them? For that kind of money you could even resurrect Beethoven!"

"I don't have to—if I keep Etude alive."

"Oh, I know, I know," said Blaystone, and Osten could hear the warmth in his voice. "But I have to laugh every time I think of that poor old snob who heads Etude—and of how grand he is about letting us sell his select list of classics! If he only knew! He should see the mountain of returns we get!"

"What did you do with the latest returns?"

"We followed your instructions and gave all the un-sold Etude LPs—thousands of them, I might add—to schools and hospitals and music libraries all over the world. Don't worry; we keep a complete accounting of all such gifts and—"

"Good," said Osten. "What else?"

"You might want to check your royalty statements, and as I said, there are tax returns for you to sign. We need you to approve some press releases, and then there's all the fan mail. Hey, in the latest batch there's even a letter from the White House. An official envelope marked 'personal.'" He chuckled. "Not bad! Not bad at all! How does it feel to have a fan way at the top?"

"How soon can I get all that stuff?" asked Osten, anxious to have the call over with.

"Anytime."

"Who will make the delivery?"

"I'm going to lunch right now; I can drop it myself. Tell me where."

"Stop your taxi on the southwest corner of Broadway and Forty-seventh Street. A guy in a Mexican sombrero and mirror glasses will be standing there waiting. Hand it out the window to him. In a plain manila envelope."

"Does it have to be a taxi? Can't I take the company car?"

"A taxi," said Osten firmly. "It'll do you good to be in the real world for a change."

"Speaking of the real world," said Blaystone, "when can it expect another record from you?"

"The real world? Or Nokturn? You're getting greedy," said Osten.

"Maybe," said Blaystone, "but so are the fans. Can you give me some idea?"

"I'm working on something," said Osten, "and I'll let you know when it's ready."

"I should hope so," said Blaystone. "After all, we are your record company."

"For the record, you are," agreed Osten. "Now hurry up and catch a taxi to meet my Zapata!"

"Yes, sir!" snapped Blaystone playfully. "Anything else?"

"Yes. Follow my usual rules. Don't tell anyone where you take all these papers. Remember: one break of our nice little pact—and no more music!"

"Have I ever failed you?" asked Blaystone solemnly. "Believe me, I know Nokturn's got a good thing going with you. Why would I want to spoil it? We certainly wouldn't want the competition to know who you are and come skulking after you with offers!" he laughed. "Now, tell your man Zappa to expect a mail drop in twenty minutes!"

"Not Zappa—Zapata," Osten repeated. "Is that it for now?"

"I guess," said Blaystone. "No, wait! When you call next time, what name will you use?"

"How about Zapata?" said Osten and hung up.

On the way out of the hotel, Osten stopped at the desk. The porter was napping again.

Osten woke him up and said, "Can I borrow your hat

and glasses say, for an hour?" He passed some bills over the counter without waiting for an answer.

"What for, man?" mumbled the porter, still half asleep. Then he eyed the money and quickly handed over his hat and glasses.

"For a quickie," said Osten. "This chick—her name's Tequila Sunshine—gets excited only if I'm wearing a big hat, dark glasses, and nothing else."

"No kidding," said the porter, intrigued, but Osten was already out the door.

The yellow cab had barely stopped at the curb when Osten approached it from behind and tapped on the window. Blaystone rolled the window down, and Osten, keeping his face concealed under the brim of the sombrero, wordlessly took a large manila envelope out of Blaystone's hand. Then he knocked twice on the roof of the cab, Blaystone rolled the window up, and the taxi drove off.

Osten dropped the hat and glasses in the lap of the serenely napping porter and went up to his room. He opened the big envelope and spread its contents out on the bed. He glanced through the royalty statements, signed the IRS documents and the transfer authorization, and carefully examined the terms of the contract between Nokturn Records and Etude Classics in which, for the next two years, Nokturn agreed to distribute Etude's records for a specified sum of money and guaranteed a minimum sale of each of Etude's labels. He then slowly scrutinized the letter of agreement between Goddard and Nokturn, signed it, and placed it and the other documents in several prestamped envelopes; these he would mail directly to Blaystone in care of a special post office box maintained by Nokturn solely to receive communications from Goddard.

Finished with business, he stretched out on the bed,

propped himself on one elbow, and riffled quickly through
the assorted fan letters selected by Nokturn for him to
look over. There was a consistency about fan mail. It
always seemed to comprise regular categories: technical
questions from scholars and music critics—to which, out
of fear they might trace him, he never replied; appeals
to settle disputes over his music that had arisen out of
conflicting reviews—to which he never replied either;
and a few serious letters of appreciation from some of his
better-educated fans—which, even though he read them
thoroughly, held no interest for him, for he had learned long
ago that there were few things in the world less imaginative than the painstaking attempts of music fans to com-
municate soulfully.

There was one envelope Nokturn had not presumed
to open. It had "The White House, Washington" embossed on it in blue, and "Personal—please forward by
insured mail only" typed next to the address: Mr. Goddard, c/o Nokturn Records, Hemisphere Center, New
York City. He tore off the side of the envelope and pulled
out several densely typed sheets of official White House
stationery, the crest watermarks clearly visible when he
held the paper to the light. Before he started to read the
letter, he turned to the end to see the signature, but it
was unsigned.

Disappointed, he turned back to the beginning, and
he was instantly absorbed by the first sentence: "You are,
dear Goddard, probably reading this in the seclusion of a
shabby hotel somewhere." He smiled, swallowed, and
read on. "You are also probably apprehensive that I am
one more of those conniving females who envy you the
peace of your self-imposed exile and who would do anything to hunt you down and share it with you for whatever
length of time you would allow. Do not worry. I have no
such plans. I love you for the richness of your music, not
for the poverty of your existence. I am not, and never will
be, some girl you once picked up simply because she liked
your music and could never guess who you were. I am like
no other woman you have ever had or ever will have. And
if you are patient enough to read this letter with the same

care that I give to listening to your music, you will know why." A weird, tingling sensation of panic—that these words had come from someone who knew him, or was about to know him—swept over him.

He finished the letter. Then, half afraid he would come across some important revelation he had missed, he read through it again. One passage near the end slowed him down. "Even though this letter reminds you that the fearful isolation you have chosen keeps you from a fuller life, where you could be yourself with someone like me, you'll probably hate it because it threatens the security of the prison in which Goddard is locked. I know how predictable and drab your real life must be when you are not Goddard—particularly when you are composing music you're not willing or brave enough to acknowledge as your own."

Osten's panic gave way to anger. Her harsh words— "poverty of existence," "predictable," "drab"—came down like lashes on his heart, and he felt his fabulous mystery turn into a prison with no exit. What right did this woman— probably just some clever White House secretary—have to tell him who he was? And how dare she assume that just by listening to his music she could know anything about him at all?

While he ran his bath and soaked in it, he listened to a popular music station on the radio, and in the course of twenty minutes heard two of his singles. He liked the anonymous climate of the hotel, with its peeling wallpaper, cracked and yellowed bathroom tiles, and overstarched towels with torn edges. He felt safe. Yet the White House letter made him recall one hotel, only three blocks away, in which he had also felt safe—in the company of a girl he'd picked up simply because she'd liked his music.

It was a year ago, and then, as now, it was hot and humid. The Great White Way of Broadway teemed with restless Saturday-night strollers, and he'd stopped in front of a record shop, one of the city's largest, and stared at the window, which was filled from end to end and top to bottom with copies of the latest Goddard album cover. Then he went inside where a crowd of buyers, mostly teenagers, were lined up at a counter waiting to listen to his records through stereophonic earphones. On the wall above, GODDARD was spelled out in foot-high fluorescent letters. He was about to leave when he noticed a soft, fresh-looking girl listening to one of his records at one of the turntables. It was not her youthful beauty, partially hidden under the earphones, that made him want to know her, but the serene, almost unearthly expression on her face. Her eyes were closed. Her body swayed ever so gently to what she was hearing.

The machine stopped, and she awakened from her meditation. Just as she was about to play the record again, a salesman stepped over and removed it from the turntable. "C'mon," he said, "give others a chance. You've listened to it four times already. Either you buy it or you don't."

The girl looked at him pleasantly, as if she were under a spell. "I guess I don't—not today," she said.

Osten approached her. "Do you like Goddard?" he asked, pointing at the record.

"I love him," she said as she focused on Osten. "I could listen to him for days."

"Then why don't you buy it and listen to him at home?" asked the salesman.

"No bread," she replied sweetly as she got ready to leave.

"Wait," said Osten. Handing money to the salesman, he picked an album up off a stack and handed it to the girl. "A gift," he said.

"Thanks," she said. "But you don't even know me."

"I sort of do," said Osten. "We both like Goddard." He started to walk out of the store.

Record in hand, the girl walked beside him. "What's your name?" she asked.

"Jimmy."

"I'm Debbie," she said. "Where are you from?"

"Out of town," he answered.

"Same here," she said. "I'm just in for the day."

"When do you have to leave?" he asked.

"The last bus is at midnight."

"Do you want to have dinner?" he asked, trying to sound casual. "We could buy some stuff in the deli on the corner and take it to my hotel."

"How far is that?"

"Two blocks."

"It's okay by me," she said with total unconcern.

They bought sandwiches and potato salad and ate watching TV. As Osten opened a beer, the girl reached into her bag and took out a syringe, a needle, and a small packet of white powder. "You want some?" she asked on the way to the bathroom.

"No, thanks," he replied, adding, "you should be careful with that."

"I only have to be careful without it," she said and giggled.

Through the door he heard her set things down on the washbasin and flush the toilet. After a short span of silence she came back and stretched out on the bed. He sat next to her and studied her silky hair, the fine contour of her neck, the outline of her small girlish breasts under her blouse.

She watched him stare. "You're sweet," she said. "So sweet. Even your voice is sweet. What's wrong with it?" She looked up at him, the pupils of her eyes shiny and dilated.

"A few years ago," he said, "I had little calcified deposits in my throat. They scraped them off and, as a result, I kind of coo."

"It sounds fine," she said, "as long as you don't have to sing." She laughed softly.

He then changed his tack. In his natural voice, he said, "But when I want to, I do sing—in my own voice. You see—I'm Goddard. I've sung all those songs." He pointed to the album on the table.

"I believe you," said the girl sweetly. "I've already met five Goddards. I believed every one of them."

Her cheeks were flushed; she stared at him, her gaze unsteady, and he stared back. Then she reached for him.

He made love to her, aware that he could hurt her and that in her narcotic trance she might not feel it. Yet her passivity excited him; he felt free to do what he pleased. The girl responded by clinging to him like a child. All his efforts to bring her to orgasm failed and she seemed only vaguely aware of his lovemaking. Afterward, they took a bath together and dressed. As Osten turned to switch off the light on their way out of the room, he heard her fall to the floor with a thud. Thinking she had passed out, he propped her against the wall and splashed cold water on her face and neck, but she didn't move, and when he leaned close and looked into her eyes, she stared back at him without blinking. She was dead.

At first, it seemed inadmissable: how could death step between them this way—without warning, cutting off the girl's life as if it didn't matter at all, as if it were a crude synthesizer suddenly unplugged from the source of energy! And what was the meaning of life, if it could be so quickly, so arbitrarily and senselessly snatched away?

Then Ostern panicked. He was terrified at the thought of summoning the police and being dragged by them to a precinct house crowded with muggers, pimps, and whores. There was no way he could explain the girl's death anyway, he told himself. He had no idea where she had got the stuff she took or how much she had shot into herself. And what would he say when the police asked him who *he* was, how he made his living, why he was staying in that particular hotel, where he had met the girl, whether they had had sex? His sperm was still in her; the police might say she had died during their lovemaking, or even that he had killed her.

He froze at the thought of what his presence here, and his unclear role in the girl's death, would mean to his father, and of his father's horror over the sensational headlines and their impact on the image of Etude Classics, the family business and his father's single most cherished possession. Even worse, he recoiled at the thought of having to explain to the world who James Norbert Osten really was. What would the discovery of the real Goddard and the ensuing hysteria of the media do to his father? To him? To his music?

Carefully, he took a towel and wiped his fingerprints from all the surfaces he had touched in the room. By the time he finished, his mouth was dry from fear and his heart was hammering. Leaving the girl's body propped against the wall, on his way out, he turned off the light and locked the door. With Goddard's record under his arm, he descended to the hotel lobby and walked slowly out to the street where his thoughts calmed down and he felt safe again.

If the White House letter awakened in him the memory of the dead girl, it was because he felt tempted now, as he had been tempted then, to enjoy someone who could be drawn to him as much for himself as for his music. Sitting in the tub, he continued to think about the anonymous letter writer. At the University of California at Davis, where he had gone to school and where he was still enrolled as a postgraduate student, anyone who wrote so well and so analytically would have been either an English or a psychology major. Was the woman who wrote it young or old? Was she the wife or daughter or secretary or mistress of someone prominent? And if she wanted to—or had to—hide who she was, why did she write her letter on the White House stationery and send it to him in an official envelope?

The letter implied that she knew why he had chosen "Goddard" for his name. That stunned him. How could she? If she chose to write again, she said, she would "write more about that and other such derivative matters." What clues had she learned from his Mexican songs about which her letter had given only vague hints? And why had she waited until now to write to him—she had obviously been researching him for a long time. Above all, in view of the fact that she had spent so much time analyzing him, why didn't she ask to meet him?

Perhaps she had important White House connections.
But even if she did, he was not impressed. Politics and power
in themselves had never meant much to him; one was like
the art of blowing glass, the other like the act of smashing
it. His father, many of whose values he had taken as
his own, saw politics as the source of most of mankind's
evils and proudly maintained that of all the arts, music
was least influenced by political considerations.

Osten looked at the White House envelope. It occurred to him that in music, the term "envelope" had
to do with attack and decay—the start of a note, its
growth, its duration, and its diminution and termination.
It was quite different from reverberation and echo,
which were much in use in the new musical technology,
in which synthesizers invaded and changed the space of
sound's natural envelope. How clever was this writer?
he wondered. Was the impressive White House envelope,
as well as the letter inside, a subtle declaration of
war on the envelope of Goddard's voice—an attempt
to agitate him and create echoes and reverberations?
Was that what she wanted? And if so, what was in it
for her?

As he put the envelope down, he realized that it bore
a remarkable piece of information: the postmark was not
Washington, D.C., as he had assumed, but New York
City, somewhere on the West Side to judge from the zip
code. Did she want him to notice that?

The more he thought about her, the more it annoyed
him that he didn't know who she was, for then, at least, he
could imagine going after her, tracking her down, beating
her at the game. The image of the dead girl returned. She
could never have written or even understood the White
House letter; she had been far too simple.

Quickly he dried off and dressed, picked up the envelopes he had to mail to Nokturn, pocketed the White
House letter, and threw all the other letters and papers
into the incinerator chute down the hall. Leaving the
hotel, for the fourth time that day he found the porter
asleep.

* * *

Osten decided, since he would be east for a while, to drive out to visit his father. Having called first to say when he thought he might arrive, he rented a car—choosing for fun, as he always did, a model he had never driven. Since having become Goddard, Osten rented almost everything he used, except for music equipment, which he always bought with cash and always kept in one place. Renting had become practically an art to him, something he enjoyed and kept on perfecting.

To avoid ever having traceable personal papers lying around, he did all of his business out of cheap hotel rooms, and when he was in New York he frequently sublet apartments for short periods, making it impossible to accumulate possessions that could lead people to him. In this country whose greatness once rested on the ability of its people to buy—often carelessly—what it produced, the best that could be said for it now, in its inflationary phase, was that what was once bought was now either for sale or for rent.

Osten drove past the Goddard Beat, the West Side disco that was named after him. He had visited it only once, a little over two years ago, and he remembered the night vividly. He had been somewhat curious to see what the famous Goddard Beat was like, but more curious by far to know how he—Goddard—would feel being there, alone among strangers, known by no one, yet known to everyone. The disco was frequented then by a mix of people—Columbia University students, Juilliard students, and many black musicians and their groupies from nearby Harlem.

The place was reverberating with rhythm, and Osten entered hesitantly. Two rock bands performed at the

Goddard Beat, alternating every hour, playing mostly the biggest and newest Goddard hits. As he walked through the crowded rooms, Osten turned to watch the band on stage go at his latest big single. In the act of doing so, he was unexpectedly tripped by a couple dancing past, and losing balance he went crashing into a small side table, knocking over two glasses and a bottle of champagne and causing the table's occupants, a thickly built black man and a willowy black girl, to overturn their chairs as they jumped up to avoid getting wet.

"Hey, you motherfucker, look where you're going!" roared the man, his suede slacks soaked with champagne, as he spun and challenged Osten.

"It wasn't his fault," said the girl, brushing the droplets off her velvet jump suit and calmly placing the empty bottle in the ice bucket beside the table.

"Oh yeah?" said the man, still furious, pushing Osten away. "Then who in the fuck—"

"Stop it, Paul," the girl said sharply as she stepped between them. "Couldn't you see the guy didn't mean it?"

As other patrons, ignorant of what had happened, turned to watch, hoping for a fight, Osten held out his hand to the black man. "I'm terribly sorry," he said. "I'd like to pay for another bottle."

The man seemed on the verge of slapping his hand aside when the girl intervened again. She quickly shook Osten's hand, then sat down as if nothing had happened. "It's all right," she said, "it could happen to anyone." She looked up at him and smiled politely, and he noted how expressive her eyes were.

"Now get lost," her companion said to Osten. "D'you hear?"

"I'm truly sorry," said Osten, but now the man ignored him. As the waiter came up with a dry tablecloth, Osten discreetly handed him several twenty-dollar bills. "Get them another bottle, will you?" he said, and without giving the couple another look he turned and walked away.

Unsettled, angry with himself and humiliated, he moved toward the stage and watched the band members perform in turn for the groupies gathered around. But in a few minutes, with no mood to guide him, he decided he had had enough of the Goddard Beat. He was about to leave the disco when someone touched him on the shoulder. It was the black girl, her jump suit clinging to her body like another skin.

"Thanks for the champagne," she said with a faint smile.

He mumbled that he was glad they had liked it, and she caught him peering behind her for a sign of her companion.

"Paul's gone," she said. "He went home to save his precious suede pants."

"I'm sorry," Osten said slowly, as he stared at her full breasts, partly exposed by the open zipper of her jump suit. When he raised his eyes, he saw that she was amused to have caught him staring.

"Don't be sorry," she said. "That's what they're there for. Women peek too." She was smiling widely now, showing two rows of impeccably white and even teeth. "And although tough guys always think we're looking for things that are big and long, that's not what turns us on."

Her self-assurance put him off. "Really. What does?" he asked, afraid as he said it that he was setting himself up.

"A cute ass." She gave him a studied once-over. "And a body that's tall and slim and leggy."

"Aren't you talking about yourself?" he bantered.

"Maybe I am," she laughed. "But also about you." She paused, then gave him another assessing look. "What do you do when you're not knocking over tables, boy?" she asked jokingly, intoning like a southern overseer.

"I travel a lot," he said. "How about you, ma'am?"

"Why, I just play, honey," she answered.

By now he was convinced she was a hooker. He had never been out with a hooker, and the thought of pulling the zipper of her jump suit all the way down and having her step out of it on her high heels straight into his arms excited him greatly. Regaining his composure, he said,

"I'm Jimmy." Then, staring openly at her breasts, he asked, "Are you free?"

"Free?" She laughed. "Of course I'm free. Slavery is no longer in, you know."

"I mean—" he stammered, "free to go out. With me." He hesitated, then blurted out, "For money, I mean."

"To go out—with you—for money?" she repeated, as if working out a puzzle. "Oh—I—see," she said, spacing the words, and then she threw back her head and laughed. She moved close to him and brushed her hips against his, sliding her hand over his buttocks. "I'm Donna," she murmured. "Tell Donna just exactly what it is you have in mind, honey."

"To eat your honey," he purred back. "For the rest of the night."

"At what eatery?" she asked.

"A hotel," he said. "Any hotel. I'm from out of town."

"I don't like hotels," she answered. "And after midnight, hotels don't like girls like me either." She gave him a long look. "What do you do for a living, boy?" she asked, intoning again.

"I study writing," he said, "in California." Then, for fear she might leave him at that news, he added, "But I have enough money," and he reached into his pocket.

She stopped his hand. "I know you do. You already bought Paul and me champagne tonight."

Touched by his sincerity, she stared at him for a moment with a gentle smile on her lips. "How about going to play at my place?" she asked.

"Where is it?" he asked, afraid she might say Harlem.

"Carnegie Hall," she whispered.

"Carnegie Hall? *The* Carnegie Hall?" He thought she was joking.

"You heard me." Her hand played now with his thigh.

"They let you work out of Carnegie Hall?" he asked, watching her intently.

"I prefer to work in. I use an artist's studio there," she explained. "Didn't you know, boy, there are over a hundred of them living there?"

"Who's the artist?" he asked, afraid she might be setting a trap for him.

"A pianist. From Juilliard."

"And where is the pianist now?" he asked.

"On a date with a stranger. That's why you and I can play there. Don't worry." She convinced him she was safe and, arm in arm, the two of them left the Goddard Beat.

In a taxi, driving down Broadway he tried to kiss her, but she wouldn't let him. "Later," she whispered. "Give us time, boy!" At Carnegie Hall, he followed her to the side entrance. A night porter scrutinized him as they got into the elevator.

She opened the door of the studio, turned on the lights, then dimmed them instantly. A large piano dominated the room. The rest of the furnishings consisted of a large double bed, a desk covered with musical scores, a bookshelf, a radio-phonograph console, and several objects of African art—tribal masks, fetish figures, and beaded bags.

"What sort of music does your friend play?" asked Osten, amused to be going through his first experience with a whore in the modest Carnegie Hall studio of a Juilliard music student.

"Guess."

"Is your friend—black?"

"Yes," she nodded.

"Then—is it jazz piano?" he asked.

"Jazz? Now what ever made you think of that?" she said, teasing him. "No—my black friend doesn't play jazz! Guess again!"

"I give up!" he answered with a straight face.

"How about you? Do you play anything else but that?" she asked, touching his groin.

"A little," he said and sat down at the piano. It was open, and almost involuntarily his hands fell on the keys. Unwilling to entertain her with a rock tune she was bound to know, he struck a few chords, then, to impress her, he awkwardly played a short passage.

She stood next to him, and when he finished he put his arm around her thighs and tipped her onto his lap.

Aroused by her nearness, he started to kiss her neck and nuzzle her shoulder.

"Schubert's Quartet number fourteen. Right?" she asked. "Also known as *Death and the Maiden*."

Astonished, he slowly pulled back. "I don't believe it! How did you know that?" he asked.

She got up and straightened her jump suit. "Black magic. What else?" she said, pointing at the fetishes.

It occurred to him that she could have heard the passage played by the Juilliard student. He started to play another piece.

"Debussy. *Prelude to the Afternoon of a Faun*," she said, and he stopped. "You play it well, boy!"

He stood up and closed the piano, suddenly glad that throughout the evening he had spoken to her only in his altered voice, for her musical ear might have unmasked him.

"Where did you learn music?" he asked.

Speaking in a southern drawl again, she replied, "Why? Ain't it right for a little ol' black girl to know what the white folks play?"

"You told me you were—"

"I told you the pianist who lives here is out on a date with a stranger," she said in a firm voice. "Well, you're the stranger. And this is where I play." She sat down at the piano and began to play, then stopped as suddenly as she had begun.

"Chopin's *Barcarole*," he said, reciting like a music student in front of his teacher. "A tender nocturne with two main phrases that render the piece two-souled, like a dialogue of lovers. The modulation to C-sharp major evokes their kissing, petting, and lovemaking. The gently rocking rhythm of the bass solo suggests they may be making it in a boat—a gondola, perhaps." He smiled. "You should have played at least up to bar 78, when they get it off together . . ."

She looked at him with unmitigated surprise. "Now how come you know all that, boy?"

"Now how come you can play like you do, doll?" he said, imitating her.

"I learned it at Juilliard."

"And I at home."

She walked over to him, and pressing her breasts against his chest, steered him slowly toward the bed. When he felt his legs touch the edge, he tried to pull her down but she resisted.

"What was a boy who knows Schubert, Debussy, and Chopin doing at the Goddard Beat?"

"Looking for his barcarole," he said. "What was a classical pianist doing there?"

"Meeting a faun," she said. "Paul, the guy you saw me with, is a music agent, and I guess I'm a prelude he might take out some afternoon to meet music publishers and shop for a label."

"Don't waste your faun's afternoons anymore," said Osten. "My father owns Etude Classics."

Music was thus the springboard of Osten's initial infatuation with Donna. He saw her as his redeemer, the first person with whom he could be himself—without feeling severed from the other side of his being, where, as Goddard, he existed alone, hidden from view.

She was also the first black person he had known intimately. Everything about her—from the shape and color of her body to her middle-class South Bronx background to her spontaneous love of music—seemed exotic to him.

Soon after their first meeting he took Donna to a black-tie reception in his father's Manhattan apartment. It was an annual event and that year it was to celebrate the thirtieth anniversary of Etude Classics.

There were about eighty people there, including the Etude executives, many of the composers and performers published on the Etude label, and assorted music critics. The appearance of Donna in a low-cut gold lamé gown with a slit skirt left the staid, distinguished company gasping.

Because this event was so important to his father, Osten had attended it every year since boyhood, and as the only child of the company's founder and president, he was known to most of those present. It was at one of these parties that, as a teenager, he had first met Goddard Lieberson and Boris Pregel, the two men whose views on life and art were to influence him long after both men were dead. As a rule, however, most of the guests were boring—doubly so, inasmuch as they were on their best behavior. Osten took a special delight in passing among them with Donna—the only black woman at the party—on his arm.

Introducing Donna to his father, he was amused to see the old man's obvious consternation at the sight of her breasts bared to the nipples by the low-cut gown. Then he took her on a round of the other guests, noticing with pleasure their unsuccessful attempts to hide their shock.

As he and Donna moved through the crowd, Osten saw Patrick Domostroy, a man he had met several times at his father's parties. Domostroy's music, as well as his concerts, had once been highly successful, but some years ago the man had stopped composing and now he lived in obscurity, surfacing only from time to time.

Middle-aged, skinny, wrinkled, and balding, Domostroy moved through the room like a starved vulture. His voice had a hint of some foreign accent, and everything else about the man seemed foreign as well—his gestures, his quick glances and frenetic way of talking, his clothes forcefully sporty, his manner overly at ease. He was accompanied by a blue-eyed, puffy blonde much younger than he. When Domostroy saw Donna, he stared at her with such intense curiosity that Osten spontaneously stepped in front of her, as if to shield her from the man's sight.

As for Domostroy, he had met Jimmy Osten on two or three occasions—always in the presence of Gerhard Osten and his guests and associates—and although they'd never exchanged more than a few words, Domostroy had found Osten's remarks about his father's company, and about music in general, uniformly naive. He also found the young man's stare annoying and his manner wishy-washy and ineffectual. The kid was a boring wimp. Mentally Domostroy called him the Lukewarm Noodle. He would have certainly avoided him now, had it not been for the young woman Osten was with. The black woman was unusually beautiful and statuesque; she was also self-possessed, graceful, and her patrician air made Domostroy wonder whether he might not have misjudged Jimmy Osten, or at least nicknamed him incorrectly.

When Osten and Donna passed nearby, Domostroy seized the opportunity to meet her. Osten made the introduction reluctantly, and when Donna recognized Domostroy's name and thanked the composer for the pleasure his music had given her, Osten regretted the encounter even more.

Domostroy made no effort to hide the impression Donna had made on him. Ignoring Osten, he looked into her eyes and said, "Had I known you would like my music, I would have written twice as much."

"You still can," she said, flirting.

"I'm flattered," said Domostroy, "and surprised. I wouldn't expect you to like my music."

"Because I'm black?" asked Donna.

"Yes—and I'm white," said Domostroy, frankly staring at her. "It's a matter of different rhythmic intensity."

Osten felt the blood rushing to his face. "This is idiotic," he said, turning to Domostroy and lowering his voice in anger. "Are you also going to talk to Donna about the Negroid natural rhythm?" He could barely restrain himself. "Come on, Donna, let's go." He took her arm, but she resisted.

"Wait a minute, Jimmy," she said, lifting her arm from his grasp. "Mr. Domostroy is right. To me, rhythm is not a musical exercise inhibited by bar lines, but an impulse—my body's own natural percussion. My ancestors were African slaves who communicated from one slave ship to another with Atumpan and Ashanti talking drums. And even though my father was a jazz pianist, the first musical instrument he taught me to play, when I was still a child, was an mbira, a thumb piano with simple metal reeds and a gourd resonator—"

"—discovered in South Africa by the Portuguese in the sixteenth century," interjected Domostroy, "and mis-

named by them the Kaffir." He paused. "Could you, by
any chance, be the daughter of Henry Lee Downes?" he
asked her.

"Yes, I am," she replied. "I was a late child. My
father died when I was fourteen. Did you know him?"

"I heard your father play," said Domostroy. "He was
a great jazz virtuoso. He could make the piano sound like
a bell or a horn."

Donna gave him an amused look. "It's kind of you to
say that, Mr. Domostroy, but what to you is probably just
black history," she said, "is to me a living rhythm—a
music like no other." She turned to Osten and said playfully, "When Mr. Domostroy listens to his past, I'll bet he
hears Elizabethan madrigals. I'm sure a Steinway was the
first musical instrument he saw at home as a boy."

"Indeed it was," agreed Domostroy. "My mother's
grand piano. She was a concert pianist." His eyes met
Donna's. "You are as articulate as you are beautiful, Miss
Downes," he said. "Are you a dancer?"

"That's enough, Domostroy!" said Osten.

"I'm not a dancer, Mr. Domostroy," Donna said calmly. "Though I like to dance." She pointed at the grand
piano behind them. "That's my Kaffir now."

"Then by all means," said Domostroy, studiously disre-
garding Osten, "play it!"

"Donna, let's go!" said Osten. "He can't order you
around," he added, almost snarling.

"As long as I'm ordered to *play*, I don't mind," said
Donna, her eyes returning Domostroy's challenge as she
went and sat down at the piano.

There was a hush, and the guests opened a circle
around her. Gerhard Osten, arm in arm with the blond
woman Domostroy had left in his care, walked over to his
son. "This is hardly the time for dancing," he said quietly.

The blond woman leaned over and, squeezing the
older man's arm, said, "But, Mr. Osten, that might be
fun!"

"Don't worry, Father," said Osten. "Most of the guests
here wouldn't know how to dance!"

His father cleared his throat and smiled nervously.
"Jimmy, I want you to meet Miss Vala Stavrova," he said.

Osten and the woman shook hands.

Domostroy, standing next to Osten's father, put in,
"Miss Stavrova is originally from Russia—the country of
classics!"

"Yes. But I love dancing rock 'n' roll," said Vala
Stavrova in a high-pitched voice. "Is she a rock singer?"
she asked, pointing at Donna.

Donna started to play, and the sound of Chopin's
Scherzo in C-sharp Minor filled the room.

"Remarkable," said his father, watching Donna play.
"Incredible, in fact. Who is she?"

"Donna Downes, Father," said Osten, speaking low.
"I introduced you to her."

"Of course you did. Where's she from?" asked his
father.

"From New York," Domostroy cut in.

"Where did she learn to play like that?" asked Gerhard Osten.

"Donna is a student at Juilliard," said Osten with
finality, hoping to silence the conversation.

"I would never have expected her to play Chopin!"
his father continued.

"Why not?" asked Domostroy, leaning toward him.
"Have you forgotten, Gerhard, that Chopin and Liszt
were the favorite composers of the black pianists in New
Orleans and Sedalia at the end of the last century?"

"I haven't forgotten," said Gerhard Osten, "because I
never knew. Interesting. What do you think of her?"

"I think she's a beauty," Domostroy answered, his
gaze still on the pianist.

"I mean her playing."

"So far, quite competent," said Domostroy, "but she
hasn't come to the hard part yet—the switch from chords
to finger work. When Chopin wrote the piece, he knew
that most pianists would never make the switch in time, so
he called for an improvisation."

They listened. When Donna came to the difficult
running passage of the scherzo, her left hand skimmed

brilliantly up four octaves, then gently lifted. She executed a split-second break between one beat and the next, settled into an avalanche of quavers, hesitated, then came rolling back down the four octaves, separating each note from the next with metronomic precision.

"She's a gifted Chopinist," said Domostroy. "You'd never guess it from her looks, would you?"

In Osten's car on the way back to Carnegie Hall after the party, Donna asked, "Did you like the way I played?"

"I'm not good at judging friends," he said. "But everybody seemed to love it. My father—"

"Your father told me how surprised he was that I played Chopin," she said. "Did you hear him? In fact, everybody told me how surprised they were by it—meaning that black and Chopin just don't match! Only Patrick Domostroy told me that I played the piece like a professional—including that impossible free-time passage that Chopin marked in the score with an X."

"You better watch out," said Osten, "Domostroy looked as if he'd like to score an X on you." He pressed down on the accelerator and they speeded up. "I didn't like the way he talked to you."

"He said I used the soft pedal exactly the way Chopin indicated."

"How?" asked Osten, a bit annoyed by her enthusiasm.

"My own way!" she said and laughed. "To encourage free interpretation, Chopin never marked the use of the soft pedal. He said fingers, not a pedal, created a pianist's touch. Chopin was the first pianist who understood the distinct and separate physical attributes of each of the fingers. Domostroy also said that I even managed to evoke Chopin's Żal."

"What's Żal?"

"A spiritual enigma—pain and rage smothered by melancholy—an emotional trademark of Poles, or any people oppressed for long periods of time. Żal permeates all of Chopin's work. Domostroy said that because I'm black, Żal will probably color all of mine as well." She hesitated. "What kind of man is Domostroy? You obviously can't stand him."

Osten shrugged. "I guess he's a bit off—like Chopin."

"Chopin was a great composer and a virtuoso performer," Donna reminded him. "His music is all that matters."

"Let's say Domostroy leads a double life," said Osten. "He lives alone in a shut-down ballroom in the South Bronx; at night he plays in some crummy Mafia-run pinball dive; and in the wee hours, when everybody else is in bed, he prowls the streets in that old jalopy of his."

"Why?" she interrupted.

"Why what?"

"Why does he do it? Maybe he has a reason."

"He's obsessed, that's the reason," said Osten.

"So was Berlioz. Otherwise he wouldn't have written his Fantastic Symphony. So were Liszt, Tchaikovsky, and Wagner. So were a lot of other talented men."

"Domostroy is a sex nut," said Osten contemptuously. "I once read an old *New York* magazine profile of him. They called him the Jekyll and Hyde of the music scene. At night he drives around in disguises—you know, phony mustache, goatee, big hat—and stops off at all kinds of odd places—underground couples parties, secret societies, encounter sex clubs. Once he was followed for hours by New York City police detectives who, after he had made some fifteen stops in such strange places, took him for a dope pusher and gave him and his car a thorough search and found nothing but some of his old music sheets! They were furious for the time they lost! He's like some sort of satyr, off on a perpetual witches' sabbath." He paused to let her react to what he had said, but she kept stubbornly silent. "Even during his heyday, Domostroy used to go for the mondo weirdo: the freaks, the psychos, the whores, even the sex changes. I think he even photographed them— as a hobby. I hate to think whom he goes after—and whom he gets!—now that he's nobody. No decent piano bar or nightclub will have him anymore."

Again Donna did not react.

"You saw Vala, the Russian bimbo he brought to the party. That's the kind he goes for," he said sullenly.

"Your father certainly seemed to like her," Donna remarked.

"My father knows absolutely nothing about women," said Osten. "My mother was his first and only love. He married her after cutting in and dancing one tango with her. And he couldn't even dance! Since her death, all he cares about is music. To my father," he said, "every Etude recording is a flashing meteor, lighting up the musical firmament and then blazing away into the future. He sees himself as the great custodian of true art. And who knows? Maybe he is."

Looking out the side window, speaking as intimately as if she were speaking to herself, Donna said, "You must love your father a lot, Jimmy."

Without taking his eyes off the road, Osten said, "I love him more than a lot. I would do anything to keep him happy."

Somehow, it was easy for long periods of time to pass between visits to his family home on Long Island. Now, as he left the city in his rented car, he realized that it had been two years since his last drive out and two years since he had met Donna. A recently completed stretch of highway shortened his trip by nearly an hour, and he arrived at Wainscott much earlier than expected. He drove up a private road lined with birches, their trunks black at the base and veined above like marble columns, and stopped at the house, a white mansion with tall, many-paned windows in its facade. He parked his rented car in the driveway between two brand-new automobiles, noting their personalized license plates: ETUDE for his father and VALA for his stepmother of less than two years.

The main door was open, but Osten hesitated and then rang the bell before entering the house. In the hall he ran into Bruno, his father's Viennese valet and chauf-

feur, who had been in service since the death of Leonore
Osten, Jimmy's mother.

"Herr Jimmy, how are you?" muttered Bruno, forcing
a smile that revealed uneven tobacco-stained teeth. Bruno's rare moments of genuine warmth were reserved for
Gerhard Osten and his youthful second wife. "Your father
and Madame are on the side veranda," he concluded
stiffly.

Before Osten spoke, he coughed to bring on his altered voice. "Thank you, Bruno," he said.

As he crossed the hall, which was dominated by a
life-sized marble statue of Bach, he braced himself for the
stress he inevitably felt in the presence of his stepmother.
He could never think of Vala as a relative, and being with
her made him uncomfortable.

The veranda was flooded with sunshine and with the
sound of Handel's *Israel in Egypt* playing on the tape
deck. His father and Vala sat reading, and when they saw
him, as if on command, they both put down their newspapers. Smoothing his flat white hair and clutching at his
back, his father stood to greet him. Vala quickly buttoned
up the front of her housecoat.

"Hello, Father. How are you, Vala?" said Osten,
stepping forward and hugging his father. Embarrassed,
Gerhard Osten stepped sideways, freeing himself from the
embrace, and then uneasily patted his son on the shoulder. Vala raised her hand, as if offering it to him to kiss,
and, awkwardly, Osten stepped over to shake it.

"How have you been, Jimmy?" asked his father, sitting down and indicating a place at his side. When he had
scrutinized his son's patched jeans, blue work shirt, and
faded suede jacket, he said to Vala, "He looks like a
cowboy, doesn't he?"

Vala smiled. "But, darling, Jimmy is a cowboy," she
said in her whining voice. Even though she had come to
the States at age sixteen, some ten years before becoming
Mrs. Osten—during which time she had been married
and divorced somewhere in Colorado—Vala had lost none
of her Russian accent. Still a trifle plump, she was nevertheless quite pretty. Her slightly enlarged pupils, framed

by dark eyebrows and thick lashes, gave her watery blue eyes a thoughtful expression.

"Well, tell us, what brings you here, Jimmy?" asked his father while Bruno served coffee.

"I just felt like seeing you both, that's all," said Osten, sipping from his cup of coffee. "Donna is sorry she couldn't come with me," he said, "but something came up at Juilliard at the last minute and she had to stay in town. She sends her love to you both." The coffee burned his lips, but he smiled and strained for a leisurely manner. "You look great, Father. You too, Vala." There followed an awkward pause. "What's new with you two?"

"Everything is as usual," said Vala, stretching in her chair. "We play a little golf—"

"She's turning into a great golfer," said his father. "You should come out and watch her play."

"I'd love to," Osten said. He attempted a compliment. "I'm sure Vala's a born golfer."

"You would not love to," said Vala. "You don't like golf." To her husband she said, "Jimmy doesn't like golf." Then to Osten, "You said once that golf is like fishing in reverse: instead of waiting for a fish to come up, you wait for a ball to sink in."

"Jimmy doesn't like a number of things," said his father with an icy edge. "Work, for one thing. Music, for another."

"My studying is work, Father," said Osten. "And I do like classical music."

"No, you don't," his father declared with some resentment. To Vala he explained, "Jimmy is not musically inclined. Goddard Lieberson used to divide all musicians into those who scratch and those who play. Well, even as a kid, Jimmy could not play piano, only scratch it, that's all." To his son, he added, "You've said yourself that you prefer language, or whatever it is that you've been studying out in California all these years, to music."

"Literature, Father," said Osten gently. "Remember what H. L. Mencken said: 'Next to music, prose is the finest of all the fine arts.' My father forgets that both the piano and the typewriter have keyboards," he said to Vala with a weak laugh.

"I distinctly remember your saying that music was cold, that it did not express anything,'" said his father.

"I was only quoting Stravinsky."

"Without understanding him," said his father. "Stravinsky was obviously paraphrasing Goethe, who saw architecture as music frozen in time, while Stravinsky saw music as time's architecture."

"The other day I heard on the radio some of the recent Etude releases—the New Classics series," said Osten in an effort to change the subject. "Quite magnificent, I might add."

"What new series is that?" Vala interrupted, feigning interest.

"They're works that were written for one type of instrument and are now being recorded on another," explained his father, calming down.

"How closely do they follow the originals?" asked Osten.

His father brightened. "Even the purists agree that harmonically and melodically they're the same. It's the most sophisticated musical transformation, and often, freed from the mental set attached to the original solo instrument, the music emerges even purer than before."

"Isn't that something like translating?" interjected Vala.

"Yes, it is," said Gerhard Osten enthusiastically, adding for his son, "Vala is right." He looked at her like a proud teacher showing off his pupil. "It's much the same, Vala, as it would be to translate Pushkin into today's English. The important thing in such a case would be to make sure that Pushkin was not damaged. Our first concern is to preserve the great works. This new series represents our only experiment in over thirty years, but it has been enormously promising so far. It seems in a way actually to make the great works greater."

"So Etude is really doing well?" asked Osten, sipping his coffee.

"Couldn't be better," said his father. "Nokturn Records has just renewed its worldwide distribution agreement with us. Nokturn knows a good thing. We're staying right at the top of the classical music market."

"Your father negotiated the deal himself," said Vala.

"I certainly did," said his father. "In the last few years, our sales have skyrocketed, and the return rate of our albums remains the lowest in the industry." He paused. "That's why I was able to negotiate with Nokturn from a position of strength. And Oscar Blaystone, the president of Nokturn, has a reputation for being one of the toughest men in the business. But I knew, and he knew, that he had to meet my terms."

"Your father was so excited by that deal," said Vala, "that I was jealous. I made him prove to me that he could get just as excited over me." She turned her face to them with a doll-like expression and smiled girlishly. "And he did prove it, too," she purred. "Didn't you, darling?"

Gerhard Osten looked at her adoringly. "Now, now," he said manfully. "You can't be jealous of Etude. I founded Etude long before you were born."

"I know," she said with a pretty pout. "Music has been your love so much longer than I have!"

"Now, Vala, that's not fair," scolded the old man. He assumed the posture of an actor on stage and began to recite, his heavy German accent exaggerated by emotion: " 'Do not let sadness come over you; For all your white hairs you can still be a lover.' That's Goethe," he announced. " 'He capers nimbly in a lady's chamber to the lascivious pleasing of a lute.' And that's Shakespeare," he exclaimed, proud of his memory, looking at Vala with such utter love that Osten had to turn away to hide his embarrassment and anger. How could his father—one of the world's outstanding musical authorities and the founder of Etude Classics—so blindly worship this brainless lump of flesh? Was it simply because he was old and dried up and she was young and soft and energetic? Was it because of Vala that his father was so admiring of Goethe, who at seventy-one proposed to a seventeen-year-old? When Santayana remarked that music, though the most abstract of arts, also served the dumbest emotion, he must have been referring to the men engaged in that art, Osten thought, as much as to the art itself.

He caught his father looking at him severely and wondered if the older man could read his thoughts. "I understand Vala's feelings about music very well," Jimmy said with sudden cheerfulness. "I go through the same thing all the time with Donna. To her, too, music is all that matters."

Vala shook her head. "If it really is all, then it's your fault, Jimmy," she said. "Listen to me. Black or white, young or old, ugly or beautiful—deep down, every woman wants one thing, and one thing only." She paused dramatically, about to tell them what that one thing was, when his father broke in.

"Donna's an amazing girl," he said. "No one would ever imagine that she could have such a sure understanding of the classics. She played so superbly at my party that time." He reflected, then went on. "If she were to place first, second, or even third at the next International Chopin Piano Competition in Warsaw, I would certainly sign her up with Etude," he said.

"Donna can't make up her mind whether she's going to enter the competition or not," said Jimmy. "She says her interest is in music, not prizes."

"She'll soon realize that in today's world, in music, as in everything else, it is success, unfortunately, that determines value," said his father sadly.

"She already has," said Osten. "That's what frightens her, I guess."

"As sexy as she is, I doubt if she's frightened of anything," said Vala. "Look at her—big bosoms, the waist of a bug, the hips of a schoolgirl, the legs of a spider . . . and those lily-green eyes! I'll bet that in any disco your Donna's an African queen!" She paused. "And as a Chopinist she's truly exceptional. For a black, I mean!"

"Well, if Donna's exceptional—for a black," said Osten, determined not to let Vala know how annoying he found her remarks, "so are you, Vala, for a Russian, loving disco dancing as much as you do. Aren't Russians supposed to be passionate only about classical music and ballet?"

Vala darted an angry look at him. "Russian or no Russian, I'm passionate about just one thing—Gerhard!" she snapped, her archness making her accent all the more pronounced.

"And that's good enough for me," said his father with a big smile, eager to dispel the tension. "Tell me, Jimmy, has that business," he said, pointing at Osten's throat, "given you any more trouble?"

"No, I'm fine," said Osten.

"Are you still having regular checkups?"

"Yes," said Osten. "The doctor says it's fine."

"What's wrong with Jimmy?" asked Vala.

"Nothing anymore," said his father. "A few years ago, just after Jimmy had enrolled at that university in California, he had a tumor removed from his throat. But his voice has never been the same since!"

"The tumor was between the larynx and the pharynx," said Osten, addressing Vala. "Along with the nose and mouth, those are the parts of the throat that determine how our voice sounds."

His father glanced at his watch. "Vala and I are dining at the club tonight. Would you like to join us?"

"Thanks, but I can't," said Osten. "I'm meeting Donna." He got up. Under the watchful eye of his father, he pecked Vala on both cheeks, careful not to brush her with his body.

His father took him by his arm, saying, "I'll walk you out," and in the hall he said, "The money from your mother's trust—does the bank send it to you regularly?"

"Yes, same as always," said Osten.

"And is it—" his father halted "—enough?"

They were outside now. "I manage fine," said Osten.

His father opened the car door for him. "You may as well know," he said, "that almost all I make goes to support Vala and me." His father hesitated again. "She recently redid the duplex in the city, you know, and you wouldn't believe what it cost me—new carpets, wallpaper, stereo, and so on. And at Etude we've been socked with all the new union scales and upped royalties." He was

speaking quickly, as if to preempt any time there might be
for questions.

As Osten waited for his father to finish, he realized
how unhealthy the old man looked. His skin, covered by a
network of veins, was yellow; his lips had a bluish tinge;
the whites of his eyes were bloodshot. Osten felt a sudden
urge to take his father in his arms and kiss him on the
forehead, to cuddle against him as he used to do when he
was a boy.

As if sensing this, his father took a step back. "Vala
has been very good to me," he said. "Very sweet. No one
else could have replaced Leonore." He lowered his voice.
"And that's why you should know—" he stopped, his eyes
downcast "—that when I . . . go, I intend to leave everything to her. Everything," he repeated, looking up, hoping to solicit agreement.

"I understand," said Osten, swallowing the wave of
bitterness rising in him. "I understand." He got into the
car and started the engine. "Take care, Father," he said
through the window as he pulled away.

Once on the road, Osten recalled the phone conversation he had had with his father the day his father told
him how happy he was that Vala had accepted his engagement ring and that they planned to marry within a
month. Osten had responded with forced enthusiasm. He
was sure, he said, that young as she was, Vala would make
an inspiring wife.

"You would be amazed if I told you how well Vala and
I have hit it off," said his father, lowering his voice.
"Believe me, those who say that age makes a difference
should see Vala and me . . . when we're alone."

"I'm sure Vala is sweet and understanding—" said
Osten.

"I'm not talking about sweetness and understanding,"
interrupted his father. "I'm talking about love, physical
love. I have even tested her love for me," he went on, like
an adolescent bragging about his exploits.

"You tested Vala's love?"

"That's right," said his father. "And chemically at that!" He paused, then announced proudly, "I came across an amazingly clever device! Mood Undies!"

"What are Mood Undies?" Osten asked patiently.

"Panties. Girls' bikini panties."

"What do they do?"

"They don't do—they test." His father chuckled. "They test excitement. Sexual arousal, that is. Each pair has a little heart sewn on the front—you know where!" He chuckled again. "The heart is treated chemically, and as you—" he hesitated, searching for words "—are intimate with your lady and her mood changes, so does the color of the heart! A little scale next to the heart shows just how hot she feels for you! If the heart turns blue, it means she is feeling really excited; if it turns green, she's just playful; brown means she's only mildly interested; and black—well, she's cold about the whole thing, physically cold, I mean. You understand?"

"Yes, Father," said Osten. For a moment he was touched by his father's naiveté, his unflinching belief in things American—even when they were so patently absurd. But then he squirmed as he imagined his father in bed with Vala. He saw them kissing and cuddling in the darkness; then he saw his father suddenly turn on the light, put on his glasses, and bend down, gray-white, wrinkled, and flabby, over Vala's curvaceous body to peek at the color of the heart and read the scale.

"Well," continued his father, "by now we've used at least a dozen of these Mood Undies, and each time, guess what color the heart showed?"

"Blue," said Osten.

"Right! Every single time." His father let out a high giggle. "And it's scientific," he reassured his son. "None of that Goethe and Erika apple of your eye' stuff—lovers finding true love in each other's letters. As long as Vala keeps her heart blue, I won't be blue!" He was speaking exultantly. "You should try Mood Undies on Donna," he whispered. "It might be interesting to know . . .!"

"I'm awfully happy for you, Father," interrupted Osten. "And for Vala. I already like her a lot," he added quickly, knowing it would please him.

"She likes you too," responded his father. "She says the more she knows you, the more she likes to picture you as Lensky, the romantic poet in *Eugene Onegin.*"

"Tell her thanks," said Osten, "even though Lensky gets killed by Onegin, his best friend, in a duel."

"Come up and see us soon, Son!" his father said expansively, and then he had hung up.

Listening to his father on the phone that day, Osten had felt crushed by embarrassment. Weren't wisdom and restraint supposed to be the rewards of healthy old age? What had happened, he wondered, to the man who was responsible for recording some of the world's best music? The man who had been honored in countless testimonials by members of the National Academy of Recording Arts and Sciences and the Record Industry Association as the unimpeachable aristocrat of the music business? The man whose closest friends were once such men as Goddard Lieberson and Boris Pregel? In his old age, his father seemed no different from some of the boys Osten had known in high school, who at one stage had thought about nothing but sex. Thinking of Mood Undies, Osten remembered how the group had talked endlessly about a special type of condom called Maiden's Death, advertised as "an invasion of ecstasy, irresistibly urging the woman to let go." Like all condoms, Maiden's Deaths were supposed to make the man feel as if he wore nothing at all and the woman to experience urges and sensations she had never felt before. But their chief and novel source of excitement was visual. Maiden's Deaths came in a variety of enticing colors: Skydive Blue, Ski White, Red Socks, Midas Gold, Golf Green, Silver Bike, and Nubian Black— each one guaranteed to make the woman frantic with desire. As vulvas painted in lush colors by courtesans of ancient civilizations once aroused male lovers, so brightly wrapped penises were meant to reverse the process in modern times.

Those gullible high school lovers who pinned their hopes on Maiden's Deaths to assist them in their sexual conquests bought the condoms in such quantities that the local pharmacy wound up supplying them at a discount. Soon, however, detumescence set in. Although the idea of the colored condoms excited the boys to no end, one obstacle rendered Maiden's Deaths almost totally useless: most of the girls who consented to go all the way insisted on total darkness—possibly because they were embarrassed to watch their boyfriends struggling to unwrap, unfold, and roll on their brilliant "pleasure invaders."

Osten wondered whether his father's behavior was the result of emotional rejuvenation or of some sort of moral and physical sclerosis. Was it possible, he asked himself, that men never really ripened with age, but only hardened in certain areas and went soft in others?

But, Osten reminded himself, his father was an incurable idealist and romantic. He recalled his father's sporadic, childlike enthusiasms for the results of various parascientific experiments, particularly the ones that claimed that by affecting man's higher cerebral centers, as well as the sympathetic nervous system, music could aid the digestive, circulatory, nutritional, and respiratory functions of the human body. Whenever his father learned that one of his friends or acquaintances was ill he would promptly dispatch to the patient a collection of Etude classical records, each one of which, he was convinced, would generate in the sick man a specific mood, helping him to combat the illness faster and better than all the doctors and their medicines combined could do.

As he drove, Osten recalled that his first impulse, after hearing his father announce that he was going to marry Vala, had been to call Blaystone and order him to withdraw Goddard's secret backing from Etude Classics, even if that entailed a costly breach-of-contract suit. If

Gerhard Osten were faced with losing his beloved business, Osten had reasoned, he might well reconsider the marriage. More to the point, since Osten had little doubt as to who in reality was pursuing whom, perhaps in those circumstances Vala would pull out of the engagement; what would she want with a man who was penniless and able to bestow on her nothing but his old age?

But, Osten had reflected, would he ever forgive himself if, confronted by bankruptcy, his father should have a stroke or a heart attack and die? Osten had instead decided to try to bring his father to his senses by invoking the image of his dead wife and reawakening his former devotion to her. He had also decided to speak to his father with shaming frankness about Vala's youth and his advanced age.

"Just because he seems old to you, why should he seem old to himself?" Donna had demanded. "There's nothing wrong with being old. Why shouldn't he enjoy himself with Vala? Look at Liszt and Wagner—they both lived with women who were young enough to be their daughters!"

Easing into the stream of city-bound traffic, Osten started thinking about Donna. Some five or six months after their meeting, when the novelty of their relationship had worn off, a nagging doubt had begun to settle in his soul. He felt it from the moment he opened his eyes every morning until he went to sleep at night.

In order for his two existences to remain valid, he had to be assured of his inspiration. He had to be filled with a need to write and perform music, a need so overpowering that everything else would either lead to it or stem from it. He believed that if he began to feel musically sterile for even a moment, he would be lost. And Donna had failed to trigger in him the need to create.

He was less and less often prompted to fly on the spur of the moment from California to New York, for even though his physical infatuation with Donna was still strong,

it hurt every time she expressed her disdain of rock music—
and of Goddard's music in particular.

He had told her, for instance, that if he were a
musical performer, he would investigate electric pianos,
the modern alternatives to the grand piano, which—with
the help of oscillators, attenuators, and amplifiers—could
create synthetic tones of a wide variety and a precise
frequency and intensity. He reminded her of the ever-
increasing use of electric pianos by popular recording stars
and ensembles, adding that at least one distinguished
piano manufacturer had even begun to develop an electronic grand piano.

But in his talks with Donna he had to be careful not
to sound too well informed. Remembering that in her eyes
he was a student of literature, at best a potential writer
with only a minor interest in music which his father forced
on him, he would attempt to talk her out of her rigid
purism only in nonspecific terms. He defended the
synthesizer as being not just another specialized musical
instrument, but a creative multi-use musical erector set,
and he quoted Stravinsky, who had once said that the
most nearly perfect musical machine was a Stradivarius or
an electronic synthesizer. Osten then speculated that the
instrument would be a boon to composers and performers;
at the merest touch of a button, they could hear full
arrangements, as well as endless variations on a single
theme; they could compress or extend a phrase, slow it
down or speed it up. All this seemed to him an invaluable
enrichment of the musical tradition—as well as a means of
transcending it.

"For all of its presets, custom voice ensembles, special effects, and computerized rhythm and sequence pro-
grammers, a synthesizer is nothing but a hybrid of a
jukebox and a pinball machine," Donna had announced
during one of their disagreements. "It turns the composer
and the performer into a kind of creative automaton serving up crude mechanical selections."

"But isn't the piano, to a degree, mechanically crude
as well?" ventured Osten. "So crude that simply by replacing its hammers with teaspoons, you can convert it into a

harpsichord? And isn't its imperfect state evident in the never-ending attempts to improve its sounding board, strings, hammers, and the action of its keys?"

"Certainly not," replied Donna. "The piano is the descendant of a whole line of stringed instruments, starting with the ancient psaltery—a gourd with strings stretched across it that the player plucked—on up through Pythagoras's monochord, the clavichord, the spinet, the harpsichord . . ." She caught her breath and glared. "Unlike all the synthesizer's musical gadgetry, which changes from week to week, the keyboard of this"—she struck a resounding chord on her piano—"was already fully developed by the fifteenth century, and no other instrument has ever matched the variety and richness of its tones."

"I read somewhere," said Osten cautiously, "that in a recent musical experiment, acoustics experts imitated—or should I say duplicated?—piano tones by tuning a series of audiofrequency oscillators to the precise frequency and intensity of struck piano strings. And when a panel of musicians and nonmusicians was brought in, they couldn't distinguish between recordings of real piano tones and the synthetic tones made by the oscillators. In fact," he went on, "the real and synthetic tones were so alike the musicians in the group couldn't hear them any better than the nonmusicians could. Each group identified only about fifty percent of the tones correctly!"

"That doesn't prove anything," said Donna, her voice rising. "The point is, every real artist knows that synthetic tones lack harmonic richness and warmth." Then she added, "In any case, Jimmy, you're not a musician, so you're talking about things you don't really know about. Believe me, there are no bad pianos, only bad pianists. And there's much more to making music than synthesizing a vibrating string!"

He felt irked and angry. After all, as a pianist Donna was just a performer, at best a talented imitator who knew nothing about the trials of composing—of writing original, vibrant music. He, on the other hand, was both a performer and a composer, and the value of his music, in sheer volume of sales, was greater than that of any previous recording artist, classical or rock. What would she say, he sputtered inwardly, if he were to tell her that? Unable to defend himself, he resorted to attacking her.

"There might be more to music than a vibrating tone," he said, "but is there really any more to the piano?" He tried to stop, but he couldn't. "After all, the instant you hit a piano key, the key throws out a hammer which is then no longer connected to the key but is flying freely, like a softball thrown through the air, beyond the reach of the pianist. Right? Therefore, for any given hammer speed, the tone is exactly the same whether the key was initially depressed by the finger of the great concert pianist Donna Downes or by the paw of a monkey from the Bronx Zoo!"

He could see that she was furious. She slammed the piano lid shut and spun around to face him. "That's the biggest load of crap I've ever heard," she said, "especially coming from you. You play the piano a bit yourself, Jimmy. Can't you tell that there's much more to it than hitting keys and activating little hammers? What about the whole art of pace and note-duration, of fingering and pedaling and attack and phrasing and coloration?" Without giving him a chance to reply, she groaned, "Oh, skip it. What's the use of talking?"

The peace between them was once again broken. Feeling out of place, all he wanted was to be alone.

At times, as he lay next to Donna, Osten felt estranged from her and believed that she, sensing this in him, must also feel estranged. It seemed to him, at such times, that they were not so much lovers as merely people who were capable of pleasing each other.

After long hours of practicing scales and doing exercises aimed at strengthening her arms and wrists and increasing the span of her fingers, Donna was often restless and excitable. Her sexual needs came suddenly and in spurts, relentless, overabundant, rushing along like a stream, leaving him on the shore. Her eyes would shine then, her cheeks would burn, and, as if she were starved and sex were an act of nutrition, she would spell out the kind of lovemaking she wanted. In such moments, he could not fulfill her wants; what she took to be her impulse and improvisation was to him nothing but calculation and repetition. It made him uneasy and increasingly passive, and he would despair at being no more for her than a mere physical diversion, instrumental at best in drawing her away briefly from the piano—which was and always would be the main instrument of her life's emotions.

Sometimes, after practicing the piano in front of him, she would suddenly fall on him and attempt to impale herself, to arouse him and make him erect, and if he did not respond at once she would push him down her body and force him to caress her with his mouth and tongue until an orgasm shook her body and the last of a string of urgent promptings died on her lips. It was as if, in return for being allowed to hear her perform, he had to become the servant of her resultant needs.

Yet there were other moments, just as frequent and persuasive, when Donna made love to him so ardently, so selflessly, that he felt himself the sole source and target of all her passion, moments when she would plead with him to drive her to respond to his impulses and his whims. But even then, after giving in to her forceful urging that he use her body as an instrument of his own pleasure, he often felt no closer to her, as if somewhere along the way she had failed to be the source of excitement for him.

One evening in her studio, waiting for her to come home from Juilliard, he pulled an album of photographs from a bookshelf and glanced through it. Among the many pictures of Donna with family and friends was one that disturbed him greatly. It showed her in a topless bathing suit being helped out of a small, obviously private pool by a young, handsome white man whose wet trunks bulged to reveal his unusually long and large member. The sight of the man, and of Donna's full, bare breasts, caught by the camera as they thrust upward with the motion of her body; the photographer's mood of sexual abandon—all this struck Osten as gross. It was a snapshot for a porno magazine, not for a personal album. Next to the slightly faded photograph Donna had glued a white square of paper with a poem by W. H. Auden typed on it.

> *Thou shalt not be on friendly terms*
> *With guys in advertising firms,*
> *Nor speak with such*
> *As read the Bible for its prose*
> *Nor, above all, make love to those*
> *Who wash too much.*

Who was the man in the picture and what were his feelings for Donna? How had she felt about him? How long ago—and by whom—had the picture been taken? Osten felt chagrined by his ignorance. He was envious of the other man's place in Donna's life, and he felt physically inferior to him. He was also stung with shame to see Donna's undisguised enjoyment at being part of this sexual show. Was it possible that she was as sexually uncurbed as Devon Wilson, the ill-fated girlfriend of Jimi Hendrix?

After hesitating for days, Osten finally brought himself to ask Donna about the man in the photograph, and Donna told him he was an actor she had once dated. Feigning nonchalance, Osten asked whether he might ever have seen the man in a play or movie. Visibly upset, Donna said she doubted it: the guy was a minor actor who played small parts in grade-B movies. Finally, when Osten asked her who took the picture, Donna snapped back that it had been taken by a friend of hers, a Juilliard student, at the friend's family pool in Tuxedo Park. No wiser for his questions, Osten wondered what had upset Donna so much—his asking her about her past, or the memory of the man who had played a part in it.

Part of him also rebelled against Donna's aesthetic taste. Even though Donna was a versatile pianist, accomplished and at ease with the work of many composers, she saw herself primarily as an interpreter of Chopin, a composer who was in her view as daring as Bach and unequaled in his harmonies.

Osten could not share her enthusiasm. First of all, there was, even to him, something incongruous about this ravishing black girl choosing to express herself in the field of classical music. Had she chosen to act in films or on stage instead of playing the piano, she could have been a star overnight on the strength of her exquisite face and figure alone. But in profile, bent over the keyboard, she was slightly grotesque, almost vulgar: her African head seemed too small, her neck too extended, her breasts oversized, her ass too round, her legs too long. He knew that it was the man in him—and the white man at that—who reacted to her in this way. He knew he might be happy to ogle such a beauty on a burlesque stage or a bed, but he was always surprised and a little disturbed to find one all dressed up behind a concert grand, and he found that he couldn't control his reaction.

Then, too, it was the music she chose to play. Osten did not like Chopin, who seemed to him a gifted amateur, a musical polyglot and a capricious, pampered wunderkind who had never developed into a classical composer. Chopin's evanescent, donnish and fragile music simply was not universal, could never inspire the masses; it belonged in velvet chambers, in elitist concert halls, in music schools. There was also an ephemeral, almost ragtime quality in Chopin that Osten didn't care for—the very quality that had made Chopin, an uprooted Pole transplanted to France, so popular a century later with the black ragtime pianists of New Orleans—who probably learned about him through the city's Francophile coterie.

In order to understand Donna better, Osten had read a few books about Chopin, only to be troubled by most of what he learned about the composer's tumultuous life. Although several biographers explained that Chopin's feverish tubercular state was the cause of his constant sexual obsession, Osten nevertheless found it impossible to condone Chopin's frantic and utterly perverse amorous escapades. To Osten, Chopin's relationship with the French novelist George Sand was of a particularly disgusting nature, since from its outset the composer must have known that the novelist was not simply bisexual, but a lesbian by temperament as well as inclination. Yet he allowed her to use him over and over again as a pawn in sadomasochistic games with her male and female friends and lovers, among whom were some of the most perverse minds of the century. Listening to Donna's passionate, sometimes frenetic, overtly sensuous renditions of Chopin's ballades, nocturnes, and scherzos, Osten could not keep himself from making free associations between the music and the composer's unhealthy life—or between Donna and Chopin.

Osten was glad to find that to H. L. Mencken, the toughest of American critics, Chopin was "another composer who is best heard after seeing a bootlegger. His music," wrote Mencken, "is excellent on rainy afternoons in winter, with the fire burning, the shaker full, and the girl somewhat silly."

But Donna was anything but silly. Again and again Osten asked himself what this smart American black from a middle-class family found so exciting in Chopin. Did she, like her ragtime predecessors in Missouri and Louisiana, perceive in Chopin's music, or in his life, some rich hidden meaning which was essential to her but which, so far at least, had eluded her white lover altogether?

Initially he had hoped that Donna would be the one to pull him out of his self-imposed sterility and involve him in her life and music. He had hoped, too, that she would also help him erase the memory of the only woman he had ever really loved—Leila Salem—who had come into his life as unheralded as the White House woman, but in quite a different way. So far Donna had done neither.

He had sensed no impending drama on that quiet day just two and a half years ago when he left his small ranch and drove out of the Anza Borrego Desert toward San Diego. He had no special purpose in mind beyond staying a day or two in a good hotel and visiting a few bookstores. In San Diego, he drove aimlessly for a while. Then he crossed the Coronado Bridge, looking down at the harbor and the heavy silhouettes of the ships of the Pacific Fleet. Soon he found himself in the driveway of the Hotel Del Coronado, where he had not been since his freshman year.

He parked his Jeep and wandered around the hotel, staring in wonderment at its Victorian excesses—the gingerbread terraces, balconies, and verandas stacked one on top of the other, the shingled roof and turrets, the splendor of the entrance.

He passed through the interior garden court, peered into the Crown Room, where a large banquet for Arab dignitaries was taking place, then walked along the Hall of History, glancing at photographs of the hotel in its various transformations over a hundred years.

In the arcade, he paused at an open record stand to look at a large display of Goddard recordings, and while he stood there a woman emerged from behind one of the stalls with a stack of albums in her arms. She was in her early thirties, tall and slender in a close-fitting dress, and from the instant he saw her, Osten was unable to take his eyes from her. She was exquisite: waves of thick corn-blond hair, a high forehead, prominent cheekbones, sculptured nose. Unconsciously, Osten moved toward her, and, assuming he was a salesman, she handed him the records she was holding.

"Can I charge these to my hotel bill?" she asked in a faintly foreign accent.

"I'm sure you can, madam," he said, taking the records. He caught her gaze, her eyes light gray and translucent, and afraid to lose her, he did not move.

He glanced down at the albums—all American rock, about two dozen of them, including three copies of Goddard's latest record.

"You have three of these," he said.

"I know," she said, her eyes still on him. "Isn't that all right?" She smiled agreeably.

"But they're all the same," he said.

"I must be his best salesperson," she said, pointing at the abstract drawing of a rock singer on the cover of the album. "I buy his records for all my friends."

"Lucky friends," said Osten with a smile. "But only Goddard? I mean, there are other rock stars."

She reflected. "Not like him. I heard him for the first time under very strange circumstances. It was during the war in Lebanon on the radio of the United Nations peace-keeping unit. And I was captivated without knowing anything about him."

"No one knows anything about him," said Osten. "People say he's crazy—or crippled—or—"

"But, you see, I discovered him on my own; I didn't even know he was a star. His music seemed to untangle something within me to bring order to my feelings and give feeling to what was nothing but order." Her eyes had not left him as she talked. "I couldn't care less who he was as a person, and what he looked like. I still don't. I can't quite explain what I mean." She took one of the albums from Osten and, looking at the faceless drawing of Goddard, said, "He is original because he makes one feel original too. Such a feeling is the greatest gift an artist can give—and only a great artist gives it."

She turned to Osten, and again he met her stare. "And you—what music do you like?" she asked.

"He's my favorite, too," he said after a full beat. "And like you, I also discovered him on my own. I heard his first record on the radio in New York. Now I know all his music." Their eyes were still locked, and to hold her, he decided to risk more. "I play a bit myself," he said.

"Really? What do you play?"

"Anything Goddard plays I can play too!" He laughed.

"Do you also sing?" she asked.

"A bit," he said. He was about to tell her that surgery had left him with a permanent throat defect—the story he had told others for years—but he decided to say nothing about it.

She glanced around. "You have other customers. I don't want to monopolize you."

He smiled forthrightly. "I don't work here. I'm monopolizing you."

"Oh, I'm so sorry! I didn't mean to—" She reached for the records, but he laughed softly and backed away with them. "May I, at least, carry them for you?"

She smiled. "That's kind of you." She extended her hand. "I'm Leila Salem."

He shook her hand, narrow and cool, aware that it was the first time he had touched her. "I'm James Osten," he said. "You have a slight accent—where are you from?"

"I was born in Lebanon, of Syrian parents," she said.

"With your light eyes and fair skin I wouldn't have thought you were an Arab."

"Perhaps not." She paused. "But you would certainly know that my husband is. He looks Arabian."

He felt confused, then betrayed. He had already lost her to another man. "Your husband?"

"My husband is the Lebanese ambassador accredited to Mexico. We're just visiting San Diego," she explained.

They looked at each other in silence, and she saw him go from distraught to resigned. "And you—are you married, Mr. Osten?" she asked.

He shook his head that he was not.

"Are you a professional musician?" she asked politely, as if to distract him from his thoughts.

"Nothing professional about me," he sighed. "I'm a student at the University of California at Davis."

"Studying music?"

"Literature. Music is just a hobby."

"I studied art, first in Lebanon, then in Madrid." She paused again. "Ahmed—my husband—is an economist." She watched him drop his gaze. "What are you thinking about?" she asked, her voice almost conspiratorial.

Without raising his head, he murmured, "About—" he stalled. "About you. I wish I could see you again."

She edged closer, until her hip stopped against the records he was holding.

She hesitated before she spoke. "Tomorrow my husband and I are taking the children to Rosarito Beach, a little resort outside of Tijuana, for two weeks. Then we'll return to Mexico City." She hesitated. "While we are in Rosarito, Ahmed will be treated by the doctors at a clinic called Rejuvene-Center."

"I've heard about them. They were allowed to conduct some medical tests with Gerovital at the University of California—injections of animal embryo and afterbirth, that are supposed to have a rejuvenating effect," said Osten.

She nodded and lowered her eyes. "The Gerovital treatments are available only in Mexico. They have not yet been approved in the United States."

Seeing her discomfort, Osten changed the subject. "I've been to Rosarito Beach," he said. "It's a lovely spot. Where will you stay there?"

"At the Scheherazade. A small villa overlooking the sea."

"How old are your children?"

"My son is eleven, my daughter nine." Her face lit up. "They love music. You should see them rock to Goddard."

"I'll be in Tijuana next week," said Osten on an impulse that left him no time for reflection. "I want to test my playing and my voice"—he laughed—"in front of people."

"You mean, perform in public?" She seemed surprised.

"Why not?"

"But why Mexico? Why Tijuana?"

"Well, they say that over twenty thousand people visit there each day!" he replied. "With that many people milling around, you don't have to be Goddard to stand up and sing," he laughed.

She smiled. "Where will you play?"

"Wherever they will have me. Some small square, or a café maybe," he said. "Any place where I—or the audience—can make a fast getaway!"

"Will you sing in Spanish?"

"Just in English. I don't know Spanish well enough," he said.

"That's a shame," she exclaimed. "I love the *musica ranchera*—the real Mexican folk songs."

Osten reflected. "Really? Do you have any favorites? Perhaps I might try them."

"My favorites right now are 'Volver, Volver, Volver' and 'El Rey,'" she said without hesitation. "You can find them in any Mexican record store."

"I'll get them tonight," said Osten.

She looked at her watch as she and Osten walked toward the exit. "I must go," she said.

The cashier, an old gray-haired man, grandly rang up her sales on the cash register and had her sign her name and room number on the sales slip.

Outside the stand, Leila Salem was politely accosted by two olive-skinned men in business suits. One of them said something to her in Arabic, and she turned to Osten with an expression of apology. "My ever-present protectors," she explained with a sigh. "A debatable deterrent to one's enemy; an unquestionable nuisance for one's friends." She paused, then gently touched Osten's arm. "I hope you won't mind if they accompany me when I come to hear you sing?"

He was almost afraid to show his elation. "Will your husband come too?" he asked.

"I doubt it," she said matter-of-factly. "Ahmed hasn't been well. He must rest and try to relax. But my children definitely will. So please don't forget to call the Scheherazade and tell me where to come," she said. She took a calling card from her handbag and handed it to Osten. "That's the name to ask for," she said. "Don't forget!"

His mind was made up; he had already envisioned what he was going to do, and even though without doing anything at all he could imagine the outcome as if it were a tune, he still felt prompted to take a chance and carry out his idea of reality. The mind, he reflected, was like an ideal musical instrument—invisible, portable, capable of synthesizing all sounds—too bad it required its listener, the body, to exercise leverage on physical reality.

*   *   *

After meeting Leila Salem, Osten drove to Tijuana, and in the biggest record shop there he bought every available version of the two folk songs Leila had told him she liked, recordings made in Spain, Mexico, and other Spanish-language countries. Then he checked out the city and its never-ending streams of pedestrians—the swarthy locals, the easy-to-spot American tourists, and the masses of brown-skinned peasants lured from the provinces to this modern boom town by the promise of construction work. Midway between the city's affluent shopping centers, on the Avenida de la Revolución and the shantytowns near the bullring, Osten found what he was looking for: a half-enclosed open-air restaurant-café that would hold about sixty people; it was housed in an undistinguished little hotel called La Apasionada.

He went inside and talked to the manager, a short, plump middle-aged Mexican who spoke fluent English. In broken Spanish—to test himself with the language—Osten told the man that he worked for an American musical instruments company and would like to use the terrace of the café for two weeks to try out a new electronic console, the latest in entertainment, in front of a live audience. He was aware, Osten said, that his playing and singing would constitute a break in the routine of the Apasionada, and he was therefore prepared to pay for the use of the terrace, as well as for a room at the hotel.

Sensing he was onto a good deal, the Mexican told Osten that he rarely allowed singers into his establishment, for, liking girls as much as he did, he believed the old saying: like bullfighters, singers get all the best girls. Then he guffawed and named a sum which, though exorbitant by local standards, Osten found quite tolerable. He promptly gave the manager a deposit—a third of the total amount—and promised to return and begin his engagement in a week.

He then drove back to San Diego, parked in front of the city's best-supplied musical instruments store, and went in. A Eurasian girl with the manner of a docile masseuse greeted him at the door. When he told her he was interested in electronic music, she escorted him to the desk of a bespectacled young salesman who, in his old white shirt, dark tie, and limp seersucker suit, could easily have passed for a scientist from the nearby Salk Institute.

The salesman introduced himself, and Osten sat down. On the desk Osten saw several brochures picturing the latest electronic music consoles.

The salesman saw his glance. "Paganini. The ultimate electone console," he said. "Phenomenal versatility in finished sound. Its own SSFS—the synthesizing sound factory system—gives you, with unbeatable authenticity, flute, clarinet, trombone, trumpet, horn, saxophone, harmonica, tuba, oboe, violin, piano, harpsichord, ukulele, banjo, viola, guitar, harp, diapason, bass drum, marimba, xylophone, vibraphone, cymbals, and brush—among others." He paused for breath, then went on. "The Paganini includes such special-effect sounds as banged pots and pans, dry seeds in a glass jar, party noisemakers, a plucked rubber band, finger-snapping, finger-tapping—" he paused again "—clanking silverware, crumpled cellophane . . ."

"I like the pots and pans and the dry seeds in a glass jar," said Osten.

The salesman brightened. "The clever Japanese have not overlooked a thing in this one," he said, handing Osten several of the information booklets. "In its automatic rhythm section, the Paganini contains"—he looked for confirmation in one of the booklets—"thirty-six authentic autorhythms: march, swing, rock, tango, rhumba, bossa nova, waltz, ballad, bolero, beguine, mambo, samba, as well as several less common Latin ones—"

"Latin rhythms?" Osten interrupted.

"Yes. A wise choice, given our proximity to Mexico and the Southern Hemisphere. You know what's really amazing?" he said. "With the thousands of musical combinations possible on the Paganini, you practically invent a new instrument every time you play it!"

"I wish I could invent a new me," said Osten.

"You almost can on the Paganini," said the salesman, glancing into the booklet. "And the Paganini is built so compactly that you can invent your 'new me' almost anywhere you go."

He took one of the booklets from Osten, wrote a price on it, and passed it back like a card in a casino. "Even the price is compact," he said, smiling. "That's why we sell a lot of these models to nightclubs and traveling rock performers, as well as to composers and songwriters. Did you know that some of these electone consoles have even been installed in the lounge sections of some of the big jetliners?" He was winding up his pitch.

Osten glanced at the figure written on the card.

The salesman began to worry. "What kind of music do you play?" he asked.

"All kinds," said Osten. "I improvise a lot."

"Then the Paganini's your best bet by far," said the salesman. "By means of its special line-input, you can feed any sound into it—anything you have taped or picked up live, or from any other electronic instrument—radio, TV, your record player, even your own singing voice . . ."

"It would have to be someone else's singing voice, not mine," Osten laughed.

"Don't be so tough on yourself!" the salesman scolded. "You may sound a bit hoarse, but so what? These days, a lot of singers and musicians use modified mouthpiece microphones. The Paganini lets you modify any external sound—including your own voice. Why don't you follow me to our music room and try out the Paganini for yourself?"

Beaming, he got up and under the indifferent gaze of the other salesmen, he led Osten through a labyrinth of desks to the music room.

With the Paganini secured in the back of the Jeep, Osten drove home through a pass between the Cuyamaca and Volcan mountains. He stopped to fill the gas tank in

Julian, once the region's gold-mining center, where the two hundred inhabitants now took pride in apple and pear orchards and dense oak and pine forests.

It was near sundown when he passed through the gates of his ranch, which he had named the New Atlantis after a book which had impressed him greatly. In it, in 1624, the philosopher Francis Bacon had described the music of the future as being created in

> Sound-houses, where wee practise and demonstrate all Sounds . . . of diverse instruments of Musick likewise to you unknowne, some sweeter than you have; Together with Bells and Rings that are dainty and sweet. . . . Wee also have Strange and Artificial Echoe's, reflecting the Voice many times, and as it were Tossing it; And some that give back the Voice lowder than it cam, some Shriller some Deeper; Yea some rendering the Voice, Differing in the letters or Articulate Sound, from that they receyve.

Situated four thousand feet up in the Laguna Mountains, the New Atlantis covered three hundred acres and overlooked the entire valley below. In addition to the two-story house Osten occupied, there was a small gate-keeper's house where his helpers lived. They were three Shoshone Indians—middle-aged brothers who had worked for him ever since he had acquired the ranch.

The Indians rushed to help him unload the Paganini. Even though every day, and for years, they sat staring for hours at a television set, they still barely spoke English, and in communicating with them Osten often had to rely on gestures and wordless sounds.

The men helped him carry the console to the big house, which, with the exception of a bedroom, bathroom, and kitchen, was an elaborate soundproofed recording facility. There, on the ground floor, the Paganini joined an impressive array of musical instruments and recording equipment—electric organs, amplifiers, synthesizers, guitars, drums, and effect boxes—all dominated by the Gershwin, the state-of-the-art, twenty-six channel, sixteen-track recording console that gave Osten complete flexibility in digital computerized recording and playback techniques.

When the Indians left to prepare his dinner, Osten went into the studio to listen to Leila Salem's favorite Mexican songs.

As soon as he heard them, he knew how he wanted to play, sing, and eventually record them. He knew it all at once because that was how his mind worked, but also because he was already seeing himself—with Leila—in Tijuana.

Here, in his own House of Sound, the sanctum of his creative retreat, he felt safe and secure. He had designed every inch of it, selected every instrument. There wasn't a single object he didn't know as intimately as he knew his own body; not one keyboard, push-button, switch, wire, patch cord, plug, oscillator, potentiometer, generator, or amplifier was alien to him. It was his secret nickelodeon, where he could cease to distinguish between memory and fantasy, the two springs of his imagination—one of the past, the other of the future. Here, all alone, a vivisector of his talent, he could instigate and control the whole creative process, from the initial source—his own songs and voice—to his arrangements for any of the electronic and nonelectronic instruments he used to produce the Goddard sound.

At times, uncertain of the direction his music should take, he would consider the enormous potential for modern music in the field of electronic experimentation. He studied the music of those composers who wired their heads to neurological amplifiers in order to transform the brain's signals into sympathetic resonances in an ensemble of musical instruments. Although he was intrigued by the technological virtuosity of these works, he always found them lacking in inspiration. He was equally familiar, and equally disenchanted, with laser and sound-sculpture experiments, as well as with all contemporary efforts to create multimedia music. In the last analysis, as a composer and performer, he knew that he had to rely solely on his own ideas and emotions and to search inside himself for the sounds and words that would express them, both for him and for all those people to whom his music could serve as echoes of their feelings.

He also paid attention to silence. He admired what John Cage had said: "The music I prefer, even to my own or anybody else's, is what we are hearing if we are just quiet."

Often at dawn, when the Shoshones were still asleep in the small house, he would drive to one of the dry washes of the Anza Borrego Desert. He would get out of the Jeep and walk into the empty reaches of stone and scrub that opened before him like a dungeon of heat and sand. In the distance the rising mist revealed the lofty pinnacles of scraggy mountains, a reddish streak against the sky's blue, and below, like dry bones stripped of flesh, the hillocks of the Borrego Badlands.

Here, where no sound broke the quiet, he would stand and imagine that one day the well of his music might become as dry and as soundless as this desert. Until then, he knew, he had to search his inner life for traces of any spring that had so far eluded him.

Osten loved his anonymity because it guaranteed his freedom, and he loved his freedom because it let him be anonymous. Even though his roots were in New York, only when he was secluded in the New Atlantis was he really at home—a disembodied spirit floating in a mysterious continuum, a mystic possessed by melody, as removed from the natural world as music itself. He could write his music and lyrics the way he liked and record them to suit himself. He rejoiced each time a digital master tape was finished and he could play it in the studio one last time before sending it to Blaystone. Such tapes gave perfect sound reproduction, free of any distortion. He was delighted by the pure sound of his voice, his words, his instruments pouring out from the quadraphonic speakers and converging on him, solitary there, slumped in an easy chair in the center of the room. Like an artisan in his shop, he would listen to what he had made, his eyes occasionally fixing on the ancient maxim he had hung as his motto on the white soundproofed wall: *Ognun 'suoi il segreti*—"Everyone has his secrets."

Once a record was made from his master tape and published by Nokturn, his music would boomerang back into his ordinary life, where as Jimmy Osten he would listen to it as everybody else did. Then he would realize all over again that only his anonymity kept the public from trespassing on him and on the stimulus that gave birth to his music, and he would cherish his freedom to start fresh and create more.

There was another advantage to his situation. If, for whatever reason, he ever chose not to record anymore, no one would ask him why; no reporters would appear on the doorstep or follow him around trying to find the cause of his creative block; and no explanations, true or false, would be expected from members of his family, from past and present lovers, from friends and associates, from his agent, from his manager, or from record company executives.

In order to succeed, rock stars—no matter how talented they were—needed the visibility provided by the media, just as Renaissance artists in their time had needed the support of rich and princely patrons. Yet Osten knew that he had succeeded alone—and had done so in spite of his self-imposed invisibility.

Best of all, the sales of the records he produced in seclusion secured the future of Etude Classics. Thanks to him, his father could live out his life a happy man, convinced that he had succeeded in bequeathing to his adopted country an everlasting legacy of classical music—the best expression of mankind's spirituality. He need never know that his bequest was financed by his son's success in rock, a field of music Gerhard Osten despised.

Jimmy Osten's commitment to his public thus ended where it had begun—at the New Atlantis. Once his music was published, it became public property, and people could then respond to it according to their own needs and means. He was no exception; he became at that point one more anonymous listener, and his critical judgment— whether he was listening in a car, a music shop, a disco, or at home; whether alone or among others—was no better, no worse, no more astute or more valuable, than the judgment of any other listener.

His denial of a public self was therefore the ultimate affirmation of his private self. Freed of Goddard, Osten could welcome new experience, let his feelings emanate honestly, be justly critical, and carve out from life's unlimited possibilities his true emotional destiny.

If, out of occasional loneliness, he had ever doubted the wisdom of his choice to remain anonymous, his doubt had vanished when John Lennon was murdered. Osten had been in New York City at the time, and he had gone to stand with the thousands of anguished mourners outside the Lennons' apartment building.

He realized that Lennon, by stepping too easily and too often into the midst of his fans—whether to sing for them, shake their hands, or autograph their albums—had unwittingly undermined his separation from ordinary people, which was the essence of his charisma.

Given an easy chance to be close to the famous man, the assassin—once a fan of Lennon's music—had seized the opportunity to kill him, as if by doing so he could usurp the very greatness Lennon had sacrificed by stepping down to the crowd, by attempting to prove himself ordinary.

Standing in that wailing throng, Osten had been happy to be James Osten and not Goddard.

The New Atlantis owed its existence to events in Osten's life that occurred at a time when he knew what he wanted to be but could not decide how to bring it about. A major cause of his indecision had been his father.

Gerhard Osten had come to the United States from Germany to escape the Nazi persecution. A classicist by

training, he had specialized in the early Greeks, beginning
with Pythagoras, particularly in their investigations relat-
ing mathematics to music. But he was not keen on devot-
ing himself to a life of scholarly research or to teaching the
classics in an American university, and he was wary of
trying to be a creative artist. He believed that an individual risked being viewed as totalitarian if he was original
enough to produce art, for the very act of imposing an
image of the world on others demanded their approval or
disapproval; it polarized people into friends and enemies,
leading them to see art not in terms of its own merit but as
an image of the artist. Just as a military hero was the
product of a war, so was an artist a product of his art,
able to say, after Alexander Pope,

> *"Yes, I am proud; I must be proud to see*
> *Men not afraid of God, afraid of me."*

Thus, life and art necessarily became confused in the
eyes of the audience, and any success the artist might
have he would have to pay for with his happiness and
with the happiness of those dear to him.

Gerhard Osten's real love was classical music, which
was to him—as it was to the ancient Greeks—as pure and
abstracted from quotidian reality as was mathematics. More
and more he began to feel that only through classical
music could he, and others like him, be lifted beyond the
memory of all the hideous events of his young manhood
and the terrible destruction of his family in the Holocaust.
Therefore, with the encouragement and financial help of
two friends, Goddard Lieberson and Boris Pregel, who
were musicians by vocation and business entrepreneurs by
occupation, he had founded Etude Classics. From then
on, music was Gerhard Osten's country, and like the
citizens in Aristophanes' *The Birds*, he was free to become
anonymous and contented in that "land of easy and fair
leisure, where a man may lounge and play and settle
down."

But under the glass top of his office desk Gerhard

Osten kept a letter written by a Jewish concentration camp inmate shortly before his death in the gas chamber.

> We are in the company of death. They tattoo the newcomers. Everyone gets his number. From that moment on you have lost your "self" and have become transformed into a number. You no longer are what you were before, but a worthless moving number. . . . We are approaching our new graves . . . iron discipline reigns here in the camp of death. Our brain has grown dull, the thoughts are numbered: it is not possible to grasp this new language.

To Gerhard Osten, only classical music offered modern man the means to repair the part of him that had been brutalized by this new language of hate and despair.

Even though Gerhard Osten seldom talked about the events of World War II, Jimmy knew that his life under the Nazi yoke had been one of constant fear, flight, and hunger. Being forced daily to seek new hiding places, having to pretend not to be Jewish, living among strangers, he must have been filled with an unending sense of terror. He had made extensive notes in a series of small notebooks during that time, notes about his life as well as about music, but not wanting to upset his son by passing on to him the story of the horror of his earlier life, Gerhard Osten had always kept these notebooks locked up. Only once had Jimmy been able to glance at them, and then he saw clearly that the notebooks had been his father's way of transcending the hideous events that surrounded him daily. What Jimmy read in the notebooks forever affected his relationship with his father. On coming of age, the son had made himself the guardian of his father.

Leonore Osten, Jimmy's mother, had died when Jimmy was fifteen, and he remembered her as a frail, elegant woman. A promising pianist when she was young, she had given up all her hopes of a career when she married Gerhard Osten, who convinced her that the titanic efforts required to achieve artistic success would destroy their chances of having a family. An invalid confined to her bedroom during the last few years of her life, she saw Jimmy only twice a year, when he was on vacation from the boarding school he attended in New England.

Thus, from adolescence on, Jimmy had had only his father for family, and he worshiped everything about him— his shyness, his soft-spoken manner, his refinement, his constant preoccupation with the sanctity of privacy—and in every way he could the boy emulated the older man.

In every way except one: Gerhard Osten detested rock. It represented for him victory of obsession over reason, emotion over logic, chaos over composition. By ruthlessly imposing itself upon the mass audience, rock 'n' roll was, for him, totalitarian in nature.

From the time Jimmy first heard rock as a boy in boarding school—he had never heard it at home, for his father would never have allowed it there—he was struck by an overpowering desire to create such music, to speak to others through it in a big, rich, compelling voice such as he, Gerhard Osten's son, for whom seclusion and cir- cumspection were the inherited principles of life, could hardly dream of possessing or displaying.

Because of his growing need to listen to this kind of music and his fear that he might hurt his father by his love of it, he chose to go to college in California, far from home but close to San Francisco, where the rock culture had exploded and still flourished.

He enrolled at the University of California at Davis, where Karlheinz Stockhausen, the master electronic music composer, had once been a lecturer. Osten was particu- larly impressed by Stockhausen's *Counterpoint No. 1*, a work in one movement for ten instruments, in which he fused six different timbres, winds as well as strings, into the single timbre of the piano. Osten was fascinated, also, by Stockhausen's experiments with synthetic composition of sound and aleatory music—music composed and per- formed to a great extent by chance. In such music—aimed at the inseparable partnership of composer and instru- mentalist—the composer selected keys and tempos by dice throws or by computer and the performer could decide on the order in which to play the principal sections.

Still his consuming love was rock. He collected every rock record and tape he could find, and when he ran out of space he transferred it all to cassettes. But his dormitory room was still not big enough to hold the cassettes and the equipment needed to play them. As his passion—and his collection—grew, he became more and more afraid that his father might surprise him with a visit and learn of his obsession, so with some of the money he received from his mother's trust, he rented an attic from an elderly widow who lived near the campus and moved his tapes and stereo equipment there.

During his freshman and sophomore years he drove to rock concerts and festivals all over California, and at the same time he devoured all the literature covering the history of rock. He became an encyclopedia on the subject. He knew every song by every rock group, from the Jefferson Airplane to the Rolling Stones, from Elvis Presley and Otis Redding to David Bowie, and he could describe every musical happening in Berkeley or Haight Ashbury or Los Angeles over the past twenty years, down to the psychedelic slides and the stroboscopic light shows. He saw the Beatles' films and the film of the Monterey Pop Festival, watching the thousands in the audience stand up and dance to the music of Janis Joplin and Jimi Hendrix; and with each viewing he understood more forcibly something his father could never accept: that rock was much more than a part of the record business; it was democratic in nature, a necessary part of the broad, popular culture of a free society, a way of life in itself—something classical music had never been or aspired to become.

Over a period of two decades, rock, the new music, had come of age. More and more the rock audience had learned to perceive rock as a serious form of musical expression, something worth listening to as well as dancing to, and the new singers and bands had responded in kind, creating music that was way beyond hootenannies and folksy rock stuff—music as good in its way as the classical music his father loved so much, music which was subtle, complex, and intellectually demanding.

Because of his knowledge of electronic music, Osten studied with particular care rock electronics, especially the guitar improvisations of Jimi Hendrix. He noticed that some groups, such as the Velvet Underground, had initially used electronic techniques to convey the psychic effect of the drug experience—as in the song "Heroin" —or to produce the new, heavy, thick sound of hard rock—as in "Sister Ray." In the song "What's Become of the Baby?" on their album *Aoxomoxoa*, the Grateful Dead modified keyboard and percussion sounds, mixing and symphonizing natural and artificial tones by means of electronics. They modulated the human voice electronically and built an entire vocal ensemble from the sound of a solo singer by recording the singer's voice and then playing it on top of itself at specified intervals. As Osten listened to the works of other rock musicians who favored electronic effects—Frank Zappa and the Mothers of Invention, Pink Floyd, Brian Eno of Roxy Music, Rick Wakeman of Yes and Keith Emerson of Emerson, Lake, and Palmer— he became aware of their original use of electronic technology in multitracking, the mixing together of several separately recorded virtuoso solo performances, frequently with adaptations of motifs from classical music. He also studied such artists as Tangerine Dream—the German group of keyboard players who used synthesizers and other electronic instruments to create a uniquely rich, innovative, avant-garde music.

Steadily and systematically, Osten taught himself to play the instruments favored by rock stars—acoustic guitar, harmonica, electronic organ. He imagined that if he mastered these instruments, as well as synthesizers that could generate their own tones, as well as modify other voices and instruments, and if he learned the techniques of threading several sound sources into a recording device, thereby creating musical montages, he might actually succeed in becoming a one-man musical event.

In time, after he had gone through dozens of musicians' guides to independent record production, it seemed only logical to him to transform the rented attic into a practice studio. There he sang, played, and recorded by the hour, hoping that, one day, he might even manufacture his own record matrices and create his own—Jimmy Osten's own—musical tradition. The old widow never disturbed him, nor he her. She was a victim of muscular dystrophy and spent most of her life in front of the turned-up TV set in the living room of the spacious house.

He had always been vaguely aware that he had a pleasant singing voice, but by the time his innate reticence allowed him to admit even that to himself, he had learned from his reading and listening that in order to succeed, a professional singer needed more than a nice voice. He had to make a forceful impact on listeners. Only a well-trained singer could produce controlled sounds with a distinct individual quality.

He began avidly to study the acoustics of the human vocal apparatus and to try out all the recommendations for developing a singing voice. He learned that most pop singers could neither darken their sounds nor open up their throats fully, and so they had to depend entirely on electronic amplification. In order to enlarge his own voice, he patiently trained himself to sound as if he were yawning and speaking at the same time; and to darken his tone and give it a slightly operatic quality, he did exercises to expand his pharynx and lower the position of his larynx.

He persevered in this way for many months and eventually mastered all the available knowledge that might apply to his own situation. He familiarized himself thoroughly with his musical instincts, with the articulation of his vowels, and with the limitless variations in sound recording made possible by electronic technology. By the time he finished college, he had no doubt about his talent; he was even ready to bank his life on it.

One thing worried him tremendously and would continue to worry him, and that was the dark, violent side of rock. He saw *Gimme Shelter*—the film of the famous Rolling Stones concert in Altamont, California—every time it was rerun, and he stared in horror as the Hell's Angels, hired by promoters to police the event, turned it instead into a display of brutality and terror that left one young black man dead and scores injured. He hated the fact that two of his idols, Janis Joplin and Jimi Hendrix, had died of drug abuse at the peak of their creativity and popularity. Osten had read that after Hendrix's death, all his notebooks and letters and private tapes, together with other personal belongings, had been stolen, and that soon after the theft the most intimate facts about him had surfaced. Devon Wilson, Hendrix's girl friend for whom he had written many of his best songs, was a heroin addict known to be notoriously promiscuous with both men and women; she was later killed in an unexplained fall from an upper-story window of the Chelsea Hotel in New York. Michael Jeffery, Hendrix's closest business associate, died in the mysterious explosion of a commercial airliner. Many others in Hendrix's immediate entourage also had died, or been killed, or gone insane. There had been other tragedies as well. Mama Cass of the Mamas and Papas; Brian Jones, an original member of the Rolling Stones; Jim Morrison, the lead singer of the Doors; Keith Moon of the Who—all had died young, and in all cases the circumstances of these deaths were mysterious and frightening. Was rock a political force, subversive in nature? Was Plato right when he wrote in *Republic*: "A revolution in music endangers the whole fabric of the most important societal conventions"? Thrilling as rock culture was, it was riddled with an excess of human trauma, and at Altamont it had even lost the dignity its collective ethos had gained at Woodstock. At Altamont also, this culture had revealed the madness it could inspire. Heavy drugs, cult worship, and maddening, suffocating lack of privacy had become ever-present dangers in the rock world—dangers that seemed almost inescapable to Osten as he contemplated making a career of rock. Every day he would come across dozens of newspaper headlines full of preposterous, excessive and hostile claims and dreadful insinuations about rock stars, their lives, their lovers, their families, their agents, managers and bank accounts. Any one of these headlines could wreck one's life. Once a rock performer's fame and notoriety turned him into a public person, the constitutional statutes which under the First Amendment guaranteed the freedom of the press allowed its reporting about a public person not to depend on the truth of the facts. Thus, even false, defamatory and factually untrue reporting was constitutionally protected, as long as the reporter wrote it in good faith and claimed to honestly believe his reporting was true.

And how could a defamed rock star ever successfully prove to anybody that the reporter who defamed him did not believe in the truth of his own reporting? One day, however, while struggling through James Joyce's inscrutable *Ulysses* for one of his literature courses, Osten came across a little song that the character Stephen Dedalus remembers:

> *I am the boy*
> *That can enjoy*
> *Invisibility.*

If only, Osten thought, he could find a way to write and sing rock music and have it known while he would remain unseen—better yet, unknown—by his audience! That would be the ideal life.

Knowing what it would mean if he ever told his father that he considered making a career as a rock performer, Osten kept his thoughts smothered, at the same time growing more and more frustrated. What added to his concern was the knowledge that Etude Classics was slowly heading toward bankruptcy. Having driven the big saloon singers out of the recording studios, rock was also causing mayhem in the classical music business—all the more reason why Osten couldn't approach his father. Finally, almost in despair, he decided to seek the advice of his father's closest friends—Goddard Lieberson and Boris Pregel.

Both were most extraordinary men. When Jimmy Osten first met them, Lieberson was already president of Columbia Records and Pregel president of the New York Academy of Sciences. In addition, between them, the two men served on the boards of directors and boards of trustees of at least a dozen major corporations, foundations, and institutions. Together they wielded tremendous influence. There was literally nothing about music, the music business, or any contemporary composer, performer, or talent, that Lieberson—who was a composer, author, technical innovator, and businessman combined—did not know; and everything he knew, he knew with the intimate knowledge of those blessed with talent themselves. Older than Lieberson, Pregel was a gifted composer, pianist, inventor, and businessman who was a major shareholder in uranium companies in Africa, Europe, and North America.

The two men had a number of characteristics in common: love of classical music, ready talent for composing and performing, formidable business acumen, and rare executive ability. Both men were handsome, with charming personalities, accessible generally yet sufficiently imposing when they needed to be. Both epitomized financial success. Both made New York their home, but in order to break the city's frenetic rhythm, both maintained peaceful retreats to which they could escape for recharging—Lieberson to the hills of New Mexico, Pregel to a lake in Switzerland. Both men considered Gerhard Osten a most valued friend, and they were protective of Jimmy Osten.

Although Lieberson and Pregel were worldly, affable, and confident, equally at ease in intimate conversation and at a podium in front of a thousand people, their friend Gerhard Osten, by contrast, seemed to shrivel in public. Almost anyone could intimidate the shy man—from his own secretary to a postman routinely asking for his signature on a special delivery letter. And whereas, to a great extent, Lieberson and Pregel had both sacrificed their composing and their other private interests for what they deemed to be matters of significant public concern, Gerhard Osten, who had never shown musical talent himself, continued at best to be a kindly supporter of a few talented composers, somewhat ill at ease in his corporate position as head of the modest firm of Etude Classics. In the course of the friendship of these three men the enterprises headed by Lieberson and Pregel grew and flourished, but with time it became clear that Etude Classics was headed for disaster. Lieberson and Pregel both held some stock in Etude, and to save the company and bail out their friend, they offered him long-term loans, but he refused them out of pride, declaring that the firm eventually would right itself.

Just about that time, Jimmy Osten called on Goddard Lieberson to ask for advice.

He saw him in the presidential suite at CBS, where Lieberson had lunch served for the two of them, and while they ate without speaking, Osten played his tapes. Lieberson, at the peak of his long distinguished career, recognized an indisputable talent. He knew immediately that Jimmy had the ability to turn the ungraspable into an artistic as well as commercial reality, and so he spoke to him seriously and tenderly about the consequences of sudden success—how it would change his own, as well as his father's, life. As Jimmy Osten listened, the concept of the New Atlantis sprang into being.

Jimmy Osten then visited Boris Pregel in his office at the RCA Building. He observed, on shelves along one wall, a simple display of fluorescent products which he knew to be the result of Pregel's long research in the field of radioactivity. In the quiet privacy of the somber room, Pregel sat with his eyes closed and listened first to what Osten had to say, then to his music.

The twilight fell. The older man's face was dimly illuminated by the light emanating from the objects on the shelves. Composer turned scientist in the atomic age, Boris Pregel now seemed an alchemist from ages past, about to transmute experience into advice. "Success estranges," he said quietly at last, then added, "and great success banishes. Be prepared for that."

In the long silence that followed, Goddard was born.

The Apasionada was not a popular hotel, and even during the steamy evenings of late spring its restaurant and terrace café were only half full. The patrons paid little or no attention to the Paganini console standing on a slightly elevated platform in one corner of the terrace, and Osten, from his second-floor room in the hotel, could see the terrace and judge when it was crowded enough for him to descend and begin his set.

Billed on the hotel's board as "Paganini Electronico," his show consisted of about a dozen pieces played on the console, all presumably to demonstrate the versatility of the instrument. He would start out with standard American pieces, mostly rock, country, and pop, all well known to his audience from being played on radio and television. He had practiced them at length at the New Atlantis and had programmed various versions into the Paganini's computerized memory system. This allowed him to play full recorded arrangements at the touch of a finger, or to play backup arrangements and sing along himself; he could even improvise again, over his own recorded improvisations, and record as he went along. Mcreover, he could add or subtract his recorded vocals, other instruments, and audience reactions at will in the event that he might want to recombine these sounds in any of a thousand ways. He found the console particularly reassuring for these first public performances, for he was still uncertain of his live singing voice; if he felt insecure, he could turn off the mike and lip-sync to his own voice without the audience's even knowing it.

As soon as there were twenty or thirty people on the terrace; Osten would start preparing himself. Even though he was thoroughly convinced that no one would ever identify his voice as Goddard's, he always felt a shiver of apprehension. Each time he went down to start his show, as small and indiscriminate as his audience was, it still posed an awesome challenge: it openly, face to face, judged his performance, and he had never been judged like this before.

During his first few days at the Apasionada, he found it difficult to remain detached from the audience. If guests fidgeted or talked loudly while he was performing, if waiters served drinks or rattled change, or if anyone got up and left without glancing at him, he was distracted. In such moments his self-assurance, tenuous at best, would flag, and he would switch the Paganini over to prerecorded music and contribute only the lightest touch of improvisation to the musical fabric. But with each performance, as he sensed greater freedom within himself—and less fear—he felt the audience's attention grow more focused and their reaction more freely expressed as well.

Every day he was tempted to call Leila at her villa, but he waited, hoping to catch her just as she was sufficiently settled in to be a bit bored by the sea, the beach, and the children. Also, he knew himself well enough to know that he had to have more practice, more self-control, and more of the conviction that he had something to offer before he could even bear the thought of her being present in the audience.

After his show each night, he would stroll through the crowded streets of Tijuana and then veer off and walk alone in the fetor and decay of one of the shantytown areas, where children begged him for money and pubescent girls stared invitingly until he lowered his gaze; where men, women, and children were mere specks in a human volcano of hunger and denial on the brink of eruption. Walking among them, he was no more a rich tourist but, rather, a solitary wanderer exiled for a time from his past. He would think of the New Atlantis then, his private island of creativity and invention that sheltered him from most human misery; and he would realize with sadness that, three centuries after Francis Bacon and his idyllic House of Sounds, the world for many was still a sty, and that all the music of the world, past, present, and future, could not shelter for an hour even the weakest child of that one shantytown in Tijuana.

He wondered if music—rock, at least—could nourish their emotions, make these people feel better and stronger and bigger. What if all of rock was a pretense, a collective scream from the spoiled children of the rich industrial nations: "a bridge over troubled water" to Paul Simon, a "safe kind of high" to Jimi Hendrix? And what if the whole rock culture was nothing but hype, perpetrated by record companies and rock stars themselves—"a communist band run by a capitalist board," as Ray Thomas had called it? "I have American ideas—I love money," Alice Cooper had said. "I have one basic drive on my side that they can't defeat—greed," Frank Zappa had seconded. And Charlie Pride had added, "I believe music is just like buying and selling groceries. Or insurance, or anything else." Was there more to rock than making money—and a great deal of noise—by means of drug-induced group hysteria?

In the hotel, Osten woke at dawn one morning and had his breakfast as usual, alone on the hotel terrace. Then he drove through the streets as they slowly filled with traffic, reached the highway, and sped along the arid coast of Baja until he came to the turnoff for Rosarito Beach. The little town was still asleep when he arrived.

The Rosarito Beach Hotel was the town's largest. As Osten stopped at its gate, the night guard was blowing droplets of morning mist off the polished visor of his cap. He yawned when Osten asked him for directions to the Villa Scheherazade, and he yawned several more times as he gave them.

As Osten drove to the villa, he could see its marble terrace and lush garden on top of the red cliff and the silhouette of a servant cleaning the large swimming pool. When he approached, he saw three *federales* guarding the villa, their cars and motorcycles parked discreetly in the bushes. They saw him, too, and as he passed the gate without slowing down and continued along the road, two of their dogs strained on their leashes and barked. While two of the *federales* watched him through binoculars, the third spoke into a walkie-talkie.

Osten stopped at the far end of the road, got out of his car, and surveyed the villa. The breeze had picked up, and he could see the Lebanese flag flapping on the villa's highest turret. Two men carrying trays crossed one of the terraces, and in a corner room someone opened a window.

He kept on watching in vain. Somewhere within the stucco walls of that building was Leila, still asleep or waking up or taking a bath. He thought of her nude; nature in its most finished stage.

He also considered his predicament. Even though

Leila seemed unapproachable, she had nevertheless yielded herself to his music. He could not deny that his music already had possessed what now he wanted to possess himself.

He returned to Tijuana and decided to give himself two more days to smooth out his performance. Then he would call Leila and invite her to come and hear him.

He was hesitant to telephone her for fear that she might have reconsidered her promise, but when he finally brought himself to call, she sounded pleased and enthusiastic, almost elated, and she said she would try to come that evening. She would be alone, she said, but she might return another night with her children and her husband.

He calmly gave her the name of the hotel and directions for finding it, and only after she hung up was he seized by the full realization that in a few hours he would see her again. Instantly he was beset by self-doubt. What if she found his performance inept or unoriginal—or just plain bad? And what if some Mexicans in the audience made fun of his versions of the two Mexican songs? Even if Leila was attracted to him, her attraction might not survive a display of mediocre art or a ridiculous—perhaps even ridiculed—performance. A further dilemma tugged at him: if he sounded too much like Goddard, she might either recognize him or take him for a cheap imitator; if he didn't sound as good as Goddard, she might not be moved.

He had to compose himself before starting his performance, for the knowledge that Leila would be in the audience had triggered in him a new wave of doubt: why, he fretted, did he feel the need to seduce a woman by his performance when up until now he had, as a strict matter of principle, detached from his life the impact of his performance as Goddard? Was it the man or the artist in him who needed a guarantee of success?

Given Leila's position in life, he could not hope for a binding relationship with her. What, then, was the nature of his need? What was it he wanted from her? A quick sexual encounter that would only reduce her, a woman who affected him as no other ever had, to the level of a mindless groupie? A long-term sexual liaison disguised as friendship? But why would she—beautiful, young, married to a man in the public eye—want to strike up a friendship with an ordinary American student? How would she explain that to her husband, her family, her friends? Unless—he hesitated at the thought—unless she came to harbor some idea that he might be Goddard. Yet if she did, and if she confronted him with it, was he ready to admit to this other identity? Up to now, he had always discovered himself through his gut reactions—and his reactions more often than not surprised him. Now, for the first time, he was concerned with extracting a moral truth from himself: was he ready, for the sake of the love of a woman who was another man's wife, to end the separation of his life from his art, the creation of which had been an art in itself, as original and exciting in its design and execution as his music?

The terrace was almost full, and hearing the audience's applause as he stepped up to the console, he felt disoriented, not even knowing where to look for Leila. Only when he sat down and began to turn the switches to activate the microphone and amplifiers did he see her, sitting alone at a table near the exit. Her bodyguards must have remained outside. Osten caught her stare, and a hot flush rose to his face. He smiled, and she smiled back and waved to him like a schoolgirl. He was tense and his mouth felt dry, but he began to involve himself with the keyboard, checking the tempo, volume, and balance while his fingers glided from one note to another, until he had the full attention of the audience.

Still tense, but composed, Osten announced into the mike—first in Spanish, then in English—what he was going to sing, purposely omitting to mention the two Mexican songs. As he spoke, he saw Leila lean forward to hear him better, a smile and a look of utmost concentration on her face.

The audience applauded again, and as they did he made certain to insert into the microphone head a voice rate changer, which would keep him from sounding too much like Goddard. Then he started to sing. In accompanying himself, he used the full range of possibilities offered by the Paganini, at the same time carefully steering away from the Goddard repertoire.

Accustomed to local amateur singers and mediocre combos, and unprepared for a forceful voice and the rich sound of a modern electronic organ in talented hands, the Mexicans went wild that night over his unusual renderings of a dozen well-known songs. They clapped, screamed, whistled, and banged the table tops; they stood up, sat down, and stood up again, hugging and clutching each other, cheering him on as if he were a rock idol. Their reaction soon silenced even a group of loud-talking American tourists who, although convinced that no good singer would ever bother to perform in a dump like the Apasionada, at least sat quietly for the rest of the performance.

During the applause Osten activated the Paganini's tape bank and set it to a recording of the two Mexican songs, for he was fearful that he might become too nervous in Leila's presence to sing them. By the time the audience had finished clapping, his mouth was no longer dry. Now his blood was racing, and he began to play and sing the first song, ready at any moment to turn off the mike and switch to tape and lip-sync.

As the tender music and the sad lyrics of "Volver, Volver, Volver" filled the room, the waiters stopped serving and most of the audience sat frozen, a number of men and women humming the familiar tune along with the singer. Osten glanced at Leila, and the look she sent back reflected a mood as sad and tender as that of the song. She inspired him, and soon all the rigidity fled from his shoulders and the tension in his breathing was gone. He sang effortlessly, his voice encompassing a whole spectrum of sweet sound and feeling and conveying it lovingly to the farthest corners of the terrace. The audience was enthralled;

Leila's eyes glistened with tears. When he came to the refrain, the Mexicans, who knew the lyrics as well as they knew the alphabet, realized that he had written his own words in Spanish, and a new wave of frantic applause swept the room.

He paused briefly, his gaze never leaving Leila's face, then he broke into "El Rey," which the audience knew as well as they knew the first song. Once again they hummed the refrain, listening as they did to his altered lyrics, and at the end they went into an uproar.

As the audience cheered and a few of the young people gathered round to take a look at the console, he switched it off and got to his feet. Hot and sweaty, he made his way to Leila through the appreciative crowd.

She looked alluringly girlish in her white-lace Mexican peasant dress, and flushed and excited, almost joyous, she extended her hand to him, and her entire body bent forward with it. "Listening to you play and sing," she said, "I felt so spontaneous!"

He held her hand tightly, all the while shielding her from the crowd, who pressed up against them and kept complimenting him on his performance. Then he moved her from behind the table and led her to a screened-off part of the café that was closed for repairs. He pulled out a chair for her beside a dusty workbench, and she sat down facing him as he leaned against the workbench. They looked at each other, a silent pounding passing between them. He sensed her presence in him as securely as if they had been together for a long time.

"I'm glad you came," he said at last.

"So am I," she said, her voice deep with emotion.

Restraining himself, he inched closer to her. She sensed his mood, recognized his advance, but did not move. Again he inched closer. Again she acknowledged his movement with her eyes.

"The bodyguards?" His voice was husky.

With a movement of her head she indicated that they were out in the lobby. Gently, he took her hands. They felt cold. She rose and he saw her lips trembling. He noved his hands up behind her shoulders and brought her closer, until only the narrowest sliver of space separated them.

"I love—I loved your voice," she whispered, her eyes on his lips.

"I love you," said Osten, burying his face in her hair. Feeling her body tense, afraid that she might pull back, he muttered words to keep her where she was. "Tell me—what you're thinking."

"About what?" she asked, her hands weightless on his neck, still reluctant to embrace him.

"Anything." The closeness of his face to her neck triggered a shiver through her.

"My favorite songs," she began. "Thank you for singing them for me. You made me cry."

His hands moved down her back and rested above her hips.

"You were so—inspiring," she said, combing her hands up through his hair. "In the best musical tradition." She sighed as he kissed her earlobe and pressed her closer. She nuzzled her cheek against his, and with her hands on his back she pressed against his chest.

"Whose tradition?" he whispered as he moved his thighs against hers. Wedging his knee between her legs, he impaled her on his thigh. She moaned and swayed away from him. Tenderly, he pulled her back.

"The tradition of the best," she whispered back. "You're a master singer. As good as anybody established." She was spacing her words with kisses and swaying back and forth on his thigh. She kissed his forehead, his cheeks, but still avoided his mouth. Then she sighed and brought her pelvic bone down on him with her full weight, twisting herself sideways, torn between the need to feel him deeper and the fear of letting go.

"I was told many times I imitate him too much," he whispered.

"So what? You're stronger than he is. Ahead of the tradition," she said. At that moment, torn no more, she took his head in her hands and pulled him against her. Her eyes closed, her body riveted by orgasm, her lips cold, her tongue searching, she kissed him on the mouth, and he responded breathlessly, tense at first to the point of breaking, then rigid no more as the well of his emotion opened up like a desert spring, sudden, fresh, and tumultuous.

Before meeting Leila, he had had a number of affairs with older women. Because they had their own lives to worry about and would not pry into his, he preferred them to the young and unattached women who were free to follow him anywhere. Most of these older women were suburban housewives—in New York, in the Midwest, in California—some of them comfortably married, some separated from their husbands, others divorced and looking for the next suitable husband. What always troubled him about these liaisons was that the women invariably saw him simply as a clean-cut youth—an incarnation of the typical TV soap-opera juvenile with a little of the beachboy thrown in, or possibly their image of a budding astronaut. To those versed in the theories of women's liberation, an affair with a younger man was merely one of many options newly available to them—like getting involved in local politics or possibly even running, against great odds, for a political office. Some of them were only following the advice of a renowned authoress who counseled: when in doubt, take a lover or redecorate your homes.

Young, unmarried girls were nearly as difficult for him. Though they might offer richer possibilities for a lasting relationship, most of them viewed him solely as a potential husband. They all seemed to follow the same scenario: the gentle entrapment of Mr. Right. This began with their prying into his life—which they perceived as a necessary condition for both openness and closeness. They wanted to make certain that he was still single; that he did not have a live-in girl friend; that he intended at some not-too-distant time to settle down with one woman, as opposed to, say, joining up with a bunch of swingers; that his financial prospects—or, since he was still a student, the financial prospects of his family—were good; that he could be easily domesticated and made a father soon; that his personality was flexible enough to share everything with a wife; and that he had never been in love—really and truly in love—before.

The scenario always grew more complicated by the end of the first week of the relationship. After taking the girl to dinner, he would promptly receive a corny, printed thank-you card with a hope-to-see-you-again-soon note, a phone call signifying "what next?", or an invitation to dinner in her apartment. This last was almost always followed by a night of lovemaking, breakfast in bed, and the suggestion that they save a weekend soon to visit good friends of hers in the country or go with other friends of hers to the beach.

In terms of sex, the gentle entrapment scenario passed through succeeding stages: exotic drinks along with unguarded language, discussions of secret sex fantasies, showers and long baths together, an out-of-the-blue bump-and-grind striptease, offers to share porno reading matter and try out some of the more acrobatic positions pictured there, and banquets of oral stimulation.

He had long since come to abhor the uniformity of social posturing and the artificiality of sexual maneuvers; without exception, all of these young unmarried women had touched the keys of his life much too lightly ever to strike a chord.

Having failed to find any lasting comfort within the narrow boundaries his secret life set for him as a lover, Osten came to rejoice more and more in the unlimited possibilities offered to him in the realm of music. Of all the arts, he decided, music imitated most faithfully the flow of man's life—to the point of being inseparable from it; rhythm and melody seemed to support and fit man like his own bone and skin. As powerful as religion, music gave ritual to life. It transformed man's feelings, clarified his emotions, and paced his thoughts.

Until Osten met Leila, music had been his only passion.

*   *   *

What astonished him about Leila was how natural she was, how free of restraints. There was not a trace of cunning or coquetry or pretense in her; indeed, the most seductive thing about her, in Osten's mind, was her guileless admission of the longing she felt for him.

By contrast with his American conquests, Leila's passionate honesty about her love for him was matched by a sexual hesitation that suggested inexperience. Even though they were never free to go to his room and shut the door, there were opportunities when, in the screened-off area next to the Apasionada's café, they could have made love stretched out on a lounge chair or leaning against a windowsill, well hidden behind the draperies. But they did not, simply because Leila did not seem to know how. He found this facet of her nature so endearing that he risked upsetting her by speaking to her about it. Blushing, she explained that in the Arab tradition in which she was brought up, the punishments for engaging in illicit sex were so great that it was quite common for both men and women to be totally inexperienced sexually when they married. Married at an early age, she said, she had always remained Ahmed's faithful wife.

She also made Osten aware that, even though her parents were Christians, as an Arab and the wife of an Arab, she was bound until death by *ird*, the specifically female honor that depended on the rigidly enforced code of Islamic sexual conduct. As opposed to *sharaf*, the code of male honor, which was flexible because it included all behavior, *ird* was as absolute as virginity, and the sole purpose of a woman's life was to preserve it until her death. Once a woman lost her *ird* as a result of having illicit sex with a man who was not her husband, she could never regain it. In the conservative circles to which Leila's husband's family belonged, a woman's loss of honor could only lead to punishment. According to Islam, because the *sharaf* of all the men in a family was affected by their women's obedience to the *ird*, loss of honor by one woman affected a number of families: the woman's own, as well as the families of her brothers and her husband. And in the case of such a loss, the only means of restoring family honor to all concerned was by punishing the guilty woman.

Thus, Leila's bodyguards became almost a symbol of Osten's relationship with her. Each time she returned to hear him perform, they were with her, their faces impassive, standing at the rear of the restaurant or behind the door to the bar or patiently following Leila and Osten if they walked into the hotel's small garden. Because of the bodyguards, she could never go with him to his room or drive with him in his car. She always had to pretend—to them and to the others in the hotel—that she was befriending the young American who performed on the Paganini only because she was impressed by his compositions and because she was keenly interested in electronic instrumentation, which was far removed from Arab tradition. In the course of three or four visits, the pattern of their lovemaking emerged with painful clarity. Their intimacy was confined to guarded meetings of the eyes, kisses stolen behind a wall or screen, hands held nervously under their table, sudden brushes of a thigh. or shoulder, the slightest of which jolted them both.

To quell any possible suspicion on the part of her husband, Leila eagerly invited him and the children to hear the young American play. Their arrival at the Apasionada—the family, governesses, and guards in three limousines escorted by *federales* in cars and on motorcycles—caused considerable stir among the hotel's patrons.

Watching the commotion from his room and knowing that the Arabs' arrival would lure some of the local press photographers, Osten put on dark glasses and a large cowboy hat before descending to the café, which—for the first time since he had started giving performances—was filled to capacity.

The Salems were waiting to greet him. Older than his wife by twenty years and slightly shorter in stature, Ambassador Ahmed Salem looked like a Bedouin in a painting. With black mustache and beard, olive skin, and long aquiline nose, he presented the greatest possible contrast to Leila. As soon as she introduced them, Ahmed became the warm Oxford-educated gentleman, managing to put Osten at ease to a surprising degree. The children, who both had their father's dark hair and olive skin, shook hands politely with Osten and in all ways demonstrated the best British upbringing. Leila's behavior was astonishing; nothing in her manner betrayed the slightest apprehension or embarrassment. With fifteen minutes left until his show, Osten invited the Salems to join him for a drink in the hotel bar, and the owner, impressed beyond belief by these guests, promptly closed the bar to other patrons. Osten ordered drinks for them and Shirley Temples for the children, and they all sat down, the children silently eyeing their parents and Osten.

The conversation turned to music. Ahmed, who knew of Osten's background from Leila, inquired politely about Etude Classics and then spoke briefly about his concern over the rapid Westernization of Arab musical tastes, particularly among the *muthaqqafin*, or cultured class. Leila smiled and explained that to a trained Arab ear most Western music seemed crude, for although there were only two modes in Western music—major and minor—there were as many as ten in Arab music, and a cultivated Arab traditionalist might well perceive most Western harmony as dissonance. Osten, who—because of Leila—had bought and played a fair number of Arab records, ventured to suggest as a reason for this that Arab music was mostly monophonic, with the melody carried by a single voice or by two voices an octave apart, whereas Western music was almost entirely polyphonic, consisting of chordal progressions and harmonizing melodies.

As they talked, Osten noted the affection and respect that Leila and Ahmed had for each other. Several times Ahmed said with pride that he made no decisions, diplomatic or otherwise, without first consulting Leila, and she pointed out that Ahmed had always been her greatest source of wisdom. Ahmed said that Leila was tremendously excited about Osten's playing, particularly his improvisational techniques. Did he know, Ahmed asked, that an Arab judged a singer by the virtuosity of his improvisations? That was true, Leila said, and except for Goddard, whose improvisations approximated from time to time the Arab ideal, Osten alone of the Westerners she had heard seemed to have a musical sensibility equal to his finest counterparts in the Arab world.

As Osten listened to her and observed her with her husband and children, he was seized by a terrible sense of guilt. What if his few moments of passion with her had damaged Leila's *ird* beyond repair? What if the music he was about to play, the words he was about to sing, were to give away his love for her? What if, listening to him, she were to betray her emotions, inadvertently exposing her love for him?

It was time to start the performance. As the audience applauded and he sat down at the Paganini, his eyes rested on Ahmed, who was bending toward Leila and whispering into her ear. Osten became apprehensive. What if Ahmed knew that his wife was in love with another man? What if he suspected that she had already transgressed against the *ird* and as a result had deprived him of his *sharaf*, which could only mean the ultimate loss for any Arab, the loss of his self-respect?

Ahmed turned away from Leila, saw Osten staring, and waved. He had a smile on his face. Was it the smile of a man who sensed that he was losing his honor, or had already lost it, and in obedience to the ancient Bedouin law of retaliation was scheming revenge?

Osten started to play and then sing, and as the patrons in the room grew wilder in their applause with each ensuing number, he saw Leila's children lose their composure and move happily to his beat. Ahmed continued to smile encouragingly, but Leila, knowing that she and her husband and children fell under the steady gaze of the bodyguards, the *federales*, and the customers at neighboring tables, remained impassive; only her eyes traced Osten's every movement.

When he sang the first of the two Mexican songs, he could see her lips moving ever so slightly, forming the words he had written for her. Listening intently, Ahmed stared straight ahead. What if he knew the songs as well as Leila and noticed that Osten had changed the lyrics? What if—even though Ahmed's Spanish was far from perfect— he understood at a single hearing the meaning of Osten's lyrics?

As before, there was a riot of applause, and to calm the audience down, Osten began to intone the opening phrases of the other Mexican song. As a surprise for Leila, he had woven into his arrangement a tender Arab motif from one of the Arab records he had studied. He played it first on what sounded like a single instrument, repeating it several times without variation according to the Arabic mode; then he sang it a number of times and picked it up once again with the solitary instrumental voice. Watching her carefully, he could see that the Arab melody had caught her off guard, rendering the familiar sad words even sadder for her, and as she listened to it, he saw tears welling up in the eyes that stared into his. He could also see that she was unaware of Ahmed's eyes resting on her face. Shifting his gaze rapidly from Leila to Ahmed, Osten saw an expression on the other man's face that filled him with dread.

At the end of the performance, Osten went outside to speak to the Salems. He thanked them for coming, and Leila thanked him in return and lowered her eyes. The children shook his hand. Ahmed's warm smile was back on his face as he thanked Osten for inviting them and said he hoped Osten would visit them soon in Mexico City. When Osten suggested that they might even get together again in Tijuana or Rosarito Beach, Ahmed, his smile still open and generous, said that unfortunately such a meeting would not be possible since he and his family were leaving for the capital the following day. When she heard what her husband had said, Leila lifted her eyes to his face; she could barely contain her feelings, but she said nothing. Osten's heart raced; only a day before she had assured him that she and her family would remain in the Scheherazade for another week.

A wave of childish anger, of adolescent jealousy, surged

within Osten. In an instant Ahmed had reduced him to
the position of spectator, powerless in the face of his own
private drama; a bystander, unable to follow and be close
to Leila, the woman he loved. If ever, Osten thought, he
were to perform in public, even once, as Goddard—
anywhere in the world—whether in tourist-jammed,
poverty-ridden Tijuana, Mexico City, or even war-torn
Lebanon, he would command crowds the likes of which
Ahmed Salem had never imagined. Then it would be
Goddard who would have the police escorts and the reti-
nue of servants and the hosts of beautiful women—Leila
among them!

Osten's mouth went dry, and he smiled. In a voice as
firm as his handshake, he thanked Ahmed for the invitation, saying that, for a while at least, his studies would
keep him in California. Sweetly he kissed the young girl's
cheek and patted the boy on the arm, and then, as if his
entire life were contained in the fingers of his right hand,
he extended it to Leila. With trembling lips she thanked
him for his music and his company. The bodyguards opened
the limousine doors, and the Salems got in, waving as the
federales rushed to their cars and motorcycles and revved
them up. Amid a squeal of sirens, under the admiring
stare of the crowd, the limousines and motorcycles pulled
away one by one. In another moment the onlookers had
dispersed, and Osten stood alone at the entrance to the
Apasionada. He felt empty, devoid of emotion. He believed he would never again see Leila Salem.

In the two years and more since their parting he had
made no effort to get in touch with Leila for fear of ruining
her life. And even though she had his address—care of his
father at Etude Classics, New York—he had had no word
from her. Not long after his encounter with her, he had
met Donna, who for a time had distracted him from the
memory of Leila. Now, sitting alone in a sublet New York
apartment, he wondered where Leila was and whether
she had heard Goddard's latest album—the one with the

Mexican songs on it. Had she been curious to know how those songs had come to Goddard's attention and why he had chosen to record them? As a foreigner living in Mexico, did she know enough about the American record business to be aware that the company that published Goddard's records also distributed Etude Classics? If so, might she assume that, thanks to his father's connections, he had been able to submit her two favorite songs directly to Goddard—also her favorite—who had then included them on his next album?

An anguished thought that he might never meet anyone like her again prompted him to call Nokturn. He went out to a public telephone on the street and called Blaystone, telling him to instruct the secretaries who read Goddard's fan mail to be on the lookout for another letter from the White House.

Almost before Osten finished his sentence, Blaystone said that two such letters had already arrived, and he asked for delivery instructions. Wildly excited but attempting to sound calm, Osten told him to have all the mail sent immediately by company limousine to the Forty-second Street entrance of the Public Library, where a messenger would be waiting. He reminded Blaystone to take the usual precautions regarding the secrecy of the delivery. Then he phoned Donna to say he would be late picking her up, got into his rented car, and drove to the library.

"You were wise to abandon the pianist in you," the White House woman had written in her first letter. "Instead of merely transposing from the piano to other instruments as the old masters transposed from the violin and the human voice, you compose with the whole orchestra in mind. Just as Chopin revolutionized piano technique, you have revolutionized the use of the synthesizer. Did you do it so that you could compose, perform, and record with no one else's help?"

She was right. He had abandoned the piano, the instrument his mother taught him to play, when he found that it restricted him. She was also right about his use of the synthesizer. But the words "so that you could compose, perform, and record with no one else's help" had disturbed him. Even though it was common knowledge that many big rock stars in the United States and England recorded their music on private equipment—several of them had complete sound studios in their homes—no music critic had ever suggested that Goddard composed, performed, and recorded alone. Most of the critics who reviewed Goddard's music seemed to agree that he must have worked with a few carefully selected performers who valued their income too much to reveal the source of it. One of the writers claimed to have learned from an unnamed though reputable source that while recording his songs Goddard sat in the recording studio behind a one-way mirror so that he could see his band without ever being seen by them.

Passing himself off as a messenger, Osten ran over to the Nokturn limousine and collected the letters. Then he got back in his car, drove a few blocks, and parked at the curb. He opened the new White House letter and started to read it through quickly.

"I have listened to your last album again and again," she wrote, "and the Spanish-language songs seem to have been inspired by actual events. Is it possible that you sang them first in public, for someone particular in the audience— someone you loved—or someone you may even still love? A married woman perhaps? You could have sung almost anywhere, I suspect, without being recognized, though I think of Tijuana as a likely spot—or was it San Diego, somewhere near the Hotel Del Coronado? Did either of these places play a role in your life? And is the *arabesque* woven into one of the refrains a dream out of the Arabian nights you and your love spent together?"

In a sweat, he stopped. What if—his heart began to beat rapidly at the thought—what if Leila was the woman who had written these letters? Yet, if Leila thought Jimmy Osten was Goddard, wouldn't she respect the camouflage of her friend and, fearing that any communication of hers might fall into the wrong hands, pretend that she did not know who he was? But what if Leila had talked to someone about Jimmy Osten's music—someone she trusted— and that person now suspected who Goddard was and was determined to excite his imagination to the point where he would reveal himself?

But if Leila ever suspected that he was Goddard—and nothing in her behavior had ever indicated that she did—would she share her suspicion with another person before writing or talking to him first? On the other hand, how could anyone else—a stranger who knew only Goddard's music—come so close to the truth? He resumed reading, terrified yet tempted to know more.

"I have come to the conclusion that Goddard Lieberson and Boris Pregel were both important in your life—so important that you adopted the name of one and make occasional musical references to the compositions of both as some sort of homage. Since both men are dead, I suppose it is useless for me to speculate on whether they knew of your secret life and perhaps even assisted you in planning for your invisibility. I have familiarized myself extensively with the work and accomplishments of both these men, and I am in the process of learning more—much more—about their lives, trusting that somewhere along the line in my research, finding out about them may lead me to know more about you—in the event that you and I ever brush shoulders."

That couldn't be Leila, he thought, and a sense of entrapment came over him. He hastily read the second letter. It analyzed his music in still greater detail, with two full pages devoted to the Mexican songs and his changed lyrics and a third page citing phrases in his music inspired by the music of Pregel and Lieberson. The analysis was nearly faultless. It had to have been written by someone with profound musical knowledge, extensive education in modern music, and—far more important—uncanny intuition.

He was fascinated by and fearful of this White House woman. If he were ever to meet her, he wondered, how could he possibly protect himself from such sensibility and avoid being unmasked by her?

If only he had an idea of who she was, he told himself, he would telephone her that minute and pretend to be Goddard's manager or collaborator. He would call her bluff and feed her a thousand false clues. Not that she would believe him, necessarily, for he knew from reading the gossip columns how many people went around claiming to be Goddard, his music collaborator, or his lover, or his manager, or even his coke dealer.

Three weeks later, when he had abandoned hope that she would write him again, Osten called Blaystone about another matter. "The President is after you again," Blaystone jokingly announced. "There is another letter from the White House."

Osten gave instructions to have it delivered by the already tested Blaystone personal delivery service, and when he had the letter in hand he raced to his apartment to read it. As he unfolded the neatly typed pages, several color Polaroids fell out. His hands trembling, he picked up the photographs one at a time, as if they were alive. The woman in the pictures was lying naked on a large bed, and the poses left no doubt as to what she was doing when the camera caught her. He could see, in a couple of the shots, a self-timing Polaroid reflected in a mirror. Looking for a clear shot of her face, he went avidly through the pictures a second time only to realize that not a single photograph revealed the woman's face.

Before reading the letter, he examined the photographs for a third time. She seemed to be in her mid-twenties—much younger than he had guessed from her letters—and her body was so perfect that it seemed to have acquired, on its own, a right to be nude. It seemed to palpitate and blush; it was firm but not hard, shiny with sweat yet cool by virtue of its faultless shape, as tempting in its purity as in its self-defilement.

He felt aroused by her, and his desire seemed to emanate not from him, not from his brain, but—like a sound from an instrument the timbre of which he did not recognize—from the pictures. He promised himself that he would go after her and find her and make her give herself to him as readily, as openly, as sweatily as she had given her body to her own hands before a camera.

Anxious to know her name and her whereabouts, he turned to the last page of the letter and saw to his dismay that it was, like the previous ones, unsigned. Then, disenchanted and angry, he started to read it from the beginning.

Still not knowing anything about the White House woman, he felt deserted by her, much as he had once felt deserted by Leila Salem. Ironically, the two of them were the only women in his life who had understood and accepted him as he was—though Leila knew only Jimmy Osten, and the White House woman knew only Goddard— yet he could not be close to either of them.

He had tried often to bring Donna closer and involve her in his life and thinking—almost as if he were preparing her spiritually to meet Goddard in him. But to Donna, most of the rock recording artists, with the exception of a few talented nightclub singers, sounded phony, the products of studio equipment and commercial hype. Possibly because she and Osten had met at the Goddard Beat, the most "in" place for such music, she invariably singled out Goddard—the man and his music—as the prime example of exploitive rock and ersatz music. Everything about Goddard, she maintained, was kept deliberately vague, from his voice to his gut-level sincerity, from his makeshift lyrics to his simplistic rhythmic intensity.

Above all, to Donna, Goddard was an aleator, a musical dice thrower, who sought musical meaning in nihilistic spontaneity and depended for his effect on free-wheeling macaronic improvisation—not for his music's sake, but for the sake of his audience, whose mood was as inconstant as the random throw of dice. He was also a cheap crowd pleaser, she claimed, who capitalized on being both a musical show-off and a personal no-show; and as for his crass invisibility act, it was no more interesting or original to her than the exaggerated visibility of other rock stars.

Both extremes, she concluded, were nothing but manipulative devices used by the big record companies to mine the music market, to con and coax the masses of ignorant whites and underprivileged blacks into accepting disco and rock and punk music as their sole emotional expression and the antidote to their spiritual impoverishment.

How different Donna's perceptions were, he thought, from those of the White House woman, who had written in the latest letter: "By steadily improvising and developing new rhythmic and melodic values, you have become a descendant of the greatest of the performing virtuosos—Bach, Liszt, Beethoven—who knew that, in music, improvisation is synonymous with the search for meaning. For centuries music has been essentially a physical—as well as a symbolic—separation between composer and performer, and between performer and audience. You will be remembered as the first artist to generate true thrall and spontaneity in an audience by fusing composer and performer and then withdrawing from them both, leaving listeners hypnotized by a pure musical experience."

According to Donna, rock and disco had failed to produce any music of lasting quality. They had merely reduced popular music to its crudest and lowest common denominator—tortuous rhythm, sexual pantomime, and idiotic "kiss, kiss, don't miss"-type lyrics. She emphatically agreed with Ralph Ellison, to whom commercial rock 'n' roll music was "a brutalization of one stream of contemporary Negro church music . . . an obscene looting of a cultural expression." She felt that the bigger the rock music business became, the more it led to the suppression of better music—the best in jazz, for instance—as greedy record companies weeded classical music and much of the superior pop music out of their catalogs so they could budget more promotional funds to keep the rock and disco industry booming.

"As a result, what prospect does a black instrumentalist have of ever being recorded?" she had asked him angrily. "Just look at what happened to that CBS record series featuring black composers from the eighteenth century to the present. After ten or twelve records were

published, the series was ended, that's what! Has Etude
Classics, for instance, ever recorded a black composer? Or
even a black instrumentalist? Has it, Jimmy?"

Alluding to the fact that Etude Classics were now
distributed by Nokturn Records, which was to her a mass
producer of musical trash, Donna also pointed out that
Osten and his family belonged to the capitalist class, the
top one percent of the U.S. population, who owned half of
the corporate stock, a third of the bonds, all the munici-
pals, and over ninety percent of the total trust of American
assets. These were the people who, in her eyes, controlled
all the corporate assets and resources of the country—while
she and her family came from the exploited masses, from
the very bottom of the lower half of the population, all of
whom held barely five percent of all the personal assets of
the country.

Aware of Osten's extravagant spending habits and
the way he threw money away on frequent trips between
New York and California that struck her as completely
unnecessary, Donna assumed he was a spoiled child
supported totally by his rich father and she openly
disapproved of both his dependence and the source of
his father's fortune. As much as she and Osten had
in common, she implied, they were divided by an eco-
nomic gulf so great that nothing—not even music—could
bridge it.

She often mentioned My Life in Bondage, the memoirs of the ex-slave Frederick Douglass, who said that
slaves loved spirituals, the precursors of the blues, only
because they reflected the fear, despair, and pain consistently felt by these uprooted people. What spirituals once
had been to the slaves, Donna said, rock had become for
black performers and black audiences; while it helped to
loosen their Protestant restraints, it also underscored their
anxiety by seeming to reconcile what they, the descen-
dants of slaves, knew could never be reconciled: the white
man's order with the black man's chaos, the white man's
wealth with the black man's poverty. Though rock lyrics
often recalled spirituals and seemed loving on the surface,

they were sexually antiseptic, exploitive, and as spiritually needy and loveless as the black man's existence in the white man's culture.

Listening to Donna, Osten felt his innermost convictions, one after another, being distorted. Her words forced him to repress—even during their lovemaking—his dream, however faint, of one day sharing himself entirely with her. Through all of their most abandoned moments a single thought worked on Osten like an isolated musical phrase: if Donna ever learned the truth about Goddard, she would have to reject him utterly, and no amount of lovemaking, tender or violent, spontaneous or calculated, could return her to the fervor she felt for him now.

In the meantime, what she felt for him now was actually invalid, owing to what she did not know—and could never guess—about his life.

When they were in her Carnegie Hall studio, Donna frequently played Domostroy's records, often when she and Osten were making love. They put her in the mood, she said, and she dismissed Osten's dislike of the composer as a simple case of male jealousy.

Reluctant to discuss Domostroy as a man, Osten focused instead on his music, always being careful not to sound too knowledgeable. He didn't deny, he said, that as recognizably weird as Domostroy's music was, it was also not easily categorized and that some of it might even be considered original. Then he told Donna stories about Domostroy that had been passed around in the music-publishing business.

As a hoax, an unknown musician from Los Angeles once plagiarized *Octaves,* Domostroy's best-known work, which when initially published had won the National Music Award, the nation's highest musical honor. To embarrass Domostroy, the plagiarist submitted it under a fictitious name and another title to all the major music publishers in the United States—including Etude Classics, which ten years earlier had initially published *Octaves*. As the plagiarist had expected, all the publishers—including Etude—rejected the work, calling it chilly, episodic, something less than a musically satisfying whole. To the humiliation—and fury— of Gerhard Osten and the amusement of everyone on Tin Pan Alley, Etude's own editors not only failed to recognize the work as *Octaves*, but they rejected it out of hand, as nonpublishable, at the same time commenting in their letter to the plagiarist that certain elements in the work brought the music of Patrick Domostroy to mind! Didn't the hoax, Osten asked Donna, only go to show that *Octaves* was what Wagner had called "soulless pen music"—a mediocre if not inferior work from the start, which had managed to get published and honored more thanks to some of Domostroy's unholy social contacts, than merit? And what about the press allegations that under the guise of needing editors for various drafts of his musical manuscripts and galley-proofs Domostroy secretly employed dozens of young musicians, many of whom were his sexual escorts as well, but who, in fact, would occasionally write his musical trebles for him?

Donna vehemently disagreed. To her, she said, the hoax indicated that even ten years after its publication *Octaves* was still ahead of its time, too original to be assessed objectively, and she reminded Osten of *Time* magazine's suggestion, that to prove that very point, Domostroy had perpetrated the hoax himself. By now, she said, every hip kid in the music business knew that the charges of a cover-up of his musical helpers were trumped up by the headline-hungry New York radical tabloid which hated Domostroy's guts for being visible, flamboyant, active and vocal on the other side of the political fence. To her, these vendettas said worlds about the state of the music business in which a serious, highly-idiosyncratic composer, because he was also a moral odd-ball, could be publicly lynched by the bunch of musical hit-men jealous of his popular success.

*   *   *

Donna's preoccupation with Domostroy continued to
pain Osten. Since their meeting at Gerhard Osten's party,
Donna had never concealed her interest in Domostroy's
music, which she found fascinating in its thematic inven-
tions and technical innovation, and now Osten blamed
himself for ever letting her meet the man. In complimenting Donna so cleverly on her performance, Domostroy
had managed, it seemed, to secure for himself a permanent niche in her psyche, and it troubled Osten when she
told him that she'd been impressed with the composer's
straightforwardness and intelligence, and would like to
invite him for a drink and listen to him some more. By
caring so much for Domostroy's music that she could
ignore the man's sinister character, wasn't Donna unwittingly demeaning the role played in her life by Jimmy
Osten? As far as she knew, Osten was a man without creative
talent whose tastes in music she did not share, and
whose music—even though she didn't know it was his—
she abhorred; yet she still shared her body with him,
perhaps only for lack of any other meaningful link.

After each emotional setback with Donna, each new
estrangement, Osten would return to the White House
letters. He read them over and over again, and they
always left him more puzzled and uncertain than before.

He was in one of these deep and uncertain moods on
the day he received the fifth and last of the letters.

"Surely I have convinced you by now that I not only
respect your double existence, but also consider it absolutely essential to your creativity. You are right to shield
yourself from all those who, if they knew who you were,
would seek to alter the conditions of your life as well as

the form of your art. Probably that includes almost everybody.

"I recently spent some time studying Chopin's letters and in them I learned that he saw his work as emanating from a soul apart, inviolable to the influences of the outside world. He wrote the following to one of his most intimate friends: 'It is not my fault if I am like a mushroom which seems edible but which poisons you if you pick it up and taste it, taking it to be something else. I know I have never been of use to anyone—and indeed not much use to myself.'

"At another time, in another letter, he compares himself to an 'old monk who had stifled the fire in his soul and put it out.' And shortly before his death he wrote: 'We are the creation of some famous maker, in his way a kind of Stradivarius, who is no longer there to mend us. In clumsy hands we cannot give forth new sounds and we stifle within ourselves all those things which no one will ever draw from us—and all for lack of someone to mend us.'

"Is that how you think of yourself? If you do, don't anymore. Let me assure you that I love Goddard for his music—in other words, your soul—and that if by accident we ever meet, I know I will unfailingly detect the soul in you without a note of music to assist me, and I will love you for it even if you turn out to be another poisonous mushroom, or an old monk, or a broken man with no one to mend him.

"I'm sure you need to remain who you are and I respect you for it. I hope you're also tempted to want to know who I am. I'm a drama and music student, and though I would love to know you, in order to convince you of the sincerity of my feelings for you, I have decided for the sake of your music—for Goddard's sake—to make this my last letter. I wish you well. Good-bye, Goddard. Good-bye, my love."

So she was not a White House staffer but—if he could trust the postmark—a New York student of drama and music who possibly used Capitol Hill connections to obtain White House stationery in order to make her letters stand out. But why, Osten wondered, would she send him five intriguing, intimate letters, as well as those sensual photographs, if she never intended to make herself known to him?

He studied the photographs again and again for hints that could lead him to her. His eyes traced the exquisite, harmonious, almost austere, lines of her body, searching in vain for the slightest clue to her identity. Eventually he realized that something about one of the photographs kept evoking in him the curious sensation that he had seen it before—long before he received it from her. Peering intently at the picture and letting his associations flow freely, he discovered at last that his sense of *déjà vu* stemmed from the picture's composition. Somewhere in his past he had seen a picture of a woman—a woman he could not recall—taken from the same weird angle, but he couldn't think of where he had seen it. It wasn't a picture of Donna, he knew, or any of the women he had dated in California, or of the perky Mexican waitress at the Hotel Apasionada who had tried to seduce him while she served his breakfast by showing him photographs of herself in the nude. It was possible, of course, that the White House woman had set the camera and arranged herself in such a way that the picture would appear composed, but this was unlikely. Osten knew enough about photography and picture taking to realize that for a shot like this, the camera had to be so close to the floor that even an experienced model could not tell without looking through the view finder what part of her body would be framed by the lens. What if the Polaroid on the tripod reflected in the mirror was a deliberate ploy? What if a skilled photographer had set up these shots with an eye to calling maximum attention to the girl's beautiful calves and thighs and buttocks and then had ducked out of range of the camera? Was that photographer—and not Goddard—the one for whom the girl had posed so intimately?

Although Osten still couldn't pinpoint the other photograph he had in mind, or the person in it, he had a feeling it was of someone he knew.

The more convinced he became that he had seen a similar picture, the more unable he was to place it in his memory. Then, just as he was about to abandon the mental search, memory sprang into motion and in a flash he visualized the photograph that resembled the one he held in his hand. It was a picture of Vala Stavrova!

Moreover, it was his father's favorite photograph of her. On one of his infrequent visits to the apartment he had seen it on his father's night table in a spot once occupied by a portrait of Jimmy's mother, Leonore.

The photograph, taken before she met his father, portrayed Vala dressed in a long-sleeved black leotard, desperate to look like a silent film star or a Soviet ballerina as she reclined voluptuously on an old-fashioned chaise longue. In order to attract attention to and glamorize the shape of her calves and thighs, the photographer had taken the picture from an unusually low angle and had manipulated the composition and cropping to exaggerate the effect even further.

The angle, composition, and cropping of Vala's picture and of the picture of the woman before him were identical. Was it possible, Osten wondered, that both photographs had been taken by the same man? It was a long shot, but Osten had nothing to lose by pursuing it. He would ask Vala for the photographer's name, then find him, and somehow learn the identity of the faceless nude.

Lest he arouse Vala's suspicion, Osten decided not to make a point of phoning her about the picture, but to wait instead until a better moment presented itself. In the meantime, he had another strong lead. If his White House correspondent was, as she said, a music and drama student, her various musical references, her knowledge of the music of Lieberson and Pregel, and particularly her digressions on the life of Chopin, might be traced without too much difficulty to courses in the history of music she might have taken recently. Since all of her letters to Goddard had been mailed in New York, it seemed logical to check out the Juilliard School first and to begin his inquiry with Donna, who not only was a student there but who, from time to time, audited music courses that interested her at other New York schools.

Casually, Osten asked Donna to find out whether the music of Goddard Lieberson and Boris Pregel was taught at Juilliard. Both men, he explained, had been close friends of his family, and he would like to be able to tell his father that their music was not forgotten. After looking through recent catalogs and making a few phone inquiries, Donna told Osten that as far as she could tell, Lieberson and Pregel were not included in any major curriculum in New York, though their music might come up in special graduate seminars. He then asked her offhandedly whether she knew of any course that devoted sufficient time to the life of Chopin to include a study of his letters. His father, he explained, loved to discuss all aspects of Chopin's life, and Osten always felt like a cipher when the subject came up; there was one letter in particular his father had referred to several times in which Chopin compared himself to a mushroom. Did Donna have any idea where he could find out about such things?

Amused, Donna told him that by coincidence, just a few weeks ago, one of her history professors had read that very letter in a piano literature workshop.

Barely able to hide his excitement, he then asked if he could sit in on classes with her from time to time in order to bone up and impress his father. Surprised and pleased by his unexpected interest in her world, which up to then he had avoided, Donna volunteered to take him with her to the next piano literature workshop.

The following day, in the hope of extracting from Vala the name and whereabouts of the man who had taken the provocative picture of her, Osten stopped by his father's Manhattan apartment on the pretext that he had to look up something in Gerhard Osten's library for a term paper he was writing. He chose a time when he knew his father would be in his office at Etude Classics.

The maid went off to announce him and, returning a moment later, led him to the exercise room which contained body-slimming and muscle-firming devices as well as two steam cabinets. The room had been a birthday present to Vala from Osten's father. Wrapped only in a chiffon robe, through which Osten could see the outline of her breasts and the darkened patch of her groin, Vala slowly pedaled an exercycle while a series of gauges in front of her monitored her speed, her blood pressure, her pulse, the distance she pedaled, and the number of calories she burned up.

Embarrassed by her state of undress and still bothered by the memory of the Mood Undies, Osten told her he would wait in the library. He started to leave, but, amused and flattered by his discomfort, she insisted that he keep her company until she had completed her required mileage. Angry with himself for finding her physical presence disturbing, he sat down on the bench and made an effort to be casually friendly.

Vala had lost weight. He noticed how slim and shapely her midriff was, how smooth her lightly tanned skin. She had let her hair grow, and it fell in abundant waves over her shoulders down to her breasts. Even without a touch of makeup, her dark eyebrows and lashes brought out the blue of her eyes and the delicate pink of her lips.

After asking him about his studies, she launched into the subject of her own progress as a figure skater. She was a natural, she said. Every time she skated at the rink in Rockefeller Center, crowds gathered and people took photographs of her, and she had received several offers to appear in films from producers who had seen her there. But, she added with a languorous sigh, all that attention only angered Gerhard and made him jealous and suspicious. As she slipped out of her robe and stepped into the steam cabinet, she asked Osten not to repeat what she had just told him. He promised not to, and a few minutes later he politely turned his face away when she emerged and—with full awareness, he knew quite well—took several steps naked to the closet to grab a fresh robe. She told him to wait while she showered, and as she closed the bathroom door, he went into his father's room, sat down on the edge of the bed, and picked up from the night table the photograph that had brought him there.

The instant he glanced at it, he knew he had been right: the similarity between Vala's pose and that of the White House nude was uncanny.

"What do you think of it?" asked Vala. He turned around and saw her standing there in a gauzy peignoir.

"I think—it's beautiful," he answered, looking at the photograph in his hand.

"I don't mean the picture, silly; I mean this," she said, indicating the peignoir. "Your father bought it for me on our honeymoon, in Paris."

"It's lovely, Vala," he assured her. "It makes you look—like Olga, in *Eugene Onegin*."

"Olga! That's not nice, Jimmy!" Vala made a sound of reproach, and then recited Pushkin's description of Olga:

> *"A lifeless round face*
> *Of a pretty Vandyke Madonna,*
> *Like that of this stupid moon*
> *On that stupid sky!"*

Osten felt himself flush. "I didn't mean that, Vala," he said. "I meant—just the Madonna, that's all! But tell me," he asked, "who took this picture? It's simply great!"

"You don't really want to know," said Vala. "Like a boy, you're embarrassed." Pretending she wanted to refresh her memory of the picture, she sat down next to him, and as she leaned over his shoulder to look at the photograph, she pressed her breasts into his back and let her hair fall against his cheek.

He asked her again in his casual tone who the photographer was, and Vala, still playful, asked, whispering huskily in his ear, why he was so curious to know. Even Gerhard Osten, she said, who was jealous by nature, had never asked her that. Was Jimmy, she teased, by any chance jealous of her photographer?

Afraid that if he pursued the matter recklessly he might not get her to tell him the truth, he did not ask again, but smiled good-naturedly and returned the picture to its place on the night table. Feeling that he was about to get up and leave, Vala stretched over, leaning on him, to retrieve the photograph, and studying it again, reminiscing, she said that this was how she looked when she arrived in America from the Soviet Union. Although her hairdo may have seemed provincial to New Yorkers, she said defensively, the best hairdresser in Leningrad had styled it for her just before she left.

Osten remained silent and continued to stare at the picture appreciatively until at length Vala blurted out coquettishly that the man who took the photograph had been in love with her. Their love had ended long before she ever met Gerhard, she assured Osten, but they were still good friends. She moved closer, pressing against his back and thigh, and he knew that if he were to displease her now she would never tell him who the man was. As he waited for her to speak, inhaling her perfume and sensing her excitement, her nearness began to excite him too. He turned toward her, put one hand on her shoulder, and gently drew her closer, until her head rested on his shoulder and her hair tickled his face. A blush appeared on Vala's cheek and spread over her neck; her breathing quickened. She was still holding the picture between them, but she restrained herself long enough to set it back on the table before framing Osten's face with her hands and bringing it close to hers. Then her lips parted and she looked into his eyes, and he saw how beautiful and innocent her eyes were. If he had ever disliked her, he thought, he didn't dislike her now.

Just as he was about to surrender to the moment, Osten thought of his father, whose lips, blue with age, had kissed her only hours before, and whose hands, dotted with brown spots, had held her as Osten was holding her now. A vague dread passed through him, and he gently disengaged himself and got up. Without a word, she also got up and wrapped her robe more tightly about her.

Uncertain of what it was that had prompted him to leave her, she followed him to the library and watched him as he looked through several books, replacing one after another in the shelves. To detain him, Vala asked him whether he still wanted to know who took the picture of her, and before he could answer, she went right on, as she so often did, and said that the picture had been taken by Patrick Domostroy—her old friend—who introduced her to Gerhard Osten the same evening she met Jimmy and Donna.

Osten was really perplexed now. Was Domostroy connected with the White House letters? Could he have photographed the nude woman?

When Osten examined the White House photographs with a magnifying glass and a fingerprint detection kit, he was astonished to find that the only fingerprints on them were his own. Was the absence of fingerprints accidental? he asked himself, or was the writer of the letters so determined to keep her identity secret that she had wiped all her prints off the photos?

Next he took the Polaroids to a photo lab and while he waited, had each one blown up to the size of an opened newspaper. The enlargements brought out more than ever the mysterious, thrilling beauty of the girl's natural proportions, and the longer he stared at her, the more entranced he became by the bewitching purity of her abandonment. Her long, full hair, which obscured her face in all the photos, also seemed in many of them to be artfully arranged over her shoulders in such a way as to conceal the contour of her shoulder line. The thought that she might remain forever faceless and anonymous maddened him, and he began to examine methodically, obsessively, her neck, her breasts, the line of her belly, the shape of her thighs, hoping to discover a birthmark, a blemish, anything that he might one day match up in a body of flesh and blood.

He noticed the unusually large aureoles of her breasts. He had seen such aureoles only once before, on a former lover, a housewife who was six months pregnant at the time. But there was nothing in the shape of the White House nude to suggest pregnancy.

On a surprise visit to his father, Osten managed to get a minute alone in the bedroom, where with his camera he quickly took a picture of the photograph of Vala. The next day he had it developed and enlarged and compared it with the enlargement it resembled. Even though Vala was dressed and the White House woman was naked, and even though the two women were photographed in entirely different settings, when he placed the pictures next to each other, the similarity in camera angle and pose was unmistakable. Still, as unlikely as it was that two photographers would be moved to capture their models from exactly the same bizarre, almost perverse angle, it was, he supposed, plausible.

While considering these matters, Osten had something else to worry him. Donna had told him that she was getting up her courage to contact Patrick Domostroy. She wanted to ask him to listen to her play and to analyze her technique. This, she said, would help her in making up her mind whether or not she should compete in Warsaw. The International Chopin Piano Competition was held only once every four years, so if she did not try this year, she said, she might not get another chance.

Osten was convinced that Domostroy would take any such opportunity to make a play for Donna, for at the party where they had met, Domostroy had shown all the signs of being attracted to her. It occurred to Osten also that Donna might inadvertently provide Domostroy with information that would betray Goddard's identity. Yet, he had to admit, he had no good reason to tell her not to contact Domostroy. And, after all, unless she had guessed more about him than she had ever revealed, what could Donna possibly say to Domostroy that would give him away? As far as Osten knew himself, he never talked in his sleep.

In the meantime, he went to Leitmotiv, Inc., the best-stocked store in New York for surveillance, security, rescue, and detection equipment, which supplied well-to-do private eyes as well as wealthy Americans, Latins and Arabs mindful of their safety. He bought a voice-activated microminiaturized tape recorder that would record nonstop for twelve consecutive hours and a parabolic microphone designed to pick up, amplify, and record sounds from as far away as one third of a mile.

In the hope of finding the White House woman before she found him, Osten became a frequent visitor at Juilliard and carefully studied all the women in the piano literature workshop in which Chopin's letters had been discussed.

Using the White House photographs as a yardstick, he quickly eliminated all those whose figures were patently at variance with the figure in the pictures, and eventually he narrowed the candidates down to about six. From that point on, the photographs were of little help. They told him that his White House letter writer was white, but nothing more. Everything else about her—height, weight, size, identifying marks—was obscured by the way she was posed, by the play of light and shadow on her body, and by the angle of the camera, which either foreshortened or extended the length of her limbs. Nevertheless, on further observation, at least three of the six likely candidates appeared to be relatively close in physical type to the woman in the photographs. The only way to be sure that one of them was the woman he was seeking would be to examine her intimately—not merely her body, which might resemble a dozen others, but also her mental environment, her musical knowledge, her taste, her thoughts and associations. Even then, the process would not be easy because all his suspicions were tenuous at best. What if the resemblance between the two photographs was accidental? What if the woman he chose to question turned out to have no connection to the White House or to anyone working there?

Then he realized the greatest problem of all: if one of these Juilliard women was the person who had written to him, would he, by inquiring too obviously about things she had said in her letters, be falling into a trap that she, or someone behind her, was setting up for him? Would he be letting her know that he was Goddard before he could be certain that she was his White House correspondent? Was he prepared to take such a risk—and of all places at Juilliard, a veritable beehive of music-business gossip? Furthermore, if he asked any of the women out in order to talk to them, how could he justify to Donna this sudden interest in her schoolmates—in the event that she found out about it? Was he prepared to risk losing Donna to find the White House woman?

That Patrick Domostroy might have taken the woman's picture made for additional complications. Even if Domostroy had taken the pictures, he might still not know what use the woman had put them to. And, if questioned, why would he reveal her identity to Osten? On the other hand, if Domostroy had taken the pictures and known why he was taking them, then either the woman was a tool in his hands, or he a tool in hers, and any attempt by Osten to question him would automatically arouse suspicion. If he went to Domostroy and began to ask him things that only Goddard could know from the letters, wouldn't he be declaring himself as Goddard? Was he prepared to take such a chance with Patrick Domostroy, a morally bankrupt man and open himself to blackmail?

During his visits to the Juilliard piano literature workshop Osten found one of the three of his women candidates particularly interesting. Her name was Andrea Gwynplaine. She was a classmate of Donna's, so it took only subtle prompting to get Donna to introduce him to her one day in the school cafeteria, his favored spot for studying the looks of his White House nude candidates.

At first Andrea seemed to Osten to be a bit taller and perhaps more slender than the White House nude; on the other hand, he knew that the odd angle of the camera would have distorted her figure. Osten thought he could see the slightly angular line of the nude's thighs in Andrea's body even though the natural wave of Andrea's hair did not match the hair of the nude. The more he thought he might have identified the woman he was looking for, the more excited he grew over the prospect of exploring Andrea's mind, for if she had written the letters to Goddard, her mind was infinitely more exciting to him than her body.

How different Andrea was from Donna, he thought. Donna was statuesque, her carnality ostentatious; Andrea was feminine and stylishly mellow. Donna's dark color, as if defying light, seemed to come out of her and stop with her, but Andrea's flesh, radiant as the light that fell upon it, was lambent to his eyes. In manner, Donna was decisive, self-assertive; Andrea was simply vivacious. Donna commanded attention; Andrea attracted it. And finally, the remote chance that Andrea might be the White House woman filled Osten with longing for her. He no longer desired Donna.

In his imagination, he had come to see the letter writer as the woman he had always wanted to have, the woman he had almost found—and lost—in Leila. Was it possible that he would realize her in Andrea?

He had to remind himself to move cautiously. If Andrea was his faceless nude, under no condition must he tip her off as to who he was, for if she had written the letters he had received, she was obviously hoping at every moment to be approached by Goddard, and any sudden interest shown in her would put her on her guard.

Yet he wanted to know her. He was drawn to her not only because she might have written the extraordinary letters, but also because Andrea was in herself enticing. Still, there was one persistent thought that made him recoil from her: the thought of Patrick Domostroy.

If Domostroy had taken the photographs of the White House nude, and if the nude was Andrea, then Osten had to face the possibility that a man he disliked intensely was a friend of this beautiful woman, possibly even her lover, at least intimate enough to have taken highly compromising photographs of her in a state of sexual frenzy. Osten himself wanted intimacy with Andrea so much that, to clear an emotional path to her, he decided he would have to take risks in order to resolve whether or not she was the faceless letter writer, and if so, whether Domostroy was the man who had photographed her.

III

⋀⋀⋀⋀⋀⋀⋀⋀⋀⋀

Once all the letters were sent, everything was up to Goddard. Trusting Domostroy's instincts about musicians and his assurances that the letters contained sufficient clues to lead Goddard to her, Andrea hoped Goddard would waste no time, and to make room for him Domostroy left her apartment as they had agreed he would and moved back to his room in the Old Glory.

He was greeted there by the stale smell of old leather and by layers of dust, and he spent all of his first day back cleaning his quarters, checking all the fuses and alarms, and resetting the dozens of electronic Rat-Away devices whose high-frequency sound kept the unfriendly rodents at a safe distance. On his second night home, he pulled the dust cover from the grand piano in the ballroom and, improvising arrangements of Goddard's Spanish songs, played himself into a drowsy state. He had expected to feel empty and bereft away from the comfort of Andrea's apartment, but to his surprise, as the days passed he actually felt elated, as if by being alone again he was suddenly free to embark on another journey, of whatever sort he might choose.

Meanwhile, Andrea waited for Goddard, or someone representing him, to show up. She scrutinized the behavior of everyone around her, and she called Domostroy at odd hours, asking him to meet her in hotel lobbies, coffee shops, or museums in order to discuss her findings and suspicions, always taking the greatest pains to make sure no one followed her.

Domostroy could not tell whether she did this because she was bored without a lover to keep her company, or because she wanted to keep her hold on him. Even though he was content to be on his own again, living by himself, listening to good music, reading a lot, and playing four times a week at Kreutzer's and looking for other jobs in between, he promised to be on call to help her whenever she needed him. In return, she said, she would spend a night with him from time to time.

Soon after he moved out, they met once in the music rooms of the Metropolitan Museum. As they passed among the display cases filled with musical instruments, Domostroy found himself wanting her again. In her loose blouse, tight jeans, and high-heeled sandals, she was the image of a seductive coed. Caught between his craving for her and his contempt for his own sexual dependence, he knew he was by no means free of her.

"How's life at the Old Glory?" Andrea asked.

"Fine, but I miss you," he said flatly.

She dismissed his words and stopped beside a collection of ancient lyres.

"Now that's something for you," she said, pointing at one of the strangely shaped instruments and reading the label. " 'The Kissar, an African lyre. In Central Africa, the bodies of lyres were made from gourds, coconut shells, or, as in the ones you see here, human skulls; sometimes the arms were the horns of a gazelle.' " Domostroy recoiled at the sight of the skeletal face of the Kissar. The top of the skull was sliced off, and skin was stretched over it; locks of human hair were stitched around the crown for decoration, and for resonance the bottom of the skull was tightly wrapped in thin dried skin.

Andrea followed the line of his stare. "Judging by the color of the hair, the owner of the skull was white. Too bad for him," she remarked calmly. "By the way, speaking of white men and African gazelles, I found out that you have another admirer at Juilliard—Donna Downes, a black pianist. You never mentioned that you knew her."

"I met her only once—and very briefly—at an Etude party," said Domostroy. He remembered Donna well, and he had always regretted that he had let time and events neutralize his memory of her. He wished he had followed his initial yearning to go after her. "How do you know that she's my admirer?" he asked.

"Donna sat down with me in the cafeteria yesterday, and—surprise, surprise!—she had an Etude Classic of yours in her small black hand!"

"Her hand may be small and black," said Domostroy, "but it's certainly big on a piano."

"Though not as big as her tits," said Andrea. "Anyway, I asked our coconut woman what she thought of you."

"I hope you didn't tell her that we know each other," he snapped. "Remember our plan. Until we hear from Goddard, no one, but no one, must know—"

"Of course I didn't tell her," said Andrea. "But there was nothing wrong with talking about your music. Lots of Juilliard students are familiar with it."

"And what did Miss Downes have to say about my music?" he asked.

"She didn't get a chance to say anything because Jimmy Osten, her boyfriend, came to pick her up, and she stopped talking."

"Ah, yes," said Domostroy, "little Jimmy Osten!"

"Do you know him?" asked Andrea.

"Not well. But his father has been my publisher for years, and visiting him, I occasionally run into Jimmy. He was so quiet and withdrawn as a child that nobody paid any attention to him. He's grown up now, and still nobody does."

"One body does," said Andrea. "Donna's."

"What do you expect? She's about to become a concert pianist and must be in need of a music publisher. Keep in mind that Jimmy's father, a rather sweet old goat, owns Etude. But his kid seems like a cold fish to me—with no feelings."

His words annoyed Andrea. "How do you know he has no feelings? Did Donna tell you that at the party?"

"She didn't have to," said Domostroy. "The night I met Donna, Jimmy and I had a little argument about music, and even though he got furious with me—or with her for agreeing with me—he couldn't bring himself to say so. Such a suppressed little cock!" he laughed. "Or is he a cuckoo?"

"That's unfair," she said. "Why make fun of him just because he has a voice defect?"

"Who cares about his voice? I'm talking about him.

> *O Cuckoo! shall I call thee Bird,*
> *Or but a wandering voice?*
> *No bird, but an invisible thing,*
> *A voice, a mystery!"*

he recited. Wordsworth.

"You amaze me with your trivia. Besides, Jimmy's hardly an invisible thing! He's definitely good-looking," she said. "Beautiful smile. Gentle eyes. Silky blond hair. And he seems sentimental." She halted, then said snidely, "But let me tell you a little story about your nigrescent venerator, Donna.

"A couple of years ago a guy named Marcello used to hang around Juilliard. Marcello was white, built like a beachboy—tall and lanky, polite, always smiling—and he never made a move to date anyone. Yet he kept hanging around with that very big, and believe me, very obvious thing of his tucked in his jeans, as if he were keeping a vigil, as if he were waiting for someone he hadn't met yet, and we couldn't figure out who it could be.

"Some of the girls—and I was one of them—fell for his looks and his manners. We fantasized about Marcello's innocence, hoping he was still waiting for his ideal love to come along and lead him gently to bed. But he kept his distance. Finally, after we had all given up on him, he found his true love, Donna Downes! A real slap in our white faces. Donna was an honors scholarship student—and the winner of just about every piano award there was—including the Elisabeth Weinreich-Levinkopf Piano Prize. Before we knew it, Donna and Marcello started going steady, and eventually our jealousy died down as we got caught up in our own studies, lovers, and commuter trains.

"Then something unexpected happened. A friend of mine said he was convinced that our Marcello was, in fact, the porn star known as Dick Longo, who had played in hundreds of 'sin-ematic' porno loops, special videotapes, and stag films, that were being shown in the peep show theaters around midtown.

"The next day my friend took me to one of the Times Square video sex emporiums where, in the privacy of the peep booth, we examined all the outstanding features of Dick Longo in *Organ Playing*, one of his naughtier sex-capades. There was no doubt about it: Longo was Marcello. I promptly bought a copy of the film, and the next day I invited all the girls who had once liked him so much to view my acquisition. Imagine their excitement at seeing him in all the splendor of his well-endowed parts." Andrea paused.

"What about Donna Downes?" asked Domostroy. "Did she know all along who he was?"

Andrea raised her hands in a shrug. "All I know is that Donna came to the screening, and as the rest of us watched the extended antics of naked Dick Longo—and of his very out-standing 'longo'. On the screen, we also kept an eye on her—watching him. Well, I'll say this much for the inky jade—not a twitch of her face indicated that she was surprised by what she saw, and none of us dared to ask whether she had known before that day that she was being fucked by the most overexposed porn stud in the country. Anyway, after that, our Black Orchid went right on dating Marcello for several months. Obviously it was to spite us." She smiled mischievously.

"Or because she was in love with him," said Domostroy.

"In love? With a porn stud?" Andrea laughed. "She couldn't have been, not if she cared for the Jimmy Osten sentimental type. Jimmy couldn't be more different from Dick Longo!"

"Don't be so sure," said Domostroy. "Pornography and sentimentality go hand in hand. They both lie about sex. But tell me more about Jimmy and Donna."

"There's not much to tell," said Andrea. "For a bi-racial barcarole, they seem to be doing fine. We all wonder, though, whether the Bantu Queen doesn't ever long for the Dick of bygone days." She smiled wickedly.

"Now, that's unfair," said Domostroy, mocking her previous tone, "making fun of Jimmy just because he might not measure up to Mr. Longo."

"Maybe he does," laughed Andrea. "Maybe Jimmy has women all over the place. He's often away, I know. Apparently he can't stand his young bolshevik stepmother and I gather the dislike is mutual. Actually, he just got back into town."

"But tell me—does Donna seem happy with Jimmy?" asked Domostroy.

"I can't tell. Just now the frail sister is in a state of nerves over whether or not to enter the Chopin competition in Warsaw. She's obviously tempted. And we all know what winning in Moscow did for that other Juilliard graduate—Van Cliburn!"

The image of Donna Downes in an evening dress bowing before the formal European audience stirred Domostroy's fantasy. How he would like to be at her side in Warsaw—a city where he had studied—the master with his apprentice, the lover with his mistress, calming her on the way to the concert hall, listening critically to her playing one last time in a practice room before she went on, making certain that her favorite piano was properly positioned on the stage, listening breathlessly to her performance, then wrapping his arms around her in the moment following her triumph.

"You like her, don't you?" asked Andrea.

"Donna Downes?" he blustered.

"Yes, Donna Downes." There was no malice in Andrea's voice.

"I like her looks. Show me a man who wouldn't!" he said, pretending he had already dismissed Donna from his thoughts.

Andrea studied him brazenly. "Do you think Donna would make a compliant apprentice in one of your sex clubs?" she asked.

"From what I've seen, Donna Downes is anything but compliant," he replied. "Ask Jimmy."

"I'm asking you," she said, and when he did not answer she continued. "What if the nefarious cyprian were to submit to you?" She spoke in measured beats. "After all, Donna is already a slave—of the white man's music. As a onetime master of that music, aren't you already her potential master?" She paused and stared hard at him. "Think what a sensation your black slave would be in Poland, playing the Grande Polonaise, at the Chopin piano competition!" She let her words sink in. "Why don't you call her, Master?" she intoned like a sultry sex kitten.

"Gladly," said Domostroy in a purposely playful tone, "but if I do, can I count on you to keep Jimmy away?"

"That might not be too difficult," she said mischievously. "The way the golden neophyte looked at me in the cafeteria, I wouldn't be at all surprised if he asked me to go out with him."

"If you do go out with him," said Domostroy, "just be careful of what you say! Remember who he is and that Nokturn, the company that publishes Goddard, is also the distributor for Etude, owned by his father. The music business is like a company town; all these people are socially interconnected, and some of them might even know Goddard."

"You still haven't said whether or not you plan to call Donna," said Andrea.

"Does it really matter?"

She waved her hand. "It just might. What would you say if I went after her myself?"   •

"Well, well. I wouldn't have suspected you of being into women," he said.

"Sexually, I can be into anyone, anytime," she said ominously. "But she just better stay out of my way."

"Out of your way?" Domostroy was annoyed. "If Jimmy likes you, Donna's hardly an obstacle. And if he doesn't—"

"Who said Jimmy? Look, I can tell you like her, and I don't want that black clit hanging around you, is that clear?" she said. "Until I know who Goddard is, you and I mustn't lose touch, must we, partner?" A thin smile of mockery played on her lips. "Even though you are back at the Old Glory, I want to know you are standing by."

"As a one-night stand?" he asked.

"What do you think?"

"I think," he said, pretending he thought she was still joking, "that if I were Donna, I wouldn't fall for you."

Andrea sensed his mood. "But you're not Donna," she said. "It's bad enough for her to be black, poor, and a woman at that. But she's also insecure as an artist. And so our sooty dame is a sexual changeling—and a hot one at that. She'd do anything to be loved. To feel needed. To become equal—even if only in the eyes of her lover." She was baiting him. "As a woman, I know more about that minx than you ever will. I'll bet you anything I could have the black pearl in my bed in a minute."

"As a man, though, I know more about Goddard than you do," he said, restraining his anger, "and even if he's a veiled Arab sheikh, I doubt if he would fall for a crude American dike."

What Andrea had said about Donna triggered in Domostroy a memory of a woman he had known some years before, whom he had still not forgotten. He'd been at the height of his popularity as a composer and performer, and probably because his name and likeness were part of the steady media diet, a movie company had asked him to play the part of a Russian composer in an epic Hollywood film. Convinced that such an experience could only stimulate his imagination and be useful to his art, Domostroy had accepted.

Parts of the film were shot on location in Spain. At the same time that Domostroy and the other featured players arrived in Seville, a contemporary music festival was about to begin there, in the Hotel Alfonso XIII, a spectacular relic of Spain's architectural past. Some well-known artists and composers would be participating in the festival, and Domostroy realized with regret that his shooting schedule—from eight in the morning until late afternoon or evening—would cause him to miss many of the major group and solo performances.

One day in the costume trailer, as he was dressing for his next scene under the watchful eyes of his barber, his

stand-in, his makeup man, and the costume supervisor,
Domostroy noticed a young woman outside. He recognized her as a member of the prop and costume unit and
realized that she was absorbed in reading a souvenir program of the music festival.

He had seen her several times before—she was pretty, with pale skin and delicate features—and he had been
aware of her shyness, her fear of catching his stare. This
diffidence put him off, and the woman, taking his aloof-
ness as rejection, had avoided him. But he liked her looks
and was particularly taken by her way of dressing; each
day she wore a different dress, and each dress seemed to
change her appearance, almost to the point of altering her
personality.

Later, when he spotted her eating alone in the cafeteria, Domostroy sat down across from her and asked her
which of the festival events she planned to attend. Pleased
by his interest, the woman answered his question and
then went on to tell him that what fascinated her most
about the festival was not just the music, but the presence
of so many composers. To her, a shy person, composing
seemed removed from actual life, and she had always
wondered whether composers might be shy people too.
Were they jealous, she wondered, of the performers, ar-
rangers, and other aggressive nibblers at their work who
were often more acclaimed and better paid than the composers themselves? She had just read an article in which a
French psychologist claimed that musicians, who are by
nature absorbed by and lost in music, are also more capable of emotional and spiritual fusion than other people—of
being at one with their sexual partners. She said that she
had always wanted to know just what sorts of events or
mental states it took to inspire a composer to write music.

In spite of her preoccupation, or obsession, with the
mystery of how music was created, she said, she had
never known a composer, nor had she ever met one
socially. She hoped that the Seville music festival, so well
attended by composers, might give her a chance to meet
at least one of them.

"You've already met one," he said, attempting to put

her at ease. "Me. Unless you think I've got a future in film acting!" he joked.

She looked at him. "Of course I knew you were a composer, Mr. Domostroy. And I know your music. It's just that I met you under such ordinary circumstances!"

"Ordinary?"

"Well, yes. There's no mystery in our meeting."

He was taken aback by her frankness. "You mean there's no mystery for you in our meeting now because you've met me before? Because you've seen me on the set of this movie?"

"Oh, no, not at all," she protested, her face flushed. "It's because you already know who I am, what I do, and," she hesitated, "even how I look—under such ordinary circumstances."

"You are still a mystery," he said. "I don't know anything about you. But I like your looks a lot. Tell me, do you really look any different under other circumstances?"

She hesitated before answering. "I do," she said shyly. "I like clothes. I like dressing up—changing myself a bit."

Taking a chance on what he had only suspected about her, he asked whether her preoccupation with clothes and costumes—as evidenced by the way she dressed every day—was the reason for her choosing a job with the film company's wardrobe department. At this, she recoiled and blushed to the base of her neck, and he quickly followed up by asking her if she had ever tried on various historical costumes. She glanced around, as if in panic that someone might have overheard him. Then, breathing quickly and still flushed, she started to rise as if to leave, but he stopped her by gently putting his hand on her shoulder. He told her that he liked her and hadn't meant to offend or upset her. It was just that, since the first time he had seen her, whenever he imagined her—was it the composer in him?—he imagined her in disguise, in different costumes. When the woman was calm again, she asked him what sorts of costumes he had envisaged and he said that it depended on his fantasy—at different times he might see her as a violinist, a nurse, a go-go girl, or a society debutante.

He said that, if she liked, he would introduce her to some of the composers at the festival; for each introduction, she might wear a different wig and dress and make-up. That might allow her to become different women, with new mystery and a fresh source of emotional fascination, for each composer she met.

Each metamorphosis, he said, would also be an act of composing a new *persona*, not unlike composing music, a comic opera of sincerity, and it would enrich her search for the self—and her sense of self-discovery. Even if she did not win a lasting place in the imagination of any of these creative men, she would feel her momentary effect on all of them and, in the process, expand Domostroy's own reality as well. He frankly admitted that even though he had only just then thought up the scheme, the prospect excited him and he hoped she would take part in it. He confessed that he already had an idea for capturing it in music: he would, he thought, call his piece *Octaves*, and it would be a series of metamorphoses of a single melody broken up and punctuated, step by step, by frequent pauses, solo voices, and silences.

Obviously flattered, the woman did not seem disconcerted by his plan, and she meekly admitted that she often wore wigs and costumes at home, but she wasn't brave enough to go out on dates in them. For her, by nature so shy, this could be the closest thing to becoming an actress, she said, to playing a new, exciting role each day—or even each night. She knew that some of the men in the prop and costume unit—hairdressers and makeup artists—occasionally borrowed wigs and clothes and even went out dressed as women. They had told her about their escapades, and more than once she had found herself envying their courage.

On the first night of the festival, Domostroy invited the woman to a café which was frequented by local musicians. Many of the visiting artists also were there, and a number of them recognized Domostroy and waved to him or came over to chat. Several spoke enthusiastically about compositions of his that they had played, and Domostroy could tell that the woman was impressed by these tributes.

The following day she told Domostroy that if he still liked his idea of introducing her in disguise, she was prepared to go along with it. She had chosen three outfits and had even picked out the accessories—wigs, coats, scarves, shoes, handbags, and jewelry.

Domostroy told her he was delighted, and that night he looked over the list of participants in the festival program and selected three composers he had met at various gatherings in the past. He promptly called them all and arranged to meet them at different times.

The first was an American, known primarily as a composer of serious pieces, but also as a songwriter. He was in his fifties and had lived most of his life in Minneapolis, where his wife had died recently. They met in the hotel bar, and the man seemed glad to see Domostroy. As they ordered a drink and began to talk, Domostroy saw the prop girl enter the bar.

If he had not known in detail what she would be wearing, he would never have recognized her. The curly blond wig fit faultlessly; a fine makeup job discreetly altered her lips and eyes; the borrowed black silk dress elegantly outlined her girlish waist, and a padded bra made her small, firm breasts look substantially fuller. Long gloves, an alligator bag, and high-heeled shoes completed the lofty image. Playing her role well, she glanced around as if in search of someone, registered slight disappointment, turned to leave, then suddenly feigned surprise at noticing the two men. She approached their table and spoke to Domostroy with astonishing assurance and poise, reminding him that she had once had the pleasure of meeting him at a benefit concert in London. Stunned at her effortless manner in carrying off the deception, Domostroy muttered some words of apology for not having recognized her sooner, and then he introduced her by her assumed name to the American and invited her to join them for a drink. Politely she agreed and proceeded to prove herself as accomplished in her conversation as in her disguise. She talked knowledgeably and at length— thanks to the reading material Domostroy had given her—

about music, the subject she said fascinated her above all others.

At what seemed the right moment, Domostroy excused himself and left. On the following day, when he asked her if she had succeeded in leaving her mark on the composer, she replied distantly, saying only that the composer had asked to see her again.

More intrigued than ever, Domostroy proceeded with the other introductions. The first was to a Soviet composer-conductor who was touring Western Europe by himself, having left his wife and three children behind in Kiev. For this meeting the woman came disguised as a loquacious redhead, a college student on vacation in Spain. Again she talked convincingly about her main interest—the history of musical form—and in an hour's time she had the Russian captivated. Domostroy pleaded a previous commitment and soon left the two of them alone.

The final candidate Domostroy chose for her was a recently divorced middle-aged German, a distinguished composer of chamber music and the author of a lengthy study of the physics and development of the entire family of stringed instruments. For him the woman had become a midwestern music critic who was covering the festival—a trim, luscious, full-breasted brunette who wore silk blouses and tweeds—and the German turned out to be by far her simplest conquest.

Soon all three composers were pursuing her, and Domostroy was amazed at how expertly she managed to keep all three relationships—and disguises—going. Several other composers had complimented Domostroy on the beauty of the three women they kept seeing in his company; one of the men came to the movie set seeking them on his own, and was disappointed not to find even one. Meanwhile, in the evenings, on her way to one romantic rendezvous or another, she would often stop by Domostroy's room and let him check out her wardrobe and makeup or coach her in appropriate dialogue. As to her amorous progress with the three men, she was reluctant to be specific. She would only say that they all seemed to be intensely interested in her and that she was pleased by the success of her disguises.

Throughout the time of her adventures, Domostroy wondered how truthful the woman was being with each of the men. Had she told any of them about her game of disguises? Had she admitted to wearing a wig, for instance?

Aware of Domostroy's curiosity, as if to tease him, the woman began to hint that she had gone to bed with all three of his candidates. At such moments, her manner itself was a disguise, and it intimidated him. In perfect control, without a trace of her timid self, she would stare into his eyes and watch his slightest move, as if she expected to find some dissembling in his voice and look and manner.

Under her scrutiny, he broke, admitting to her that he wanted very much to know more about her and her conquests of the three men. When she answered him, she was no longer cryptic. In a voice quite empty of emotion, she described in minute detail how she let each man make love to her without ever letting any of them fully undress her. She also told Domostroy that during these simultaneous love affairs, she felt herself to be an entirely different woman with each man, but that the three men now appeared to her as one and the same man. With the American, she said, she was inventive and demanding, and she would usually straddle him to bring him to orgasm; with the Russian she was docile and submissive, almost in a trance, and she would let him excite himself by rubbing against her; with the German she was fresh and innocent, and she would tease him until he begged her to let him rip off her clothes. She would often go from one lover to the next, right in the same hotel, during the same afternoon or evening. Because sex, like music, was sensual and direct, she said, she had the feeling that she was the composer and they mere performers of her sexual music.

When the festival ended, most of the participating artists, including the American and Russian, promptly left Seville. The German, however, decided to stay a bit longer, and Domostroy wondered whether the man had made this decision on his own or at the woman's request.

In another week the German left too, and Domostroy looked forward to seeing the woman abandon her last disguise. But she did not. One night she came to his room so well disguised that he could have passed her on the street without recognizing her—although he certainly would have wanted to meet her.

"And for whom are you wearing this costume?" he asked.

She came close to him. "It's for you," she said. "Aren't you about to compose your *Octaves?*"

Years later he met the woman again, and it was then that her name was linked with his in a trashy magazine article about a weekend he spent with her at a couples' club.

"Why don't you call her?" Andrea's words reverberated in Domostroy's mind all day. When he got home that night, he wrote a note to Donna Downes, care of Juilliard, asking if he could see her. But when several days passed and she did not respond, he assumed she had decided against seeing him, and once again he resigned himself to his routine—but he thought of her often.

Donna was young, beautiful, gifted. And now he also knew that she was drawn to him because of his art—he remembered all too well what Andrea had said—that Donna had been carrying one of his albums. If Donna found his music fertile, then he had already gained access to her as an artist. But he desired her, and what he now wanted as a man was to gain access to Donna as a woman.

On occasion Domostroy went after odd jobs to supplement his income and to break the routine of his solitary existence. Going out into the world somehow recharged him. He would photocopy his capsule biographies in *Who's Who in America* and *Who's Who in the World* and send them out with brief notes, saying that he was available for special engagements. These notes went only to nightclub and hotel managers, dance hall operators and small-time agents who would know little and probably care less about his failure of the last decade.

Through one of the Cuban waiters at Kreutzer's, Domostroy had also made contact with some members of the Free Cuba Fighters, a loosely organized group of Cuban patriots living in America, ranging from well-to-do businessmen to aged veterans of the Bay of Pigs invasion. Hardworking professionals for the most part, of quick intelligence and uncanny commercial drive, these Cubans proudly declared themselves the "Jews of Latin America," a claim they supported by their vigorous work habits. Although they had often asked Domostroy to play at weddings and small parties, he was surprised when one of them called and offered him an unusual amount of money for playing at their annual formal party, which was to be held at the Harmony, one of Manhattan's newest and most elegant hotels.

Dressed in his tuxedo, Domostroy arrived at the hotel on the appointed evening and left his car, an oddity in the long line of double-parked chauffeur-driven limousines, in the care of one of the uniformed attendants. Then he made his way through the vast marble lobby, feeling a bit intimidated by the crowd of expensively dressed men and ostentatiously bejeweled women who mingled there.

After reporting to the manager, he was promptly escorted by a security guard to a suite on one of the hotel's top tower floors. He had to show identification at the door, and after two powerfully built, tuxedo-clad Cubans frisked him thoroughly, he was allowed to proceed into the magnificent suite where the Free Cuba Fighters were gathering for an evening of amusement. One spectacular salon led to the next, and since the doors between them all were open, he was free to wander from room to room, although as he did so he realized that security guards were stationed throughout at regular intervals.

In the center of the largest room, Domostroy saw a white fiberglass enclosure, some twenty feet in diameter, its sides about three feet high, with a floor of spongy rubber matting. Nearby stood a portable scale in a wooden case, and the room's corners were filled with clusters of empty cardboard carrying cases. At the room's far end stood a Paganini console, which, Domostroy realized, was brought there for him. He had played such an instrument only once before, the previous year, at the Music Fair Exhibition where its versatility and sound fidelity had surprised him.

More and more Free Cuba Fighters continued to arrive, the men in tuxedos, the women in extravagant evening gowns. A number of the men carried extra-wide attaché cases made of wicker or polished wood and equipped with combination locks. Domostroy watched each of the men calmly open the case he had brought with him and transfer its contents into one of the larger carrying cases grouped in the corners of the room. The contents were all the same—fighting cocks, the evening's only serious fighters, their feathers rainbows of red, orange, black, yellow, and beige with iridescent ruffs billowing around their necks, their legs and beaks tied to prevent them from hurting themselves.

Helpers tended the birds, carefully affixing spurs and identification bands to the legs of each rooster. A man beside Domostroy took it upon himself to explain that these spurs were of different sorts, depending on the kind of fight the bird was bred and trained for. Some spurs were made from dead roosters' legs, honed to razor-sharpness and cured for strength, designed to slide in and out of the opponent's body. Others were made of metal; of these, the "gaffs" looked like bayonets, while the "slashers" were single-edged and sickle-shaped.

At a table near the pit, the helpers neatly laid out assorted cockfighting paraphernalia; pads for cleansing and healing, waxed nylon strings, leg bands, leather gaff sheaths, moleskin tapes, additional rubber mats, sponges, plastic garbage bags for the dead cocks, as well as supplies of dextrose for injecting strength into wounded birds and antibiotics to guard them against infection.

Waiters in white jackets circulated with trays of drinks. Domostroy helped himself to a Cuba Libre, and as he watched the activity in the room he recalled hearing once that with bettors shouting, pitmen screaming, and bystanders cheering on the birds, cockfighting was a noisy sport. His reason for being hired for the evening now became clear to him: with the help of the Paganini—which could sound like a whole band—he was supposed to drown out the sounds of the cockfight and declare to guests on the floors above and below that patriotic Cubans were dancing and cheering and singing to the music of a native combo.

As the birds were outfitted for battle, their owners argued the pros and cons of using gaffs and slashers. Two men near Domostroy talked about the fighting cock's extraordinary instinct to battle other cocks—always, everywhere, without any apparent reason. It was an instinct so deep, constant, and overpowering that no human, however savage or motivated, could comprehend it. One of the men described an incident that had occurred at his cousin's cock-breeding farm in Florida. During a violent hailstorm, heavy winds blew down most of the pens and coops, freeing the birds, and by the time the storm was over, most of the birds were dead. Freed from their prisons, they had fought each other to death on the spot.

Domostroy walked around, listening as the women in the room chatted with each other about jewelry and fashion, exercise classes and rejuvenating cosmetics, and the men talked intently about fighting cocks.

Most of the men at the party were middle-aged, a few already gray or bald, generally of average height and slightly heavy around the hips, with firmly masculine features and energetic, flamboyant mannerisms. The women, shorter than the men, their plump round figures exaggerated by tight gowns, were vivacious and feminine, with elaborate hairdos, heavy makeup, and bright shades of red lipstick. The men's excitement over the coming cockfight soon spread to most of the women, particularly as the initial bets began to be placed. Several of the younger women eyed the Paganini, anticipating the time when the fights would be over and the men would turn their attention to women, music, and dancing.

The man who was to act as referee stepped forward

and called for the first two pitmen, and two men with aprons over their tuxedos and fighting cocks in their hands got into the fiberglass enclosure, the cocks twitching, readying themselves for battle. A stir of excitement filled the room, and at that moment the referee gave Domostroy the signal that it was time for music.

As Domostroy struck the first chord, the pitmen handed their roosters over to the referee, who examined the spurs on their legs, weighed them, and declared them eligible and properly matched according to regulations. From his position behind the console, Domostroy then saw the cocks struggling to peck each other, as the guests, screaming and shouting and placing last-minute bets, crowded around the pit. The pitmen set the cocks down a few feet apart on the spongy mat floor and scurried out of the pen; instantly, tails stiffly erect, feathers ruffled in fury, the birds moved in on each other, circling, staring angrily. Then they collided. Savagely tearing and exchanging blows with their beaks and spurs, they beat their wings frantically and became airborne for an instant, their legs stretched out like those of attacking eagles. As they came down, they rebounded, sinking their spurs into each other, until blood began to seep through the feathers on their necks and torsos. They went on raking each other, landing blows, hooking their spurs, wrestling each other sideways to the ground, flying up, falling down, and half blinded by blood and torn feathers, tipping over, colliding again, their torn muscles hanging out, until one bird suddenly collapsed, barely twitching in the pool of its own blood, and its opponent, in the final rage of victory, rushed to it and with one faultlessly aimed strike of its beak dealt the prostrated enemy a mortal blow. With the fight over, the guests collected on bets, and the owner of the winning bird scooped it up triumphantly and carried it off to examine its injuries, while helpers tossed the dead bird into a refuse bag. Just then, the pitmen introduced two new birds for the next fight.

To smother the continued clamor of excitement around the pit, Domostroy was asked to play louder, so he turned the Paganini up to full volume and began to improvise.

Soon, a sound indistinguishable from that of a rock combo was blasting through the console's six stereo speakers, and by means of its preset tone selectors and autorhythms—Latin rock, patchanga, merengue, bossa nova—Domostroy was giving the Cubans every romantic song he knew, rendered with a Latin flavor in a variety of instrumental voices including flute and celesta. Although the noise around the pit did not diminish, and the rounds of fighting and betting and cleaning up went right on, a group of the Cuban women began to gather around Domostroy and dance with each other, applauding the player for his best selections.

He was in the middle of a slow dance piece when a pair of strong hands covered his eyes from behind, a scent of delicate perfume invaded him, and a woman's voice menacingly whispered in his ear, "Guess who?" He pressed the foot pedal that automatically maintained his preset beat and said, "I can't!" but even as he said it he knew there was something familiar about the voice, although he couldn't conjure up the image of the woman who went with it.

"Well, try," she said, and that was enough.

A flash of excitement burst within him. "Is it Donna Downes?" he asked.

"That's me!" she said, laughing happily and removing her hands. She told him to keep playing, and as he turned toward her he saw her in her full splendor—her hair piled on top of her head and fixed with little sprigs of fresh flowers, her neck and shoulders bare—wearing a long violet gown that wrapped her body snugly down to the middle of her thighs and then fell loosely over her knees and ankles. Before he could think of what to say to her, another fight climaxed in the pit and a roar of excitement filled the room. Domostroy automatically increased the volume of what he was playing and speeded up the tempo, and unexpectedly, Donna sat down next to him and began to play along. Under their four-handed improvisation, the music blasted the room.

Soon an intermission was announced, and everyone was invited to the buffet supper in the next room. In the pit, men replaced the rubber floor covering and tied up the plastic bags containing the bloody corpses of dead roosters. Still uncertain of what to say to Donna and timid in her presence, Domostroy offered to escort her to the room where the buffet was laid out.

In the next room a gray-haired Cuban beckoned to them. Whispering that he was her date for the evening, completely at ease, Donna introduced Domostroy to him and to her other friends as someone whose music she had known for years. In the party's din the word *music* must have been lost, for her friends all seemed to assume she and Domostroy had known each other for years.

The Cuban was a retired widower who lived near Donna's parents. He had met Donna through them soon after he moved to America, but, he added quickly, only recently had he thought of asking her out. Cockfighting was his great passion, he confessed, and that was the reason he lived in the South Bronx, an area where cockfighting had become so popular that the local state assemblyman, to please his Hispanic constituency, had tried several times—unsuccessfully—to introduce into the New York State legislature a bill aimed at legalizing the sport.

Their conversation was interrupted by an announcement that the second round of fights was about to begin, and Domostroy excused himself and returned to his post at the Paganini. Much later, when Donna and her friends were leaving, she came over to say good-bye. She told him that she had received his note and intended to call him soon; she was thinking of entering the upcoming Chopin competition in Poland, she said, and wanted to talk to him about it, as well as about Warsaw, where, she remembered reading, he had studied music at the Academy as a young man. Even though she said it with warmth and feeling, Domostroy felt she was simply being polite and would probably not call. After all, why would she respond to his desire?

*　*　*

A few nights later, he was having a nightcap at the bar in Kreutzer's when Donna showed up looking for him.

With her figure outlined by her faded jeans and pullover and her hair falling freely over her shoulders, she looked girlish and free.

They moved to a corner table in the empty dining room, and for several moments Domostroy remained silent, feeling intimidated by her presence. When she told him that she had often been tempted to call him after their initial meeting at the Etude party, he became braver and loosened up enough to tell her that he had often thought about her too. He had been surprised, he said, to see her at the cockfights, and he asked whether she regularly attended such bizarre events. She answered that, given the life she had been born to, very little struck her as bizarre or extreme. The cock's rage to kill was its whole life, she said, so it was only natural that the cockfighting pit should be its means to death. What was bizarre to her, she said, was that there were so many black people, born into the countless ghettos of America, whose rage to live could never be fulfilled, at least not in the pits of Harlem or the South Bronx.

When he did not answer, she began to talk about her life, as if to explain herself to him. She told him that she was presently living—on and off—with Jimmy Osten. Then she asked Domostroy why he had written her the note and what he wanted from her. He replied that he wanted to talk to her because he had a sense that his music was not remote to her; that, through her, he too might arrive at a point where he no longer felt remote from it—or from himself.

"What is it that you want to know about me?" she asked, and he sensed that she expected him to ask her about her musicianship, her studies, or her piano-playing plans, but for some obscure reason that was not at all malevolent, he went straight to the truth.

"Tell me about your life with that actor."

Taken aback by his words, she stared at him for a sign of hostility, but when she found none, she appeared miserable, overcome by disgust.

"Who told you about him?" she asked sullenly, then checked herself. "I'm sorry—it doesn't matter, does it? But why do you ask?"

"I want to know you, Donna," he said quietly, "and because I might not have another chance, I feel it's important to ask you about someone you cared about."

She searched his face for signs that she could trust him. Then she composed herself and began to speak, her voice calm, her eyes resting on his, gauging his reaction as she surrendered herself to her past.

"Please keep in mind, Patrick, that I can't explain what I'm about to tell you," she said, placing her hand on his, unconsciously smoothing his skin with the pads of her fingertips as she spoke.

"Recently, leafing through some magazines in the Juilliard library, I came across a scientific article about female sexuality. It said that when a woman gets excited sexually, whether by physical contact or through her imagination—the amount of vaginal blood and the rate of her vaginal pulse both increase. Yet the researchers found that during orgasm, although the rate of the vaginal pulse increases, the amount of blood decreases, and even though this information was obtained by the use of sophisticated research techniques, medicine has not been able to offer an explanation for it."

She stroked his hand, as if expecting him to answer her, and she stared at him. But he did not answer. He watched her hand on his, and the thought that she would soon go home filled him with anxiety.

"If such a simple physical thing is still a mystery to science," she said, "I guess I'll never know what it was about Marcello that made me love him."

Domostroy felt the incomprehensible world of her past rise like a barrier between them. Her green eyes stared at him without expression, and meeting her gaze, he wondered whether that barrier would ever crumble before the groundswell of his feeling for her.

She had been in love for the first time, she said, when she was twelve. She and the boy used to slip out at night and meet in a burned-out building near her family's apartment in Harlem. The boy was sixteen and white, and he always acted frightened, probably because everything around him was black—the night, the mood, the burned-out building, the girl he was squeezing. They met and kissed and petted a number of times, until barely a week after he had deflowered her with his hand, one night the boy's parents sent the police after him. She and the boy were found necking in the ruins, and because the policemen were white, her boyfriend was no longer alone in the blackness. They herded Donna into a police van as if she were a stray dog, took her to the station, and charged her with soliciting for the purpose of prostitution. She was locked overnight in a cell with two other women—black prostitutes who treated her as tenderly as if she were their daughter—and then she was released in the custody of her father, who made her promise never to see that white boy again.

The incident taught her that even though she was not guilty of soliciting lovers, she could still be arrested for it. By the time her family moved out of Harlem and into a more affluent South Bronx neighborhood, she had developed spiritually; now her sexuality was no longer awkwardly clitoric; she was rid of shame, defiance and fear, and openly resentful when other boys tried to fulfill her manually. In her erotic life she saw herself as sexually precocious. The knowledge did not disturb her. She liked the idea that she could be as carried away by sex as some of her high school friends were by coke and hash, and even then, in her mid-teens, she decided that she would always be the one to take the initiative: she would solicit only those lovers who seemed to be worth the experience.

She went about her life with that decision more or less fixed in her mind, and one day, years later, she noticed a handsome man outside the Juilliard library. He seemed to be waiting for someone, and even before she saw his face, she couldn't help seeing what his tight jeans revealed. Extreme virility, whether of duration or size, didn't interest her much, however; it was only when he looked at her that she was attracted, for his face was boyish and his expression shy and innocent.

As soon as he saw her he began to stare, and she found his intentions so obvious and his stare so comical, that she burst out laughing. He spoke to her then, asking her why she was laughing at him. He seemed hurt. She apologized instantly. Their affair began with laughter and apology.

Marcello told her that after being orphaned in early childhood, he had been brought up by a series of relatives. He had worked at a variety of part-time jobs, most recently for a videotape company. Lacking formal education beyond high school, Marcello was nevertheless well informed and well read, and although he was not overtly musical, he seemed to respond instinctively to good music. He was a patient listener during the long hours when Donna practiced the piano, and throughout their relationship he made an effort to learn more about music. But even with his many likable traits, it was as a lover that Donna enjoyed Marcello most of all.

Just as she was occasionally surprised to find a piano that could reveal to her, by virtue of its construction and tuning, a new beauty or a hidden sense in some composer's work, or to discover a room that, because of its special resonance, could alter her perception of tone and clarity in musical sound, so was she surprised to meet in Marcello a being who—for the first time in her life—elicited a response from her that was wholly sexual.

"Until I met Marcello, most of the men I had run into were pretty much alike," she said, eyeing Domostroy thoughtfully. "Usually, my date—black or white, no matter—didn't think there could be more to me than what he saw. But once he found out there was, to prove to me he wasn't after a quick lay, he would take me out a lot—clubs, discos, restaurants—anywhere but home. Then, if I liked him, we would often end up at his place—or mine." She attempted a smile, but it dissolved and she looked haggard.

"When we were finally alone, free to step out of our clothes and free from the roles they imposed on us, my date would usually go down on me, with that humble, slightly remorseful stare—puppylike and eager to please.

You see, to make me feel the pleasure was, for him, a form of usurping power over me, of turning me into a slave of my own uterus. Then, when I reassured him that he was doing all right, he would go on making love to me as if I were an insatiable, racially double-dealing ogress, never taking a chance, never surprising me with something he would want me to do for him, always afraid he might begin to use me for his pleasure alone. And every time I saw that anxious stare, I would feel as if I were hidden from him in the dark, watching a spectacle being performed by a stranger."

She halted, and when she spoke again her voice seemed lifelessly even. "All that time I felt that there must have been something in me—in what I'd said or done—some invisible score I'd written for them to enact that made every one of those men so passive, so obsequious. Yet, even though I became fed up with them and disgusted with myself, I wouldn't—or couldn't—do anything about it. You know, Patrick, that in matters of sex it's often easier to turn down what you feel than to go after what you want.

"That was the mood I was in when I met Marcello. . . ."

Marcello understood her very well, she continued. In their first weeks together, whether they were alone or in public, he would constantly surprise her, constantly insinuate his will by touching her body, sniffing her hair, warming her neck with his breath, brushing against her breasts or thighs or buttocks, rubbing her groin with his hand or knee, all the while communicating to her body that it was a hiding place for innumerable stealthy urges from within, until at last she came to expect her every ordinary moment to be turned by him into a state of sexual tension, an act of frenzy, stripped of everything except feeling. At that point it was enough for her just to follow him, no matter where he chose to lead her.

One place he led her often was a downtown bar called Dead Heat. Located in Soho, in the basement of an old warehouse building, Dead Heat appeared to be one large room with a stone floor and rough black walls; it had a circular bar in the center, a section of tables and chairs,

and a small dance floor, all lighted by a few small red
lamps hanging in tiny iron cages, which cast moving circles on the ceiling and walls whenever they swayed. At
the far end of this room, usually unnoticed by the new-
comer, two corridors led to the most essential area of
Dead Heat, called the Jam Session, which consisted of a
dozen catacomblike rooms, vaults, stalls, and cubicles, all
with walls and floors of rough black stone, all lighted by
small, bare red or blue bulbs, separated in a few cases by
a doorless toilet. Furnished with a few wooden stools,
wooden platform beds, and old metal bathtubs, the larger
rooms of the Jam Session could hold fifteen to twenty
people, the vaults about ten, and the stalls and cubicles
five or six at most.

Open after midnight—and only on weekends—the
gloomy, inhospitable place attracted people who came
there to use its stark, savage spaces for their stark and
savage rituals. It was a gathering place for people who
dressed in leather or rubber; for women who wore heavy
makeup and high stiletto heels and were accompanied by
anemic-looking lovers in sweatshirts and shorts; for men in
tank tops and shorts who liked to show off their muscular
bodies, as well as the frail beauty of their scantily clad, if
clad at all, female or male lovers; for people seeking
partners who were as wild and momentary as the love
they craved and whose only real stimulus to intimacy was
to be found among a steady stream of strangers. At Dead
Heat the beautiful mingled with the deformed, the old
with the young, the naked with the clothed.

Donna would sit with Marcello at the bar or at a table
off to one side, or she would cruise with him through the
corridors, talking little, watching the other patrons. Whenever Marcello noticed a couple—a man and a woman, two
women, or two men—straying from the main room and
starting to make their way to the Jam Session, he and
Donna, and others, would follow. The couple would go
into one of the empty rooms off the corridor and start to
stroke each other, and immediately the other men and
women, as many as the room could hold, would jam and
press in around them and watch in silence, like a huge

predator the lovers could not escape even if they wanted to.

The first time Marcello took Donna to Dead Heat, she was surprised to see how many of the people there— particularly the men—knew him. They came up to him and shook hands or waved at him from across the room, or they pointed Marcello out, whispering to one another or to their female dates as if he were a celebrity. When she asked him what he had done to be so popular, Marcello told her that he was one of the Dead Heat regulars and that the people there were simply friendly.

One night, after they had had a drink or two at the bar, Marcello slowly got up, took her by the hand, and led her down one of the dark corridors. As she followed him obediently, she could feel the presence of a crowd behind them, somber whispering bulks, a moving forest of silent male and female trunks, an excited eager procession escorting her to the outermost reaches of experience.

Pushing her gently ahead of him, Marcello turned her into a large room at the end of the corridor. He lifted her by her hips as he might lift a keg and set her on a table near the far wall. She closed her eyes. He rolled her dress up over her breasts and neck and pulled down her panties, and as they slipped over her feet, he spread her legs. Rubbing his groin against hers, he massaged her breasts, and with her eyes still closed, she joined him in a long kiss. She sensed the crowd in the room, hovering and sullen at first, almost silent, like frothing foam, then stirring, coming nearer, tightening their circle around the table. When she opened her eyes, she saw them all staring at her from the darkness. With no warning, Marcello slid into her, and as she folded her hands around his neck, she screamed in pain and pleasure. The crowd made a noise too, a single long sigh. As Marcello pushed rapidly and insistently in and out of her, opening her like a fresh wound, the faces in the crowd all came nearer, like sentries closing their ranks, until they pressed against the two of them. Engrossed in the feelings aroused in her by Marcello, she barely felt the multitude of hands on her, hands which seemed to belong to no particular body, or at times, to everybody, and kept on feeling her feet, stroking her calves and thighs and breasts, brushing over her shoulders, caressing her hair, her neck, and cheeks. Lost in a single sensation, her body one with the body of the man driving into her, she could feel herself drifting away, abdicating to an inner, infinitely pleasurable turmoil, a mass glowing with its own heat, and she felt she was leaving this swarm of lifeless figures who, while laying their hands on her body, could only gaze at her from afar, from the cage they could not leave.

Donna looked at Domostroy, trying to gauge how he had judged her.

"Later, when it all ended," she went on, "and Marcello and I returned to the bar, I was still excited," she said. "My whole body still oozed sex, and I spun from one orgasm to the next. Like heartbeats, they kept on coming— for as long as he kept on touching me, for as long as I wanted to go on." She halted. "And I didn't mind having people around either. I felt there was something sad in all those men and women cruising alone, back and forth through Dead Heat, in all those couples who held hands but couldn't really feel each other, and in all those women who dress like men and those men who maybe should have been born women. Sometimes I wanted to laugh at them. Such pathetic creeps, I thought, such spiritual nobodies, such sexual frauds. But when I looked at them again, I felt I could cry for every one of them, so lonely, so desperate, so condemned to watch love they themselves could not—or were afraid to—enact.

"It must take courage for them to come to this awful pit, I thought, to these bowels of sex, and by coming here to acknowledge to themselves and to others that watching Marcello and me and other couples like us was the only way they could participate in love, the only way to hear its music—even if they couldn't play it themselves."

The next time Marcello took her to Dead Heat, he led her again into the Jam Session, and again the quiet footsteps of strangers followed them in the hazy distance. This time he turned and backed into one of the largest vaults—damp, rectangular, empty of stools—and turning

her around, pulled her in after him. With his back against
the far wall, he continued to pull her, unresisting, until
her back was pressed tightly against his chest and groin.
Then, facing the human mass that moved relentlessly in
on them from the corridor, she could feel Marcello behind
her, his hands under her skirt caressing her ever so
faintly, while in the bleak half-light the crowd stared,
quiet, enrapt. Then, at last, he sank into her from behind
and she yielded to the sensation of him in her, of being
impaled, and leaned down and back and onto him. Her
blouse was unbuttoned, her wraparound skirt spread open
behind her, falling primly in front like an apron or a
shield. As she felt herself following his movement, the
crowd moaned. Her flesh sealed with his, she swayed back
and forth with him, lingering in the moment, clinging to
his flesh convulsively, while the crowd jammed clumsily
into the black cavity of the vault until they threatened to
fill every inch of it. Like a monstrous centipede, men and
women, breathing and sweating and pungent in the darkness, sought her with their hands, groping for her hair,
her breasts and belly and thighs. She couldn't hold them
off, and Marcello's hands had to rescue her, roughly ma-
neuvering the intruders away, one after another, slamming the door to her shut, the door that a moment before
he had so willingly opened.

Donna glanced at Domostroy and went on talking, as
if she was reluctant to give him time to speak. In the
weeks that followed, she said, she often asked Marcello
why he kept wanting to return to Dead Heat and make
love to her there in front of strangers.

"Marcello told me he was not like most men, who
need privacy for their sexual feasts. He said he could get
sexually high only by making love to me in the presence of
strangers. To him, the real excitement of sex came from
bridging the sexual distance between lovers, not at home,
where there was nothing—and no one—to distract them,
but in places like Dead Heat, where their intimacy or
even the mere performance of it, was constantly threatened,
tested, onstage, on trial, almost under siege.

"Dead Heat was like a church to him, housing ecstasy

and ritual, at once corporate and personal. Making love to me there, he said, was like walking a high wire without a net. Even the prospect of going there aroused him. He always wondered what the sex would be like on a particular night: whether there would be many 'eunuchs'—single, docile men who would kneel in front of me on his command and kiss my feet—or 'cannibals'—those dominant sex freaks of the Jam Session whom his presence kept at bay but who were always ready to snatch me away and, before Marcello could find me, get to me all the way, one after another, as they had often done with other men and women abandoned in the labyinth of crypts at the Dead Heat.

"If I went along with Marcello for such a long time, it was because, with him, I had begun to think of myself as more alive than ever and of him no longer as my lover, but as one of those who watched me from the darkness.

"But," Donna went on, "Marcello kept on swearing that he loved me, saying that if I loved him too, I shouldn't be put off by what we'd done at Dead Heat. He said that even though he made love to me in front of the people there, I should know that all they could do was watch. His body was between theirs and mine, and as for them touching me, didn't the sand touch me too when I lay on the beach? These people, he said, were human sand. He told me I was, sexually, the only woman in his life; he was freer and more fulfilled with me than he had ever been with any other woman."

Donna admitted she never knew much about his whereabouts during the day. While she was at Juilliard or practicing at home, his video jobs kept him moving around, and on the few occasions when she did try to phone him at the number he gave her, no one ever answered. Eventually they agreed that he should move in with her, and when he did she was astonished at how few belongings he brought with him—one suit, a few shirts, two pairs of slacks, two pairs of shoes, and a toilet kit. Was that all there was? she wondered. Then she noticed that he didn't carry any credit cards, or a driver's license, or even an address book and he never got any phone calls or received any mail. When she asked him about this, he said he was a free-lancer, successful enough to be free of such mundane things as appointment books and monthly bills. He insisted on being paid in cash, he said, and he paid cash for everything he bought.

He was an indefatigable lover, and Donna found his lovemaking so persistent, his orgasms so frequent, his sperm so plentiful, that she never doubted that he was faithful to her. Moreover, she never detected on him the slightest trace of any perfume or lipstick or powder but her own.

Then one day, said Donna, Andrea Gwynplaine, a fellow student at Juilliard, invited her and some other students over to the apartment of Chick Mercurio, Andrea's boyfriend, to see *Organ Playing*, a porno flick that was supposed to be a parody of a Broadway musical. When the movie started, Marcello—billed as Dick Longo in the credits—appeared on the screen, naked, in front of a mirror in a theater dressing room, masturbating himself with one hand and a grotesquely fat, platinum-blond woman with the other.

The shock was so sudden, so extreme, that for a moment she refused to believe the evidence before her. But she kept on watching as Dick Longo went through a string of sleazy starlets, demonstrating his—apparently proverbial—ability to produce a fresh orgasm at every twist of the flick's idiotic plot. As Andrea and her boyfriend and the other students in the darkened room cheered the hotter moments of the film and made crude jokes about the bodily parts of its stars, Donna slowly realized that it was she, not Dick Longo, who was the main star of the screening.

When the lights came back on, none of those in the room indicated to Donna in any way that they had recognized Dick Longo as her boyfriend, Marcello. For their added amusement, Andrea began to distribute Xerox copies of a porno magazine interview with Dick Longo, profusely illustrated with stills from his movie in which the star admitted to having made hundreds of porno loops every year for the past three or four years, and boasted

that not a single working day of that time had passed
without his having had—on cue, in front of the camera—at
least a couple of orgasms. Sensing the other students
gazing furtively at her, Donna felt naked before them, as if
they were the strangers of Dead Heat who had just succeeded in raping her.

Donna paused and looked at Domostroy, expecting
some reaction, but he sat motionless, crushed and dis-
armed. He was wondering whether Andrea had told him
the truth when she said that Donna went right on living
with Marcello long after she discovered that he was Dick
Longo. If it was true, what hellish need in her, Domostroy
wondered, could have made her punish herself so? What
was Donna's private organ playing?

As if sensing his thoughts, Donna continued her story.
She said that she went home after the screening and
waited for Marcello to show up. She knew just what she
would do when he entered, clean and freshly shaven and
amorous as usual. She would grab a kitchen knife, the
longest one she had, and like an addict in a rage of hurt
pride, embarrassment before her friends, shame and
anger of being, for him, just another wide-open cunt, she
would stab and slash and cut him as long as his body kept
on jerking and twitching and turning, until his blood filled
his lungs and throat and drowned out the last gurgle of his
life.

But, she said, when at last he did come home, freshly
bathed, smelling of cologne, sporting a new haircut, and
wanting to kiss her exactly as she had imagined, all she
could manage to do was ask him, just like that, why in all
their time together he had never told her that every day,
when he left her, he went off to fuck all those white and
black and yellow cunts, front and back, one after another,
one next to the other, one on top of the other, on cue in
front of a camera, to be paid in cash for every hard-on, for
every orgasm—all during the time he was supposed to be
in love with her?

All he answered was that, as he had told her from
the start, he loved only her. He said that fucking all those
countless cunts was his job; that when he was with them,

his prick was no different from a masseur's hand; and that only with Donna he was utterly himself, able to bridge that sexual distance which, until he had met her, had remained open like a chasm between himself and the dead heat of his life.

She neither screamed nor kicked him out, nor did she end the relationship until several more months had passed.

With sudden clarity she saw that during their months together it was she who, with palpable abandon, enjoyed the temporary lifting of the burden of sexual consciousness, the obliteration of responsibility. It was she who had been using him in order to experience herself through him. Now, because of what she had learned from being with him she was whole. Marcello had been, she said, nothing but a bystander in the process, one more lecherous paw reaching out to touch her from the dark recesses of Dead Heat.

Domostroy had always been convinced that in order to compose well, a good composer had to write to satisfy himself, not others. Because he had refused, at the peak of his career, to yield to the critics and go on writing as they wanted him to write, they had bombarded him savagely each time he produced an original work. That had caused the listening audience—fickle always, but especially so in the age of disco and television—to abandon him. After a malicious nation-wide defamation campaign launched against him and his work by one particularly hostile musical coterie, without creative prompting from his peers, the critics, or the public, he had finally stopped writing altogether, annoyed that his creative record could no longer be set straight.

He knew that he wanted Donna, for in the hour she spent talking about her life, she revealed to Domostroy truths about himself he never had suspected. As he listened to her, he came to see that the state of his mind and the pattern of his life would be arbitrary from this point on unless he could go on being replenished by her. He sensed that he might be able to ensnare her by subtle, roundabout tactics, but that seemed cowardly, a bit like writing music to please the critics or to prove to himself that he could still displease them. The other way was to go after her directly, without psychological dodges or intellectual filters, straight from the gut of his being, from the vortex of his psyche, the way he once wrote music. If he displeased her then and lost her, as he had once displeased and lost his critics and his public, at least he would not have lied to her or to himself. As his father used to say, "When rain falls, logs rot, but roots grow deeper." Domostroy wanted to send out sound roots in his dealings with Donna.

Finally, he left it up to her. He thanked her for giving him so much of herself and told her matter-of-factly that he would be glad to discuss the Warsaw Chopin competition with her; that there might be something out of his long experience which she could use in preparing for it. She asked him if there was a piano where he lived, and he told her there was—a concert grand—and that she was free to use it at any time, alone or with him as her audience. They arranged for her to visit the Old Glory a week later, on one of Domostroy's days off.

When the appointed day came, he found himself restless. He went over the Old Glory a half-dozen times, dusting the piano, checking the liquor and ice in the kitchen, rearranging chairs and tables. In the event that she might spend the night, he changed the sheets and pillowcases on his bed and put fresh towels in the bathroom.

A few hours before she was due to arrive, Domostroy had taken an added precaution to ensure her safety in the area. He drove to the nearby baseball lot and hunted up the leader of the local gang, known as Born Free. Living alone as he did at the Old Glory, Domostroy regularly bought their protection, for even though he knew that the owner of the Old Glory sent monthly payments from Miami to his old friends on the South Bronx police force to keep an eye on the unsold ballroom, he also knew from firsthand experience that the Born Free gang—referred to by the local citizenry as the Born to Burn—were the actual rulers of the neighborhood after dark. This time because he wanted to take no chances, Domostroy was several days early with his monthly payment.

Not that such an arrangement was foolproof. On several occasions, arriving home late at night, Domostroy had been aware of huddled figures watching him from recesses in the walls or from behind the scrubby bushes. He knew full well he was an easy target, and he was never sure whether the figures were Born Free members or intruders taking advantage of the gang's absence.

He heard a car drive through the gate, but today he had little doubt as to who might be storming the drawbridge of his fortress. Donna was right on the dot, and as he stood there looking out of the window and watching her little white sports car raise a tunnel of dust as it sped across the empty parking lot he remembered that the South Bronx was Donna's native land and that she probably knew her way through its maze of parkways, avenues, and streets even better than he did.

She was at ease when he greeted her. As he shook her cool, firm hand, she bent forward and, ever so briefly, kissed him lightly on the cheek. When he felt her lips on his face and the slight pressure of her breasts against his chest, he was seized with a shiver of rapture that lasted no longer than the kiss, but long enough to rob him of his carefully collected composure. To hide his excitement and apprehension, he motioned for her to follow him to the bar, telling her that it once held two hundred patrons each evening, and as he showed her around the huge ballroom, he carefully avoided the narrow corridor, flanked by storage vaults, that led to his modest living quarters.

But she had come, carrying her music, to play the piano for him, and it was the grand piano on the stage in the ballroom that quickly absorbed the two of them. Domostroy raised the lid and asked her whether, considering the sorry state of most pianos, she knew how to tune and test for voice and brilliancy all the registers of a piano. Donna admitted that she had always had to rely on the help of a professional tuner.

Domostroy warned her that a concert piano was not

like an unmade bed, which any maid could make, and that
if she decided to go to Warsaw, she would do well to be
able to adjust any piano she played, particularly the one
assigned to her for the competition, for evenness of tone
and volume throughout the keyboard. This could be done,
he said, by means of the soft pedal and a tuning instrument, and she ought to know how to do it by herself if she
had to, or with the help of a tuner.

Like music critics, tuners were also known to be stubborn men, Domostroy told her. They might insist that,
since they didn't tell her how to play the piano, she
shouldn't tell them how to tune it, but she must be firm
with them. He also told her that once the pitch, the
volume, and the timbre of the piano had been tuned to
her liking, she should stand far back from the instrument
and listen again. Many pianists considered the piano stool
to be the only good listening post, but Domostroy was
convinced they were wrong. Regardless of where she would
play in the future—whether in the best concert halls of
the world or in acoustically less perfect auditoriums—she
must always ask her tuner to play for her while she stationed herself as far as sixty feet away or in the fourteenth
row of the concert hall, for only then could she know how
her piano would sound to the audience; and if it didn't
sound good, Domostroy insisted she should have the tuner
adjust it until it did.

Such a test was absolutely essential, said Domostroy,
because the physical characteristics of a concert hall—the
size and shape of the stage, the slant of the walls and the
roof, as well as the type of absorptive or reflective surface
they had—seriously affected the reverberation and diffu-
sion of sound.

In preparing for her visit, Domostroy had deliberately left a few small adjustments to be made in the
tuning, and now he was pleased at how deftly Donna
recognized what was needed and then followed his instructions to make the slight changes that were necessary.
She was close to him, bending over to see inside the piano
and observing how he held the tuning instrument to check
the position of each hammer and the condition of the felt

that covered it. The sight and nearness of her body aroused him. His mouth felt dry, as if desire had drained him of saliva, and to distract himself he began a meticulous demonstration of tuning.

One comment he wanted to make before she started playing, he said, was that when he first heard her play at Gerhard Osten's, he had noticed her use of the pedals, although original, seemed to be at times uncertain. His own view of the role of the pedals in Chopin's music, he remarked, might be helpful to her.

She kept silent and he pursued his point. He reminded her that even though Chopin never marked the use of the soft pedal, he realized better than most composers how important all the pedals were in coloring the sound of keyboard compositions. If used subtly and creatively, the pedals allowed the pianist to achieve rich and varied orchestral effects. But, Domostroy warned, pianists who misused or overused the pedals in an effort to cover up weaknesses in their fingering and touch only succeeded in calling attention to their deficiencies, for the slightest imbalance in technique was prolonged and exaggerated, not concealed, by improper use of the pedals.

He then asked her to play several pieces that demonstrated Chopin's fullest creative use of the pedals, starting with the Ballade in F Minor.

After closing his eyes and listening for some moments, he stopped her and asked her to repeat again and again bars 169 through 174, which called for a particularly subtle use of pedaling. Chopin started each of the initial three bars with a little splash of pedal, followed by a fast bass run without any pedal, followed by a succession of legato notes in the right hand. Domostroy told Donna not to use any pedal on the smooth right-hand notes, and when she admitted that she had always been baffled in trying to play them legato without a pedal, he told her that it was because she didn't have sufficient control in her fingering. Rather than wash the passage, he suggested, she should release the pedal as indicated in bar 169 and then, at the third sixteenth note of beat three, pedal almost imperceptibly for a split syncopated second; that would allow her to make the right-hand notes smooth while retaining an over-all effect of dry sound.

He then had her play a series of selections: the beginning of the Nocturne in F, to see whether her pedaling muffled the melody in the right hand; the Nocturne in E, which demonstrated Chopin's unique contrasts between pedaled and unpedaled sound; the Prelude in A Minor, which, except for one short passage near the end, was all without pedal; and the Prelude in B Minor, in which Chopin had initially indicated normal pedaling every second beat in bars 2 and 3—played with the left hand—but then had crossed out the markings, leaving all three opening bars in his autograph edition under one shockingly long pedaling blur.

She finished and sat looking at him like a student nervously waiting for comments from her teacher.

Being careful not to put her off, he said that he sensed in her playing two opposing forces: a desire to be free of Chopin's written notes and dynamics so that she could improvise—an impulse she probably inherited from her jazz-playing father—and a need to be letter-perfect and to adhere rigidly to every mark on the dense Chopin scores, which certainly came from her classical schooling at Juilliard. With sufficient practice, and with her obvious talent, Domostroy went on, there was no reason why she couldn't learn to fuse these drives and negotiate Chopin's most difficult passages, not only with precision, but with all the ingenuity and energy of the born jazzman. To achieve this, he felt she needed to concentrate on developing greater suppleness and strength in her back, shoulders and arms, as well as in her wrists and fingers. He also offered to show her special exercises to improve her knuckle mobility, and told her frankly that she needed to practice more, not only rehearsing and polishing the Chopin pieces, but doing more exercises and scales to refine her overall technique. He recommended to her certain exercises of Cramer and Clementi, two men who influenced Chopin's technique and his understanding of the piano, as well as works of Czerny and Hummel and Leopold Godowski's versions of Chopin's Etudes, particularly his twenty-two studies for the left hand, which contained a C-sharp minor version of the so-called "Revolutionary" Etude.

Donna listened to him carefully, and if she was surprised or hurt by any of the criticism implicit in his advice, she managed not to show it. Instead, she asked what he thought of her chance of winning at the Chopin piano competition in Warsaw. He answered with equal directness that, unless she improved her technique and increased her strength, her chances in his opinion were slight, but he added that he felt she could achieve much in a few weeks if she really worked at it.

Now she stood up, and he led her outside. It was warm and sunny, and they strolled slowly around the Old Glory, crossing the parking lot and walking until they reached the tall wire fence. Beyond, as far as the eye could see, lay a dead ghetto of burned-out tenements, black ruins scarred by broken windows and boarded-up doors, the drooping old stoops and the backyards piled high with stones and charred rubbish. They walked along a path inside the fence, and at their approach a rat scurried out of the tall grass and ran towards the ruins.

Domostroy glanced at her from time to time. In the past he had always seen her in artificial light, but here, in bright sunlight, her skin gleamed. Under the delicate lines of her brows, the long oval arches of her eyelids shone as if lighted from within, and her eyes, shaded by thick lashes, were leaf green. He kept glancing at the faultlessly etched hollows under her cheekbones, and at the subtle play of light on her lips, so full and smooth they threatened to burst open. Her beauty overwhelmed, almost stifled him; it was regal, yet unaffected, as pure as the soul within.

Someone whistled shrilly from the roof of an empty building, and when Domostroy looked in the direction of the sound he saw three members of the Born Free gang waving at him. He waved back.

"I went to school not too far from here," said Donna as they turned to walk back. She waved at the ruins. "Those black holes were always there. I walked through them often, alone or with other kids, playing hide-and-seek, fighting, chasing cats and rats, and often being chased by the riffraff who would come looking for skirts. I used to crawl into smelly trenches like those, waiting and waiting for my boy lover."

They walked in silence except for the sound of chirping sparrows that foraged on the ground and in the bushes.

"One day I heard my father singing an old blues song," she said and intoned:

> *"Come along—*
> *Done found dat new hidin' place!*
> *I'se so glad I'm*
> *Done found dat new hidin' place!*

And I said to myself that I never wanted to go back to those pits, so I made up my mind to look for 'dat new hidin' place' myself, and I knew it was going to be music. From then on my life in bondage was over."

She reflected for a minute, then smiled. "You know, whenever I try to think of myself as a serious musician, I always remember a poem by Paul Laurence Dunbar that was printed on a sampler my mother had in our kitchen:

> *G'way an' quit dat noise, Miss Lucy—*
> *Put dat music book away;*
> *What's de use to keep on tryin'?*
> *Ef you practis twell you're gray,*
> *You cain't sta't no notes a-flyin'*
> *Lak de ones dat rants and rings*
> *F'om de kitchen to de big woods*
> *When Malindy sing. . . ."*

As she finished the poem he sensed a conflict in her. He could tell that she was grateful to him for today and that she probably felt she should show it by staying with him a bit longer, possibly even letting him make a pass at her. But he didn't make a pass. Even though he wanted her, and even though, knowing that she was about to leave, he felt forlorn, he didn't attempt to detain her. He

did not want to become her lover because of any gratitude
she might have felt, and—even more than that—he didn't
want to share her with Jimmy Osten, the man in her life.
Firmly—to her surprise, he imagined—he led her to her
car and opened the door for her.

As she slid into the seat she put her hand on his arm.
"When will I see you again, Patrick?" she asked, a bit
uncertain of herself.

"Anytime you want," he said brusquely. "Just come."

"But I don't want to intrude. You have your own
work to do."

"No, I don't," he said. "Come over anytime."

"I might take you up on that," she said, starting the
engine. "Would three times a week be too much?"

The prospect excited him, but he didn't want her to
know it. " 'We will be held accountable for all the permit-
ted pleasures we failed to enjoy,' " he quoted the Aggada
and chuckled to put her, and himself, at ease. "That's
good for a start," he said. "When do we begin?"

"How about tomorrow?" she said, and he sensed in
her eagerness to let him know that his offer to help had
pleased her.

"Remember me to Jimmy," he said.

"I will," she said. "Though I doubt he has forgotten
you!" She drove off, her hair blowing in the breeze.

His feelings in utter disarray, Domostroy walked back
to the ballroom. When he turned and looked behind him,
she was gone. The parking lot was empty. Even the Born
Free members were no longer at their post.

Donna did not hide her visit to Domostroy from
Osten. She even told him of her plans to work with the
composer so that she could get as much help and advice as
possible in preparation for the Warsaw competition. Osten
could not challenge her right or her need to seek musical
help, but he resented the fact that Domostroy was the
person she had chosen to go to for it. He knew of
Domostroy's reputation and by now he was suspecting

more and more that Domostroy was the man who had photographed the White House woman and might have collaborated with her on her letters to Goddard. Finally, disturbed by Domostroy's interest in Donna, Osten decided to investigate the composer's motives, and one evening when he knew that Donna was with Domostroy, Osten rented a car and drove to the Old Glory.

Whenever he had driven in the South Bronx before, he had been on his way to somewhere else, but now, looking for a specific address there, for the first time he became aware of how closely the South Bronx resembled the slums of Tijuana. Except that in Tijuana, at least, the slum dwellers lived with the hope, misplaced though it might be, that their city, because it was so close to the wealthy United States, might one day grow into a metropolis and that their lives would become as new and straight as the new buildings and highways that were springing up all around them. There were no new buildings or highways, and no such hope, in the South Bronx.

He found the Old Glory and circled it once, slowing down when he saw Donna's car parked near the entrance to the dance hall right next to an old convertible, almost certainly Domostroy's. He knew she would be there for the whole evening, so he decided to bide his time and wait for twilight to give way to darkness.

He drove for a while through some desolate stretches, his radio blasting the latest rock blues, killing time until the moon floated out and the black walls of the ballroom turned silverish in the lunar radiance.

He parked his car outside the chain-link fence and walked into the tall grass that grew beside it, his parabolic microphone in one hand, a lighted flashlight in the other. Placing the microphone on its tripod, he aimed its dish in the direction of the light that was streaming out of the windows of the huge ballroom. He flicked on the microphone and, pressing a button, activated the machine's tantalum wind filter, which would eliminate all unwanted outdoor sounds. Then he attached the microphone to a small cassette recorder, and as through the earplugs he began to pick up the first sounds from within the Old

Glory—either Donna or Domostroy playing Chopin on the piano—he hunkered down and leaned one shoulder against the fence.

Except for the recorded piano sound, there was stillness all around him. Behind him, rows of burned-out buildings stretched away in silence. Before him, the vast gray floor of the parking lot shone eerily, and the Old Glory, with its arches, columns, carved surfaces, balconies, and sloping roofs, rose like a phantom castle.

He sat on the ground and expectantly moved closer. Just then, without warning, something hard hit him on the back of the head, and as he fell forward in the wet grass and his thoughts grew dim, he was conscious of harsh voices. Barely aware that he had been attacked from behind, he lapsed into darkness.

He came to, uncertain of where he was or how long he had been unconscious, his head feeling as if it were clamped in a vise. He was sitting in an old naugahide armchair next to a grand piano, and when he looked up and saw Donna bending over him with concern on her face, at first he assumed he was in her Carnegie Hall studio. Turning his head, he saw Patrick Domostroy holding the parabolic microphone and the tape recorder, and next to him three swarthy young Hispanics in yellow caps with BORN FREE printed on them.

"Are you all right, Jimmy?" asked Donna, patting him gently on the shoulder.

He reached up and felt a lump on his head, then glanced at his hand to see if there was blood on it. There wasn't. "I'm fine," he said, remembering out of instinct to alter his voice.

"I thought you were a student of literature—not a spy," said Domostroy, walking toward him.

The Born Frees flashed broad grins.

Osten looked at the floor. He felt like a kid caught stealing in a candy store, and the thought that he must appear ridiculous to Donna and Domostroy filled him with shame.

"I don't give a damn what you thought," Osten said

sharply. "And don't think I don't know what's been going on here!"

"What is that supposed to mean?" asked Donna, recoiling from him.

"What it says," Osten said, seizing the chance to play the deceived lover. "That you're a cheater and a liar! Well, aren't you?"

Donna's face became flushed. "You don't know what you're saying!" she stammered. "How can you be so unfair to me—and to yourself? I'm here to play piano. Don't you know how much that means to me? You have no right—no right—" She turned away, hiding her tears.

"That's some guerrilla bingo set you've got to spy with," said one Born Free, rolling his shoulders as he took a few steps closer to Osten.

"Why don't you give it back to the CIA, man?" taunted another.

"You're wasting it here, man. This ain't El Salvador. Not yet!" gibed the third.

"Take it easy!" said Domostroy to calm the gang. "He's not working for the CIA. He's just spying on her." He gestured at Donna. "She's his girl friend."

The gang members snickered, and Donna looked at Domostroy with reproach. "Patrick, please."

"He's right, Donna," Osten interrupted, anxious to mislead Domostroy. "He's right," he repeated slowly, getting up. He stretched his shoulders, winced, and looked her in the eye. "I wanted to find out what was going on between you and your music teacher." He glared at Domostroy, and the three Born Frees grinned with glee.

"You've got some nerve, man," said one of them. "You were trespassing without a visa, didn't you know that?" He looked at his pals with a wink. "This is Born to Burn country, this is abroad, man; this place split from Uncle Sam long ago, and you could get hurt by sneaking around like this. Next time we catch you, sonny boy, it will really cost you!"

"Next time I'll know what to do with you!" snapped back Osten.

By now Donna had regained her composure. She was

no longer sad, just angry. Controlling her voice, she said, "There won't be any next time, Jimmy. I think you better go now." Her voice quivered with emotion as she added, "I don't want to see you again."

"Wait, Donna," said Domostroy, "don't be too hard on him." He laid the microphone and recorder on the chair that had been vacated by Osten. "He was only trying to protect you. He was probably worried about your being out here . . . alone . . ." His voice trailed off.

"That doesn't mean he can follow me around and spy on me," said Donna, glancing at Osten then quickly turning away from him and facing Domostroy and the others. "He had no right—no right whatsoever—to do that. No one does." Her firmness seemed to leave her, and she sounded as if she might cry again, but she hastily composed herself and pushing aside a chair that blocked her way, she walked to the piano and sat down. "Let's work, Patrick," she said calmly as her fingers struck a chord on the keyboard.

Osten picked up his possessions. "I'm sorry, Donna," he said. He paused. "Maybe one day you'll understand how I feel."

One of the Born Frees snickered. Another, imitating Osten's croaky voice, said, "Maybe one day, man, we'll kick the shit out of your tight ass."

A wave of rage and humiliation swept over Osten, and turning to Domostroy, he said, "Tell your Foreign Legion to go fuck themselves." Then, still angry, he turned to Donna. "As for you, Donna—you deserve a better lover than a cheap nightclub act!"

"Why don't you just leave," Donna replied, her back to him.

He wheeled and started for the door, but one of the Born Frees blocked his path and switched open a long knife.

"Let him go," said Domostroy, barely controlling his fury. "Let him take his spying toys and go bug someone else."

When Osten was gone, Domostroy shook the hands

of the three young men. "Thanks for keeping an eye on the place," he said. "You did a great job."

"Our pleasure," said the tallest of them as he settled his cap on his head. They went laughing and chattering from the ballroom, and at the doorway the tall one turned and gave Donna a long look.

Outside in the fresh air, Osten became aware of his pain. It radiated through his skull and went all the way down to his left shoulder, affecting the movement of his arm. When he got to the car he found that someone had stolen his jacket and his wallet, which contained, in addition to more than a thousand dollars, his university ID and his California driver's license.

He threw the microphone and recorder on the back seat, got in, and headed back to Manhattan. He drove slowly, fearing that his rotten luck and his splitting headache might cause him to have an accident along the way.

In sifting out his thoughts, Osten discovered that what upset him most was not the loss of Donna, but his failure to accomplish what he had set out to do. He had no doubt that Donna had meant what she said and would not see him again, even though he doubted she was Domostroy's mistress. Frustrated at finding that he had no control over her, he also felt a sense of relief so suddenly that he was free of her, for the anxiety their relationship caused him by now had eroded the love he once felt for Donna. And though he was halted for the moment in his attempts to find out what—if anything—Domostroy had to do with the photographs of the White House nude, at least he was free to pursue Andrea, the possible subject of those photographs and the potential writer of the letters, about whom he had so far only been able to fantasize. Even if she turned out not to be the White House woman, she was still eminently worth going after.

At his sublet apartment, he chased two aspirin with a bottle of beer and put a compress of ice cubes wrapped in a towel on his head. He then tacked the enlarged photographs of the nude he hoped was Andrea up on the walls and studied them for an hour or so. Drowsy and numb by then, he promised himself he would call her first thing in the morning. Then he fell asleep.

When he awoke, the lump on his head was bigger, but the pain had diminished. Before calling Andrea, he was seized by doubt as to whether he should tell her what had happened to him the night before, and he decided finally that since there was a good chance she would learn about it from Donna, he had better tell her himself.

Andrea seemed surprised to hear from him. Trying not to betray how much he wanted to be with her, he asked lightly if she would see him for dinner that night. With seeming innocence, Andrea asked if he was planning to bring Donna. He answered that he meant dinner for just the two of them because Donna and he had split—and not under the most agreeable circumstances. As he described his encounter with Donna and Domostroy, painting himself as an innocent jerk lost among villains, Andrea's giggles of appreciation spurred him to embellish the story and he began to laugh along with her.

Before hanging up, they made a date for that night.

" 'Consort not with a female musician lest thou be taken in by her snares.' That's Ecclesiasticus, the Book of Wisdom." Andrea was speaking to Domostroy on the phone. "I had dinner with Jimmy Osten last night," she went on. "How come you had your hired hoods beat Jimmy up in front of 'Brown Sugar' Downes? Was it because you're fucking her now and wanted to show off?"

" 'Women, indeed, are the music of life.' That's Richard Wagner!" he retorted. "What's more, I resent your racist remarks about Donna."

"Oh, you do, do you?" she replied. "Now let me tell you who's the racist here. Why do you think you like Donna Downes? Because of her wonderful talent and her Juilliard schooling? Bull! You went after your tawny temptress, Mr. Hypocrite Whitecock, not because her music

made your white cock hard, not because the Harlem oda-
lisque was your spiritual soul sister, but because she was a
black go-go girl and for you, and for every other white
male sexist, black skin means slavery and black cunt means
whoredom. You tell yourself that you want Donna because
of her music and talent and other shit like that, but in fact
you want to fuck the cunt of a chocolate chippie slave.
Like any other white master going after a black ghetto
hussy, you're turned on only by her talent for entertaining
you! Deep down you know it! And your Black Carmen
knows it too!"

"Are you studying drama, or soap opera?" he asked.

"I've also been studying you, remember?"

"Then you should know that I met Donna Downes
through little Jimmy Osten—her other 'white master,' as
you so crudely put it. Or was Jimmy really in love with
her?"

"I doubt if he was ever in love with her," said Andrea. "He tells me he's had his eye on me for three
months—even before Donna ever introduced us."

"You didn't, by any chance, buy him his surveillance
toys and send him to spy on us, did you?"

"I didn't have to. He's probably sick of her screwing
around behind his back when he's away at school." She
paused. "By the way, as a lover, Jimmy has one advantage
over you," she broke off casually, as if to tease him.

"He's young," he ventured.

"Age doesn't matter," she said. "But his vulnerability
does. By not hiding it, he brings out the nurturing instinct—
the most fertile ground for sexual giving and receiving in a
woman."

"Emotional maternity wards are just not my beat,"
said Domostroy harshly.

"Just as well," said Andrea. "That's where Jimmy has
beaten you."

"I'm not in a contest with Jimmy Osten, or for that
matter, with anyone else," he said, trying to change the
subject. "The mother in you may enjoy taking up with the
boy in him, but I'm convinced it's bad for our plan. What

if Goddard should turn up and find little Jimmy milking your maternal breast?"

"Stop calling him *little*! Unless you want me to ask Donna how you compare with Dick Longo."

"You do that, and I'll—"

"You'll what?" she challenged him.

"I'll call Jimmy and tell him about you and me."

"He won't believe you," she said.

"Will he believe the photographs I took of you?" he asked. "I have copies of all of them."

"So what? They're faceless!"

"Some aren't. You were just too preoccupied playing with yourself to know what pictures I took!"

"If you do that, Patrick, I'll—"

"You'll what?" Now he was challenging her. Abruptly, realizing they were getting nowhere, he became conciliatory. "Let's stop this nonsense, Andrea. I swear I haven't slept with Donna. And I had nothing to do with the gang beating up Jimmy Osten on his childish mission impossible. I hope he knows that."

"He was very curious about you," said Andrea blithely. "In any case," she said, calmer now, "you're right when you say that he can't stay in my apartment. Goddard wouldn't appreciate it, if he ever shows up. And of course, Jimmy's accustomed to all that space in California."

"California? Why California?" Domostroy asked.

"He's studying literature and creative writing at the University of California at Davis. Postgraduate work toward his Ph.D. Boy or no boy, Jimmy's an intellectual type, you know. So if your precious Donna has left him out and alone, I just might hang around—even hang onto—him for a while."

"You go ahead and do that," he said, trying to sound offhanded. "In fact, be good to the boy. After all, what's good for the Ostens is good for Etude, and what's good for Etude is good for me. I'm still in their greedy hands, remember." He laughed. "Just be on the lookout. And let me know if anything unusual happens."

"Like what?" asked Andrea.

"Like Goddard showing up He's certainly a bigger

fish to catch than Jimmy." He chuckled. "I spent a lot of time luring Goddard with my brilliant letters and your dirty pictures. I wouldn't want to think that all my efforts were wasted because he turned up and found you in bed with"—he groaned in mock grief—"little Jimmy Osten!"

"Keep in mind," said Andrea, "that I paid you for your efforts. So I can waste them if I want to." Not amused, she hung up.

"Have you ever met Andrea Gwynplaine?" Donna asked Domostroy after one of their practice sessions at the Old Glory.

For a moment Domostroy was tempted to admit the truth. Why should he lie to Donna, the one woman he could so easily love. Why should he let his secret and insidious arrangement with Andrea threaten his open and trustworthy involvement with Donna? To what degree was he bound by his pact with Andrea?

"Andrea Gwynplaine?" he repeated. "The name doesn't ring a bell. Who is she?"

"Haven't I mentioned her to you? She's a drama student at Juilliard who also attends lecture courses in the music department," said Donna. "I think Jimmy was very impressed by her, and he's been after her ever since he started coming to Juilliard with me to sit in on lectures."

"When was that?" asked Domostroy casually.

"About a month ago."

"A month ago? Are you sure he didn't meet her earlier?" he blurted before he could stop himself.

"Of course, I am," said Donna. "It was right after Jimmy asked me to find out whether Juilliard taught the music of Goddard Lieberson—whose name I knew because of his connection with CBS—and of another composer whose name escapes me . . ." She halted. "I know," she said, "Boris Pregel, a contemporary of Lieberson's. Do you know their work?"

"Yes, I do. I even knew them." Domostroy's heart

pounded with excitement. "But go on with the story," he said, afraid she might lose the train of her thought.

"Well, actually Jimmy wanted to know whether Lieberson and Pregel were taught in music courses anywhere in the city. I checked through all the course catalogs, but they weren't—not this semester anyhow."

"Is that so?" said Domostroy, encouraging Donna's talkative mood. "I didn't know Jimmy was so musical."

"Oh, yes. He is, surprisingly. He also asked me to find out if any New York music school offered a course in Chopin's life. I guess he did it for my sake."

"And did you find him such a course?" asked Domostroy.

"Yes, I did. Piano Literature, given right at Juilliard. I took Jimmy to the next couple of lectures."

Domostroy felt lost. First, according to Andrea, Jimmy Osten studied at the University of California at Davis. Karlheinz Stockhausen had once been a visiting professor at Davis and had exerted considerable influence there. One of his students later became the creative light of ELMUS, an ensemble which, with the help of digital electronic instruments, developed music of an unusually high energy level, particularly in terms of percussion. Some of Goddard's melodies and arrangements, Domostroy remembered, bore striking similarities to ELMUS's music. And now here was Osten, who had gone to school right where ELMUS originated, hanging around Andrea, the girl who was the bait for Goddard, asking questions about Pregel and Lieberson and Chopin letters! The only reason Osten would want to know about Lieberson and Pregel would be if he had seen the letters. By now Domostroy had no doubt that there was a direct link between Osten and Goddard. Otherwise how would Osten know exactly what was in the letters to Goddard? Did he know Goddard personally? Was there a connection between Goddard and Etude Classics? Was there some way Jimmy Osten—with the authorization of his father or someone at Nokturn— could get to read Goddard's mail before it was delivered to Goddard? Then Domostroy thought, What if Goddard never received the letters? What if Jimmy Osten had intercepted them and then gone out to look for the White House letter writer on his own?

And now another thought started to trouble him. Why would Osten, who had gone after Andrea only a month ago, now claim to her that he had noticed her three months ago? Was it so she wouldn't connect the time of their meeting with the time Domostroy had mailed the first White House letter? And why would Andrea unquestioningly believe his claim and repeat it? Could there be a conspiracy between Andrea and Jimmy Osten? On the other hand, how could Osten possibly suspect—if he did—that Andrea was the White House woman? Could Osten be Goddard's emissary? And if he was, who had been so clever as to send him to spy on Domostroy and say that he was spying on Donna instead? And unless Andrea had given everything away, Osten would have no way of connecting him, Domostroy, to the White House letters. Finally, as improbable as it seemed until now, could Osten be Goddard?

"What are you thinking about?" Donna asked, interrupting his thought process.

"Oh, I don't know," he said, hesitating. "It's just that from my old days with Etude, I always think of Jimmy Osten as such an innocent kid." He paused. "What's wrong with his voice, by the way?" he asked, still uncertain.

"Some years ago he had a tumor removed from his throat," said Donna. "His father told me it was serious surgery. It left Jimmy's larynx scarred and permanently altered his voice."

"In any case," Domostroy went on, "I didn't think Jimmy was the type to spy on people." He paused, then attempted once again to sound detached. "Has he ever spoken of Goddard?" he asked.

"Goddard Lieberson?"

"No, Goddard, the rock star."

"Very seldom. And if he likes him, he hasn't said so. Even though he and I met at the Goddard Beat, he knew how I felt about rock."

It now occurred to Domostroy that Osten could have

written music and even lyrics for Goddard. After all, ghost-writing was not limited to literature.

"Given Jimmy's family background," he asked, "do you know if he's ever written music or played any instruments?"

"Jimmy is into writing, not writing music. Musically, he's very naive," said Donna. "As for his piano playing—well, his mother taught him to play a bit, that's all."

Reassured by her tone that she had told him the truth and was not herself connected to what Domostroy began to perceive as Osten's conspiracy, Domostroy then asked, "Do you suppose Andrea Gwynplaine put Jimmy up to spying on us?"

"Could be," said Donna pensively. "I wouldn't be surprised; she thrives on intrigue."

Domostroy pretended to reflect about that. "What kind of person is this Andrea Gwynplaine?" he asked.

"Beautiful," said Donna. "Bright. From an old Tux-edo Park Mormon family. They were once very rich, but she says they no longer are. Apparently, that's why she's studying drama. She wants to be a Broadway producer so that one day she can make millions on her own and put her family, and herself, back where she thinks they belong—at the top of society."

"That's quite an ambition," said Domostroy. "Is she talented?"

"Let's say she's devious," said Donna, adding with a smile, "and in drama that's talent."

"Devious? In what way?"

"In a mean kind of way," said Donna. She hesitated. "I don't know if I should tell you."

"Don't tell me if it's a secret." He could see that, at the moment, she was torn between these two sides of her nature.

"It's no secret," she said. "I've already told you what she and her friends did to me that time they invited me to watch Marcello in a porn film. Well, there was another incident, even worse. Andrea engineered it."

"What was it?"

"Well, underneath all the talk about her fine old

Mormon family," said Donna, "Andrea has a real taste for
what's sick and kinky. Especially, I gather, when it comes
to sex. She used to date Chick Mercurio, the leading
member of the Atavists, and soon after Chick made the
cover of *Rock Stars* magazine, he was busted for drugs.
Then awful stories about his life started to come out in the
press, and no one would book him for concerts anymore.
He was finished. It was from reading all the stories about
Chick that we came to realize that even though she wasn't
mentioned in them, our sweet Tuxedo Park debutante had
been into some very strange doings while she'd been
dating him. And I don't mean taking ludes, drinking beer
with a straw, painting her nails black, wearing rubber
garter belts and leather jackets; I mean sex with chains
and whips." Again she hesitated. "Andrea apparently enjoys hurting and humiliating people."

"Nothing wrong with that," interjected Domostroy,
"as long as her lovers enjoy the theatrics of it and nobody
gets harmed."

"Some were, though," said Donna. "About the same
time Andrea was going out with Chick Mercurio, she
started dating Thomas, an investment banker—young, good-
looking, New England family, pinstripe suit, vest, the
whole Wall Street thing. Well, dear Thomas showed Andrea only the best—the best theaters, the best restaurants,
the best parties—but she complained to her friends that
he bored her stiff and that he was just as unimaginative in
the sack as he was everywhere else. One day he invited
Andrea and some of his friends to his fancy Park Avenue
duplex for drinks, and Andrea happened to use his private
bathroom upstairs, instead of the guest bathroom. There,
in a drawer, poking through his things she came across
several porno magazines folded open to the classified
pages—full of sexual personals. Thomas had circled several ads from sexually dominant women who spelled out
their sexual specialties and professional services in great
detail, and in his precise handwriting he had written cryptic comments in the margins alongside! While he enter-
tained his friends in the living room, Andrea snooped
around his bedroom until she found a golf bag full of

implements that would have delighted de Sade and Sacher-Masoch. That discovery freaked her out because, as she told her friends, in his sex with her, dear Thomas had always adhered rigidly to the faith, you might say—his position strictly missionary. Feeling outsmarted, to teach him a hard lesson, Andrea embarked on an elaborate plan. She asked Chick to photograph her, naked, in a wig and high boots, with her hair straight down over her breasts and a leather mask over her face—and she placed the picture in several of the sex magazines Thomas bought. She included a typical blurb—'Mistress Valkyrie: The Balcony of fantasies, fetishes, and other pleasures. Only the refined should apply'—and gave a post office box number. She ran the ad for several weeks and waited, and at last, among the many replies she received from interested clients, she found one—long and sincere!—from Thomas pleading for an appointment. The joke might have ended there, except that his letter was rather graphic. It contained descriptions of his fantasies and of the rather unusual sexual activities he said he needed for release and fulfillment, and he volunteered to pay generously for them.

"Andrea decided he would pay indeed, and writing to him as Valkyrie she told him that before they could meet privately, he must first pass a submissiveness test, which, for her own professional safety as well as her client's pleasure, she required of all her potential customers. For bait she enclosed a Polaroid photo of herself—cut off at the head—posing in the typical skintight patent-leather costume of the sexual dominatrix. She ordered him to dress in a tuxedo and go to the Till Eulenspiegel, a seedy midtown hotel, at midnight the following Saturday. There, on the mezzanine level, he would find an empty niche behind a heavy green drape,—her favorite Balcony, she said—and he was to stand in it with his face to the wall and wait for her. She asked him to write back and promise that he would obey her instructions, and Thomas replied, assuring her that he would.

"In the days that followed, Andrea kept going out with Thomas as usual, not once letting him suspect what she had discovered about him.

"The next Saturday at midnight, Andrea arrived at the Till Eulenspiegel with Chick Mercurio and a group of her punk friends. They all went up to the mezzanine without making a sound and gathered in front of the green drape. As Mercurio readied his camera, Andrea—dressed in her extravagant leather costume—put on a leather mask and went into the niche, drawing the drape behind her. There was her dear Thomas, dressed in evening clothes and smelling faintly of cologne, his hair neatly combed and his face turned to the wall, waiting to meet his new Domina.

"Andrea—that wretched bitch—told everyone exactly what happened next. Towering like an Amazon on her high-heeled boots, she hugged him roughly from behind and dug her gloved hands into his chest. Whispering harsh but sensual epithets in a slight German accent, she bit his neck, kissed his earlobes, and pressed her leather-clad body against his, and soon he was moaning with excitement and begging her to let him turn around and see her. But she ordered him to stay facing the wall. She slowly loosened his belt and, caressing him inside his pants with her gloved hands, she let his pants and shorts work themselves down to his ankles. She kept playing with him until he started whining and pleading with her to make him submit in any way she chose. When she had him aroused—and very visibly so—Andrea quietly pulled the drape open and stepped out, exposing poor Thomas to her dear friends.

"Only when he heard the shrieks and guffaws of his live audience did poor Thomas turn and see that he was on display and was being photographed, but by then it was too late for him to do anything but reach down and pull up his pants. As he did so, he realized that among those laughing hardest was Andrea, his haughty girl friend, got up in the skintight outfit he knew so well from the photograph she had sent him."

A faintly nauseous feeling swept over Domostroy. He regretted ever having met Andrea, ever having let her lead him around. How stupid he had been to go along with her scheme and submit to her sexual manipulation.

For her sake he had done everything he could to make
Goddard curious about the beautiful woman who wrote
such intriguing and perceptive letters, curious enough to
take up the challenge and go after her—and be trapped.
Little had he, Domostroy, known that Andrea had already
carried out one such scheme—including even a faceless
photograph—all on her own, for nothing but sadistic kicks.
What, Domostroy wondered, had she in store for him
now? And what place in her intrigue was Jimmy Osten,
Andrea's newest slave, playing?

He winced. Knowing what he now knew about Andrea, the best thing he could do would be to forget the
whole affair. He had his own life to live, and he couldn't
care less who Goddard was.

When Domostroy was with Donna he was careful not
to do or say anything that might reveal his feelings for her
and thereby throw her off balance. He knew she needed
to concentrate completely on preparing for the Warsaw
competition. Several times in her piano sessions with
Domostroy, panicking at the thought that in Warsaw she
would be competing with the best young Chopinists in the
world, she threatened to withdraw from the competition,
but each time Domostroy calmed her down and convinced
her that, if only for the sake of the experience, she had to
go to Warsaw and perform there with all the artistry she
could muster.

As the date of her departure approached, Donna began
to come every morning to play for him, and he always
behaved as if he were her teacher, concerned only with
honing his student's talent and developing her confidence
to display it to others. Whenever he caught in her gaze
the slightest need of him as a man he took great pains not
to betray how much he wanted her.

But then he noticed that his feigned detachment unsettled her, and he could tell that she was waiting for his
feelings to change; this was particularly evident in the
days following the unexpected intrusion of Jimmy Osten

into the Old Glory. One day not long after that event, she gave Domostroy two photographs of herself. On one she had inscribed, "Dear Patrick, know that I'm always with you", on the back of the other she had written words he had once used in speaking to her: "Since I met you, I think of beauty as being you, not of you as a beauty."

Under his tutelage she played better and better, making the old ballroom reverberate with magical sounds. At times her sheer virtuosity and certainty of touch made Domostroy think of a remark of Schumann's: "A good musician understands the music without the score, and the score without the music. The ear should not need the eye, the eye should not need the ear." The more he listened to her, the more he became convinced that she could do very well in Warsaw, and given a lucky selection of pieces for the finals, she might even place second, third, or fourth.

If he doubted her chances of winning first prize, it was principally because he suspected most judges of inverse prejudice—of being afraid that if they awarded the first prize to a black, they would be silently accused by the public and the other contestants of having acted out of a desire to rectify a system of social injustice many centuries old, not out of impartial judgment of musical talent.

But he also doubted whether any other young pianist could match Donna's energy and bravura when it came to playing Chopin. As he sat and watched her play, he had the eerie impression that in these few weeks she had unconsciously been doing battle with the restrictions history had placed on her race and was determined now to throw them off, all by herself, through the power of her art. Could there be, he wondered, another pianist competing in Warsaw whose ambition matched such a sense of purpose—or such a desperate need to have it accomplished?

In the time since Donna had begun working with him, her fingering had improved remarkably. At times her fingers seemed to float over the keyboard like delicate seaweed timidly swaying in the incoming tide; at times they fell upon the keys, as harsh as sea coral. He noticed that now, when she played Chopin's Etude in A Minor, she actually reverted to a technique used by Chopin himself—sliding the long third finger over the fourth and fifth, particularly when her thumb was elsewhere and the third finger could play a black key. Under Domostroy's careful scrutiny she was also striving to avoid any unnecessary hand movement; in the smooth, sustained phrases, she now played as many notes as she possibly could without shifting her hand, and when shifts were required, she effected them with maximum ease and always made them coincide perfectly with breaks in the phrases. He was astonished at her musical intuition and at the freedom with which, as if she were a ragtime pianist, she could alter standard fingering when the need arose. He marveled at her precision when, in order to counteract the plodding angularity inherent in the mazurkas of a rigid musical era, she would use to the fullest all the exotic accents provided by the chains of side-stepping dominant sevenths; and he was impressed by how free she made herself with the sharpened fourth, the accented bass, the unexpected triplets, and the continuously repeated one-bar motifs.

To illustrate to her that speed was not the only means of achieving pace, and tempo never to be gauged by a stopwatch, alone, Domostroy made her listen to various recordings of the finale of the B-flat Minor Sonata, one of the most difficult of all Chopin passages. Although Rachmaninoff and Vladimir Horowitz each took precisely one minute and ten seconds to play it, Donna agreed with Domostroy that Rachmaninoff's version sounded faster and more dynamic. Domostroy concluded the lesson by telling her that if, as Beethoven remarked, tempo was the body of performance, then the black musical tradition of ragged time, and the boogie and blues of the Harlem pianists, of Duke Ellington, Luckey Robert, Fats Waller, and, much later, her father, Henry Lee Downes—must make her aware that, in the end, it would be her interpretation of Chopin's dynamics—her phrasing and pedaling—which together would create the impression of pace. As he spoke, he realized to his own astonishment that, just as musical genius had displaced Chopin to a period far

ahead of his time, Donna's musical talent had displaced
her, guiding her instinctively back in time, until she exactly matched up with the genius of the Pole.

Domostroy woke up each morning anxious not to miss
the first sound of her car, conscious of the hour only in
terms of the time he spent yearning to be with her again.
As long as Donna stayed with him, she, like her music,
filled his being, and each time she closed the piano ready
to leave him for the night, he felt anguished at the very
thought she might not want to see him again. Anxious not
to betray what he felt, each afternoon he would escort her
across the dusty dance floor to the door and then out to
her car, careful not even to brush against her body.

In the time between her leaving the Old Glory and
his own departure for Kreutzer's in the evening, he always
felt aimless, overcome by a dull fatigue, a sort of inner
stillness in which all hope that his life might change seemed
to ebb away. Alone, he would pace back and forth in the
parking lot, studying each of the slabs of concrete as if
they were pieces of a domino; or he would go back to
his room, and as a gleaming twilight enveloped the lot,
the adjacent field, and the charred buildings beyond, he
would stand at the window watching the beginning of the
night.

Even while he was working, the memory of Donna
would not leave him, and the hours he spent at Kreutzer's
were simply a long tunnel through time, leading him to,
or, it seemed to him often, separating him from Donna's
arrival the following morning. The thought that someone
might come along and take her away from him was his
constant fear, even though he knew—and told himself so a
hundred times every night—that there was no way he
could ask Donna to share her life with him. What could
she possibly want of him? His age alone offered no
prospect of reversing, or even delaying, the obvious outcome of his life.

And yet he wanted her. He wanted her because she

was young and because he was not; he wanted her to need him, and through her desire—even if it were only for a borrowed moment—to see himself once again as a man worthy of love. His longing was also sexual, for only by physically possessing her, could he ever hope to gain—even at the risk of humiliation and rejection—a sense of being himself again.

Each night after work he would drive across the bridge to Manhattan and go from one after-hours bar to another, from one adult club to the next, like a stray cat, alert to every sound, killing hour by hour the time that separated him from Donna.

In the morning, his quest for her sealed behind a conventional smile, he would greet her with a simple handshake and a friendly kiss on her cheek, then go directly to the pieces they would work on that day. Never once did he let his tone betray how agonizing it was for him to maintain this cool indifference.

As the time approached for her departure for Warsaw, Donna became more and more disturbed. In a mere matter of days she would be competing in a foreign country before an audience of strangers and a panel of judges whose cold, unbiased assessment of her playing would influence the whole future course of her life.

Her cushioned existence at Juilliard—where she had always had a strong sense of being worthy of attention—was now threatened. In the real world, she might well come up against failure, even disgrace, and it seemed to her that neither her family nor her friends—of whom she had few enough to begin with—could understand her entrapment, much less give her comfort and advice. She knew that Domostroy could give her that, yet, as if to hurt her, just when she needed to know how he felt about her and her chances in Warsaw, he had chosen a self-imposed coolness as his way of being with her.

Preoccupied with these thoughts one morning, she sat down at the piano and, in preparation for strenuous exertion, unbuttoned the top of her blouse and loosened the belt of her skirt. Without looking at him, she began to play the great A-flat Polonaise, remembering to hold back any unnecessary exuberance in the opening phrase but then exploding into life in the next four quavers with such strength and passion that the sounds which seemed to radiate from under her fingers sent quivers and vibrations to the farthest corners of the vast ballroom.

She stopped halfway through the piece, thought for a while, and then started to play the *Etude in Thirds*. Domostroy watched her left hand and recalled one of the first lessons he had given her. He had told her that because the main melodic lines in most music written for the piano were in the high register—meant to be played by the right hand—many pianists, even extremely accomplished ones, involuntarily treated the left hand as important only when it carried the melody; they tended to slacken the thrust of the left hand when executing slow notes with it while at the same time playing notes at double or triple the speed with the right hand. Handling such a passage now, Donna showed that she had taken the lesson to heart.

Breaking off, she moved easily into "The Wish," the gay, subtle mazurka, the words of which, "If I were the sun in the sky, I would not shine except for you . . ." she had often heard Domostroy quietly humming.

Again she stopped midway in the piece and switched, this time to the Waltz in F Major, which, because of the feline shifts in the first three beats of its principal eight-quaver motif, had been nicknamed "The Waltz of the Cat."

She stopped once more, then closed the piano. Wordlessly she folded her arms and laid her head on them, hiding her face from him. She could hear the sound of Domostroy's heels echoing on the parquet floor as he got up and walked over to her.

He restrained his impulse to sit next to her, denied himself the luxury of inhaling the scent of her body. Instead, he remained standing and leaned against the piano.

"Why did the cat stop waltzing?" he asked.

"I don't feel like playing," she said.

"Why not?"

"What's the use?" she whispered in a resigned voice, her face still hidden from him.

"The use? To play well," he answered softly.

"For whom?" She spoke into her arms without looking up.

"For others. For those who, like me, want to hear you," he said. "To give them pleasure. To make us feel something that, without you, we might never be able to feel."

She straightened up, and when she looked at him he saw that she had tears in her eyes.

"I don't care about the others," she said through her tears. "They can't live my life for me or think my thoughts." Her lips trembled, and tears rolled down her cheeks and fell on her blouse. "Why, Patrick? Why?" she asked in choked tones.

He moved closer until he was standing next to her. In the bright shaft of light that fell on her from an overhead spot, she looked like a statue made of liquid bronze.

"Why—what?" he asked.

"You used to care about me," she said in a small voice, "and you don't anymore. Why?"

He gave her a gentle pat on the shoulder, no different from a buss on the cheek.

"I care about you—more than I care about anyone—or anything else," he said very slowly, still in charge of his feelings.

She raised her head and turned toward him. Full of light and tears, her eyes seemed pure green. She bit her lip and said, almost in a whisper, "You care, yes. But I thought when I first came here—you were in love with me."

"I still am," he said, removing his hand from her shoulder.

He turned and walked a few paces away from her, stopping in the shadow, afraid that she might read the emotion in his face. "I love you, Donna. More every instant I'm with you."

"Then . . . why didn't you . . . haven't you"—she fumbled for words—"ever asked me to stay with you? You must know how I feel about you!" she burst out.

He walked back to the piano and stood facing her.

"If I haven't, Donna," he said, "it's because I was afraid that one day, when you were strong and secure, you might look back and think I had used you when you were frightened and weak and dependent on my help."

He halted, then gave in to his own truth. "As long as I'm not your lover, you know I love you for more than just your beauty."

She stood up, glanced around, and silently, calmly, took the pin out of her hair and let the thick, shiny mass fall over her shoulders. Then, with her back to him, unhurriedly, as if executing a long and docile musical passage, she unbuttoned her blouse, unzipped the side of her skirt, took them both off, and lay them on the piano bench. She stepped out of her shoes, then her panties, and turned to him.

He thought she would come to him, but she didn't. Naked, the shaft of light cascading down over her shoulders, breasts, and thighs, she swept her clothes off the bench, sat down at the piano, opened it, and began to play. The doleful, madly lyrical sound of the Scherzo in B Minor grew and grew until it flooded the huge ballroom with Żal, that Slavic mood of hopeless rancor.

Looking at her and listening to her play, Domostroy knew that what he had been waiting for would finally happen. The moment seemed now subject only to his wish, yet he felt himself making an effort to postpone it, fearing that when it came, he might become impotent, or, like the men she had talked about in her life—passive, eager to please, unable to impose or receive. Instead, after letting his gaze wander over her body, he stared at her slender hands and her supple wrists, and he watched her fingers, suddenly stretching whole tenths with ease, expanding to summon a third of the keyboard, so strong and quick and mobile that it seemed as if they were free of her arms, moved at last by the same spirit that made her breathe.

Domostroy knew that to overcome the sense of inwardness and achieve lucidity needed to produce harmonious sound, the player had to be perfectly at ease, coordinating his own physical rhythm with the flow of the music. The slightest stress affected the player's hands, wrists, and shoulders and hampered the performance, diminishing the quality of the sound, harmony, rhythm, and melody. Now, he could hear, the longer Donna played, the more tense and uncertain of herself she became.

His sexual impulse on edge, he forced himself to concentrate fully on her playing, noticing that everything about her—her hunched shoulders, her rigid neck, the stiff movement of her legs, her soundless sighs, even the way she lifted her hands from her lap to the keys—indicated anxiety, a sense of doom, defeat, surrender. Within minutes, her music was as out of breath as she was. The energy seemed to have gone out of her playing; the sound that had been flowing through her from within had lost its buoyancy and seemed to come only from the music sheet over the keyboard, as separate from the pianist as she was from the instrument she played.

If she were to leave for Warsaw right now, he thought, her inner turmoil would destroy any chance she might have of winning or even placing high in the competition. He knew that no amount of warming up, no physical or mental exercise alone, could ever remove such deeply implanted disquiet or free her from her stage fright long enough to win.

He moved toward her, a player himself now, reaching for the keys, in full expectation of what he was about to do and longing to do it, but filled with fear that his touch might go awry and spoil the very first measure, out of which the entire piece would have to flow. He must try now to do what every pianist tries to do at the start of a concert—let himself be moved by an impulse coming no longer from his hands or wrists or arms or shoulders but, rather, from the deepest place within him, his soul.

He stopped and stood only inches behind her, but

she went on playing as if she were not aware of how near he was. And even though he stood so close to her that he could feel the warmth of her body and smell her scent, it seemed to him that he was standing away from himself, and that by touching her he could bring himself back to his own reality, which for so long now he had been afraid to confront alone.

Reaching out, he touched the nape of her neck and pressed his fingertips gently against her skin. A ripple ran through her, but she continued to play. Her flesh was firm to his touch but as he pressed harder it seemed to soften, and he wondered whether its initial resistance had come from her or from some weakness in his tactile sense, some failure to judge how much force to summon through his own hands and arms and shoulders in order to caress her. He slid his hands over her shoulder blades, and her shoulders and torso shifted subtly in response. As she kept on playing, his familiarity increased with each gesture, and he grew more secure in his movements, until he felt the tension within him dissolving, his inhibition dissipating, and he knew that only his clothes remained an obstacle to the full freedom of his contact with her. Now that his sense of himself was no longer a blur, he could delightedly stroke her neck and shoulders and spine with the fingertips of one hand while he undressed himself with the other.

Naked, he brushed his chest and belly against her back, and she shivered and leaned back in order to meet his pressure, and then her hands were no longer steady on the keyboard. She stopped playing, and uncertain what to do with her hands, she turned and faced him. He took her by the shoulders and held her steady, as though he were afraid she might topple over, and an overpowering sensation of need and anguish rose within him. All that mattered to him now was to infuse her with his presence and to make his being incarnate with hers.

Gently he turned her around to face the piano, and she placed her hands on the keys and began at once to play "Spells," a sweet, sad song by Chopin. The ten-bar phrase of the strophic melody brought back some of the words which he had sung as a boy listening to his mother preparing for her own Chopin concert in Warsaw:

> *When I sing with her, I'm in awe;*
> *When she goes away, sorrow without measure;*
> *I want to be merry*
> *And I can't!*
> *Without doubt,*
> *These are spells!*

Leaning over her shoulder, careful not to press too heavily on her, he let the tip of his hard, protruding member touch her back, further proof of his nearness, as he kissed her neck, her chin, her ear, and brushed his cheek against her hair.

As he bent over her, his elbows touching her shoulders, he let his hands play with the lightest touch on her breasts, the cushions of his fingertips barely sliding over her nipples, leaving them standing up hard and pointed, then over the aureoles, then under her breasts, over her rib cage, down toward her navel, then back, then downward again. His fingers descended hesitantly along the skin on either side of her belly and moved between her thighs to her groin. His hand pressed more firmly now, until the palm of one hand settled over her groin and his fingertips descended again, stroking, spreading and entering her flesh.

With his chest pressing on her back, his face next to hers, his hands between her thighs, Donna kept on playing, her body swaying under his touch, languorous, on the way to being overcome by desire.

Just when her torso seemed no longer willing to support her arms, and her hands seemed to resist movement as if separated by an invisible accordion that she could no longer open and close, she began to play "Out of My Sight," one of Chopin's expressive two-strophe songs set to a poem by Adam Mickiewicz, which she and Domostroy both loved. She had often sung it for Domostroy while she played it on the concert grand:

In every place, during every
day and night,
Where with you I wept, where with
you I played,
Everywhere and forever I shall be
by you,
For there I left a piece of
my soul.

Not allowing her to interrupt her playing, he sat next to her on the bench. Lifting her gently, he moved under her and slowly lowered her onto his thighs, entering her, filling her flesh with his, steadying her yielding body with his chest, rocking rhythmically with her, sliding in and out of her, drawing her tighter until she began to shiver and tremble and moan feverishly. Her fingers lost their fluid motion then, and her hands dropped from the keys, no longer airborne, no longer free to move on their own.

He lifted her again, pushed the bench away, and lowered her to the floor. With their clothes for a cushion and the empty seats of the ballroom as their audience, she clung to him at once tender and giving, brutal and selfish.

They drove to the airport in his car, Donna's two large suitcases—one filled just with evening gowns for her competition performances and state dinners in Warsaw—taking up most of the backseat. She sat close to him, and he drove with one hand, keeping his other arm around her shoulders and occasionally mussing her hair or touching her neck with his free hand. Wordlessly she took his arm from around her shoulders and clasped his hand between her thighs. With her chest rising and falling and her breath quickening, she moved closer to him, bringing his hand deeper into her, warming it with the heat of her flesh. Clinging to him, she leaned her head on his shoulder, raised her eyes to his face, and emitted a low moan through dry, parted lips.

Even though she had asked him to go with her to

Warsaw, and even though he could have made the trip
with the money he had saved from Andrea's payments, he
had decided that it was important for Donna to be in
Warsaw on her own, without his censoring eye and ear,
with only the audience she yet had to conquer.

Her mother and four younger sisters would be waiting for her in the departure lounge, she said, and she had
been told that the press would be there to interview her.
Domostroy convinced her that she should greet them
alone. At the airport he pulled the car up to the curb, got
out and opened the door for Donna, handed her luggage
to a porter, then turned from her and slipped back into
the car as her relatives and the reporters, cameras flashing, started to advance on her. Always eager for visual
novelty and memorable faces, the media had found in
Donna Downes the perfect subject through whom to cover
the much-publicized Chopin competition.

By the time Domostroy had parked the car and entered the terminal, Donna was surrounded by a solid wall
of camera crews and reporters, who had managed to steer
her family off to one side. He could barely see her for all
the shoulders and elbows in the way, but whenever he
caught sight of her, she looked intense and beaming, and
she answered the endless questions with poise and quiet
self-assurance. He saw her glancing around, looking for
him, but each time she did he ducked out of sight, having
decided that the moment belonged to her alone.

Her interview ended when the pack of press people
disappeared to cover the arrival of a plane bringing back
the bodies of American servicemen killed somewhere in
Latin America.

Accompanied by her family and a few friends from
Juilliard, Donna moved slowly toward the boarding gate,
still looking for him. He followed behind, hidden by a
group of beefy East European bureaucrats who were march-
ing in a block toward the gate. When she had given up
hope that he would get there in time to see her off, she
said good-bye to all the others and reluctantly moved to
pass through the security checkpoint. Then he stepped
out and waved, and like a child surprised by a gift, her

expression changed. She ran to him and hugged him, and while her mother watched in embarrassed wonder, mildly disapproving, and her little sisters giggled and gazed wide-eyed, Donna kissed him lingeringly on the neck, on the eyes, on the mouth, and he, now oblivious of the stares of her family and the other onlookers, let himself kiss her too, his arms around her, his mouth on hers.

Then it was time to go. She pulled away, and looking only at him while waving at her family, she walked through the gate and down the long passageway. He watched her until her tall silhouette was swallowed up inside the corridor that led to her plane. Smiling and giving a modest nod to her relatives, he turned and started for the exit, but after a few steps he was accosted by a short bespectacled woman in thick-soled sneakers and a broad-brimmed hat with straw flowers on it. "Excuse me, sir," the lady entreated, her pale watery eyes magnified by thick lenses. "Wasn't that beautiful young lady you just kissed somebody famous?"

"Not yet, Madam," Domostroy replied patiently, "but she will be by the time she comes back."

"I thought so!" the woman cried triumphantly, flashing her dentures. "I thought so," she repeated. "I can always tell a famous person!"

IV

∧∧∧∧∧∧∧∧∧∧

VI

Andrea had agreed to meet Osten again that night for dinner. In the afternoon he went to his bank to cash a check, and while he was there he started for the safe-deposit vault, thinking that he would examine the White House letters once more for thoughts and phraseology that might prove revealing But he changed his mind, deciding that he would do better to take the automatic minisensor tape recorder with him.

He met Andrea at the Stage Fright, a cozy restaurant near Lincoln Center, known for its good menu and hand-some staff—all actors and actresses who worked there between engagements. In an organza blouse and close-fitting silk skirt that outlined her body, with her hair falling in long waves over her shoulders, Andrea looked stunning, and once again he thought how much taller and better proportioned she was than the nude in the photographs.

They talked about Donna's departure for Warsaw, which they had both seen on TV Then, as if to distance him further from the memory of Donna, Andrea told him about Donna's affair with Dick Longo, the porno star, and the story made Osten laugh even though he felt a twinge at discovering the identity of the well-endowed man from Donna's photo album.

Seized by the need to be close to her, Osten told Andrea that after meeting her for the first time in Juilliard's cafeteria he had been curious to know whether she was dating anyone steadily And now that he knew her a bit better, he admitted to wondering whether there was someone as important in her life as Donna had been in his until recently.

For a moment Andrea looked somber. Then she said she had no boyfriend. Most of her time was taken up by her studies, and many of her weekends she spent with her parents in Tuxedo Park, the place where she had grown up, which held only pleasant memories for her. Maybe one day, she said, he might drive up there with her to swim in their pool under some of the oldest oak and cedar trees in the state.

The more they relaxed with each other, the happier he was that he had not read the White House letters again in order to study the words and phrasing in them. This way he could listen to Andrea without ulterior motive, lost in the enjoyment of her clear, well-articulated ideas and the pleasant sound of her voice—so different from Donna's speech, which, owing to her upbringing, he had found somewhat mannered.

"Why didn't you ask Donna about me?" Andrea asked matter-of-factly. "I'm sure she would have come up with some old school gossip," she added as an afterthought.

"Much as I liked your looks," he said, "at that point I wouldn't have risked making Donna jealous."

They stared at each other in silence.

"After you and I spoke briefly in that cafeteria, though, I began to think about you often," Osten went on. Then a memory stirred him, and he said quietly, his eyes downcast, "I started to see you—in front of me—even when I shouldn't have."

"When?" she asked in a low voice.

"When I was making love to Donna," he said, meeting her stare again. "I would close my eyes and feel I was with you. I couldn't stop myself. There you were—like a premonition."

"A premonition . . . of what?" she asked, subdued by his frankness.

"Of falling in love," he said, and only after hearing his own words did he realize how simple and direct his desire was. "With you," he added, reaching out and gently putting his hand on hers. He felt her pull away. "That's the first time I've touched you," he said softly, almost apologetically.

"I like you, Jimmy Osten," she said slowly, weighing each syllable. "A lot. I liked you even when you were with Donna. I was a bit jealous of her. I felt—and hoped—that there was no real energy between you two. That you were together but not with each other, as far apart as black is from white. I'm glad it's over. Glad for you, and—why lie?—for myself, for us."

They soon had no more to say of how they felt about each other. Instead, he asked her to tell him about her life, and he listened, enraptured, while she talked of her flying lessons, her forays into skydiving, her experience of reviewing music for *Soho Sounds*, the avant-garde rock music paper, and most of all, her hopes of becoming a producer of Broadway plays and musicals.

The evening flew by. Driving Andrea home, he noted that she sat as far away from him as possible. He took it as a signal that she was not yet ready for further intimacy, although all during dinner he had given her every indication of his desire.

He respected and even admired her reserve. Taking his cue from her, getting out of the car to escort her to the door when they arrived at her building, he left the engine running.

"Aren't you coming up?" she asked, her voice again perfectly matter-of-fact.

"Isn't it too late—for you, I mean?" he stammered, suddenly uncertain of himself.

"Not at all," she said. "I don't have any classes tomorrow. What's more, I'm an insomniac! 'Macbeth has murdered sleep,' " she quoted.

While Osten parked the car across the street, she waited for him at the front door. In the car, his gaze fell on the bag containing the tape recorder. He hesitated. His instinct told him to forget about it. Not since his time with Leila had he been so eager to be with a woman, and he recoiled from the idea of treating Andrea as though she could be an accomplice to someone as perverse as Patrick Domostroy. Furthermore, Osten noted, nothing she had said to him so far sounded remotely similar to any of the thoughts or phrasing in the White House letters.

Still, in that split second before slamming the car door, he thought that if there was the slightest chance that Andrea was the letter writer, he had to know it, and he quickly and unobtrusively grabbed the tape recorder out of the bag and slipped it into the inside pocket of his jacket. Then he rejoined Andrea.

As he climbed the stairs, feeling acutely conscious of her nearness, he regretted that he couldn't be honest with her and simply tell her who he was and why he had to conceal his identity.

He liked the orderliness of Andrea's apartment—the well-chosen antique furniture, the neatly arranged notebooks, the family photographs in silver frames, the dusted shelves of books and records. She got out a silver box that held a plastic bag of pot, a packet of papers, and a little cigarette-rolling contraption. As she was showing him her collection of antique perfume bottles he came and stood behind her; then, with a step forward, he took her by the shoulders so that their bodies touched. He turned her around to face him. She hugged him gently, looking into his eyes for a moment, and then went to open a bottle of wine, talking to him over her shoulder all the while, saying that although she needed more sleep than most people, she had great trouble getting enough of it. She then asked him if he'd like to put on a record, adding, jokingly, that she had a few Domostroy records in case he'd care to refresh his memory of that composer. As he bent down to look at her record collection he quickly hid the tape recorder behind a pile of albums. Its automatic timer would activate it the following morning.

He glanced through her records, noting with pleasure her complete collection of Goddards. He was tempted to play one, but decided against it and went over and turned on the radio instead.

She brought the joints and wine, got out an ashtray and a silver roach holder, and sat on the bed next to him, sinking into a bank of pillows and tucking her legs up

under her. They began to smoke, and the smoke drifted
slowly about the room.

"Speaking of the devil, have you ever met Patrick
Domostroy?" he asked, watching her closely.

"No, I haven't," she said, "but I know a few things
about him." She seemed so at ease that he felt she was
telling the truth. She sipped her wine and passed him the
joint. "My parents met him a number of years ago in
Tuxedo Park. He used to date a woman writer who lived
near them. Is he an interesting person?" she asked, gazing
at him. Then she laughed. "Not that I expect you to be
objective on the subject!"

"I'm not." He laughed too. "Even my father, who
never says anything bad about anybody, doesn't think
much of Domostroy's way of life."

"How about his music?"

"My father calls it overly visceral," said Osten,
"rudimentary and premeditated. He attributes these quali-
ties to Domostroy's unnatural preoccupation with sex."

She seemed genuinely interested. "What kind of sex?"

"I don't really know," said Osten, "but I remember
some years back—I was just out of high school, I guess—
when Domostroy horrified all the guests at a party of my
father's with a filthy story about Chopin."

"I wonder if he told such stories to Donna," said
Andrea, laughing.

"She wouldn't like it. She idolizes Chopin."

"What was the story?" Andrea asked.

"Everybody knows that Chopin was into sex—George
Sand and all the rest, right? But because he had tubercu-
losis, many of his adoring contemporaries said he couldn't
help it. They put him on a pedestal and used his disease to
excuse his peccadilloes. According to Domostroy, to preserve Chopin's good name—or what was left of it—his fans
kept a whole body of letters, memoirs, and other written
accounts from being made public. But Chopin's more
objective contemporaries wrote about the composer's relationships, and these documents were preserved in archives
and libraries. They've been gone over by many critics and
historians, including Domostroy himself."

"Why would Domostroy do all that research?" said Andrea.

"I guess in order to write a book about it, now that he can't compose anymore, and possibly to prove his own point—which, I gather, is that fucking around is one way of getting rid of one's chaos, isolation and timidity. And for a genius that's good for art! I read a few books on Chopin myself, and I found out some strange things about him. Chopin was involved with a certain Marquis de Custine, and with Custine's rather slimey circle of friends."

"Was Custine as bad as that other marquis?"

"The Marquis de Sade? Hard to tell. De Sade made up most of his sexual antics, but Custine didn't have to: he and his friends—Chopin among them—acted theirs out.

"It was Custine who had turned his spectacular villa into a scene of perverse doings where Chopin was often the *pièce de résistance*—though he didn't resist very hard.

"Domostroy claimed—in all seriousness—that excessive sex prolonged, or even engendered, Chopin's artistic life. It combated his insularity and routine. It made him less withdrawn. According to him, the disease kept Chopin's temperature so high that he was in a constant state of sexual heat, and any sexual activity raised his body temperature even more—enough to kill some TB bacilli, so that his body's resistance to the remaining ones was strengthened! Supposedly, after an orgy, Chopin actually felt better and was therefore able to go on writing music and performing and, of course, go on fucking around! All of which he did—without any consideration at all for his sexual partners, many of whom he no doubt left with TB—before herpes, the most infectious disease going! Pretty sick, isn't it?"

"Fucking around? Or suffering from TB?" asked Andrea gaily. "You obviously love all these literary rumors. You must be awfully good in your field."

They had finished the second joint. As if their movements had been choreographed, they moved toward each other. His hand slid under her hair and he embraced her neck; her arms encircled his shoulders. Gently, he laid her down next to him and, leaning on one elbow, looked into her face. The marijuana made her eyes shine so that she seemed to be daydreaming. The mood of his earlier longing for her reasserted itself and, as memories of watching her passionately from afar turned into present thoughts, he tenderly swept the hair off her cheeks and neck, and lowered his face to hers, kissing her forehead, her cheeks, her neck and her shoulders, but not yet her lips, giving her the chance to kiss him first and start him on a chain of events from which, once it began, there could be no pulling away.

She did kiss him on his lips, first slowly, then more rapidly, her tongue touching his, pushing, then pulling back, her mouth pressing on his, her hands behind his head, bringing him closer as she slid one thigh under him. He was engulfed in her now, with one hand on her breast, the other kneading her thighs, lifting her skirt, his fingers feeling the heat of her groin, the moisture of her flesh.

Still kissing, reluctant to stop touching, they started to undress, twisting and entwining their bodies. She slipped out of her blouse and let him pull off her skirt and panties, and with her bare feet she rolled his pants and shorts down to his ankles so that with his own feet he could free himself of them.

She was naked now, open to him. As he glanced down the length of her body, the drug took hold of him and the image of the faceless White House nude came between Andrea and him like a transparent curtain. Dimly, before he took her, he realized that, similar as the two women were, there was no proof in the photographs that the woman either was—or wasn't—Andrea. But all that mattered now was the relationship that he was about to initiate by entering her flesh with his own.

Osten woke up around noon. Andrea was still asleep. He got out of bed and went quickly into the bathroom, being careful not to waken her. He felt queasy and he had an awful headache; the pain in his temples began throbbing from the glare of the bathroom light. The pot had not agreed with him, either because he was not used to smoking so much or because it was stronger than the stuff he occasionally smoked in California.

He dressed quietly and got ready to leave. Andrea's face was turned away from him. He would let her sleep. He crouched down in front of the shelves and reached behind the records. Instead of removing the tape recorder—his initial reaction—he reset it.

In spite of his headache, he felt exhilarated. Even though he only vaguely recalled what had taken place during the night with Andrea, he knew that he had been at ease and happy in their lovemaking. He remembered her saying how free and abandoned he made her feel, and later, when the pot had raised them to frantic, passionate heights, he knew he had gone further with Andrea than he had ever dared to go before with a woman.

He went to his apartment and took a long bath, and while he soaked he recalled after some effort that Andrea had talked a lot about her fascination with the occult. He also remembered something about automatic handwriting. With both of them high on pot and lovemaking, in a cloud of incense, and with one small candle for light, she had made him write something with his eyes closed. Almost in a trance, in a silly, abandoned mood, he had written—what? He could not recall. Was it his name? A phrase from *Macbeth*? He remembered Andrea saying that his handwriting would tell her more about his thoughts than he ever could.

He had found Andrea as natural as Leila, and fun to be with—full of delightful contradictions: a serious student of drama, bright and well informed about music; at the same time, she was a believer in magic and astrological signs, charmingly naive.

She had played him her favorite records—mostly Chick Mercurio. That had amused him, for it made him remember that when Goddard's first record went on the airwaves and hit the record shops, its spectacular sales promptly topped the sales of Chick Mercurio and the Atavists, the most popular punk rock group of the moment, and nudged them out of the number-one position on all the charts. A few weeks after that Osten had read in the papers that Chick Mercurio had gone berserk. The New York police had picked him up with enough heroin in him to supply a platoon of addicts. He was hospitalized, and tales of his sordid sex life filled the columns of the sensational press for several weeks. As a result, Chick Mercurio and his group disappeared as rapidly as they had emerged.

That was some six years ago, and if Andrea still played the Atavists, she obviously did not spend much time keeping up with the changing tastes of the country. At least she listened to Goddard too, he told himself, something that Donna never did.

And even though Andrea was mainly a drama student, with music as her minor subject, Osten was impressed as much by her thoughts about musical form as by her physical beauty. She was a firm believer, she had said, in musical innovation, and she felt that Western instrumental music was impoverished in terms of pitch. She believed that only the new electronic equipment and sound could lead to real rhythmic and melodic freedom—perhaps to the rediscovery of new values of intonation.

He wanted to call her, but she had said she would be busy for a day or so. Meanwhile, every time he thought of the tape recorder, he grew embarrassed and apprehensive. He promised himself that he would remove it the first chance he had. Andrea was no less proud than Donna, and if she were to discover that he was spying on her, it would wreck any chances of his ever being with her again.

Osten stared hard at the enlargements of the White House nude, trying to decide whether anything in the shape and texture of that body matched his fresh image of Andrea—nude, inspiring, relentless in her lovemaking—an image he was reluctant to let fade.

He felt eager to be with her again. There was something so reassuring in her easy acceptance of him. She hadn't pried into his past, questioned his social and aesthetic values, or found fault with his family background—all of which Donna had done. And unlike Donna, who focused her talent and creative energy on the piano to the exclusion of virtually everything else, Andrea had many other interests and an abundance of charms and accomplishments. She had shown Osten her poetry, and he had found it as profound as her sexual limericks were funny; her caricatures, drawings, sketches, and designs were all well thought out and faultlessly executed; and her attempts at writing plays and screenplays, she had told him, were considered promising at Juilliard. Even though he was just getting to know Andrea, he had already discovered striking differences between her and Donna. Donna's disposition was somber, obsessive; Andrea was easygoing, carefree. Donna was all seriousness; she had no time for jokes or games, and would never indulge in such learned superstitions as astrology or palmistry. Andrea, playful by nature, loved such things and did not need to hide her interest in parascientific fields, for she obviously had numerous serious interests as well. Osten smiled on remembering her utter conviction that she could gain valuable insight into his subconscious mind by minutely studying his handwriting. For Donna, sexual passion was a force so excessive and intense that she could not control it or share it properly; it conquered her from within long before her lover could claim her for himself. But Andrea, beautiful and passionate as well, brought to sex both reserve and assurance; she was happy letting her lover bring about her surrender to physical pleasure.

In a flash, Osten foresaw a time a few months, or possibly weeks off, when he would take Andrea on a trip through California. He would show her the splendor of the Anza Borrego Desert, with its oases of fan palms and rugged canyons and steep ravines, and he would identify for her the strange, far-off cry of a coyote. Then he would take her through Julian to the ranch on the nearby hill. Slowly, pretending he was not sure of the way, he would maneuver the car up the driveway and through the gate. He would stop at the main house, and they would get out,

and as if he had never been there before, he would open
the door for her—to the New Atlantis and to his entire
past.

The phone woke Osten. It was Andrea.

"Please, help me," she said, her voice shaky. "I'm in
trouble."

"Where are you?" asked Osten. He felt groggy and
disoriented, and a glance at the clock told him it was late
evening. He had slept all day.

"At the Old Glory. You know, Domostroy's place—
where you went the other day . . ."

That threw him. Only yesterday she had told him she
didn't know Domostroy.

"What are you doing there?" he asked.

"I'll explain when I see you. Please, Jimmy, you must
come right away—do you remember your way? Take the—"

There was authentic urgency in her voice.

"I know the way," he interrupted. "Don't worry. I'm
leaving right now."

In the car, his mind was racing. If Andrea knew
Domostroy, she might actually be the one who had written him, Goddard, all those astounding letters. He hoped
she was, for then at last he would have someone lovely,
intelligent, well educated, and refined to love. And hadn't
she already admitted to her love for him? With her fascination for drama and music, she was the perfect partner to
share his creative secret. Then his thoughts strayed to
Domostroy. What was his role? Was he only her photographer—or had he played another part in what might be
a plot to unmask Goddard? But whose plot was it?

The gate to the Old Glory was open, and two cars
were parked at its entrance, the door of which also was
open. Osten parked next to Domostroy's vintage convertible,
and ran inside. All the lights were on in the ballroom, and
the grand piano gleamed on the stage. The musicians'
stands and most of the furniture were covered with dust
sheets, making the place look like an abandoned stage set.

As Osten entered he heard rapid movements behind him, and when he turned he saw Patrick Domostroy, pale and disheveled. Standing behind Domostroy, wearing tight rubber gloves and holding a gun against his back, was a dark-haired man in an open shirt and baggy pants. The man's face, in spite of the large dark glasses, looked faintly familiar to Osten. Next to them, in a sweater and jeans, stood Andrea, also wearing rubber gloves and holding a gun, which was unmistakenly pointed at Osten.

"How are you, Jimmy?" said Domostroy, his lips white.

"Shut up," said Andrea. "Take your jacket off—slowly," she told Osten, "and drop it on the floor."

"What is all this?" Osten asked, still uncertain as to whether or not they were joking.

"Do what she says," said the stranger, his gun still at Domostroy's back. When Osten hesitated, the man screamed, "Do it! Now!" and his voice echoed through the ballroom. As he screamed, Osten recognized him, for he had seen that same face only recently on one of Andrea's record album covers.

"You're Chick Mercurio, aren't you?" said Osten, taking off his jacket and throwing it at Andrea's feet. "What is it you want?" he asked Andrea. His chest was frozen with the dread of losing her.

Still training her gun on him, she bent down and with her left hand felt the pockets of his jacket. Then she reached into an open attaché case on the floor and pulled out the tape recorder he had left in her apartment. "Surprise, surprise!" she said, holding it up. "We won't need this anymore, will we?" She smashed the recorder against a table, and reaching into the attaché case again, she pulled out a writing pad.

She threw it to Osten, and he caught it. "There's a pen inside the cover," she said, and when he had found it, she continued. "Sit down and write the following."

Puzzled by the scorn he heard in her voice, Osten became resentful.

"What if I won't?" he asked her. "Will you kill me?"

"Don't tempt her," said Mercurio. "Just do what she says."

When Osten still did not move, Andrea gripped her gun with both hands, spread her feet wide, and aimed at his groin.

"Write!" Mercurio screamed.

"Write, Jimmy," Andrea seconded in a quiet voice, "or I'll shoot you right in the gut."

"What do you want me to write?" asked Osten, picking up the pen and sitting at the nearest table, searching his mind for some reason that could bring Andrea and Mercurio together.

" 'Dear Andrea,' " she dictated as Osten began to write. " 'I was here around four o'clock, but you weren't home, so I'm leaving this under the door. Patrick Domostroy has asked me to see him tonight. He says that if I don't come' "—she waited for Osten to catch up with her— " 'he will tell others who I really am, and I can't let that happen.' " She paused once more, then continued.

" 'Ever since he smoked me out with those clever White House letters he wrote to me care of Nokturn, he has been blackmailing me for money, wh.ch I have always paid him. Now he wants more, and if I don't deliver, he threatens me with exposure. I can't refuse to talk to him, but the man is insane and I would feel safer with someone at my side when I see him.' " Andrea stopped again, and in the silence of the ballroom, Osten could hear only the sound of his pen.

" 'For that reason' "—she resumed dictation—" 'I hope that you and Chick can come to the Old Glory in the South Bronx, where Domostroy lives. I'll be there around eleven o'clock tonight. It's urgent. Love, Goddard.' " When Osten finished writing and started to put down the pen, she said, "That's not all!" She reflected for a moment, then went on. " 'P.S. Please keep the papers I gave you well hidden. I don't trust Domostroy!' "

Osten finished and looked up at her. "Is that all?" he asked.

"No!" Andrea snapped back. "Toss me the notebook."

He threw it on the floor next to her, and she picked it

up and put it in the attaché case, from which she took some legal-size sheets covered with dense typing. Pointing her gun directly at his head, she walked over and lined up the folded-over pages in front of him, then quickly backed away. He smelled her perfume. It reminded him of the last time he had smelled it on her body; that seemed long ago now.

"Sign them—the original and each copy—as both James Norbert Osten and as Goddard," she commanded. "Every place there's a cross. And no tricks with the signatures!"

Osten signed the documents, dropped them on the floor, and kicked them over to Andrea, who picked them up, examined the signatures, and replaced them in the attaché case, a jubilant smile on her lips.

"May I ask what I've just signed?" Osten asked Andrea angrily.

"Your last will and testament, that's what, dated three months ago," said Chick Mercurio. "All drawn up by a legit lawyer and stamped by a notary public."

"Thank you, Jimmy," Andrea said. "I see you signed them properly and in good faith."

Osten stared at her blankly, stunned. "Meaning?" he asked with contempt.

"You idiot! Don't you remember signing your name for me at my place when I told you all that stuff about automatic writing?"

"I was stoned," said Osten.

"I should hope so," Mercurio snorted. "That pot was a lot stronger than any regular grass. You had to have been a zombie!"

"He was," said Andrea, laughing disdainfully. "He was like a sleepwalker. He didn't even know where he was! Twice he called me 'Leila' and did everything I told him to do, including singing 'Volver, Volver, Volver' for me in Goddard's voice!"

Osten noticed Domostroy staring at him.

"I'm amazed, Jimmy," Domostroy interjected, "at how you can change your voice. I would never have guessed you were Goddard."

"I use a modified microphone for singing and my

gruff voice for talking," said Osten, changing to his normal voice, and in answer to Domostroy's puzzled frown, he said, "though, honestly, I doubt that anyone listening to even my normal tone would think of Goddard!"

"Fascinating," said Domostroy. "And I even suggested to Andrea once that Jimmy Osten was nothing but a 'cuckoo . . . a wandering voice . . . an invisible thing . . . a mystery!' Now I feel like a fool!" He laughed.

"You shouldn't," said Osten. "Here I was ready to call my next record 'Andrea'!"

"Enough of this," said Chick Mercurio, prodding Domostroy with the gun. "Andrea, you watch this one here while our Iron Mask music man and I retire to the kitchen for a talk."

As Andrea trained her gun on Domostroy, Mercurio stepped over to Osten. "Come on," he said with a sweep of his gun. "To the left and through that door over there! Move!" he screamed, jabbing Osten roughly with the gun.

"Chick, do you have to?" asked Andrea.

"Yes, I do!" Mercurio called back as he pushed Osten into the kitchen.

"What is your friend going to do?" Domostroy asked Andrea in a falsely genial tone. "Eat Jimmy alive? Or cook him first?"

"Since when have you been so concerned about Jimmy? You were never afraid that Donna would eat him, were you?" she asked. "How is our Sepia Snatch by the way?"

"You know she's in Warsaw." Domostroy was suddenly concerned about Donna's safety. "And she knows nothing about us, believe me, Andrea," he pleaded.

She nudged him with her gun. "I hope not—for her sake!"

He suppressed his anger. "Tell me, how did you find out that Osten was Goddard?"

"I suspected him the minute he showed up with Donna at the piano literature class where we'd been studying Chopin's letters. You and I quoted one in the last letter to Goddard, remember? That tipped me off, especially when he looked over everyone in the class and began to zero in on me. He obviously suspected I might

be the girl in the pictures. That's when Chick and I went
to work making up a will for Jimmy to sign, just in case.
And then Jimmy told me that he first noticed me three
months ago. He lied: when Donna introduced us, she said
he'd been in town only for a month or so. The night he
came to my apartment I felt something in his pocket—and
when he was asleep I checked his jacket again and it
wasn't there anymore—so I knew he had hidden something in the room. Then I found the tape recorder. Now
why would Jimmy Osten want to spy on poor little me?
And during the night, high as the sky on my special brand
of pot, he wondered aloud if my tits would get bigger and
their nipples larger if he were to make me pregnant, and
made a big thing out of my shaved cunt. And finally,
humming that Mexican song in his real voice! That was the
giveaway! I knew it was time to check his signature and
handwriting in preparation for this event!" She paused,
then added as an afterthought, "That's all I ever wanted
in the first place!"

"And thanks to me, your 'Godot finally come and
we'll be saved,' " he quoted, hoping to soften her.

"Not 'all'. Just I and Chick."

"Tell me," Domostroy went on, "do you and your
friend intend to kill Jimmy and me—and arrange it to look
as if we killed each other? Or—in keeping with my supposedly uncurbed snake-charming nature—will I kill myself after I've killed him?"

"You'll see," said Andrea. "After all, I'm the drama
student here!"

"And now you have graduated to crime. That's a cruel
Endgame!"

" 'Cruelty is an idea put in practice.' That's from
Artaud," she laughed. "In practice, then, as you and
Jimmy leave the stage, by Goddard's last will and testament I become the sole legal heir to his entire current
estate—including, of course, all future royalties from his
music. How many millions did you say our invisible boy
was worth? Fifteen? Seventeen?"

"I didn't say," said Domostroy. "You must have gotten that information from one of your other sources. Tell

me something—why did you pick me in the first place?"
he asked her, not certain whether he wanted to know her
answer.

She looked at him with an expression of disdain and
pity.

"You probably think I picked you because you've
seen a lot and been to a lot of places and met a lot of
people. But you're wrong," she said. "You weren't even
the first. Before you, I hired, one after another, three
other men in the music business, each one better informed and more accomplished than you, and a better
fuck too. But they all failed to find Goddard. So I zeroed
in on you, Domostroy, because—for all of your music and
experience—you were always a loser, and I knew I could
get you cheap. Furthermore, you're such a selfish, calcu-
lating, obscene son of a bitch that I somehow sensed you'd
be mean enough to flush Goddard out!"

Just then a piercing cry of pain echoed in the ballroom, and Domostroy shuddered. Without a word Andrea jammed her gun into his back and prodded him to
walk toward the kitchen. Without a word he obeyed.

There they found Jimmy Osten standing with his
head partially inside the walk-in freezer, his mouth open
and his tongue, extended to its full length, stuck to the
frozen metal wall. A frightful moan came from his chest.
Behind him stood Chick Mercurio, dangling his gun and
laughing at Andrea's look of astonishment.

"Chick! What are you doing?" she yelled.

"All I have to do is give one hard pull, Andrea," he
said, "and we can get a good look at the most hidden
tongue in America!" He reached for Osten and was about
to pull him away from the freezer when the door behind
Andrea burst open and two of the Born Free gang ran in,
pistols in hand, training them from close range on Andrea
and Mercurio.

"Drop the gun!" one of them shouted, and in that
instant Mercurio turned to the voice that had called out
and fired point-blank. As the Born Free tough collapsed
on the floor, blood gushing from his belly, he returned

Mercurio's fire with deadly accuracy, striking him in the throat.

Almost simultaneously, Andrea fired at the other Born Free and blew his chin off. A second before he sank to the floor his finger squeezed the trigger of his gun and sent a bullet ripping through her chest. In a moment Mercurio was in a spasm, with blood pouring out of his mouth; Andrea lay motionless on her back, her eyes dimming and a widening circle of blood seeping out from under her sweater. Then, all became still and quiet.

Too shaken to move, Domostroy stood there numbly, watching the blood from the bodies begin to form a pool: they were all dead. The collapse of his and Andrea's plot came so suddenly, so fast, and so furiously, that it left him blurred, cheated and betrayed, an overly irrational or naively contrived ending in an otherwise niftily designed adventure story. But then a fear stirred him: if Andrea had lived, he could have been tried as her accomplice in the Goddard extortion scheme. He wondered if any jury on earth could possibly have found him innocent. He imagined day after day of sensational headlines and never-ending press and television accounts of all the lurid aspects of the deal he had struck with Andrea to unmask Goddard. The past brouhaha of his alleged secret musical collaborators was comical by comparison with what the media could do with this hideously bloody drama. He thought, too, of Donna, an innocent bystander, dragged into all this simply because she had responded to his love. A judge could well have sent him to jail for years, ending his life as he had lived it till now.

Domostroy forced himself to step closer and bend over Andrea. With his thumbs he closed her eyelids. Then he touched her neck. She was warm, as if resisting surrender to the void. He thought of her when she had been his, filling the space and time around him with vibrant beauty, her flesh—so doomed now—a source of joyous surprise each time she let him touch it. If it were in his power, he wondered, would he want to bring her back to life? To embark with her on yet another adventure?

A stern inner voice told him the question was an idle

one. She was dead. The kitchen's fluorescent lighting gave her loosened hair a bright sheen; her lips, parted by her last breath, were pale, her face white. He turned to Chick Mercurio. Faithful to his pose in life, even in death the singer had kept his eyes covered by the dark glasses, and his hand was still holding on to his gun. Nearby the two dead toughs lay grotesquely still.

Osten's strangled moan brought Domostroy back to full awareness. Gagging, swallowing sour bile that suddenly filled his throat, Domostroy found the switch to the freezer, turned it off, and began soaking towels in warm water and applying them to Osten's tongue, gradually freeing the delicate tissue from the metal surface.

Shaking, Osten turned and looked at the four bodies, his face as pale as theirs; then, without a word, he skirted the pool of blood and walked out of the kitchen.

Domostroy followed.

In his room, Domostroy helped Osten, his body still racked by shivers, to apply an antiseptic to his tongue and his burned lips.

"I have to call the police," said Domostroy, trying in vain to control his own trembling. "You'd better take off—fast."

"Won't you need me as a witness?" mumbled Osten, barely able to speak with his swollen tongue and torn lips.

"One witness should be enough," said Domostroy.

"What will you tell the police?"

"I'll tell them," said Domostroy, "that my old friend Chick Mercurio and his girl friend, Andrea Gwynplaine, came to visit me. And that some Born Free members, friends of mine who keep an eye on the place for me because I live alone, arrived unexpectedly. Each side thought the others were intruders, and before I managed to intercede, they panicked, pulled out guns, and opened fire. The police can see the rest. That's all."

"Won't the police wonder why all your friends were armed?"

"Maybe. But they also know that plenty of people are armed in the South Bronx," he said.

"I suppose that's good enough," said Osten. "Before I

go, will you answer one question?" He looked Domostroy in the eye.

"What do you want to know?" asked Domostroy.

"Were you in on this?" asked Osten. "Did you help Andrea and Mercurio find Goddard?"

"Only Andrea," said Domostroy. "All she told me was that she wanted to meet you."

"And the letters?"

"I wrote them," said Domostroy.

"You wrote them all?"

"Yes. All. Except for the quotes from Chopin's letters." He smiled.

Osten gave him a long look. "Then—" he faltered for a moment, visibly moved, "you have understood me, and my music, better than anyone else ever has."

"Maybe there're others who understand you just as well! Think of what insights you might be missing in all the fan letters you have no time to read!" said Domostroy. "By the way, what made you think that I had anything to do with the whole thing? All the clues in the letters led to Andrea. There was nothing—and no one—except Andrea that could possibly have led you to me."

"Yes, there was. Just one thing. The pictures," said Osten.

"The pictures? But they were all of Andrea. There wasn't a single trace of me in them!"

"There was one. The uncommon angle in one of them," said Osten.

"What angle?"

"You once photographed Vala Stavrova from the same angle—the camera's angle—from low, near the floor, in order to catch her thighs, I guess. I'd seen the picture you took of Vala; it's in my father's bedroom. I even thought you might have repeated that strange angle on purpose, to lead me to you if I didn't find Andrea!"

"I didn't," said Domostroy. "I wasn't even aware that the angle was strange! But Vala! What a slim chance!"

"No slimmer than any other," said Osten. He picked up the battered tape recorder and carefully put it into Andrea's attaché case.

"Are you sure you won't need me to back you up with the police?" asked Osten.

"Positive," said Domostroy. "In any case, you have your name—Goddard—to protect."

Osten looked at him. "You won't tell anyone what you know about me?" he asked quietly.

"What for? What I know about you won't make me or my old music any hotter," said Domostroy.

"Thanks," said Osten. "My father tells me that Etude sales have picked up substantially in recent months. And in spite of that old bogus exposé, your records are still the pride of their Contemporary Classics list!"

"Good," said Domostroy. "Too bad I don't write music anymore. Where will you make it next?"

Osten picked up his jacket and the attaché case. "In the New Atlantis," he said. "The House of Sounds."

"Francis Bacon's?" Domostroy asked. "I once lived there too!" He laughed.

"How about you? What will you do?" asked Osten.

Domostroy stood up and buttoned his jacket. "I'll just stay here—and wait for Donna," he said.

"I hope she wins in Warsaw," said Osten. "Tell her I wish her luck."

He walked out of the ballroom, and only when Domostroy heard his car leave and knew Osten was safely away did he pick up the phone to call the police.

There was no TV at the Old Glory, and Domostroy wanted to catch Donna on the late-night talk show she was scheduled to appear on, so he went over to Kreutzer's. It was his night off, and to avoid being recognized by reporters, who had been hounding him for days for a statement about the murders, he wore dark glasses, a false mustache, and a hat. Even though the initial impact of the shooting of Chick Mercurio, Andrea Gwynplaine, and the two Born Free gang members had died down—GORY AT OLD GLORY one early headline had read—the police investigation was still going on, and Domostroy's name and occasional pictures of him were still appearing in the press.

As he thought of Goddard—now that he knew who he was—Domostroy imagined him quite secluded in his daily life, even though as a musician he was in touch with millions of people. Like Domostroy, he probably had few acquaintances and fewer real friends. Yet by remaining hidden from his public, Jimmy Osten could at least make what he wanted of his life and keep his art in the jukebox. Domostroy, on the other hand, because of his former celebrity as a performer and composer, could never separate his life from his art; and since his composing had ended, his life had become his only art—aimless as the path of a steel ball in a pinball machine. To Goddard, the public success of his music undoubtedly would always be a source of pleasure and reassurance; for Domostroy, bereft of his will to compose, the sources of pleasure and reassurance had narrowed to an occasional feat of sexual intimacy—as challenging now in its originality as writing music once had been.

With a painful twinge, Domostroy recalled the time in his own career when he was pursued around the clock by interviewers, music company executives, TV and film producers, and fans. What if he, like Goddard, had decided then or earlier to escape all publicity and live his life in seclusion, or in disguise? Would he have done this to save his music, or by appeasing his enemies and detractors save himself from the notoriety of a public scandal? But such speculation seemed useless. Yeats was well aware that the artist's notion of his life was, by nature, inseparable from his art, when he wrote:

O chestnut-tree, great rooted blossomer,
Are you the leaf, the blossom or the bole?
O body swayed to music, O brightening glance,
How can we know the dancer from the dance?

Now he began to ponder what his life would be like if he were Goddard. Would he withdraw to the safety of a remote estate by the sea or to a faraway country retreat?

Or would he, out of perversity, prefer to inhabit the Old Glory? Would he, out of boredom or creative necessity, challenge his fate from time to time by performing in public, perhaps in the very same pinball joints he was forced to perform in now?

The more Domostroy imagined himself as Goddard, the more convinced he became that, were he indeed the mystery star, he would live his life just as he lived it always, giving in to what was natural in him. For life lived against the spiritual prompting that gave rise to it was like a stream running uphill, bound in time to flood its own source.

To Karlheinz Stockhausen, whose electronic compositions so clearly influenced Goddard, a musical event was without a determined beginning or an inevitable end; it was neither a consequence of anything that preceded it nor a cause of anything to follow; it was eternity, attainable at any moment, not at the end of time.

Whether one liked it or not, weren't life's events like that too? Domostroy wondered.

The TV suspended over the bar was on, but no sound came from it. *Tuning to Time* had just started, but Donna was not scheduled to appear until later in the show.

On the stool next to him sat Lucretia, a hooker he had often noticed in the place, who, for reasons that escaped him, had never in any way encouraged him to make use of her charms. Lucretia was black, good-looking, in her late twenties, and she always dressed in the subdued manner of an eastern coed. Owing to her discreet manner and proper appearance, the management of Kreutzer's tolerated her hanging out there. In spite of Domostroy's disguise, Lucretia recognized him instantly, and putting her hand on his arm and assuring him that he was her guest that evening, she ordered him a Cuba Libre and a champagne cocktail for herself. After taking a few sips of her drink, she moved closer to him. "I'm sorry about that freaky accident at your place," she said. "What a terrible thing, having your friends kill each other like that! And that Chick Mercurio—he was so cute!"

Domostroy lowered his head as if in grief.

"I read in the paper about Donna Downes, that black piano player," she resumed in a confidential tone, "and how she said that you helped her quite a bit. She said you were like her guiding spirit, that without you, there was no way she could have won that big prize in Warsaw." She paused. "That was a nice thing to do—help a black girl make her way in the world."

"Donna Downes is a hard worker," said Domostroy a bit harshly. "Believe me, she owes nothing to anybody."

Lucretia gave him a skeptical glance. "Was there something between you two that you don't want to talk about?"

"There was nothing," said Domostroy, annoyed.

Lucretia assumed a conspiratorial look. "Tell me," she said, "are you married?"

"I'm not," said Domostroy.

"Any kids?"

"None."

"Is your family still alive?"

"No. All dead."

She thought for a moment. "How did they all die? I mean—from a disease?"

"Some from War, others from old age," said Domostroy. "Why do you ask?"

"Never mind," she answered firmly. "How old are you?"

He told her his age.

She gave him an appraising once-over. "You've got too many wrinkles for your age!" she said. "And you look tired. How do you feel?"

"No complaints." He was amused.

"That's because you don't smoke and don't eat a lot, and you take good care of your body," she said. She hesitated. "Now, I've got something you just might be interested in," she blurted out.

"What's that?" he asked, struck by her determination.

"I'm thinking," she said, "of having a baby. I'm the right age to have one." She gave him a long look.

He said nothing.

"And I want my baby to have the best of everything," she said. "I can afford it. I've worked the streets ever since I was twelve, and I've saved a lot. Now, I mean, a lot," she repeated. "It's all safely stashed away," she reassured him, a slight warning in her tone.

He watched her as she spoke.

"I could get married," she said, "but the guy would surely want to know what I'd done before. Mind you, I'm not ashamed of being a professional girl. It's just that I don't need a hassle. All I want is a father for my kid. That's all. A father—not a husband."

"I understand," said Domostroy, nodding.

She gulped the rest of her drink. "Now, if you and I were to go on a trip—" She paused to see if she was going too fast for him, but he smiled at her. "Just the two of us. A trip to some of those countries you see on TV. Like Hong Kong or Brazil? Maybe even around the world. In eighty days!" she added with a laugh. Then becoming serious, she went on. "I've got enough money for both of us to enjoy everything. Boat, plane, train, first-class travel, fancy food, the best hotels, the nightclubs—you name it. And I'm healthy. I'm clean. No herpes. No clap. None of those female infections. I take good care of my body. I know I'm also a good lay—that's one thing you learn to do well in my line of work—no John has ever complained." She paused. The bartender handed her another drink and she sipped it. "You wouldn't regret making a baby with me. I'll even show you my money in advance if you don't trust me."

"I've seen you around," said Domostroy. "I know you're not a cheater."

"You get what I mean, don't you?" she asked.

"You want me to stick with you until you've got a baby in you."

"I want you to stay with me until my kid is *born*, mister," she stated firmly. "All nine months. And then I want to have my baby in the best clinic there is, in one of those countries—Switzerland or Sweden, right?—where they treat all babies, black and white, alike. A baby, white or black, needs a lot of love right from the start." She stared at him steadily.

"And then what?" asked Domostroy. "What do we do after that?"

"We come back here," she said as if she had already lived the experience, "and you go your way—and I go my way. The kid stays with me."

"Do I get to see you and the baby—afterwards?" he asked.

She sighed. "No, you don't. It's my baby then. As far as you're concerned, we never had it. That's the deal. What do you say?"

He waited a moment. "Why me?" he asked.

"You've got music in you. It said in the paper that you used to write music, play the big time, make big dough, be on TV, even in the movies! I want my kid to be like that—to make it on his own, depend on no one. But I ain't no piano player; I've got no talent to give him." She paused. "Also, I bet you'd be good to a black girl. You helped that Donna Downes!" Again she paused. "The paper also said you've traveled a lot and knew important people—you'd know where to go and what to see. You could get the best doctors and the best clinic. And if you took me there as your lady, they'd respect me and the baby right from the start. All I know" —she moved her hands in a weary circle—"is the South Bronx. I haven't even been to Atlantic City!" She finished her drink. "We could leave anytime. All you'd need to do is tell me what kind of clothes and suitcases I should buy. For both of us, I mean—"

"I'll be frank with you, Lucretia," he said, moved by her candor. "I would like nothing better than to go with you, but I can't. I wouldn't be good enough company anyway. You deserve the best."

He could see that she was hurt, but she tried to cover up her feelings by striking a pose and applying fresh lipstick. She paid for the drinks, tipped the bartender, and slowly turned to Domostroy.

"Is it," she asked, "because of me?"

"It is not," he said with utter conviction. "Believe me, it is not."

She looked at him long and hard. Satisfied, she asked, "Another woman?"

He nodded, and a smile softened her face.

"Would it be that girl—Donna Downes?"

He nodded again.

"I thought so," she said, and she got up and walked over to the jukebox. She read through the list of selections, then dropped a coin and pressed a button. As she headed out of the bar, the room filled with the soft sound of the blues of Champion Jack Dupree:

> *I woke up this morning, found my baby gone,*
> *I woke up this morning, found my baby gone.*
> *Well, she wrote me a letter,*
> *sayin' one day I'll be back home.*

Domostroy's eyes returned to the TV set over the bar, its sound still turned down because of the jukebox. He watched the host of the show make signs of introduction and point at a curtain upstage. The TV audience applauded and Donna entered—all in silent motion. Once more, looking at her from afar, as if he had never met her, he became aware of her unequaled beauty. In a long black gown, her hair swept into a crown, she could have been a star on a Hollywood movie set. Domostroy watched as she sat down to chat with the host, an affable, good-looking Californian, as also an amateur musician known, on occasion, to play the piano to amuse his viewers. Although no sound came from the TV set, Domostroy could tell Donna was talking about her victory in Warsaw and her plans for the future.

Even before her return, Domostroy had watched television news clips of the competition, including shots of Donna's astounding victory, and he had read numerous newspaper accounts of it. In contrast to the chilly demeanor of the other competitors and the aura of rigor that permeated the recital hall, Donna, from her first appearance on the stage, had been herself, entirely at ease, more spirited and more lissome than any other player, but also the most finished as an artist and the most dependable; and from under her fingertips music had emerged that was just as lusty and exciting and immediate and emotionally charged as she was.

From the start she had dominated the piano—and the audience and judges—with the astounding dynamics of her musical stride, her thorough knowledge and control of the score, and her rare ability to convey her feelings fiercely and directly to her listeners.

He had watched and heard her play Chopin's Seventh Etude in C-sharp Minor, one of Chopin's greatest, most nostalgic works, but also the longest, most complex, perhaps most difficult cantabile for the left hand ever written. In her hands the etude's two melodic themes, two voices— the impulsive male, the soulful female—had been brilliantly distinct, as reluctant to fuse as to separate, passionate in their remote keys, hushed in the quiet interludes, then culminating with classical precision in the immense breadth of the dominant theme. As he listened he recalled a time when she had played this etude for him and he had recited Chopin's words of advice: "One's aim is not to play everything with an even tone. The property of a developed technique is to combine a variety of shading."

In Warsaw, Donna had not forgotten her lessons at the Old Glory. He had seen how composed she was when the computer tallied the votes of the jury and declared her the clear winner, how graceful and dignified she remained in accepting her prize. He had admired the tact and wisdom of her short speech and been profoundly touched by her brief mention of Żal; she had said it was a quality she felt she shared, through the music of Chopin, with all the people of Poland. He had seen and read about the reception given her at Żelazowa Wola, the composer's birthplace, and about the open-air concert she had given in the shipyards of Gdansk, the birthplace of Solidarity, where she was surrounded by thousands of working men and women who cheered her as if she had come out of their own ranks to win the coveted prize.

Then he had met her at the airport, amid the incredible hullabaloo the media staged for her arrival, and had driven her, tired but excited, straight to the RCA Building to tape the talk show he was now watching.

The show's host made a gesture of invitation; Donna rose, and the cameras followed her as she walked to the center of the stage and sat down at the grand piano. While she played, the camera angles alternated: there were images of her hands on the keyboard, close-ups of her face, long shots of her body, and close-ups of her feet on the pedals.

As he watched Donna play on the screen, watched her calm, studied movements and her perfect poise, he thought of the other side of her he knew. He remembered her as his lover, who after piano practice had run to him desperate in her need. He thought of her, her cheeks flushed, taking her clothes off with a moan on her lips, then helping him undress, throwing off the pillows and bed cover, pulling him down onto the bed, sinking to his groin, her hands and mouth on him, twisting and straining and stretching, until he would lay her down like a baby with a fever, and prompted by her clenched teeth, her thrashing legs, the shaking of her hands, her sudden cries, her rumpled hair, the look in her eyes, her flailing body, he would spear her with all his strength, his feelings flowing into her from the center of a persona that seemed no longer his own—from an archaic self, a self without a name, whose existence he knew of but could not identify. He remembered her in what seemed like a sensual trance, wrapping herself around him, clinging to his shoulders and thighs as though an inch of space between them would create an unleapable chasm. Then her lips and tongue would seek his mouth, and she would scream and cry at his every movement. After recoiling in an orgasm, she would rush back to him, pleading for more, drenched in sweat, weeping; she would hug him, only to disengage herself, almost brutally, and then, biting her tongue, her eyes cast down, her fists clenched, she would hit him again and again on his face and chest until, in order to defend himself, he would pin her down, his arms on hers, his knees over her shoulders. She would stop for an instant, and then, pleading, grabbing his hips, she would crawl under his legs and bury her head between his thighs. At her climax, screaming and crying, her orgasm ripping through her, she would strain under him, her breath ragged, her lips dry; she would not let him pull away from her but would cling to him, quaking, refusing to stop, urging him to move against and inside her, to restore the tension she felt slipping away, to prolong the release that was already fading.

On the television screen, Donna finished the short piece, bowed gracefully to the audience, and then went back to chat again with the host. She was his final guest, and at the end of the show the two of them got up and waved at the audience, their silent image quickly obliterated by a beer commercial. Domostroy finished his Cuba Libre, gave his place to a standing customer, and stepped away from the bar.

At the billiard table two pool sharks argued over a point of strategy. In a telephone booth, a drunken middle-aged woman, screaming incoherently into the receiver, caught Domostroy's curious glance and, furious at him, kicked the door shut. Next to the billiard table three youths apathetically fought star wars on the screen of an electronic computer game, and in a space adjacent to the bar an elderly black couple hesitantly tap-danced to the rock from the jukebox.

It was late, almost too late to do anything but go to sleep, and he wasn't sleepy. By now, back at her Carnegie Hall studio, fatigued by her TV performance, Donna must know that he would not be coming to be with her, that she would sleep alone.

Once again, he thought of the note Donna had sent him from Warsaw: "If you haven't guessed it yet, I love you. If I am reluctant to admit it even to myself, it is because I am unsure as to where I stand in your life."

His decision not to see Donna weighed on him like a heavy cloak. The awful events at the Old Glory had stained his reputation; the gossip columns had brought back the past in allusions to his unsavory conduct. Even his music had come, once again, under attack, being described as derivative and unwholesome with a tendency toward disagreeable dissonance. It was obvious that his presence would not benefit Donna's public image, and so he decided to leave her alone. She had to be alone, in order to go from one success to the next, as she undoubtedly would; just as he, a witness to failure—which might one day still befall her, as it might any artist—had to remain alone, in his own refuge.

He had nothing to do, nowhere to go. He could always take the car out. He'd heard about an artist's loft in Soho where a group called A Better Way to Love held after-hours encounters—but it was raining, and he dreaded driving all the way downtown with his windshield wipers on, their measured sweeps reminding him of a metronome.

He turned to a pinball machine, a popular model called the Mata Hari, its ONE TO FOUR CAN PLAY and GAME OVER signs still flashing from the previous game. The Mata Hari's lighted glass panel portrayed a scantily clad woman reclining voluptuously on a sofa and triumphantly handing a document to an elderly gentleman. The picture's caption read, "The secret map, Baron!" Domostroy's eyes lingered on the woman, young and slender, the curves of her body delectably smooth and sensuous.

He dropped a coin into the slot. Where GAME OVER had been a second before, BEGIN GAME now began to flash at him. He pressed the button, and the first ball popped up into the shaft, but for a moment Patrick Domostroy could not make up his mind whether to play it or not.

ON KOSINSKI

Jerzy Kosinski has lived through—and now makes
use of—some of the strongest direct experience
that this century has had to offer.

TIME

To appreciate the violent, ironic, suspenseful, morally demanding world of Jerzy Kosinski's novels, one must first acknowledge the random succession of pain and joy, wealth and poverty, persecution and approbation that have made his own life often as eventful as those of his fictional creations.

He was born in Poland. The Holocaust of World War II claimed all but two members of his once numerous family. During the war, sent by his parents to the safety of a foster parent in a distant village, he eventually found himself fleeing alone from place to place, working as a farm hand, gaining his knowledge of nature, animal life—and survival.

At the age of nine, in a traumatic confrontation with a hostile crowd, he lost the power of speech. After the war, reunited with his ailing parents he regained his voice in a skiing accident.

During his studies at the state-controlled Stalinist college and university in Poland he was suspended twice and often threatened with expulsion for his rejection of the official Marxist doctrine. While a Ph.D. candidate in sociology, he became an aspirant (assistant professor) and grantee of the Polish Academy of Sciences, the state's highest research institution, where he specialized in the study of individual versus collectivity and the sociology of American family life. Attempting to free himself from state-imposed collectivity, he would spend winters as a ski instructor in the Tatra Mountains, and summers as a social counselor at a Baltic sea resort.

Meanwhile, secretly, he plotted his escape. A confident master of bureaucratic judo, Kosinski pitted himself against the

State, which had already refused to grant him and his parents permission to emigrate to the West. In need of official sponsors, and reluctant to implicate his family, his friends and the academy staff, he created four distinguished—but fictitious—members of the Academy of Sciences to act in that capacity. As a member of the Academy's inner circle and a prize-winning photographer (with many exhibitions to his credit), Kosinski was able to furnish each academician with the appropriate official seals, rubber stamps and stationery. After two years of active correspondence between his fictitious sponsors and the various government agencies, Kosinski obtained an official passport allowing him to study in the United States under the auspices of an equally fictitious American bank "foundation" and to pay for his ticket to New York in local currency. While waiting for his U.S. visa, expecting to be arrested at any time, Kosinski carried a foil-wrapped egg of cyanide in his pocket. His punishment, had he been caught, would have been many years in prison. "One way or another," he vowed, "they won't be able to keep me here against my will." But his plan worked. In December 1957, following what he still considers the singularly creative act of his life, Kosinski arrived in New York able to—as a result of his sociological studies—read and write in English without any difficulty, though only with a rudimentary knowledge of spoken American idiom. "I left behind being an inner emigré trapped in spiritual exile," he says. "America was to give shelter to my real self and I wanted to become its writer-in-residence." He was twenty-four years of age—his American story was about to begin.

He started his life in the United States as a part-time truck driver, moonlighting as a parking lot attendant, a cinema projectionist, a photographer, and a driver for a black nightclub entrepreneur. "By working in Harlem as a white, uniformed chauffeur I broke a color barrier of the profession," he recalls. Studying English whenever he could, he perfected it well enough to enroll as a Ph.D. candidate at Columbia University and obtain a Ford Foundation fellowship. Two years later, as a student of social psychology, he wrote *The Future Is Ours, Comrade,* a collection of essays on collective behavior—the first of his two nonfiction studies. An instant bestseller, it was serialized by *The Saturday Evening Post* and condensed by *Reader's Digest* He was firmly set on a writing career.

After his publishing debut he met Mary Weir, the widow of a steel magnate from Pittsburgh. They dated for two years and were married after the publication of *No Third Path,* Kosinski's second nonfiction.

During the years with Mary Weir (which ended with her death) Kosinski moved with utmost familiarity in the world of heavy industry, big business and high society. He and Mary traveled a great deal—there were a private plane, a multi-crew boat, and homes and vacation retreats in Pittsburgh, New York, Hobe Sound, Southampton, Paris, London and Florence. He led a life most novelists only invent in the pages of their novels.

"During my marriage, I had often thought that it was Stendhal or F. Scott Fitzgerald, both preoccupied with wealth they themselves did not have, who deserved to have had my experience," Kosinski once said. "At first, I considered writing a novel about my immediate American experience, the dimension of wealth, power and high society that surrounded me. But during my marriage I was too much a part of that world to extract from it the nucleus of what I felt. As a writer, I perceived fiction as the art of imaginative projection and so, instead, I decided to write my first novel about a homeless boy in war-torn Eastern Europe, an existence I'd once led and also one that was shared by millions of others like me, yet was still foreign to most Americans. This novel, *The Painted Bird*, was my gift to Mary, and to my new world."

His following novels—*Steps, Being There, The Devil Tree, Cockpit, Blind Date, Passion Play* and *Pinball*, all links in an elaborate fictional cycle, were inspired by particular events of his life and written in Kosinski's own unmistakable, highly individual style. He would often draw on the experience he had gained when, once a "Don Quixote of the turnpike," he had become a "Captain Ahab of billionaire's row." "Few novelists have a personal background like his to draw on," wrote the *Los Angeles Herald Examiner*. Translated into many languages, his novels have earned Kosinski the status of an international underground culture hero, accompanied by official recognition: for *The Painted Bird*, the French Best Foreign Book Award; for *Steps*, the National Book Award. He was a Guggenheim fellow, received the Award in Literature of the American Academy and the National Institute of Arts and Letters, as well as the Brith Sholom Humanitarian Freedom Award, the polonia media National Achievement Award, and many others.

While Kosinski was constantly on the move, living and writing in various parts of the United States, Europe and Latin America, tragedy persisted in his life. On his way from Paris to the Beverly Hills home of his friend, film director Roman Polanski, and his wife, Sharon Tate, Kosinski's luggage was unloaded by mistake in New York. Unable to catch the connecting flight to

Los Angeles, Kosinski reluctantly stayed overnight in New York. That very night in Polanski's household the Charles Manson Helter-Skelter gang murdered five people—among them Kosinski's closest friends, one of whom he financially assisted in leaving Europe and settling in the States.

For the next few years Kosinski taught English Prose and Criticism at Princeton and Yale. He left university life when he was elected president of American P.E.N., the international association of writers and editors. Reelected, after serving the maximum two terms, a special resolution of the Board of P.E.N. American Center stated that, ". . . he has shown an imaginative and protective sense of responsibility for writers all over the world. No single member of the American Center can possibly be aware of the full extent of his efforts, but it is clear that they have been extraordinary and that the fruits of what he has achieved will extend far into the future . . ." Since then, Kosinski has remained active in various American human rights organizations and was honored by the American Civil Liberties Union for his contribution to the First Amendment's right of free expression. He is proud to have been responsible for freeing from prisons, helping financially, resettling or otherwise giving assistance to a great number of writers, political and religious dissidents and intellectuals all over the world, many of whom openly acknowledged his coming to their rescue.

Called by *America* "a spokesman for the human capacity to survive in a highly complex social system," a politically engaged, socially visible and vocal Kosinski has had his share of public notoriety and headline-making controversies. He was often labeled and criticized by the media as an existential cowboy, a Horatio Alger of the nightmare, a penultimate gamesman, the utterly portable man and a mixture of adventurer and social reformer. In an interview for *Psychology Today*, Kosinski said: "As I have no habits that require maintaining—I don't even have a favorite menu—the only way for me to live is to be as close to other people as life allows. Not much else stimulates me—and nothing interests me more."

Traveling extensively, on an average Kosinski wakes up around 8 A.M. ready for the day. Four more hours of sleep in the afternoon allows him to remain mentally and physically active until the early dawn when he retires. This pattern, he claims, benefits his reading and writing, his photography, and practicing of the sports he has favored for years—downhill skiing and polo, which, as an avid all-around horseman, he plays on a team—or one-on-one.

As a screenplay writer, Kosinski adapted for the screen his novel, *Being There* (with Peter Sellers, Shirley MacLaine, Melvyn Douglas and Jack Warden) for which he won Best Screenplay of the Year Award from both the Writers Guild of America and the British Academy of Film and Television Arts (BAFTA); he was also seen on screen giving a highly praised idiosyncratic performance as Grigori Zinoviev in Warren Beatty's *Reds*.

A critic once wrote of Kosinski that he "writes his novels so sparsely as though they cost a thousand dollars a word, and a misplaced or misused locution would cost him his life." He was close to the truth: Kosinski takes almost three years to write a novel, and in manuscript rewrites it a dozen times; later, in subsequent sets of three or four galley and page proofs, he condenses the novel's text often by one-third. As Kosinski's publishers often attest, it is such high principled scrupulousness that leads to the remarkable consistency of voice of all his novels. Kosinski said that "writing fiction is the essence of my life—whatever else I do revolves around a constant thought: could I—can I—would I—should I—use it in my next novel? As I have no children, no family, no relatives, no business or estate to speak of, my books are my only spiritual accomplishment."

"Learning from the best writing of every era"—wrote *The Washington Post*—"Kosinski develops his own style and technique . . . in harmony with his need to express new things about our life and the world we do live in, to express the inexpressible. Giving to himself as well as to the reader the same chance for interpretation, he traces the truth in the deepest corners of our outdoor and indoor lives, of our outer appearance and our inner reality. He moves the borderline of writing to more remote, still invisible and untouchable poles, in cold and in darkness. Doing so, he enlarges the borders of the bearable."